WHISKEY WOODS

LOOK FOR THESE EXCITING WESTERN SERIES FROM BESTSELLING AUTHORS WILLIAM W. JOHNSTONE AND J.A. JOHNSTONE

The Mountain Man
Luke Jensen: Bounty Hunter
Brannigan's Land
The Jensen Brand
Smoke Jensen: The Early Years
Preacher and MacCallister
Fort Misery
The Fighting O'Neils
Perley Gates
MacCoole and Boone
Guns of the Vigilantes
Shotgun Johnny
The Chuckwagon Trail
The Jackals
The Slash and Pecos Westerns
The Texas Moonshiners
Stoneface Finnegan Westerns
Ben Savage: Saloon Ranger
The Buck Trammel Westerns
The Death and Texas Westerns
The Hunter Buchanon Westerns
Will Tanner, Deputy U.S. Marshal
Old Cowboys Never Die
Go West, Young Man

Published by Kensington Publishing Corp.

WHISKEY WOODS

WILLIAM W. JOHNSTONE
and J.A. JOHNSTONE

PINNACLE BOOKS
Kensington Publishing Corp.
kensingtonbooks.com

PINNACLE BOOKS are published by

Kensington Publishing Corp.
900 Third Avenue
New York, NY 10022

PUBLISHER'S NOTE: Following the death of William W. Johnstone, the Johnstone family is working with a carefully selected writer to organize and complete Mr. Johnstone's outlines and many unfinished manuscripts to create additional novels in all of his series, like The Last Gunfighter, Mountain Man, and Eagles, among others. This novel was inspired by Mr. Johnstone's superb storytelling.

All Kensington titles, imprints, and distributed lines are available at special quantity discounts for bulk purchases for sales promotion, premiums, fundraising, and educational or institutional use.

Special book excerpts or customized printings can also be created to fit specific needs. For details, write or phone the office of the Kensington Sales Manager: Kensington Publishing Corp., 900 Third Avenue, New York, NY 10022. Attn. Sales Department. Phone: 1-800-221-2647.

PINNACLE BOOKS, the Pinnacle logo, and the WWJ steer head logo Reg. U.S. Pat. & TM Off.

Kensington Books Hardcover Printing: July 2026

Pinnacle Books Trade Paperback Printing: September 2026

ISBN: 978-0-7860-5236-3

ISBN: 978-0-7860-5237-0 (ebook)

10 9 8 7 6 5 4 3 2 1

Printed in the United States of America

The authorized representative in the EU for product safety and compliance
is eucomply OU, Parnu mnt 139b-14, Apt 123
Tallinn, Berlin 11317, hello@eucompliancepartner.com.

WHISKEY WOODS

CHAPTER 1

Jedediah Stark, a lean, whip-hard man in a faded blue sweat-stained shirt beneath worn leather braces, leaned back from raking a steel poker over a bed of hardwood coals.

He watched them for a moment as they pulsed and glowed beneath a wide steel pan. This, as very few folks knew, was one of the tricks the Stark family had used for generations of making whiskey, first back in Tennessee, then there at Whiskey Woods, the longtime family ranch outside of Glen Rose, Texas.

Stark stood up straight, stretching his back and letting out a long pent-up sigh, sounding like steam from a worn valve. He rubbed the small of his back and squinted, drops of sweat sliding down his forehead.

Jed, third-generation Stark to live most of his days and nights on this land, was a tall, broad-shouldered fellow with a gaze difficult to look away from if you were a lady and daring to meet eye to eye if you were a man.

He tugged free a rumpled red kerchief from a trouser pocket, mopped at his sweat-stippled brow, and thought about how fine a nice long, cool drink of water would taste then. Movement to his right, below the long eave of the open entrance to his still, caught his eye.

He shifted his gaze and squinted out into the hot, midafternoon sun cooking the dooryard. There lay his old droop-eared, long-boned red hound named Redeye. The dog was a solid, if lazy beast, but performed admirably the only real task asked of him—to lend a cold eye and a gruff bark of warning to strangers.

So far as Jed knew, Redeye was past the ten-year-old mark, but it didn't really matter. The beast had been born old, as if he had had no youth nor prime middle years. For a whole long time, for as long as Jed had known him, which was most of the beast's life, Redeye had acted as if each movement cost him an incredible amount of effort. It seemed only by the grace of good fortune was he able to perform the task of rising, walking slowly to his water bowl or his grub. Once sated and filled, it was all the hound could do to drop, as if clubbed on the head with a sledge, into another of his lengthy, snore-filled snooze sessions.

That it had turned out to be another hot day, especially for April, was not a surprise to Jed, but this hot this early in the season only meant more of the same in his experience, born of roving this spot all his days thus far.

All that was save for three years during the cursed war when he was called away and was nearly killed every moment of it, or so it had felt. And at the end of it, or at least of his time in it, never had a man been more relieved to return to his place of birth.

From then on, he vowed to never roam further than thirty or so miles from it again. Glen Rose was as good a town to live near as any other, and Whiskey Woods an ideal homeplace.

The thousand-acre ranch had been established by his grandpappy, Hawcliffe Stark, long years before on reaching the region from Tennessee and deciding to sink roots.

Jed cast his gaze once more on ol' Redeye, who had roused himself enough from his usual slumberous pose to raise his head from the dirt, droopy hound dog eyes taking in whatever it was he had first heard.

Normally, on a steaming day such as this, the old dog would slump, slow-walking, from shade spot to shade spot, only to collapse once more as if shot. It never failed to elicit a chuckle from Jed.

As the whiskey maker wiped sweat from his trim beard, he saw the dog not drop his head back to the earth but do the opposite and force himself to sit up. Must indeed be something out of the ordinary, thought Jed. He looked again, visoring his eyes against the day as he walked closer toward the sunlight from where he had been toiling before the fire at his still.

Jed looked up the long, winding lane that led from the plateau above the ranch toward the road that led to the town of Glen Rose. He had learned as a boy to always trust a beast's attention, no matter a dog, a cat, a cow, or a horse. They sensed disturbances, differences, far sooner than humans could.

He continued to squint up the road, glancing back once at Redeye, whose flopping ears now showed slight boldness, as if they had sprouted a little dignity. He saw the first possibilities of telltale puffs of someone, or something, approaching the ranch along the dusty roadway. He adjusted the angle of his big visoring hand against his forehead.

"It's likely Loud," said Jed, not looking over again at his silent conversation pard, ol' Redeye.

Loudon Paley was his newspaperman friend, a chubby Easterner who had made his way West some years before, seeking the woolly and the raw, grist for his story mill, revenge tales resulting in foolish gunplay and unnecessary mayhem.

What the man had found instead was a town, one Glen Rose, Texas, pretty enough, and sizable enough with 216 residents and another couple of hundred in the immediate surrounding area.

What he also found was that Glen Rose had need of a newspaper. In fact, it had never had one, and as the self-proclaimed "Whiskey Making Capital of Texas . . . and maybe the world,"

Glen Rose seemed ripe and ready, at least to the residents and to the puffed-up mayor, Fendall Hawkins, to welcome the services of a back-East-educated journalist.

Much to Loudon Paley's lasting regret, he had, in a fit of whiskey-fueled pique, agreed to be that man and to fulfill that role for Glen Rose. Regret because nothing much ever happened in Glen Rose.

And as Paley was a chatty type and not prone to sitting in the shadows and listening for news, he found himself knowing lots of people but not having all that many friends.

Somehow, Jed wasn't quite certain how it came to be, he and Paley had become friends. For Jed's part, being with Loud was simple enough. Jed was inclined toward quietness, and as Loud was, well, *loud,* they struck a perfect balance.

Many afternoons, practically year-round, Loud could be counted on to visit Whiskey Woods, on foot or more often to ride his old mule, Alice, out to the ranch for conversation and a sip of whiskey from the shop bottle.

But as Jed continued to watch the clouds of dust puff up and grow, closer and larger, he noticed that whoever it was, for it surely wasn't Loud, was neither a single man afoot nor a rider on horseback—or muleback.

As Jed continued to watch and sip tepid water from a canning jar, he saw steady plumes of dust rise up, closer, ever closer on this hot day. It was someone in a buggy. A small, two-wheel buggy. And this was no person intent on doing anything but getting to the end of the long, winding lane quick.

It wouldn't be his sweetheart, Lilly, because she would be busy at the diner. Besides, he'd seen her the night before and hoped to do so again this night.

Of course, Jed received visits from folks every few days, and sometimes with more frequency than that, but he knew well the schedules of all the saloon owners and others who made regular trips to Whiskey Woods to buy whiskey.

This was not one of those days and, from the approaching look of this buggy, it was not one of his regular visitors. But within another half a minute, Jed Stark knew who this visitor was. And despite his predilection for calmness, level thinking, and even acting in his life, Jed felt his guts tighten a smidgen. For he realized that this visitor was one Merlin Sheldrake.

And Sheldrake, while he had only been to the ranch two previous times, had been there for the same reason each time. Jed didn't think this time would be any different. The man would once again make him an offer that most other folks in the region, or perhaps the state, would be hard-pressed to refuse. Sheldrake wanted to buy Stark's distillery, his whiskey, the recipe—everything about it.

For certain the land would never belong to anyone but a Stark, at least not while Jed lived. And with even more certainty, he knew that they would never sell the distillery and certainly not their family recipe for Whiskey Woods whiskey. Never ever ever, even if he was killed defending it. He would take it to his grave.

And if Jed was that certain about that point, then his mother, Minerva Florabelle Stark, known as Minnie, or by Jed as Mama, or to folks who knew the family well enough, Mother Stark, was doubly certain. For they were the only surviving Starks of their line in the world, and that coveted recipe was not written down anywhere. Never had been, no sir. It resided in his head and in his mother's head, and that was it, that was all.

It would die with them. And then where would his so-called rivals be—the folks, such as Sheldrake and other whiskey makers, who thought they could make a golden liquid half as good as Whiskey Woods brew?

Jed sighed and rubbed a hand over his weary face. This was not something he had suspected was going to happen yet again, and it was certainly not an encounter he was looking forward to. For he would have two knob-headed folks to deal with.

Sheldrake and Mama. The thought that they were similar in so many ways made Jed chuckle. And doubly so when Jed mused on Mama's reaction should such a proclamation ever crawl out of Jed's mouth.

Life in Glen Rose had been fine before Sheldrake came to town four years earlier. He recognized that this area of the country was growing as more folks moved in and settled.

With that fact in mind, he reasoned rightly that Glen Rose, famous for its whiskey-making traditions and culture, would be an ideal place to set up operations for the whiskey production and distribution arm of his business holdings, of which booze was the fastest growing and most lucrative.

Jed knew that the man had made much money as an industrialist and railroad man in the upper Midwest and had been slowly broadening his empire. The rangy whiskey maker sighed in silence and walked into the sunlight from the darkened, albeit hotter, interior of the whiskey shed. It was a largely open-sided affair with long, low overhangs of roof that in the infrequent wet times kept the rain from soaking him while he worked.

The cooler months were such that Jed was plenty warm even without the protection of much in the way of walls, as he spent much of his time tending the fire and receiving plenty of heat.

In fact, the winter months were about the only time when Jed felt about right, not too hot and not too cold. The ever-present urge to make successful, consistently Stark-tasting whiskey kept the man from caring all that much about his own comforts.

"What are you thinking, eh, dog?" said Jed, barely glancing at Redeye, who sat erect now and was working up a growl deep in his old chest. That didn't bother Jed much. Redeye looked to be more of a menace than he was.

Despite Sheldrake having met the dog on two previous occasions, the rangy hound remained unimpressed with the rich fat man, an attitude of which Jed approved. It was an attitude, to Jed's relief, that his dear surly Mama shared with the dog.

As if his very thoughts cued her, Mother Stark strode on down from beneath the shade porch of the house. She looked, as Jed knew she would, tight and hard and working up a case of mean. And she was toting Ol' Shredder, a single-barrel shotgun that had been in the Stark family, according to Mama, "since Methuselah was in knee pants."

The gun—so named because it had been known to make a ribboned mess out of whatever it was that it was aimed at and its trigger squeezed at—was now aimed and ready.

This was due in part to the fact that the shells Mama used were nasty things brimming with lead nuggets the size of a child's fingertips. And when she gave that trigger a tug, Ol' Shredder spoke like a dragon that had been kept shut up in a dark place for far too long. It would roar and growl and cough and belch flame and smoke, and it would spit those maiming nuggets as if for the pure enjoyment of it.

Jed also noted, with mild relief, that she had not yet cocked the vicious barking thing—which, with Mama as the wielder, didn't mean all that much. The woman was adept at ratcheting back that hammer and sending a dose of "Mother Stark's spicy mix!" at anything or anyone she deemed in need of her attention.

"Mama," said Jed in a low, even voice. "You don't even know what he wants yet."

She swung her gaze from the fast-approaching dust-clouded buggy and fixed her big son with a hard eye. "I know and you know what that thieving brute wants. And you know and I know he ain't about to get it. But I do know what he's going to get. Held my trigger finger at bay for far too long where that fat rascal's concerned. No more, I say!"

Jed sighed. "Mama, don't kill him. Stark or no, the local law, as you well know, is no friend of ours. Marshal Chiswick will lock you up on murder charges quick as a wink."

"I'd like to see him try!" she said, cackling and squaring off.

Sheldrake's buggy, driven by the man himself, slowed and turned so that all he had to do was stay seated and address them from there, as he had done on his two previous forays out to Whiskey Woods. But then Jed noted that Sheldrake set the brake and looped the lines. It looked as if the fat man in the fine but dusty suit was about to step down.

Yep, he was, and it was not a pretty sight.

"What in tarnation do you think you are doing, Sheldrake?" said Mother.

The man did not reply until he grunted himself down, half backward, out of the buggy.

In a none-too-quiet voice, Mama said to Jed, "That backside of his looks like two pigs fighting under a blanket!"

Red-faced, out of breath, and now facing them, Merlin Sheldrake once more stood on the firm earth of the Stark's dooryard. "Well now, it is nice to see you both again, I'm sure."

Redeye hadn't yet moved, but Jed noticed the dog was tense all over, every muscle tight and set to hurtle his lean form into a lunge. The growling sound he'd made earlier had only increased in volume.

The hound's floppy ears were angled back, as if he were already darting forward at tremendous speed—something that Jed had never considered would be possible for the beast. All it would take is one step from where Sheldrake stood and that dog would be on him like stink on dung, thought Jed.

And if it happened, he didn't think he would work too hard to stop the beast. He would come to Sheldrake's aid, but Jed didn't think he would hurry himself at it. Time might tell, he thought, getting small pleasure from watching everybody work through their various stances.

He regarded the smile on the rich man's fleshy face, pink

and clean-shaven save for a thin fancy-man mustache that always looked to Jed to require more effort than it was worth, given its meager showing.

Sheldrake turned to Mama with what Jed had to assume was intended to be a winning, ingratiating smile. "Mother Stark, I must say it is lovely to see you. Why, you look younger with each week that passes, I do declare!"

As Jed watched, doing his best but not succeeding in suppressing a wincing smile, he was about to say something to help suppress the ruckus that he knew was on its way. He was too late.

"First off," growled Mama from somewhere down deep in her throat, the sound she was making matching that steady menacing gurgle that Redeye had maintained all the while Sheldrake had been there, "You didn't answer my question, curse you!"

Sheldrake's smile began to slip but he yanked it back up again and began to splutter, but the old woman cut him off because she kept right on talking.

"You great, greasy-jowled, slop-bellied fool! What makes you think you can set foot on Stark land?" Even as she said this, she raised Ol' Shredder from the near waist height she lugged the heavy thing at, taking her time and seeming to enjoy the fact that Sheldrake's beady eyes were locked on the thing, the brows rising with the gun.

"Why, my dear lady," he said, offering a slight bow, his derby shucked and clutched tight to his chest. His gleaming bald head was pink, and Jed saw the sweat bead there.

On anyone else he might think the man was sweating extra out of nervousness, but with Sheldrake, Jed didn't think so, not given the bold, swaggering way Sheldrake normally carried himself in life.

The fat man held up his free hand, palm out, and wagged it

as if he were waving bye-bye to them, which Jed wished he would do, and soon.

"My dear, dear Mother Stark!"

Jed winced again.

"And that's another thing, you pathetic mess! What in the name of all that is kind and decent in the world gives you the right to address me as anything other than Mrs. Stark? Huh? I ain't dear or sweet to you, and I certainly ain't your mama, and for that I count myself among the luckiest of folks."

Mama certainly was worked up today, thought the whiskey maker. Speaking of, he had things to do and this unexpected and annoying visit had best get to its inevitable end. Jed cleared his throat, and Sheldrake looked over at him, with what Jed thought was a begging look, as if Jed might rescue him from the hole he'd dug for himself.

Nothing doing, Jed thought. "See here, Sheldrake. I have things to do, and standing here listening to you jaw and seeing you sweat and stammer and not get to the point is nothing but annoying. Hop to the game, man, or get gone."

"Right, yes, sir, Jed, eh, Mr. Stark." Here Sheldrake glanced quickly at the old woman toting the shotgun before looking back to Jed. "The reason I am here," he straightened and stiffened his back, seeming to remember that he was not a mewling, pathetic man but a wealthy, confrontational businessman who always gets what he wants. "I came here today with nothing but the best of intentions."

The old woman snorted and spat at the dusty earth before her boots.

"Mama," said Jed. "Let's let the man speak his piece."

She mumbled something but didn't commit to a yes or no.

"Yes, yes," said Sheldrake. "You see, I know my previous offers to purchase your fine whiskey recipe fell short of the mark you have in mind, and I respect that. I really do! That is why, on reflection and consideration of the fact that you have been an established presence here in the Glen Rose region for a good many years—"

"None longer!" howled Mama.

"Yes, well, I drove all the way out here on this stifling day to make you a third and final offer." Here he had to once again hold up his hands because he saw on Mrs. Stark's face what what was coming. "No, no, please, ma'am, please let me finish."

He glanced at Jed, who nodded.

"Thank you, sir. Now my final offer effectively doubles," here Sheldrake's voice faltered as if the words were causing him no small amount of grief to utter. "I . . . I offer you double the amount of my last offer. I daresay you recall that figure, Mr. Stark?"

Jed eyed the man through squinted eyes, his arms folded over his chest. He didn't really recall the specifics of that offer, aside from recalling that the amount was substantial even then, and double that was nothing but a foolish figure, to be sure. But it was no use, never would be. But how to convince the man of it? Sheldrake was a hard learner.

"Look here, Mr. Sheldrake, we both appreciate—"

"Ha! Curse your hide, Sheldrake!"

Jed sighed and glared at Mama, then back to the visitor. "We both appreciate your coming out here on this fine day, prettier than a picture if you ask me," said Jed, digging a little at the fat man's complaint about the day being sweltering, "but as we told you last time, and the time before that, the Stark whiskey recipe is not for sale. We like it here fine, and we like what we do, making whiskey. That's it, that's all, man. I'm sorry you wasted your time."

Jed wasn't really sorry. The man was a grown fellow—overgrown, more like. Sheldrake made his choice and so did Jed, a whole lot of them on this day alone.

"But I don't think you understand me, Mr. Stark!"

Sheldrake's tone, Jed sensed, had shifted, changing from soft and placating to something with a harder edge. Not much, but it was there. "What I am offering you is twice the amount of cash. And for that all I want is a piece of paper with the recipe written on it. Naturally, too, for that amount of money, I have to ask that you both not share that recipe with anyone else for a period of, say, a dozen years. But!"—here Sheldrake held up a thick, pink index finger, as if prodding the underbelly of the air itself—"since we are, shall we say, friends, and since we are both men of the world and seem to know one another's mind, I am prepared to make certain, albeit limited, concessions."

Sheldrake tapped his chin and pooched his lips a moment as if deciding between pie or cake at a diner. Finally, a smile broadened on his face, and he nodded. "Yes, here is what I am prepared to do: I will allow you both to retain ownership of this pretty homestead the Starks have carved for themselves here.

"You will not, of course, be allowed to make whiskey yourselves for another dozen years, it's true, but with money such as that, only a fool would wish to continue working like a galley slave, eh?"

He chuckled and regarded them.

Jed wanted to ask the man if he was funning them, but he knew the answer. He was surprised that his mother hadn't jumped down the fat man's throat almost at once. He glanced at the old woman and saw a rare sight, indeed.

Mama Stark was staring at the fat stranger, her shotgun halfway poised to deliver, the hammer uncocked. But it was her mouth that surprised Jed. It was sagged open and her eyebrows were raised high. He knew about what she was feeling. He himself could hardly believe what he'd heard.

Jed cleared his throat. "Sheldrake, you have to be joshing

me." He advanced a half step on the man, Redeye tight to his right knee, advancing with him with steady dog half steps.

"As long as Starks are on this land, we will make whiskey. With our recipe. And we will sell our whiskey. That will never change, and we aren't going anywhere," said Jed, advancing. He paused when he was within a foot and a half of the red-faced, sweating man.

He'd only come this close because he was not a little worried that after all that insulting blather, Mama was about to twitch on that trigger and turn the richest man in these parts into a slopped, oozing, bloodied heap of dying fat man.

A sheen of oil, likely grease oozing from Sheldrake's pores, slicked the fellow's features, a look that made even the normally placid Jed want to punch the man. It smacked of laziness and overindulgence and craven cowardice in the face of life's everyday challenges. None of these were something Jedediah Stark tolerated in himself, and barely so in others.

He made exceptions, of course, for folks who were good at heart, such as his chubby pal, the newsman Loudon Paley. Loud liked his pie, perhaps a pinch too much, but he was intelligent, challenging, and worried about the plight of the less fortunate in life. And Loud woke up each day, Jed was convinced, with an earnest desire to help other folks. A good man.

On the other hand, given what Jed knew of Merlin Sheldrake, he had to say that there was very little kindness or good-hearted intention to the man. He was a loud-mouthed, brazen braggart with one urge and one urge only—to own everything he desired.

The closer he drew to Sheldrake the more Jed realized the fat man also had an awful stink wafting off him, like a ditch critter gone bloated in the sun. Time to get him gone.

"Look here, Sheldrake, I'm not your friend, I don't know your mind—a freakish thought at best—so I will tell you now, for the last time, we don't want to sell our whiskey recipe. The only thing we sell is the whiskey itself, to folks we know and folks we like. Now we didn't ask you to come here once, let alone three times, each time with the same unwanted offer. Stop it and go. Now."

As Jed spoke, he straightened and knew his face was growing redder with the heat of the moment. His right arm assumed a long, straight point to it that whiskered by the fat man's head and aimed at one thing—the fool's silly little buggy.

For one, two, three gulps, all Sheldrake could do was work his thick wet lips like a banked fish, his eyes round and wide.

He was about to speak when Jed, in a lowered tone, said, "If you don't do as I say, and do it right now, Mr. Sheldrake, I will have no choice but to turn Mother Stark loose on you."

As if to slam the point in place, like a well-smacked nail, from slightly behind and off to Jed's right rose up the deadly, oiled, throaty cold clicking of a shotgun hammer knocking back all the way to the deadliest position of all.

"And I ain't never, not once, failed to hit my target, mister. Keep that in mind, you great sloppy oaf. Now do as my son says and get gone!"

Standing less than an arm's length from Jed—who was a head taller and a good deal fitter, leaner, and more muscled than Sheldrake—the rich man looked up at him, then over at Mother Stark, his newly narrowed eyes locked on her sneering face. And he did something that once more surprised the two Starks.

Sheldrake spoke, this time in a low, cold, grating voice that rivaled the steely ratcheting of the shotgun's hammer in menace. "And I have never, not once, failed to get what I want in life, woman." The words curled from his mouth like smoke on the slightest of breezes. "I will have your recipe. Or I will see you both barking in the netherworld, begging for my forgiveness. Keep that in mind."

He turned and walked to his buggy and climbed up into it

with a smoothness and speed that Jed thought impossible for the fat fellow, considering his bumbling entrance and descent from the same buggy not long before.

Sheldrake gathered up the reins and looked over at them. "Keep it in mind, but not too long. Merlin Sheldrake won't be kept waiting." With that he smacked the lines hard on the horse's rump and the buggy lurched forward.

Mama walked over and stood beside Jed, and they both watched him maneuver the buggy in no hurry out toward the end of their wide yard.

For one of the very few times in his life, Jed found himself wondering if what he was doing was worth risking the lives of those he cared for, not the least his mother. And sure, the Stark recipe and name and home, too. Not to mention his own life.

More to the point, he wondered why it was that when backed right up to the wall, he and Mama didn't do anything more than stand there like turtles sunning on a log and listen to the great blustering fellow.

He looked down at Mama and to his surprise he saw a smirk on her face as she watched the slow, low cloud of dust that was Sheldrake's buggy roll away from them.

Then the old woman raised the shotgun the last few inches to her shoulder, snugged her cheek down, and touched off the trigger.

The shot whipped forward, parting the air like a clot of kill-crazy bees.

Jed saw that she had aimed a pinch high, no doubt in hopes of having the pellets arc down on the retreating buggy. Nothing sounded as if it met with its half-heartedly intended target.

Neither one spoke for a time. Then Jed said, "I will hand it to Sheldrake. He isn't one to give up on a thing."

"It's because what we do we do better than anybody in these parts. Heck, in the entire country. Maybe even the world!"

Jed smiled. "I think the Scots might have something to say about that."

"Bah," she said. "They're always whining and yowling about how great their whiskey is. I don't see it, myself."

"You don't drink the stuff, Mama." said Jed, smirking as he tidied up for the night.

"That doesn't matter a whit. I know what I know."

Jed did not respond, knowing, after a lifetime of such traded comments, there was no arguing with Minnie Stark and coming out on top. She would not, could not, be bested.

Chapter 2

"Won't sell to me, eh?" Merlin Sheldrake, now no more than a distant puff of dust on the Starks' horizon, snarled, and smacked the lines hard against the back of the poor horse he had rented for the buggy ride on out of town. He sneered at the straining beast, his seething rage at being dismissed by the Starks now unchecked and boiling; the fat man slapped the lines with renewed vigor on the horse's sweaty, dust-caked back.

"Work harder, you pathetic excuse for a steed! I rented your foul hide, and if I want to, I'll shoot you and pay the stable man his fee, which no doubt would be a gouging price!"

He shifted in his seat to break wind and then, emboldened, renewed his lashing and sputtering. "Never in my life have I had a problem buying anything and everything!"

He mused on the fact that it was true, he had owned about everything a man could own in his years as a wealthy businessman, from a sheep farm to a riverboat, from a smithy to a railway, from a bakery to a brick factory, and all manner of businesses and critters in between. His latest and most interesting, not to mention most lucrative, series of investments had been of the boozy variety.

While it was true he had made the bulk of his vast fortune in railroad investments, it was the purchase and consolidation of a handful of regional distilleries that kept the money gushing in, and that feeling of a constant and increasing source of cash with minimal effort, save for paying the oafs who worked for him, was the single most thrilling feeling Merlin Sheldrake could imagine having in life.

Innovation, he knew, was not among his top traits, but as he always told himself and others when he was buying their businesses, "Who needs innovation when you have money?" Then he would take their business, fold it into others, and kill what parts and pieces he determined were useless to him. And all of this process brought Sheldrake what he considered to be the second most important ingredient in the business world—the death of competition. The first, of course, was profit.

He had experienced it over and over again, and he never tired of rendering a competitor into a dead thing before the might of his growing empire.

Early on in his forays there, Sheldrake had decided to base his booze-making in and around Glen Rose, Texas, for good reasons. The region certainly was a good attractant. But mostly his decision had to do with the town itself, and more specifically with the Stark family's key role in the town, which was long known as the whiskey-making capital of Texas.

This Sheldrake took as a challenge. "I will have Stark's recipe or I will—no, no," he said out loud, a grim smile creeping on his wide fleshy visage. "That is no way to behave, man! For have you ever failed in attaining what you seek? No, I say!"

He smacked the lines hard, a fresh cut of dust pluming, and the buggy wheels skidding as he began chuckling with newfound enthusiasm for the thrill, the only real thrill in life, the quest, attainment of the prize, then defeat of a foe!

Trouble was, no matter how much of a fleeting feeling he had while driving, the truth was out there. He had indeed never had a problem buying what he wanted. Not until he met the vexing, stalwart Jedediah Stark. And his foul, cursed mother, Minnie Stark.

The quest had become far more than a business proposition to him. He did not mind admitting that it had become the very singular and sole challenge of his life and one he did not intend to lose.

That they made the best whiskey in all the land was undeniable. And yes, Jed was willing to concede that perhaps it was the best whiskey in all the United States . . . and beyond? Who knew? But the point was, Sheldrake knew it was most certainly the finest amber nectar he had ever tasted, and he considered himself a connoisseur of such things.

It should be good, as the Starks had been making their divine whiskey for many generations, as he had learned when he had begun sniffing around Glen Rose four years ago. And all of it was made right there, outside of Glen Rose at the Stark family ranch, named teasingly, annoyingly, braggingly, Whiskey Woods.

Trouble was, Stark and his evil mother would not sell their recipe. No matter how generous his offers had been. Over and over again, they had forced him, the swine, to raise his offer. He had even sweet-talked that vile old thing, to boot. And all to no avail.

But that really did not matter. He must succeed for one reason only: The Starks' whiskey was eating into his profits and thus, into his soul, and this was not something that Merlin Sheldrake could abide.

"Merlin Sheldrake is not the sort of man to take no for a final answer! Not a cent of it, no sir!" He lashed the horse harder, and it whinnied and lunged, desperate to get away from the sputtering, gibbering, shouting, cursing mad creature behind it.

"And so, what will you do about it, Sheldrake, my boy?" he asked himself. And again, he smiled. "If I cannot obtain the recipe by legal means, which to date I have been prevented from doing, curse them, then I will resort to other means. They have left me no choice—any man with a brain would do the same!"

He let loose a long, howling cackle that fluttered up and curled away on the dusty breeze they were making as the horse and its frightening cargo raced back to Glen Rose.

CHAPTER 3

"But you're not wearing a gun!"

The man who spoke squinted and looked at his friend, Jed Stark, as his friend hefted and lugged bulging sacks of grain off a wagon stacked with them as if they were goose-down pillows.

Watching Jed made the speaker, Loudon Paley, fend off a wave of exhaustion. It seemed that since arriving in Texas four years earlier, he'd never not been hot and tired.

"Nope."

Loudon paused and considered this response. "You mean nope you're not wearing a gun or nope I am incorrect and you are wearing a gun?"

Jed said nothing and continued to lug the big burlap sacks, sliding them off the smooth-worn planks of the work wagon's bed.

"Because, if the former is true, then, well, that puts you in potentially a great deal of trouble, I do believe, and I don't mind saying so." He raised a stubby index finger skyward as if to indicate that his point was a thought descended from the heavens.

Then Loudon cocked his head to the right. He rubbed his smooth chin and continued: "If, on the other hand, the latter is true, well . . ." he leaned back in his seat atop an ancient great scar-topped chopping block of a stump. "Then that of course is the most reasonable. Even though this does not extricate you from being in a great deal of trouble, of course. But at least then you will be armed and better able to face said trouble."

The tall, lean man lugging the sacks sighed and let his arm rest on the next sack in the wagon. "Nope, I am not wearing a gun. And now you have me saying it."

"Saying what?"

" 'Wearing a gun.' My word, you don't wear a gun like a shirt or a flower in your hat band or some such. You carry the cursed thing, either in a pocket, on your trouser waist—if you're wearing a belt or braces—or from a sling over your shoulder, or in a holster."

"Oh . . . well, frankly now I am confused."

The tall man smacked his big work-hardened hands atop the next sack, dust rising. "Welcome to the party."

"Party?" said the chubby man atop the stump. "I wasn't aware you were hosting a soiree."

"I'm not."

"But—"

The tall man ignored him and lugged another sack inside the dim low-roofed barn. When he walked back out, he glanced at the man atop the stump, who had tugged out a red kerchief and was dabbing his face. "Loudon, help me with something I think I am seeing—are you sweating?"

"Of course I am sweating."

"Why? You haven't worked in all the time I've known you."

"Amusing, as always. And it's hot here, in case you haven't noticed! In fact, everything about this place, this so-called Texas, is hot. I have no idea why I ever moved away from the stunning wonders that comprise the great Commonwealth of Massachusetts."

"Me, either."

A lull of a minute drifted over their conversation, then Loudon sighed. "I do believe I missed out on the great heyday of gunplay and brutality of this vast frontier."

Jed rolled his eyes and continued to lug sacks.

"Furthermore, I feel I am, or was, tailor-made for such a life." Paley nodded, as if agreeing with himself. "Yes, I am a newsman, but what news is there in reporting on committee meetings about town parades, or whether it was Fergus the drunk's intent to pass out and hit his head requiring doctoring, or if he fell, hit his head, and then passed out? And who really cares?"

"I bet Fergus does," said Jed.

"Bah," said Loudon. "I should be deep in the throes of covering gunplay and malintent!"

"What you should do, Loudon, is stop reading so many of those dime novels. They're bad for your head." The slightest of grins crept across the lean man's lined, stubbled face.

"Bah, again! And also, I will posit that I have indeed worked the entire time you have known me. In fact, I work every day. Like a dog digging for a long-buried bone, like a miner seeking hidden ore, like a—oh, I don't know. But I assure you I never stop working, in fact! My mental abilities are so finely honed that I actually work even when I am snatching at the few scant hours of sleep I have been able to train myself to gain in order to keep this slightly rumpled body you see before you moving forward through this heat-infested, snake-addled place in which we live!"

"Huh," said Jed. "Anyway, what makes you think I need a gun?"

"Well, don't you have a gun about the place?"

"Sure, I have a gun. Got a few, as a matter of fact. But a gun's for one thing and one thing only."

"Yes, to protect oneself."

"Nope. It's for killing. And when I need to make meat, why,

I fetch down my shotgun for the birds and small varmints or my rifle for deer and such. But a man isn't game."

"I'm not so certain others would agree with you on that score."

"Huh. What score would that be?" Jed narrowed his eyes. Of course, he knew what Loudon was on about, but it was so much fun getting the pudgy newsman worked up. All he had to do was keep stepping on the man's conversational toes and Loudon would keep on backing up and backing up until he couldn't go any farther.

Soon enough, Stark knew that Loud would find himself snugged tight in a corner, and then Jed would smile at him and shake his head and go on about his business, leaving the sputtering Yank to yammer and grumble. Then they'd break off and have a cup of coffee.

And if Mother had been in one of her baking moods, maybe even a wedge of something toothsome, like her famous seed cake.

"On the score of—oh, well you know exactly what I'm talking about, Jed! Merlin Sheldrake or one of his emissaries from the Sheldrake Distillery will be back, and they won't be offering you kindnesses and money next time. Heed my words! The next time, if they don't hear what they want to hear, that's when the situation will turn foul. You heed my words!"

Jed sighed. "Sure, Loudon, I know what you're talking about. I'm no fool. Mother would not raise one, and she'd slap silly you, me, or anyone giving thought to that notion—you know that as well as I do." His grin slipped away, and his voice grew colder, lower, brittle sounding to Loudon.

"But I can tell you something that I doubt you know, which is that killing a man, or a woman, another human, any other human, is not a pursuit that should be looked on as a light thing. It is something that most men, if they have sand at all, will carry with them forever. And it is a heavy burden."

Jed stared at Loudon, his eyes so narrowed they seemed to the journalist to be nearly closed. The lean Texan said no more, but that stare was a fixing thing. Loudon had been acquainted with Jed Stark long enough to know that when the man's usual quiet, easy way skedaddled, as Jed would say, the fellow was making a point that a listener would do well to heed.

"I take it you know firsthand of what you speak," said Loudon after a long quiet moment. He pretty much knew the answer, but it led to something the two friends had never discussed.

Jed was as close a friend as Loudon had ever had, and he suspected he was as close to a friend as Stark had, other than Jed's girl, Lilly Chu, the comely woman—and amazing cook—who owned and ran the Glen Rose Café.

Jed let Loud's comment hang in the air like a bad smell for a long moment.

Loudon was about to stand up from his customary seat on the stump and stretch his back and begin making noises about going home. That always prompted Jed to remember they were going to have coffee and cake.

But on this day, Jed made no mention of a snack. He cleared his throat and spoke. "I was in the war, don't mind saying. Nothing civil about it. I reckon that was some blame fool journalist—no offense intended, Loud—who came up with that fool word for it. It was anything but. I saw all manner of men dead. Women and children, too, as a matter of fact.

"About the only thing I learned in all of it was that nobody was right, and everybody was wrong, because the killing of another human is a harsh thing. *Raw* ain't the word for it. Sure, if you have to defend yourself, why, you go to it. But don't put yourself in a position where you have to in the first place. And war does that to a man. Day in and day out, weeks, months, years. Lifetimes."

"Sometimes it can't be helped," Loudon said, in a voice that was almost a whisper.

"Maybe that's true, although talking a thing through beforehand should take as long as it needs to take. I tell you what, Loud. If anybody sees the bodies of men strewn all over a battlefield, bloated from setting out in the sun and such, why, they would easily take them for those overfed, underworked politicians out in Washington.

"Those demons do little more than make life a righteous mess for the rest of us, the starving, ribby wolves we're all forced to become, all on account of men who decide war would be a good thing but who don't have to do a thing about it themselves other than sign the death papers for all those they send to battle."

Jed simmered and grew quiet. Loudon wasn't certain how to respond because he'd rarely seen his friend, Jed, in such high dudgeon. That was more along the lines of his old mother's way of doing.

Then as before, when Loudon was about to speak, Jed spoke again, this time in that low, wavering voice. "I saw a whole lot of dead, as you have gathered. But I also made my share of living men dead, too. Laid them low who were as alive as I was one second, then, like that"—Jed held up a thick-knuckled, work-scarred hand and snapped the thumb and middle finger together—"they were dead. About the only thing I offered them as a kindness was a well-placed bullet. One shot that ended it all. I don't believe any of the men I laid low suffered much at all. That's all I could offer them. Cold comfort, I know. But that's all I could do."

Jed turned away so that his back faced Loudon. The big man groaned and his shoulders sagged beneath his begrimed work togs. He raised his big hands, scooped off his hat, and stuffed it under his left arm. Then he ran those hands up and down his face, up over his thicket of wild, wavy brown hair with the beginnings of gray streaking through, and shook his head as if he'd doused himself in a freezing mountain freshet.

Then Jed settled his hat atop his head once more, and without turning back around walked toward the wide open doors and into the sunlight once more. Over his shoulder he said, "Don't much feel like coffee today, Loud. See you tomorrow."

With that, Jedediah Stark strode out of the barn, across the cluttered dirt yard, and kept on walking. Loudon knew from past experience, although few such moments had occurred, that Jed needed to stretch his pins, as he called it. For him that meant walking miles and miles to wherever he felt he needed to get to and then turning and walking those same miles and miles all the way back. And that, as Loudon recalled, would be well past sundown.

The newsman slid from the stump, looked around the shop, and making his own way out the door, across the yard, and in the opposite direction taken by his chum, Loudon Paley climbed aboard Alice, his mule. He made his way back to town and his now slightly less boring and perhaps a little more humbled life as Glen Rose's sole newsman.

What Loudon could not know was the deep effect his seemingly innocent questions and comments had had on Jed Stark, Texan, son, bachelor, quiet man, and whiskey maker. But first and foremost of all those things, Jedediah Stark was a man who had once been a soldier. He had fought in a war that, at the time, he had felt was justified enough that he ought to do his part, the same reason and excuse as all his friends had used for joining up.

And while a good many of those men ended up dead, others came home, and by all appearances—although Jed didn't much keep up with them—from what he'd seen and heard of them, they came home all right, picked up, somewhat where they left off, new lives, somewhat in the old places.

He wondered if he was the only one who felt as he did—weighted down by the memories of killing, the violence, the . . . the raw foolishness of it all. Men killing men because other men told them to. And when it came down to it, in the end, it really was all about money. Didn't anybody do anything for the love of doing it anymore?

By then, with such heady thoughts swimming in his begloomed mind, Jed found himself out past the pecan grove, not far from the family camp, as it had always been called. It was more of a fine small house, with a small whiskey-making still off to the side. And not far from that, eastward, there was the cave.

It was a naturally formed grotto, which was what Jed's mother always called it, although by Jed's way of thinking it was far bigger than the word *grotto* might indicate—although he wasn't about to argue with Mama.

It was an irregular space hollowed out by who knows what and who knows when, but it had some sort of artwork on the walls, crude and faint, sure, but it was there. It depicted what looked to Jed to be scenes of long-ago hunts of critters that were far larger than the folks hunting them. And to his mind and experience, those beasts were no longer around. Likely they had been driven off or hunted to the point where they no longer lived probably anywhere in the world.

Seeing that art always made him wonder what manner of beasts there had been in the world that might never have been seen and so painted or chipped into cave walls anywhere.

"Think of that," he'd told his mother one evening over dinner, many years back, when he had still been mired in his teenage years. "Why, to know that there were likely deer like those that we hunt nowadays, but maybe twice as big! It's almost too much to think on."

He had mused like this for some time, when his mother said,

"You know, boy, if you don't lay off that crazy thinking, like those fanciful deer in your head, you will end up dead!"

"How do you figure that, Mama?"

"Because," she said, "you will sit there wondering and tapping your chin with your fingertip, and you will never take a bite of the food that I spend hours making, and you will wither like gourds on a vine that hadn't tasted rainfall in months. You want that?"

"No, Mama," he had said, grinning. "I guess I don't."

"Good," she had said. "Then eat your stew, and go about all that high-and-mighty thinking when you are doing something else. But not when you are helping me make whiskey. That takes all the brains you were born with, and considering that your dear departed Daddy—a smart man, but a lazier man you'll never find—plus the brains of all the Starks in your past, I'd say that you have a considerable amount of brain, indeed."

Jed thought back on that long-ago conversation with his Mama, not all that different than any number of conversations they had had over the years. He paused, eyeing the disguised entrance to the Stark cave, where they stored years' worth of fine whiskey, his hands wadded deep in his trouser pockets. He let out a long breath and glanced about his surroundings.

The cabin looked good. Of course, he knew that Mama trailed on down there at least once each week. Sometimes, when he made his way back into the house for a snack or a sit-down in the shade, he'd call to her and she'd not respond. He knew she was likely down at the cabin. It was one of her favorite places to be, and increasingly so as she grew older.

She had told him that once he decided to settle down and have himself a wife and a child or two of his own, she would move to the cabin and spend much of her time there. That made good sense, and he'd nodded in agreement with the plan. Even if he was in no hurry to fulfill his end of that deal.

The pecan trees were looking all right, too. It was early but looked to be a promising year for them. Beyond the grove, the Paluxy River flowed low and steady. In all his years of living here, save for those three years in the Confederate States Army, Jed had never seen it run dry. That was a funny phrase, now that he thought on it. If it was dry, it wouldn't be running, now, would it?

A wry smile cracked his grimy, dusty face. He pulled in a deep breath and filled his lungs with the clean, smooth, if somewhat heavy air of this fine parcel of land in the middle of Texas.

Not for the first time did he utter a near-silent thanks to his old, long-dead grandfather, Hawcliffe Stark, Mama's papa, for settling this land.

That fine fellow had persuaded a pretty young thing by the name of Bethelza Hubbard to marry up with him, and together they hewed out a life here. Despite the fact that Bethelza was a teetotaler, she did not mind, and in fact wholly supported her husband in his goal of carrying on his family's line of work of whiskey making, a pursuit he had brought along from back east, in the hills of Tennessee, where his family had been whiskey makers for untold generations.

In time, Hawcliffe and Bethelza had begotten Minerva Florabelle Stark, their only child. Minnie was a beloved daughter who grew up pretty, but scrappy and tough. By most counts she was—and continued to be—tougher than any man around. She also came into her own as a whiskey maker. Her mama and papa were proud of her.

The only thing she ever did that made them groan was to become with child by Arthur Bigelow-Watts, a drummer of nostrums and tinctures, and a mooch and a layabout and all-around slouchy character. His only redeeming traits had happened to be that he was jovial, tall, nearly always smiling, well-spoken, and as handsome a man as that part of Texas had ever seen.

He stuck around for a spell, and they were about set to wed, Arthur prodded, with reluctance, by her Papa's double-bore. Fortunately for all of them—even Mama, as she came to admit to Jed in later years—Arthur up and died. He had been drunk on Stark whiskey one fine afternoon and fell off his horse. He landed head first on a flat rock and snapped his weak neck.

"Second-best thing ever happened to me," Mama would say.

And when he was younger, Jed would say—even though he knew the answer—"What was the first, Mama?"

She'd bend down and smooch his forehead. "Why, you, of course! Only useful thing Arthur Bigelow-Watts ever did in all his days was to leave you on my doorstep."

They'd found Arthur, reeking of whiskey fumes, eyes closed, and a smile on his face. Were it not for the odd bent angle at which his head lay, he might have been asleep, said Mama.

Then she would add, "Which was his normal state, anyway." Then she'd laugh and smack her knee and chunk another log in the stove.

She may have inherited her love of whiskey making from her Papa, but she inherited from her Mama a much-appreciated ability to bake pies and cakes and breads. In fact, there wasn't much she couldn't turn her hand to in the kitchen. She also inherited Bethelza's distaste for the very thing for which the Stark family had become known—the very whiskey she was so good at making.

Folks never believed that she was not one for partaking of the thing she made. In fact, she never had. So how did she know it was good? That was a question she'd been asked a whole lot in her lifetime of being a whiskey maker. How she could tell if it was a decent batch or whether it should be dumped into the hogs' trough?

"Well, first off, Starks don't make whiskey for hogs. Also, if I were to answer your question," she'd say, casting a sideways glance at the asker, "I'd be a fool. And that's a title I will leave to others—a good many I've met over the years."

The person asking the question would then wonder if they had been insulted by the shrewd old woman.

Jed paused as he made his way back up to the main ranch. Something deep down and far off, yet right in the midst of his brain, too, nibbled at him. It was something he could never explain, nor did he much care to—instinct, he'd heard it called.

He knew that it was a feeling, a notion, a way of being that all animals had. And as humans were critters, no different than dung beetles or rattlers or mules or crows, and they all were smart enough to abide by the notions their own guts and minds were telling them to abide by, why Jed Stark held in place.

His left hand slid down with all the speed of a quick, stiff breeze, to rest on the hilt of his big wide dagger-blade hip knife. He let his fingertips untie the leather keeper thong holding it in place.

If there was trouble in the offing, and something told him that if it wasn't trouble, it was at least something not quite right—that is to say, something out of the ordinary—then he would need to be ready.

Jed paused at the edge of the homeplace clearing and surmised the situation, his left hand atop his knife's handle, and he looked over the unexpected scene before him.

What he saw was his dear Mama, standing hipshot and ramrod-spined, with her favored weapon in perfect, gleaming condition, from its polished mahogany stock to its blued barrel—Ol' Shredder. She had the trigger cocked on that beast and elbow propped against her muscled, trim frame, her granny hair worked back in a neat-as-a-pin bun.

"What's all this then, Mama?"

He spoke as if he were asking if she had happened to bake any of his favorite molasses cookies that morning, and she answered him in kind, albeit without turning her tiny gray head. "Oh, what it seems, son, got me pair of varmints in my sights."

"Oh?"

"Yep. Caught 'em skulking, I did. I'm thinking they are coyotes, from the looks of 'em. But they don't look too healthy—nasty things, all patchy fur and lean-looking. And untended. I expect if I were to draw any closer, I might detect a stink off them that would rival that of a week-old sun-popped skunk. You reckon, son?"

Jed took a step forward, working his tongue over his teeth as if he'd finished a fine big meal. And for a flicker of a moment, he thought back to a chat they'd had that very morning about how quiet it had been since Sheldrake's visit and consequent raging threats some days before.

"Might be the calm before the storm, Mama," he'd said.

"Bah!" the old woman had said, from the cookstove. "Like I said, he's all hot air and nothing more!" Then she'd chuckled and kept on stirring her latest tasty treat.

Jed paused again and squinted at the two wide-eyed men who were exchanging glances, from Jed to the old woman with the shotgun and back again. "I expect you might well be right, Mama. They have the look of stench about them. My guess is it comes from a certain fat whiskey man."

"Now son," said the old woman. "I thought I told you that on Stark land, we don't refer to anybody who participates in the making of pig swill and then bottling it as a whiskey man, nor woman nor child, neither."

"My apologies, Mama. Yes, we did discuss that some time ago. Slipped my mind, what with the new pair of slavering dogs we got hereabouts and all. Speaking of, I was thinking I might fetch them out of their underground lockup, you know, give them some exercise, a little time to stretch their legs and run about the place. Critters that big got to eat, you know, and try as I might, I can't seem to haul home enough mule deer to keep them satisfied. Besides, they do like to bring down their own game. Especially when it's on the run."

"Now that is a good idea, son. You go on ahead, I'll deal with these two wastrel critters. Likely they have the hydrophoby, anyway. I reckon I'll put them down and be done with it. Do us all a world of favors."

The building fear on the faces of the two captives was almost too much for Jed to witness and keep a serious face. They were working themselves up from trembling chins and quivering lips to twitching opening mouths gasping like those of banked fish and on up to eyebrows rising so high they looked to be part of their hairlines.

Jed was on the verge of letting loose a hearty guffaw when noises from the two men beat him to it.

Their squeals began at about the same moment, one higher in pitch than the other. Both men stood spraddle-legged with their shaking hands held up above their heads. One of the men had lost his hat. Likely, Jed surmised, when Mama had surprised them with what he guessed were sharp hot words and the oiled, steely clicking of the hammer ratcheting all the way back.

"Now look here, folks . . ." said one of the men, but he didn't get the chance to continue, because another voice cut in and stomped all over him. Redeye, locked in a tense stance tight to Mother Stark's skirts, let a low growl curl up and out of his throat.

"No! You look here, you weasel-faced rat man!" said Mama.

Jed sighed. "Mama, you sure do have a way with words."

"Why thank you, son. I do try. I surely do. It's nice to get practice in with men such as this."

"Uh oh, did you call them men, Mama?"

"I must be slipping in my dotage, son. It's been happening of late. First time I noticed it was when my poor old rheumatism-addled fingers began twitching and jerking with the barest of warnings. It was a stiffening, tingling sort of feeling in my arm. Believe it was this arm, the one connected to my trigger finger, don't you know. And my word, I do believe it's about to happen again! Why, you should have seen the way my fingers danced and played havoc. There wasn't no controlling them, son, I tell you true!"

Jed shook his head. "I am sorry to hear that. But yes, I do recall when that happened. I believe you were holding that skinning knife and the thing fairly shot across the room and out through the window. It was as if you had somehow grown a whole extra set of arm muscles, the force of that throw was that mighty. And what's more, do you know what I found when I went on out in the yard?"

"No, son, tell me what you found."

"Well, now, I will," said Jed, scratching his chin and warming to his topic. "I found that your skinning knife had sliced clean on through the neck of that ornery old rooster. You recall the one, the very one that pecked the eyes out of that copperhead, you remember?"

"Oh yes, he's the bird we ate. I recall we ate that snake, too. Going to miss that bird. He was a good snake catcher. And as you know, I am partial to a good fry up of snake."

Jed nodded in silent agreement.

"Oh, please folks, we didn't mean no harm!"

"You hear that, son?" said Mama. "I do believe one of them can talk. Will wonders never cease?"

The other one licked his lips and said, "We can both talk. I mean, me, too!"

"Well, now," said Jed. "Might be we could be convinced to set you back loose in the wild, but only if I find out what it was you two critters want here." He eyed them both with his head leaned back, as if assessing them.

The men looked at each other, and then the taller of the two, who had done most of the talking up to that point, licked his lips, but looked away and remained silent.

Jed sighed. "Let me help you with the big words. You were sent here by Merlin Sheldrake—"

"That useless fat oaf!" growled Mama, interrupting Jed.

He waited. When she didn't continue, he resumed.—"To steal something from us. *Something* being our family whiskey recipe."

Again, he waited, and again they looked everywhere but at him.

Redeye unleashed another low-throated growl that forced both intruders to pull their heads back.

"I'll consider that as a yes from you both. I understand why you don't want to admit to participating in such a lowdown, craven, cowardly act. I would appreciate it if you'd take a message back to your boss man."

"Filth!" growled Mama.

"Well, Mama, that wasn't the word I had in mind, but come to think on it, I can't disagree with you. Now, where was I? Oh yeah," Jed rasped a big, callused hand over his beard stubble. "What I need you to tell Sheldrake is that if he pulls this sort of game again, we'll lay low the messengers and then come straight on for him. Because this game has about come to an end. You two got that?"

Neither man said much but stared at him as if considering what he said.

"Any of the words too long for you?"

Finally, the taller of the two said, "No, no, we understand what you said, for sure. Only—"

"Only?" said Jed.

"Only, well, the boss, he don't want to hear that, see? He's liable to do to us what she seems to want to do."

Mama stifled a snort of laughter, but her shotgun never wavered. "I grant you, he has plenty of guts, but not a bit of them are anything it'd take to do for you two vermin! His guts are sloppy and fat!"

"Now, Mama, I do believe our guests are asking for our help."

The taller of the two nodded, then the other followed suit, eyebrows high in hope.

"I'd say," said Jed, "that you had best tell Sheldrake what I said. If you don't, why, I'll have no choice but to come for you, too. So you think on that. Now"—Jed bent low and made as if to lunge at them, then shouted—"git gone!"

They spun, a string of whimpers burbling out of them both, their boots churning the dusty lane, making, Jed had seen earlier, for two horses tied nearly out of sight, well up the road.

He and Mama were sharing the beginnings of a chuckle when the taller of the two intruders, thinking he was out of range, slowed and half spun and shouted back at them, "You ain't heard the last of Mr. Sheldrake!"

"That little pig!" snapped Mama, hoisting Ol' Shredder and touching the trigger.

The brute gun did its intended job and delivered a fast, whistling storm of lead bees. Despite the distance and aided by Mama's proficiency at hitting running targets with the thing, the shot arced up and then down, like low, unspeakable rain. It peppered the two men with stinging, nonmortal wounds that drew specks of blood from the backsides, and howls and yips and yowls from the mouths of the two bolting fools.

She lowered the shotgun and kept her eyes on the now limping, retreating men. "They ain't nearly as musical as coyotes."

"But a heap more amusing," said Jed, smiling.

Redeye groaned and laid down right where he stood.

"Pup's fatigued," said Jed.

"I'm a mite tuckered, myself. Dealing with vermin will do that to a soul."

"Well," said Jed. "I sort of wish you hadn't done that, Mama."

"Done what?" she said.

"Shot at those fools."

"Whyever not?" She grinned. "It was fun."

"Maybe so, but you all but guaranteed a return visit, and I doubt it'll be the two of those weasels next time."

"Good." She licked her thumb and wiped dust off the barrel. "I'll be waiting." She glanced down at Redeye, who was snoring. "Can't speak for him, but me and Ol' Shredder, we'll be ready and willing."

CHAPTER 4

Another day passed with little more commotion about Whiskey Woods than a raised eyebrow from an exhausted Redeye. He noted the fleeting presence of a heat-dazed jackrabbit as it wandered by, seeking respite from the midday sun.

Late afternoon found Jed scratching his chin and mumbling to himself in the whiskey shed. His day's labors had largely been tamed when he heard a voice behind him. "Uh huh."

It was Mama. He turned to see her shaking her head and her arms folded above her apron.

"What's that mean?" he said.

"Means you're mooning."

"Mooning?" Jed knew what she meant, but he half-bristled, anyway.

She nodded. "Yep. Like a confused bullock."

"Aw, now, Mama, I—"

She held up a halting hand. "You about to argue with your Mama? A woman who bore you and who always knows best. A woman who is never wrong, even when she might be—which has never happened, by the way?"

He smirked and snorted.

"Get on to town and visit with Lilly. Never needed prodding before."

He rubbed a big grimy hand over his neck. "Well, I don't know . . ."

"Well, I do."

"You sure you'll be all right here alone if I mosey on into town? Might could go for a slice of pie at Lilly's."

Mama's eyebrows rose, and she looked as if she was about to work herself into a lather.

Jed smiled. "All right, all right. Checking, Mama." He walked over and hugged her.

"Jed?"

"Yeah, Mama?"

"You might want to bathe before you head out. You're a pinch whiffy. Lilly's tough, but she has a nose."

"Yes, Mama. Heading to the back porch right now." Jed strode off with long steps, humming.

Mother Stark smiled and looked down at the dog. "I expect even if a pretty she-hound wandered on by, you'd have trouble lifting your head, huh?"

Redeye snorted, and one back leg trembled in his sleep. "Born useless," she said, smiling and walking back to the house.

Jed's ride the twenty or so minutes into Glen Rose proper was a quiet one. He'd spiffed up decent enough, scrubbed himself everywhere he needed to and tugged on a fresh shirt, ragged the dust off his boots, and pulled on his town vest. After he mounted up, his mother had handed up to him a small familiar-looking wooden box no larger than his hand, tied in twine.

"Loop that on your saddle horn. It's for Lilly."

"What is it?"

"If you must know, it's a goodly wedge of my corn bread."

"Mama, you know Lilly is a pretty good baker herself."

"Where do you think she learned it from?"

Jed knew better than to say something about Lilly's own

Texan mama, now long dead, who by all counts had been one fine cook herself. He held his tongue, nodded, touched his hat brim, and rode on out. Wouldn't do any good to tell Mama to be careful and watchful. She'd like as not touch off a round to escort him on his way.

It was deep dusk by the time he made it to the Glen Rose Café, one of the few eateries in the small Texas town that didn't serve liquor as a staple and food as an afterthought. Lilly had opened the place years before as a young woman, spunky and new to town after rambling on her own for a few years following the death of her Chinese father. He'd been a rugged man who died under less-than-acceptable circumstances while working at the profession at which he was a reported master, that of head blaster for the Sutherland and Woolsey Railroad.

As was Jed's custom these past six years or so—since not long after he and Lilly had become a "doting pair of doves," as Mama had put it (kindly, he knew)—once he'd led his mare into the two-horse stable in the alleyway behind the café, Jed showed up at the kitchen door.

He waited until he saw that Lilly was back in the kitchen from serving out front. He'd forgotten this was Polly Doherty's night off, which meant Lilly was extra busy. He nibbled his bottom lip and knew he should have waited another day.

He held there a moment, looking in the screened door at her, a pretty woman whose head was chest height to him. She bore a full figure well and was as no-nonsense as Mama.

Lilly's long, straight black hair, beginning to show the barest hints of silver in the last few years—which, with a wink, she swore Jed was responsible for—was pulled back in a tail behind, although slips of it had sneaked out and hung before her face as she filled bowls of stew from a steaming pot atop the black cook stove.

Jed could not resist; he rapped his big knuckles once, twice on the doorframe, all the while keeping his eyes on her.

Lilly looked up at him and that lovely wide smile he liked so very well spread on her heat-reddened face as she recognized him through the screening. "Come, come!" she motioned him on in.

Jed didn't need any more invitation than that and stepped inside. She crossed the small room and, as she always did, reached up with both hands and hugged his face as he bent to her for a kiss. "Oh, I am pleased to see you," she said.

Before he could reply, she spun back to the stove. "I'm run ragged tonight. Wouldn't you know it?" But she was smiling. She nearly always was, which was one of the many traits he admired so in her.

"Can I lend a hand?" he said, guessing she would shoo him into the dining room, regardless.

But she surprised him tonight. "Only if you don't mind ladling stew and making sure that last batch of biscuits doesn't burn. Shouldn't be but ten minutes or so until the hubbub dies down."

"I do not mind. As it happens, Mother Stark showed me a thing or two in the kitchen."

"How is she?"

"Fiery, same as always."

Lilly smiled. "What's that?" she nodded as she placed bowls on a tray.

Jed handed her the string-wrapped box and rolled up his sleeves. "From Mama, for you."

Lilly untied the string and opened the box. "Corn bread!" she said, her eyes smiling.

"You act like it's gold," he said.

"Better than. Your Mama's corn bread is the best I've ever had." Then her smile faded as she lifted the slightly warm wedge from the box.

"What's wrong?" said Jed, checking the biscuits.

"There's a letter in here, addressed to me." She looked at Jed. "From your mother."

"Huh. Open 'er up."

Lilly did and found not a note but a recipe. Across the top it read: "Stark Family Corn Bread."

Jed looked at it over her shoulder and whistled low. "She really likes you. And trusts you. That's not something she would share with most anyone." He kissed Lilly atop her head and went back to the stove. "Heck, I don't even know that recipe." He heard nothing and looked back over to see her staring at the paper. "Uh, Lil?"

She looked up with slightly teary eyes and a smile on her face. "Yes?"

"Your customers?"

"Oh, yes, right, right." She folded it and stuffed it in her apron pocket. "I'll study this later," she said.

"I'm sure you will. Later later, I hope."

"Oh, I don't know, been a long day, stranger . . ." She smiled and hoisted the laden tray. "By the way, did you bring any of your finest?"

He winked and nodded. "In my saddlebag. I didn't want to overwhelm you, what with the corn bread and all."

"How do you know a girl doesn't like to be overwhelmed now and again?"

Jed turned back to the stove as she left, telling folks out front: "Oh, calm down, your food's here!"

As Lilly had predicted, the rush dwindled, and thirty minutes later found them seated in the midst of a half-filled dining room, Jed enjoying an ample wedge of warm mince pie with cream drizzled atop and a cup of coffee alongside.

Lilly sipped a glass of water and nibbled a warm biscuit. "I heard what happened yesterday out at your place," she said.

"You did? Well now, boring news travels, doesn't it?" He kept eating.

"Jed"—she laid a work-reddened hand atop his wrist and spoke in a low voice—"don't make light of it. Your lives were threatened. And not for the first time."

He regarded Lilly, looked her right in the eyes. "I appreciate what you're saying, Lil," he said in a low tone, "but what would you have me do?"

She went back to picking at her biscuit and, not in keeping with her usual bold demeanor, did not look at him when she said, "Maybe wear a gun? I don't trust that Sheldrake, not one bit!"

Jed set down his fork and sighed. "Neither do I, Lil, but we've talked about this. You know how I feel about that sort of thing. You wear a gun for anything other than hunting wild game and you are inviting trouble into your life." He wiped his mouth with a green-and-white check napkin. "I saw enough gunplay between men in the war. More than enough. Why is it that everyone is trying to get me to arm myself all of a sudden?"

"Everyone?" she said.

"Yeah, you and Loud. You're about the only folks I know well, anyway."

She smiled. "Well, he's sensible sometimes. I'll give him credit."

"He come by earlier, did he?" said Jed, as he sipped his coffee.

"Of course. The man would starve if I closed my doors. And don't think I didn't notice you changed the topic, mister."

He smiled and was about to respond when he saw her own smile dwindle as she looked past him toward the door. Jed looked over his left shoulder to see two familiar men walking in and making for an empty table in midroom, trying not to appear as drunk as they were. One of them walked with an interesting, mincing gait.

"You know them?" said Jed.

"No, not really. They haven't been in town long. Took breakfast here yesterday. Somebody said they work for Sheldrake." She looked at Jed.

He sighed. "Yeah, they do, indeed. That's them, the two from yesterday."

"Oh," she said. "Hmm, one of them is not walking so good, more than being drunk."

Jed smirked and sipped his coffee.

"Jed Stark," she whispered, "what did you do?"

"Not me. Blame Mama." He leaned toward her and winked. "Peppered their backsides to help escort them home."

"Oh, she is a fiery thing."

From one of the newcomers, a long belch rose up. The other giggled, then the belcher said, in too loud a voice, "I get any coffee here?"

A half dozen other patrons looked away, back to their own plates and companions, resuming their own talk in lowered voices.

Any mirth on Jed's face slipped away. She patted his arm. "Don't worry. It'll be fine. Drunken fools happen all the time. Let me tend to them, and they'll wander on out of here." She got up and straightened her apron as she walked over to their table.

"About time, missy!" The man smacked a hand on the tabletop, and the other fellow giggled again.

Lilly noticed that the giggler was sitting awkwardly on the side of the chair. "You look to be in pain, mister. Tell you what, you can use the whole seat. I won't charge extra."

The man looked up at her, a dark scowl narrowing his eyes. "I don't want back talk, especially from the likes of you!"

Seated, Jed spun in his chair and saw his sweetheart's face darken and her jaw set. He pointed a long finger at the man. "That's enough out of you!"

The belcher looked up at Jed and a smile spread on his face. "Well now, lookee here! If it ain't our friend, the moonshiner!"

"Not a friend," said Jed, through tight teeth, his voice low and grating. He eyed them both and noted that Lilly had walked away, likely hoping to defuse the bubbling tension in the café with a couple of cups of coffee.

"Yeah, well, from what I hear you and your ol' mama ain't nothing but moonshiners."

"You'll have to work harder than that to insult me, mister." Jed leveled his cold gaze on the speaker.

"Ha!" said the drunk. "Makes no never mind to me, big man." His comments tailed off in a giggle.

Jed held his tongue. All eyes were on the usually quiet, soft-spoken man. He pulled in a deep breath through his nose and stared at the newcomer. "It's true I am no moonshiner, although that is an honorable pursuit. What I am is a whiskey maker, a distiller of legal whiskey, something my family has been doing for a whole lot of years back, as most folks will be able to tell you."

Jed Stark stood, gently shoving back the chair so that it squawked and stuttered on the smooth-worn puncheons. "I am, in fact, a whole lot of things. But one thing I am not is a man who will tolerate ignorant insults, not at me and certainly not at a lady. As for my mother, if she were here, she'd tell you all manner of things and then run you out by her own self."

The insulter snorted back a chuckle and did nothing to hide his smirk as he shook his head.

Jed squared off before the man, a good six feet between them. "But seeing as how Mama isn't here to defend her good honor, I reckon I will have to do that for her."

With the coffeepot in hand, Lilly walked over.

For the first time, the newcomer's confident, breezy, arrogant air slipped a pinch, and the right side of his mouth drooped as his eyebrows rose.

Jed strode another step forward. "First, apologize to the lady," he said in a low, even tone, but with a hard edge, sounding like steel grinding on steel. "Both of you."

A patron two tables away shifted in her seat and the insulter snapped out of his momentary state of surprise.

With effort, the drunken man pulled on his former smug look, but not fully. Because on Jed's face he saw a look of granite, as if something had been decided and would not be altered.

He was reminded once more that Jed Stark was not a slight man, as his seated demeanor had seemed to indicate.

"I—I guess we won't do that," said the chattier of the two men. "No sir, we won't do it."

"Last chance," said Jed.

"Tell you what," said the man, rising on unsteady legs. He looked over his left shoulder. "Get up, Clem." The other man also rose, wincing as he did so.

"We had about enough of taking orders from you. And we certainly ain't going to apologize to any half-breed China woman, or whatever she is!"

Jed covered the six feet or so between him and them in what seemed a single long step. At the same time, his wide, muscled right ham of a fist arched up and caught the chatty nearer man under the chin. The fellow stiffened, his eyebrows rose, and his eyes looked to the ceiling.

As he struggled to catch a breath and stay upright, he swerved to his left, toward the table. Jed's fist flashed again and slammed into the side of the man's face, up high on the cheek bone, directing the fellow to fall away from the table, which he did, slopping to the wood floor with scant grace.

It was only then that folks from the other tables reacted, with gasps and pushing their own chairs back in efforts at self-preservation. But they were at it seconds later when the second man, he of the sore backside, lurched himself forward at Jed. "Hey! You can't do that to Rollo!"

"I already did, Clem," said Jed, and doled out the same treatment to this wobbly fellow.

Clem dropped as if it had been planned, atop his chum. Both men lay in an unmoving heap between tables.

"Jed! Are you all right?" Lilly hadn't moved from her spot a few feet from the table, her pot of hot coffee poised.

"Me? I'm fine, Lil. Sorry about the ruckus. I tried to make sure they wouldn't break any furniture."

She smiled. "You did fine, Jed." She moved to the other tables to pour cups of calming coffee. The other patrons, most of whom Jed was familiar with, having lived his entire life outside of Glen Rose proper, all looked at him with wide eyes. No one was speaking . . . yet.

Over her shoulder, Lilly said, "Finish your pie and coffee, Jed. Then maybe you can take out that trash before it starts to stink any worse than it does now." She snorted back a laugh, and Jed smiled, shaking his head.

He did not wait, but set to his task right away, lest the fools awaken and cause further unwanted commotion. As he suspected, when he muckled onto the collars of the two men and glanced over, he saw that most eyes were on him. Jed knew he had instigated the more violent aspects of the situation, but in his estimation, the strangers had required the attention he gave them—and a whole lot more.

He dragged them over to the door, opened it, then dragged them on through. Once outside, he paused again to close the door behind him but Lilly appeared and winked at him. "Thank you, honey," she said in a low voice, then closed the door.

That wink warmed him all the way along the trip to the marshal's office, halfway down the long main street. It seemed to Jed that the route had stretched in length somehow since he'd last been in town. "Or you're getting old," he mumbled as he dragged the two men on down the boardwalk.

He made it to the door beneath the swinging sign that read GLEN ROSE LAW, MARSHAL CHISWICK.

Jed knocked once out of courtesy. He'd seen light from inside, so he was sure someone might be in there. As he looked in, he was a bit disappointed to see that Marshal Chiswick himself was in, and not his assistant, Deputy Thompson.

Jed had known Lawrence Chiswick his entire life, and they had never gotten on very well. That Chiswick became the local law did not surprise Jed, as Lawrence had been prone as a youth to being a bully always hungry for dominance in any situation, from schoolboy games to the hijinks of young manhood.

Jed, on the other hand, had been quiet but had stood out because he had increasingly been large for his age, broad of shoulder and fleet of foot and fist, although he had never sought the prowess he had evinced his entire life, nor the dominance that resulted.

Instead, he had sought to see each task well done and quietly, and he had always enjoyed his own company. This was something Chiswick seldom seemed to seek, so often had Jed seen him holding court and blathering his various opinions to anyone who was unfortunate enough to be caught by the bloviating lawman.

The two old acquaintances exchanged glances. Jed nodded. "Marshal, how do."

"Jed Stark." Chiswick also nodded. "What you got there, Jed?"

"Trash, in a manner of speaking." He dragged the two unconscious men in and let their shoulders and heads drop the six or so inches to the jail floor. "Drunk and disorderly at Lilly's. Insulting folks and such."

"Nothing unusual in that, Stark. That's about what everybody gets up to at night in Glen Rose." Chiswick looked down at the two men on his floor. "I do believe they have been accosted. You the cause of this?"

"Yep," said Jed, "for good reason."

The marshal leaned his head to one side and snorted.

"You weren't there, marshal. I was. And so was a dining room full of folks."

"That's right, I wasn't there." He looked down at the men again. "And I do believe I know them."

"I expect you do, seeing as how they are in the employ of Merlin Sheldrake."

"What's that mean?"

Jed shrugged. "What I said." But Jed and Chiswick both knew what was left unsaid. That the lawman, as well as Glen Rose's mayor, another local boy they had both grown up with, Fen Hawkins, were wedged tight and deep in Merlin Sheldrake's back pocket.

Everybody knew it, and most folks in Glen Rose, if not pleased with the fact, were at least willing to overlook it as long as Sheldrake continued to honor his loudmouth promises of spending a whole lot of money in town.

And to date he had, with much of it having been doled out on behalf of his growing whiskey distillery and warehouse, not too far out of town, northeastward. A goodly amount of the building materials, as well as the manpower to assemble those materials, had come from Glen Rose businesses and the local populace. As long as there was money and work, it seemed that Sheldrake could do much as he pleased.

And to top it all off, Sheldrake had stopped shy of promising the arrival of a railroad right into Glen Rose. And everybody knew that nothing said prosperity and good times more than a railroad station in a town.

The lawman shook his head. "What all do you want me to do about them?"

Jed didn't answer with words, but the men eyed each other a long moment.

Chiswick sighed. "All right, drag them into the cell, and they can sleep it off. But I see no reason to hold them past the morning."

"Up to you," said Jed, relieved that his dragging was over with. He'd begun to regret knocking them cold.

"You're sure right it's up to me. I am the marshal here. You'd be wise to not forget it."

Jed, as was his custom, paused a moment before replying. That moment gave him time to hold his tongue from letting loose the thing he really wanted to say, which in his experience was often a sharp word that could be unkind. No sense letting folks get under his skin. He'd never seen the point in it.

"Why, Marshal Chiswick, I don't believe there's a soul in Glen Rose who could forget that fact."

Jed left the two men on the floor of the cell, laid out side by side in an untidy sprawl. He clanged the door behind him and tipped his hat to the lawman with a smile as he opened the front door and stepped out onto the boardwalk.

He made his way back to Lilly's, rubbing his chin and wondering for the first time what the future might bring to him, Mama, and Whiskey Woods. It sure seemed as if Merlin Sheldrake was tightening some sort of grip he had on the little town Jed had once considered to be a fairly sleepy place. And with it, Jed felt the squeeze of that grip, and he wasn't so certain he liked it. Not at all.

He spent a few hours with Lilly, some of them helping her to close up the café and then clean up the place, sweep the floor, wipe tables, and tidy chairs while she worked in the kitchen to prepare for the early morning breakfast crowd. That was certainly what it was called, for while Lilly Chu had gained justifiable fame for the tastiness of her cooking, it was for her ample breakfast plates that she was most known.

And making all that food required a whole lot of preparation. And that required time, something that became shorter the closer they got to morning. "Good thing for me that Polly comes in early to help."

"Lucky for me, you mean," said Jed, wrapping his big arms

around Lilly. Since she owned the building itself, a modest two-story affair, it was a small thing to lock up the café and climb the stairs to her own rooms. Jed always liked visiting with her there. She kept a tidy place, sparsely furnished but comfortable, and with a pleasant mix of but a few curious possessions that had belonged to both her Texan mother and her Chinese father.

She talked about them little, but with affection, and Jed knew that she missed them. In a way, he was pleased to know that he was one of the few people in the world she might consider to be as close as family, somehow. It also frightened him a bit. He knew he should make a decision about their relationship someday soon, but somehow, he never got around to it.

Hadn't Mama always said that if a thing worked, leave it be?

"What are you thinking, Jed?"

"Hmm? Oh, not much. This Sheldrake foolishness, I reckon."

A few long moments of silence passed between them, then Lilly said, "Doesn't it bother you, Jed?"

He let out a thoughtful long breath. "It's irksome, but that's not the same thing, is it?"

"No, I guess it isn't."

"It's a funny thing, though," he continued. "Everybody seems more worried about what Sheldrake is going to do with the Starks than the Starks are. Meaning me and Mama."

"Why do you suppose that is?" said Lilly.

"I reckon it's because we know something nobody else knows."

"What's that?"

"That the recipe he wants so much, for our whiskey, isn't even written down."

"No?" she said, a bit surprised.

"Nope. It exists, all right, but in my head and in Mama's. Nowhere else. It's never been written down, in fact."

"Well," said Lilly, "that's what makes it so special. And so funny, then."

"How's that?"

"That the thing Merlin Sheldrake wants so badly doesn't exist in the way it would be most useful to him."

"I guess so. Never thought of it that way. But yep, you about said it. The recipe he keeps trying to buy and then trying to steal doesn't exist. It's the funniest of jokes."

CHAPTER 5

"The annoying thing about Stark is that he's honest, curse him." Porter Sneed looked through the blue haze of cigar smoke that perennially clouded before him, his pink, clean-shaven face widening in a chuckle.

The two men to whom he spoke, Whistler Denny and T. M. McCloud, also chuckled and nodded in agreement.

Sneed was the loudest of the three men, all of whom were in the same trade, that of peddling whiskey to bar owners. They worked for large outfits, all of which were based elsewhere than Glen Rose. But the town, located in the heart of a vast whiskey-making region, as well as being the heart of that region, had always been a place for the three men, although rivals, to meet up and discuss the vagaries and headaches of their business.

They also were able to divvy up the region such that each man and, more important, the company he represented, was able to have a go at a roughly equal share of the whiskey pie, as it were.

Not to say that each man didn't then try to weasel into his chums' accounts when and where he could. But that was considered fair and expected among the three. After all, this method had always worked fairly well for them all. Until Merlin Sheldrake showed up, that is.

He'd lumbered into town laying out money and cash-paying jobs for all manner of refurbishment projects and brand-new building tasks, too, such as the mammoth distillery he'd built barely outside of town.

Soon the three men found it nearly impossible to compete with the man who owned whiskey-making enterprises up North and back East, as well as a rail line. And he had a coin purse that never seemed to empty.

It was all the three men could do to stay in business in the town themselves. At least each man could draw cold comfort from the fact that they had vast territories where they sold their companies' liquors that stretched far beyond Glen Rose and the surrounding region. But for how long?

For Sheldrake had begun to flex his reach outward in a wider, vaster way, and to best them at their own long-played game. Then, a couple of years after his bombastic arrival, he had summoned them to the Money Tree, or as he called it, his private club. He fed them and tried to pour liquor into them, but it was his own blend, and it was bad booze.

But that didn't even matter, for Sheldrake was the richest among them, by far, and more important, he was set to bring a rail line to town. Considering he had already bought up the two competing freighting outfits, the three drummers found most of their whiskey orders were in the hands of Sheldrake. Once the train came in, he'd have the entire region locked up tight.

Sheldrake's whiskey, even as bad as it was, anchored every warehouse at freight yards for vast distances around Glen Rose. And on top of that, he owned several of the freight yards, too, including the one at Glen Rose, which he made into the largest in the region.

No, Merlin Sheldrake was not someone they had enjoyed having as a competitor. But now he was far more than that. He was in many ways their boss, precisely because he controlled when and how their clients' whiskey made it to them. In other words, they were beholden, in almost every way, to Merlin Sheldrake.

Porter leaned forward and folded his fleshy hands before him on the polished tabletop. In a lowered voice, he said, "And the annoying thing about Sheldrake is he's not. Honest, I mean."

He leaned back once more, nodding at the truth he'd spoken. The other two men glanced at each other and offered quick nods, but did not say a thing.

As if the mention of his name were a cue from a stagehand, Merlin Sheldrake flung the door to the room wide and, fat hand gripping the brass knob, regarded the three shocked faces looking up at him. He assessed each in turn, and did not offer a smile or a word of greeting.

Finally, he did smile, only with his mouth, and entered the room. "If I did not know better, I'd swear you gentlemen were talking about me." As he said this last bit, he locked eyes with Porter Sneed and let his smile fade.

"Now," said Sheldrake, smacking his hands together and resuming his slow walk about the perimeter of the room, a back of the action chamber that was closed to all but Sheldrake's business interests, and any others the rich man might choose to invite in.

He'd bought the old, worn Glen Rose Saloon and renamed it the Money Tree Tavern, and spent a tidy fortune in fixing it up in and out. Then he hired a burly man from elsewhere as the bartender. The man was a brute, with a gleaming bald head and waxed mustaches. There were women in fancy dress as well, but they weren't there for sporting with the clientele.

In fact, once the novelty of visiting the Money Tree had dulled, most men avoided going there, as it was expensive and did not serve Stark whiskey. Plus, the barkeep was a menacing looking fellow, and the women weren't interested in much more than looking nice. And with no poker playing allowed, it hardly seemed worth the effort to frequent the place.

What's more, when he was in town, which was more often than not these days, Sheldrake could usually be found there, smiling a fake smile and eyeballing everything and everyone, and making the situation feel downright strange, especially when all a fellow went in there for was a glass of cool beer on a hot afternoon.

As a consequence, the Money Tree was often bereft of people other than the scant number of employees, which suited its owner fine. In fact, it made an ideal place for Merlin Sheldrake to use as an office and a place from which to conduct business.

"I do hope you men were considering spending some of your time talking about the Starks' Whiskey Woods brand of whiskey. Because it has one significant flaw—it does not yet belong to Merlin Sheldrake."

He scowled and looked at each man in turn. They fidgeted in their chairs and looked everywhere but at the fat man.

"The thing you three men need to understand is that while all of you at one time or another, and more than once each, from what I have been told, have been authorized by your employers to purchase Stark's whiskey business, recipes, the whole deal, not a single one of you has succeeded."

Sneed perked up. "And you have, Sheldrake?"

Again, Merlin Sheldrake scowled at the one of the three he disliked the most. "No, not yet. But I will. And soon."

"How?"

"Never you mind, but it's going to happen."

"From what I have heard, you tried yet again to convince the Starks that they needed to sell to you, but it didn't work out too well. And then your men tried the same and met with Mother Stark herself. And her best friend, Ol' Shredder."

Sneed cracked a smile and risked a look from his chums up

at Sheldrake. The big man's reddening face jellied Porter's innards, and he looked down at his fumbling fat hands again.

"Well, I am going to succeed, I tell you that here and now. One way or another the Starks will be driven out of business and will no longer be a burr under my saddle."

"You said that, what was it, two, three months ago?"

"This time, I assure you, Whiskey Woods booze will be mine. Or it will be dead."

"Seems a shame," said Sneed.

"A shame?" bellowed Sheldrake.

"Well, yes, I mean that whiskey is pretty much the best of the best. Heck, saloon owners from beyond Glen Rose buy it because their customers want it, and if they don't carry it, they don't get the business."

"And you think that's acceptable," said Sheldrake, almost breathless.

Sneed shrugged. "Jed Stark is fair. He doesn't gouge anyone with his prices. He knows his whiskey is superior to most anything else available, so he charges a little more than most, but it's not an unfair rate, especially considering the quality of it. Even at that, most folks hereabouts and from farther away, too, think pretty highly of Jed Stark's whiskey. And his mama's before that, and—"

"And her father's before that!" said Whistler Denny, eyes wide and already regretting contributing to the conversation.

"That's right," nodded Sneed. "Jed Stark's grandpappy began the trade, and from what I heard, he brought the skill to make decent whiskey with him all the way from Tennessee or some such. Back where they really know their business, I tell you."

"So what?" growled Sheldrake, smacking the chair back before him, which happened to be the very chair T. M. McCloud was seated in. The small, meek man jumped and a squeaking noise rose up from his mouth.

"I don't care if people like Stark whiskey! I don't care if Jed Stark is all but an angel among mere mortals!"

"Sure, none of us much like the fact, and our bosses surely don't, but there's nothing we can do." Sneed shrugged again, looking to his fellows for confirmation that his words rang true with them, too.

They offered small nods.

"Besides, it's competition, Mr. Sheldrake," said T. M. McCloud, in a quiet but steady voice.

Sheldrake resumed stalking the room, and angled around the table, then he turned and looked at McCloud through narrowed eyes. "I choose my competition, gentlemen. That's the only reason any of you have employment with your so-called bosses. Because I choose to allow it. Never forget that. And never forget that when I want something, I stop at nothing to attain it. And I want the Stark recipe, and what's more, I want them out of business, to boot. And I will stop at nothing, gentlemen, to see that it happens."

"What does that mean, Sheldrake?" said Sneed.

"You mind your own business."

Sneed reddened and pulled in a big breath. "I think that's precisely what I am doing. What we all are doing, am I right, boys?" Sneed felt good and riled and had no concern about showing it. "What will you do with the recipe once you get it? Set up an even bigger production plant and have at it?"

Sheldrake barked a harsh, quick laugh. "Hardly."

"What then, Sheldrake?"

The fat rich man's eyebrows rose. "I'll burn it."

"What?"

"Burn the paper it's on, and then wipe out any trace of Whiskey Woods whiskey."

"But—but it's a premium whiskey!"

"So? So's mine."

Whistler Denny and T. M. McCloud did their best to suppress laughs, and Sneed snorted.

It was well known that Sheldrake's whiskey was so poorly made that it was barely worthy of the word *whiskey*. He had been known to color it with tobacco, use gunpowder and snake heads, and mix in all manner of cheap ingredients to kick it off, as the saying went.

His swill would get a man drunk, but at best it would also leave him hunched and howling in an alleyway. At worst, well, some men had succumbed to the darkest of sleeps due to the poisons the rotgut had inflicted on them.

"But, gentlemen," Sheldrake flashed a smug smirk as he strode slowly around the table, behind the seated men, his thick, fat man's hands smacking hard on the back of each chair and sliding along it before dropping off and slowly moving to the next.

The seated men glanced at each other over their shoulders. Merlin Sheldrake was not a man it served to turn one's back on.

"I didn't say I would begin with that approach. Stopping at nothing means I have to begin somewhere, right?"

The three whiskey drummers, already with brows raised high in concern, now glanced at each other again, uncertain of what this comment meant. They considered this for too long, apparently, because Sheldrake's voice cut in on their shared concerned silence. "Right?"

"Sure, yes, makes sense," said Whistler.

"You bet it does."

The normally quiet T. M. McCloud cleared his throat.

"Yes, T. M.? You have something of use to offer this conversation?"

"Well, yes sir. I mean I don't know, sir. But, well—what does all this have to do with us, Mr. Sheldrake?"

"Ah, a good point," said the fat man. "You see, I have you, as they say, over a barrel. Each one of you, and your companies, too. What I will require of you is your undivided support in this endeavor."

"You mean," said Sneed, "to support the next phase of your campaign to drive the Starks out of business."

"That is precisely what I mean," said Sheldrake.

"But, well—why? Why should we support you in this?"

"Because if you do, I will pass along significant deals on the various whiskeys and other liquors I sell. And this means you will make a whole lot more money than you are now."

While the drummers wanted no part of Sheldrake's increasing zeal, they knew what he said was possible. After all, he was the most powerful man in the region.

"But what—what if we would rather not?"

"Rather not?" said Sheldrake, eyebrows arched. "Rather not what? Rather not make money?"

The questioner, Whistler Denny, turned an even deeper shade of red and looked at his hands.

"Rather not support your efforts to wipe out the Stark brand," said Sneed, feeling an increase in annoyance with Sheldrake.

"Ah, well," said the rich man. "That would be . . . most unfortunate for each of you. Yes, most unfortunate, indeed." He let that notion hang in the air of the room, then he smiled. "Now if you all will excuse me, I have to go listen to another bunch of fools regarding some recent diplomatic work I asked them to attend to."

Again the men exchanged glances. This time, Porter Sneed said, "Now hold on a minute, Merlin."

Now it was time for Sheldrake's eyebrows to rise. Nobody ever called him that, not even the women he paid to share his bed.

Sneed saw Sheldrake's face and color began slipping down and away from his own smooth-shaven, ruddy cheeks. "Oh, no offense, Mr. Sheldrake. What I mean is . . . well, we always show up here at your request. And I don't think any of us"—

here Sneed glanced at his fellow whiskey men—"uh, I'm not so sure any of us appreciate being called fools."

"Oh," said Sheldrake. "I didn't realize I had done such a thing. Called you fools, you say? Huh. No, no, I would not refer to my colleagues in the whiskey trade as fools. At least not those I consider my equals." He tapped his pursed lips with a forefinger and glanced at the pressed-tin ceiling, as if some obscure answer to some unspoken question was written up there somewhere.

Sheldrake reached the door and paused, glancing back at them all. "Oh, and by the way, Porter?" Sheldrake waited until he had the man's attention, as well as that of Whistler and T. M.

"I heard what you said earlier, and I did not appreciate that snort of opinion about me or my fine whiskey. In future, if any of you drummers so much as mutters a thing against me or my Sheldrake's Finest brand of whiskey—and I say this not as a threat but as a statement, a bald fact—that will not be tolerated.

"Rest assured I, Merlin Sheldrake, will stop at nothing to uphold and protect the hard-earned, stellar reputation of Sheldrake's Finest Whiskey, and that it continues on untarnished. Right?"

The brief silence was accompanied by wide eyes and sagging jaws. Then, as Sheldrake was about to repeat his last word, Whistler stuttered out, "Oh, y-yes, right, then—Mr. Sheldrake."

The big whiskey titan grinned wide. "Good, good. I'm pleased to hear we all agree with one another. Now," he smacked his pink hands together and rubbed them, "time for a meal and then to hear what my fools have to say. Gentlemen," he said, tipping his head at the three seated men. He grasped the door handle, yanked it open, and left them all sitting there.

Much of a minute passed in silence before any one of the men spoke.

Finally, in a soft voice, McCloud said, "Any of you all ever seen Sheldrake so worked up? I have known him a long time, and he's always been a prickly pear, but hoo-boy, lately he's a riled viper."

"It's that Stark. Pain in the backside is what he is. Why he doesn't up and sell to Sheldrake I'll never know. Heck, as much money as I've heard Sheldrake has offered Jed Stark, the man and his old mother have to be pure loco. No other word for it."

Chapter 6

"Well," said Merlin Sheldrake. "It's nice to see that you two dolts have decided to stop hiding from me! Marshal Chiswick informed me that you idiots—"

"Now hang on, Mr. Sheldrake, see, that . . . now that ain't right, right there." Rollo eyed his boss, then lost his nerve and looked at his boots once more.

Sheldrake returned the stare and continued. "You two idiots even made a hash of things with the Starks at their ranch. This did not come as much of a shock to me, and frankly, I am only surprised that I had not foreseen this turn of events. Because when I first hired you two buffoons, I did so with trepidation. You did not impress me in the least, despite the fact that you came recommended to me. By another fool—I see that now. My initial disappointment in your individual and shared intellect at our first meeting has only increased since then."

Sheldrake eyed them and then sighed. "Alas, when I can find other men with more competence, which, frankly, should not be that difficult, then I will release you from my employment. You will, of course, be paid, but not the complete amount we had initially agreed upon. Precisely because you have failed me twice now."

"Twice? How you figure that?"

"First, and most importantly, at failing to retrieve the Stark whiskey recipe from Whiskey Woods, and second, last night in the Glen Rose Café, you made yourselves out to be even bigger idiots. I, frankly, did not think that was possible. But there it is." Sheldrake hung his head and shook it as if he were in the deepest throes of abject disappointment.

"The only question remains now is: What am I to do with you? You have failed me twice, and I dare not risk a third time. I dare not, and yet I am tempted to. I admit that, and I say it knowing full well it rubs hard against my better judgment. But there is a sliver of possibility for you two . . . men. The thinnest sliver, I admit, but it is there.

"But before we go on, tell me, because I must know, although I can hazard a winning guess, how it is you both came to be wincing with every move? You both appear to be sullied about the face, with you, Rollo, looking worse than Clem. But you, Clem, look to have some new sort of predilection for unkempt clothing. Particularly in your nether region."

"Huh?"

Sheldrake sighed. "Your trousers, man, around back, they appear to have been met with force. Let me guess . . . by the stinging assault of a few well-placed lead nuggets from a certain old woman's well-aimed shotgun. Am I incorrect?"

Neither man wished to be the first to speak, although they each knew the boss man despised not being answered. Finally, Rollo looked up, his fingertips out of reflex rose to pat his tender face. "Yes, sir, Mr. Sheldrake, we did as you said, but that old woman, Minnie Stark, she come out of that cabin of hers with her shotgun barking low and mean! Not much we could do but make for cover. Seeing as we were there on a mission of kindness, as you put it, we didn't think we needed to defend ourselves. So we had to bolt on out of there, away from her."

"I see. And your face, Rollo?"

"Well, that happened afterwards. Down to the diner."

"Let me guess, by the old woman again?"

"Oh no, sir," said the taller of the two hirelings, not interpreting the faintest of smiles on Sheldrake's face.

"But," interrupted Clem, "it was another Stark, though. It was Jed Stark, and you know what sort of man he is."

"And?" Sheldrake's eyebrows rose.

"And what?" said Clem.

The whiskey baron sighed again. "And what sort of man is Stark, then?"

"Oh, well, he's a Stark. You know."

"No, no, I do not. Why don't you tell me, then?"

Another long moment of quiet ended when Sheldrake sighed. "Very well, gentlemen. It is time to move ourselves to the next step in this most important of games."

"What game is that, Mr. Sheldrake?"

The big man rubbed a temple. "There is only one thing in all of life and living that means anything. Now listen closely because anyone who has to be told this should be done away with should they require a second explanation. I trust I am clear on that account."

The two men exchanged confused looks but nodded, acquainted well enough by now with the boss man and his odd, wordy ways.

"Good. The most important thing of all, and frankly I belittle it when I refer to it as a game, is this, gentlemen: the acquisition of power and the acquisition of money. And although they may sound as if they are two separate things, they are not. They are one and the same; one leads directly to the next, and they are the game, the only thing, the very reason any of us are here at all."

"How do you figure that, Mr. Sheldrake?"

"That is an interesting question, Rollo. Particularly as it comes from someone such as yourself."

Rollo narrowed one eye and looked at the ground a few feet ahead. He wasn't sure, but he might have been insulted. Have to think on that later.

The boss man was forever saying things like that, and they sure sounded like barbs. And from about any other man Rollo had ever met, most of them in barrooms, that sort of thing would earn the fellow a riser to the chin. But with the boss, even though he was a fat man, and soft all about—only thing hard on him was his nose—Merlin Sheldrake was powerful.

But there was something more than that about him, too. And Clem agreed with him on this point, too: Merlin Sheldrake was downright frightening when it came to it.

Sheldrake clearing his throat in a false and loud way popped Rollo's thoughts. The hired fellow jerked back in surprise to see the boss man staring at him. That meant to Rollo he'd been lost in his mind again. That was forever happening, even when he was a child.

"Enough blather. I have decided," said Sheldrake, regarding the two men with narrowed eyes, "that I will retain your services, but only on a trial basis. If you succeed in this latest task, then I shall have good reason to find my faith in both of you renewed, and I will not only keep you on as employees, but I will raise your pay."

Rollo and Clem traded grins, despite their battered faces and twinging backsides.

"Yes, I thought you would like that, you jackals." Sheldrake chuckled. "However, if you should fail at this task, then I will have no choice but to—well, let us agree, shall we, that it would be in your best interests if you did not fail me. Succeed . . . or else."

There was something convincing in the boss's tone, a cold, hardness matched with the steely look he gave them. Any sense of tolerance, however false, Sheldrake had shown them now slid from him, leaving a face that looked to be hacked out of raw stone.

The two men could do no more than nod in mute silence. The fat rich man had a way of knocking their pins out from under them, driving in the last unassailable words of a conversation with frightening force.

They agreed to not fail him, because they knew, without having to be told, what the consequences would be. They agreed to all this even before they knew what it was they were agreeing to do. Had they known, they reckoned they would agree to do the job, no matter how distasteful they found it, precisely because of the very real ice-cold dagger of fear they each felt.

"Good, I am pleased to hear and see that you buffoons understand me completely. Now, you'll need to leave me because I am busy and you two men will soon be. I suggest, as you wait for word from me, that you will refrain from blathering in public. If I hear that you have mentioned our conversation to anyone, you will be—well . . ." He chuckled. "That will amount to failing. And we all know what that means."

Neither of the two men actually knew precisely what it meant, but they had a solid idea it would not be pleasant. Once again, they nodded their agreement. As they took their leave, Rollo paused in the doorway.

"Um, I, or we, have a question, Mr. Sheldrake."

"Yes?"

"Well, what's the thing you want us to do?"

"I will let you know when you need to know, but in the meantime, continue to report to me each morning. There is plenty here at the distillery and warehouse that needs attention, the sort of work you two are equipped for."

"Yes sir. All right, sir. We'll see you in the morning." Rollo made his way through the open door and Clem followed, then stopped and turned, looking back at Sheldrake. "Boss, what's a jackal?"

Sheldrake snorted. "Find a mirror."

Chapter 7

"That was something, Mama."

"What do you mean?"

"Sharing that corn bread recipe with Lilly."

She shrugged. "I trust her. Besides, if she's going to be the next Mrs. Stark, she'll know all the family secrets, anyway."

"Now, Mama. Nothing's been decided on that score. Heck, nothing's been said yet."

"Then it's about time, don't you think?"

Jed narrowed his eyes. "I'm going on out to check the still."

She chuckled as he walked out of her kitchen. "He's feeling it, all right. Sooner than later he'll do the job. Hee hee!"

Jed filled the next few hours working out in the shop and then in the whiskey shed, a close, always warm place Jed had felt at home and warm and safe and comfortable in his entire life. But although he worked elbow-deep in the morning's whiskey making, Jed found he could not settle his mind to the thing.

More and more his thinking turned, not of his will but on its own, somehow, to thoughts of his Lilly. It was true she was a beautiful woman, and if pressed perhaps with a pistol barrel to his temple, Jed would have to admit that Lilly bested his own Mama in the kitchen. Barely.

But this was not a question he would ever be forced to answer. And if he somehow did, well, Jed reckoned the only sensible thing a fellow in such a spot could do would be to run. Low and hard and fast.

And the more Jed let his mind have loose rein that morning—then on into the afternoon—the more he realized he missed Lilly, although it had only been a couple of days since he'd been into town. He'd have to disappoint Mama that night and skip supper here at the ranch. He needed to make for town and—hold on there, pard, he told himself, wasn't that what Mama wanted him to do?

As for Lilly, he wasn't so certain about her in that regard. Sure, it was all but agreed they would someday be a husband-and-wife team, wasn't it?

Well, no, he admitted. They'd never actually discussed it in those raw terms, but he was going along fine, and he suspected or assumed she was, too. Had he been wrong all these years?

No, not with Lilly. She seemed to feel toward him like she always had. And she didn't seem to want any more from him, did she?

These thoughts and more left Jed muddled beyond measure. By late afternoon, he'd all but made up his mind to forfeit the trip to town that evening. He was tuckered out, anyway. And besides, he didn't want to give Mama any more of a reason to think she won whatever argument they hadn't had in the first place.

"Redeye," said Jed, looking down at the dog, who was doing what he did best, holding down his little patch of earth. Jed had to hand it to the old hound, he was dedicated to his craft of making certain that worn groove he'd carved for himself years before in a corner of the dirt floor of the whiskey shed didn't up and fly off.

"Hey, Redeye!"

The hound cracked an eye, saw that it was Jed Stark staring

down at him, recognized that the man was harmless, and let the lid close once more.

Jed grinned and shook his head. "Well, at least you're true to who you are. And that is a good reminder that I should be, too. A man can't be anything but what he is, eh, dog?"

Jed banked the fire and checked the mash and water, then glanced at the dog once more. "It sure was nice catching up with you, Redeye. Let's do it again some time."

The dog broke wind, and Jed strode to the house, his mind made up. At least about going to town. He would, and that was enough. Would have to be for everyone else, too.

Scarcely an hour later, spiffed and feeling tired but fine, Jed rode into town, making for the Glen Rose Café. He walked in the front door to find Loudon visiting with Lilly, no doubt to share gossip. They were both inclined that way. Jed nearly made it to the table before either of them noticed him.

He smiled down at Lilly. "Hello, Lil. You look good tonight."

"Thank you, Jed. But you're a liar. My hair's a mess, my apron's filthy, and I didn't sleep well last night. Been up since four. But if you lie to me again, I might find the energy to pour you a cup of coffee and—"

"And perhaps, while you're back there, you might find more pie?" said Loudon, unafraid and unashamed to interrupt when there was the potential for pie in the conversation. Especially Lilly's pie.

Jed tossed his hat on the near chair, and said, "I can get the coffee, Lil. No need to wait on me."

"Yeah," said Loudon, speaking into his coffee cup. "Not like you two are married or anything."

From the sudden silence at the table, which emerged as if conjured, the comment turned out to be one of the more awkward things the chubby newsman had said in the past week, and he was not known for his tact much of the time.

Lilly excused herself, her face looking a mite redder than usual as she bustled to the kitchen to fetch coffee and pie.

"What on earth is wrong with you, Loud?"

"What? Well, what do you mean, Jed?"

But they both knew that Loudon was aware of his poor choice of words.

For the second time in mere moments, another awkward silence descended on the once-chipper table. And then Lilly returned, smiling, looking weary, Jed had to admit, but looking so very pretty.

No, he would not mind in the least coming into the house from a long day at the ranch to find Lilly in the kitchen, singing as she often did while she cooked, and looking over at him with that very same smile he was now seeing.

"Oh, you two," she said, sitting down once more. "I have a couple of minutes before I need to make the rounds," she waved her hand at the other half-dozen tables, all of them filled. It was not surprising—Lilly's café always seemed to look that way.

"Loudon was about to tell me something juicy about Sheldrake's men," she said. "The two that were in here the other night, in fact."

"That right, Loud?" said Jed.

"Oh, yes, well, indeed it is true. What sort of newsman would I be if I went about telling lies all the time?"

Lilly sighed and looked at Jed. "You know those two men you knocked cold the other night and dragged to the jail?"

"Yes," said Jed, half grinning. "But I thought you said Loudon hadn't told you anything yet?"

"Well, not much yet. Anyway," she said, waving off his question. "They were set free!"

Jed sipped his coffee. "I figured so. He pretty much told me he was going to." He shrugged. "Not much to it, anyway. They were drunks making a scene." He sipped again.

Loudon nodded.

"But," continued Jed. "I suppose it verifies, in some thin way, what we all know, which is that Chiswick is an employee of Sheldrake. Heck, he might well be paid by him, too."

"Those are bold words, Jed," said Loudon, bending over his pie and speaking in a lowered voice. He glanced around at the other diners. "Nobody seems to have any interest in our conversation," he continued, now almost in a whisper. "If they did, they are keeping their eyes on their own business. Good."

"Loud? You all right?" Jed tamped down the urge to smile. "Might be you are spending too much time in the dime novels again."

"No, Jed!" he whispered again, unaware that his whisper was quickly becoming louder than his lowered voice. "I am merely protecting what might well be one of the most important news stories of my professional life!"

Now several people at nearby tables did glance his way. Loudon's eyes widened and he said, "It's that story I'm working on about the barking dogs, um, outside of town. I—I can't seem to work up the perfect tone for it . . ."

When he looked back to his table companions, he saw Lilly and Jed chuckling in silence and shaking their heads.

"Well, I'm glad that you two seem to find amusement in this topic!" Loudon had once more lowered his head and keeping his voice at a level that only Jed and Lilly might hear, he plowed ahead. "I, for one, do not think that a wealthy, bloviating bombastic fool who slops into town and attempts to turn everything before him into something he can possess to be a particularly promising turn of events, or is in any way a good thing for Glen Rose! But if you do, why then, by all means, chuckle to your hearts' content. I—"

"Loud," said Jed. "Loud, calm yourself, man."

"Yes," said Lilly. "Calm down, for heaven's sake, and eat your pie with a smile on your face in the knowledge that we are in complete agreement with you. Okay? Now, I have to get back to it. You two stay as long as you like. I won't be far if you need anything."

She walked away and winked at Jed over her shoulder. Despite knowing it was a thing she did, one of her playful ways and one of the many things about her he liked, he felt himself blush.

Loudon smiled. "I know I made a slip of the tongue earlier about you two—and don't take this the wrong way, mind you—but you two are like a married couple."

Jed nodded, realizing he'd been a tad prickly on the subject. "Yeah," he nodded, "feels that way at times, too. Not in a bad way, though."

"Good to hear," said Loudon, eyeing with sadness the nearly empty plate before him.

Jed reckoned he could go on, but never having been the sort of fellow who sought advice from others or to talk with others about much he considered a private matter, Jed held his tongue on that subject.

But another thought came to mind, about his newsman friend, and he voiced that thought. "You know, Loud, I can't help but notice you've been touchier lately than I've known you to be. If there's anything you want to talk about, you know where to find me most any time."

"Oh, I appreciate that, Jed. I do. What I've seen happen to this town and its people since—since that man arrived is a shame. It's gone far beyond worrying, but it seems that people will do about anything for a chance at making money."

Jed shrugged. "It's understandable. Times can be tough now and again. Most folks hereabouts don't have a whole lot, and what they do have they value. So, when somebody comes in and waves cash money under their noses, they sit up and start sniffing."

"Yes, I understand all that, I'm that way myself, although it's not a trait I am proud of."

"Only natural," said Jed, enjoying a bite of pie himself.

"True, but I'll tell you what isn't natural—it's this feeling I've been getting about Sheldrake." Loudon bent his head low again, matching his voice to it and glancing around once more before speaking. "I think something's about to happen."

"Like what?" said Jed, sipping his coffee.

"Like—well, I don't actually know. Yet. But"—he tapped the side of his nose and nodded—"a newsman always trusts his instincts. I'll find out, you bet I will."

"Well, I'll give Sheldrake this much: He seems to make things happen. Busy as he is, it's a wonder he's so fat." Jed smiled.

"I'm serious, Jed. Why, it might well have to do with you and your whiskey."

"Oh, that's not news, Loud. Sheldrake's been trying to buy us out for a few years now."

"Yes, but he seems more frantic now, more desperate, and only where you Starks are concerned."

"Maybe one of those deals he always has cooking isn't going so well, that might account for the more-sour-than-normal look on his homely face. Anyway, I wouldn't worry about it, Loud. You want some friendly advice from a fellow who doesn't like to offer such things?"

"Sure, Jed."

"Head on home and rest up. Maybe don't read a dime novel before you drift off to sleep. It's bound to taint your dreams." He smiled.

Loudon stood and rummaged in his pocket. He pulled out a handful of coins and laid more than enough down on the table beside his pie plate, empty save for a scatter of crumbs.

"I do believe I will take that advice, Mr. Stark. And with that, I bid you, and—" He turned to see if Lilly was close by. She was back in the kitchen. "And will you tell your sweetheart that I said the pie was exquisite, as usual, matched only by the fragrance and splendor of the coffee?"

"Well, I'll tell Lil you enjoyed the pie and coffee. How about that?"

"Close enough. See you tomorrow, Jed."

"Night, Loud."

Later, after he had helped her clean up and close up, Jed and Lilly stood leaning against her worktable in the middle of the kitchen. He realized he was bone tired and thought that Lil looked it, too. It would be an early night for both of them.

As if reading his mind, she said, "What are you going to do now, Jed?"

"What do you mean? Oh, I'm fixing to head on home. Make sure Mama hasn't shot up the place, or more strangers, while I was gone." He grinned.

"Aren't you worried?"

"About what? Sheldrake? Bah, he's a money hound, nothing more. He finds out he can't have what he wants, he'll ease off one of these days."

"But he's been after it for a long time now."

Jed shrugged. "Some folks are slow on the uptake."

"Then your distillery truly isn't for sale and never will be."

Jed jerked his head back, instinct forcing his eyebrows high. "Course not. We've been over this. What a silly thing to say."

Lilly chuckled. "I was checking to make sure you haven't softened."

Jed pressed close to her and nuzzled his bearded face into her neck. "Don't you worry about me going soft, woman."

She giggled and shoved him away. "Run along now, Mr. Stark. I have an early start to my day, not like some folks I know who lay about in bed until all hours."

"Oh, so that's what you think I do, is it?" He grinned.

"I didn't say so, but now that you bring it up, yep."

"Now look here, ma'am," he said, allowing himself to be pushed backward onto the door mat out the back door of the diner, off the kitchen.

"Good night, Mr. Stark," she said and closed the door in his face.

"Good night to you, my dear." He smiled and turned, whistling, walked back to his horse, intending to mount up and ride back home at whatever pace Maggie, his mare, or Mags, as he called her, chose.

That's when he heard a voice from the dark before him and to his left. Jed halted, gripped by a sudden unexpected tension. His right hand slid down along his side to rest atop the hilt of his big dagger-blade hip knife.

"Jed? Jed Stark, that you, old friend?"

Jed groaned. Fendall Hawkins. Mayor Fendall Hawkins. The windiest fellow ever to live in Glen Rose, Texas.

Jed turned. "Fen, how you doing on this fine evening?"

"Oh, you know, I am fair to middling, as they say. Fair to middling. Course, I am getting on in years now. This old body of mine is starting to let me know I ought probably to slow down, you know?"

Jed gathered up the reins and walked the horse along the back lane, on up to where it joined with the main street. "Correct me if I'm wrong, Fen, but weren't you and me together in school?"

"Well, yes, but I meant, well rheumatism tends to run in my family, you see . . ."

"Oh, you don't say. I'm sorry to hear that." Jed was thankful it was dark. He didn't want the pooch-bellied little man to see him grinning. Oh, but it was fun to play with folks. He knew he should watch his words, especially with the mayor, as the man also owned two saloons in town. Neither was a particularly savory place, but then again, what saloon was, when it came right down to it?

Jed supplied Fen with whiskey for both establishments and, to his credit, the mayor always paid him on time, unlike several other of his customers. Jed had been forced to gently threaten to cut off deliveries to them until they paid their outstanding debts.

"Yes, yes, I have quite a history with it. It's my legs and back, you see, and—"

Jed glanced over at the man and decided he wasn't really all that bad, all things considered. He always was smarmy, but he wasn't really a bad man, even for a politician, which had never been one of Jed's favorite sort of folks.

Jed had known Fen his entire life and they were within a few months of being the same age. Despite being acquainted with the man for so long, or maybe because of it—he didn't quite know which it was—but he didn't trust the fellow.

The whiskey maker knew from experience with Fen that if he wanted to get on home that night, he'd have to steer the conversation. "Say, what were you doing out back of Lil's and the stable at this time of night?" Or any time, thought Jed.

"Oh, well, I—I was so busy all day that I didn't have time to make a thorough assessment of everything in town I needed to earlier."

"Assessment of what?" said Jed, curious despite himself.

"Oh, Mr. Sheldrake, he—" The mayor stopped himself there and for a brief uncharacteristic moment didn't offer further words.

"So, how is your employer these days, anyway?" Jed knew it was a low blow, and not something he would usually utter, but Jed was feeling suddenly perturbed. He had been having a fine evening, despite the chatter about Sheldrake, and this fool had pinched out the warm glow he'd felt on leaving Lil for the night.

"My employer! Why, Jed, you—you cut me to the quick, you do! My employer, as you well know, is the town of Glen Rose, nay, the *people* of Glen Rose, and—"

By then they had reached the western end of Main Street and Jed paused, intending only to listen long enough to interrupt, claiming an early day. Then he'd mount up and ride as fast as he might on out of there, away from Fen and his windy excuses for everything.

But the mayor was chatty, a state Jed knew that Hawkins always seemed to enjoy being in. Jed sighed and noticed that Fen was now talking about town offices and the difficulties of attracting folks to live in Glen Rose.

He also noticed that Fen kept glancing along the west road, as if he were expecting to see something appear any moment. Jed even found himself doing it once or twice. It was almost as if Fen was wasting Jed's time intentionally. As if he were trying to keep him from heading for home. But why?

Finally, Jed could take it no longer. Intentional or not, and rude or not on his part, he mounted up even as the annoying little man stood too close to his horse. Then the cursed man laid a hand on Jed's left boot as he kept right on talking.

"I have to go, Fen. Give my best to your family. G'night." And Jed heeled his horse and clicked with his mouth and turned the horse, the mayor talking as he rode away.

"But—but Jed, I, uh—"

The last thing Jed thought he heard the mayor say was, "Oh dear . . ."

He wanted to stop and shout back to the man, to ask him what he meant by that, but with Fen it likely meant very little. The mayor was a whole lot like a worried old lady in so many ways.

Well, most old ladies, anyway. But not the one who'd birthed and raised him. His thoughts turned back to the ranch and to his mother. Jed had been more than a little concerned lately about leaving Mama alone at the ranch, but then again, she was the toughest person he'd ever met.

He dispensed with his initial relaxed thought of letting Mags choose her own speed on the road out of town and back home to Whiskey Woods. The mayor had bled the savor of the evening for him, leaving Jed feeling edgy, annoyed, and maybe even a little worried, too.

Why was everybody so blamed worried about so much in life, anyway? Everyone he knew seemed to be that way, except perhaps for him and Mama. Must be the way she raised me, he guessed. And it was likely because of the way she was raised.

"Starks are confident people." He'd heard that bold, brief proclamation with frequency from Mama all through his growing up years. And he felt it, too, but mostly he didn't think much about it. It was a thing that was always there, much as the wind or the water or the snakes were always about. Not good or bad, just there.

In his experience, most folks only noticed things when attention was paid to things. And that often happened when others pointed them out to you. Or when others saw or realized a thing for the first time. It often made them fearful, because that new thing was unusual to them. Yes, he'd seen that sort of behavior many times.

The oddest had been when it happened to men who had seemed otherwise to be big and strong and confident. But when they faced something strange to them, instead of regarding it as a new curiosity, they looked on it instead with suspicion, through narrowed eyes. That was too bad, for one of the things in life that Jed Stark was fond of was experiencing something, anything, new.

CHAPTER 8

Jed felt a growing clot of something—worry, more likely than anything—blooming in his gut. He wasn't inclined to give over to such infrequent feelings, but this time it was enough to heel Mags harder and bend low in the saddle. "Let's go, girl. Might be nothing, but then again it might be something! Hee-yaa!"

The horse, his favorite mount, responded as she always did, with a snort before complying with his wishes, as if she were letting him know that she would do as he bade her but on her own terms. It was a trait he admired in the big brown beast.

They thundered down the narrow cartway toward Whiskey Woods, a route man and horse had taken in the dark of late night or in the small hours many times, and rarely in much of a rush.

Jed was inclined in life to not rush about, if he could help it. In his estimation hurrying at most anything nearly always resulted in some sort of headache on down the road.

But tonight was different. The mayor's oddness—odder than usual, anyway—and everything else odd happening of late, made Jed realize that feeling in his gut might well be more right than wrong. He'd hurry and deal with the headaches later.

Within minutes, they came to the one fork in the roadway,

and veered right, southward, putting them on the lane cutting into Whiskey Woods land. The lane angled deep, winding around boulders and outcroppings and over gentle swells and down into draws before veering southeastward and on into the ranch proper.

After the turn they passed the stand of cottonwoods, normally a welcome presence in the darkness. But tonight, although he knew the trees were there, Jed did not slow. For something faint, barely the whisper of a scent, tickled his nostrils and then was gone. He pulled in a deep breath. Nothing. But he had not imagined it.

They barreled on, the horse sensing more than seeing the way, and Jed bent low and hugged the beast tight, all the while flexing his nostrils as they topped the next and final rise before gullying down again at the approach to the homeplace.

And it was there, atop that slight rise in the land, that he saw it. On a night of much darkness, there was a low, pulsing glow above the land, right about where the homeplace sat, and had for far longer than Jed's memory stretched back.

"Oh no," he murmured and, without needing the urging she received from him, Mags doubled her hammering efforts, risking a snapped leg and worse as they thundered toward what Jed knew was one of the worst things that could befall a man—his place, his family's long-time home, was ablaze.

The closer they drew the brighter the sky's throbbing hue of orange and, down low, purple. "Oh no!" was all he could say, and then they cut tight and fast around the inside of the wide bend, the last stretch, and within moments emerged into the dooryard to see his worst fears come to life.

The Stark homeplace was ablaze, the stable, the whiskey shed and still, and across the yard, the house, all of it engulfed.

He leapt from the mare's back as the horse slowed, but did not stop, her gallop from this freakish new danger, instinct driving her away. Jed stumbled and nearly went down on his left knee, and his hat, after all that hard riding, popped off his hat and landed somewhere in the glowing dark. Even after all that, Jed knew that anything he might do at this point was fruitless. The building would not be saved, not by one man.

"Mama!" he bellowed gulping in a lungful of smoke, coughing and retching and spitting and repeating the word over and over, howling it until his voice was a ragged, blown-out thing.

All the while, Jed ran from spot to spot, stumbling and shouting, reaching out for anything he might grasp, knowing not what he might do, but knowing he could not feel this helpless much longer.

The crack and snap of long-dry timbers and planking filled the air about him along with the thick rolls of black smoke and the glow of the savage flames licking upward into the darkness.

The stink of it, no longer the pleasant smell of a woodfire, clouded his senses and he bellowed on, noting but barely seeing, despite the glow of the fire, animals, his meager collection of stock, running, it seemed, in all directions about him.

Jed heard the screams of horses, along with their three cows and one bullock. He heard chickens squawking and geese cackling as he staggered forward, squinting and shouting, "Mama! Mother Stark!" and even her given name of "Minnie! Minnie Stark!"

But of his beloved mother, Jed saw no sign. He cut wide around the fallen, sagged but blazing ruin of the east end of the barn and beneath it, the low crushed and blazing tumble of the place he spent his happiest of days, the Stark family whiskey still. And then he saw something low and light colored along the earth not ten feet from the blazing tumble of timbers.

He dove at it, reaching his mother's side and feeling for her as much as seeing her.

The brutal fire's one redeeming quality, in his estimation, was the brightness it afforded him in that moment. He felt he was able to discern that Mama was, at the worst, or so he hoped, knocked unconscious and not dead.

"No, Lord," he gagged and pawed at her, lifting her tiny, frail body, in his powerful arms. "Not dead, not yet, not this way . . ."

He ran with her, back up toward the lane, the one direction he saw and knew to be free of flames, and laid her in the brittle grass.

"Mama!" he bellowed, stretching her out on her back and gently but firmly jostling her, holding her chin and wiggling her head. And then he saw and felt the left side of her head above her temple and ear. It was wet and thick there, sticky. Blood.

She'd taken a knock, and her silvered hair, too, was singed and burned away in spots. He eased off on jostling her and bent low over her face shouted, "Mama! Mama, can you hear me?"

He kept this up and thought he felt breath there, sensed the rise and fall, however slight, of her chest as she breathed, this spicy, bold little woman who knew no fear.

He held his right ear close to her mouth. "Mama?" he bellowed.

And she pulled in a harsh, ragged breath and coughed. "Ain't . . . deaf!"

And with that, Jed Stark felt the deepest moment of relief in his entire life. It was even more of a relief than when he had learned that the war had ended all those years ago.

"Mama!" he shouted, tempted to grasp her by the shoulder and crush her to his chest, but fear of hurting her further stayed the instinct. He held her small shoulders in his big hands and said again, "Mama!"

"I—" She coughed and turned her head to the side and spat. "I know . . . who I am, you fool!"

Despite the awful scene, Jed had to grin in the glowing night. That flicker of happiness was brief, however, for as his mother tried to rise, shoving up onto her left elbow, she wobbled and collapsed back to the earth.

"Ohh," she said, her eyes closing and her head slowly working from side to side. "The animals, check the animals—I think I got them all out."

"That's good, Mama. Real good," he said, glancing up and around him at the flaming wreckage. Good because no structure looked to be left upright.

"Mama, look, don't move any more, promise me!" He gentled her to a flat position and rose to his feet. "I'm going to fetch water. You stay put."

She tried to laugh but coughed. "House needs water, barn needs water, the still needs water, not me . . ."

"Let me worry about all that." And Jed was off, scissoring his long legs to the well, located on the far side of the house, on the northeastern upslope corner. The little well house remained untouched and he sent the wooden pail down fast and hauled it up again, dripping and the rope creaking.

Never in his life had he so quickly nor so willingly fetched water, a task that many times in the past he had complained about, albeit in a near silent voice as a youth, mumbling his annoyance with yet another chore.

That his mother invariably heard him and barked a quick, "Jed!" was not deterrent enough. As he grew, he had come to enjoy the task, although in his usual way he was never quick at it.

But on this night, Jed Stark moved faster than he ever had. Not that it would matter much, he thought, because the Stark family homestead was being consumed by this ravenous beast of a fire. Even in the short amount of time Jed had been there, it had doubled in intensity and in size. And with painful obviousness, he admitted it all looked irredeemably engulfed and unsalvageable.

As Jed hauled the bucket back up, he looked behind him,

oblivious to the clucking and whinnying and howling of the beasts, to witness the last part of a wall of the only home he had ever known groan and collapse, sending skyward a rush of sparks.

A horse raced past him, its mane steaming or smoking, he knew not which. He recognized the steed as King, the bold gelding, who appeared to be running a race with the devil and losing, instinct nonetheless urging the horse away to some place of perceived safety.

"Good luck," growled Jed as he swung the bucket up out of the well, jammed the carved drinking dipper into it, and raced back to his mother.

He was tempted to get her even farther from the flames, but found that she had done so herself, somehow, and was resting against a big cottonwood tree, his favorite one to climb up into as a boy. "Mama, you . . . fool!"

Jed had never talked to her that way, but in that moment, he was angry with her—but relieved, too, to see she had more gumption and ability than he thought she might.

"I'm all right, son." She coughed and leaned back. "I'll let that crack slip by for the moment." She chuckled, then coughed. "But not a second time." She smiled up at him and he ladled water to her.

She drank her fill and shooed him away. "Go, go, you've spent enough time on me. Check on the beasts. Oh, Redeye! I haven't seen him!"

They both looked toward the flaming mess of the house. The porch where the lazy critter slept much of the time in the night was all but gone.

"I expect there's no sense in me telling you not to move, then," he said, shoving up off his knees once more.

He ran to the house, looking everywhere he might at once, hoping he would see the dog, but in that he was disappointed. He spun, making his way toward the barn in time to see a flaming chicken running, then slowing and finally stopping. It offered up a high-pitched screeching sound and then fell over, kicking. By the time he reached its side, it had expired. Then it, too, was enveloped in flame. It sickened Jed, and he ran by, shouting for his dog.

"Redeye! Redeye! Here, boy!" he bellowed, over and over, his voice already a raw, hoarse thing from having called for his mother and foolishly sucking in too much smoke as he did so.

His shouts went unanswered, and his gut knotted. He would feel much the same about the horses, cattle, any of the beasts they kept, really. The Starks had always been overly fond of their critters, as Jed's mother had said of herself, him, and her predecessors. In that comment there was pride, never shame.

Jed rushed all about the place, feeling more hopeless and helpless with each step he took. He called to the hound, and when he remembered, occasionally to the other beasts, all named save for the chickens—all but the largest, a cockerel named Bull.

Mama never wanted to name the beasts they would end up eating, and all the chickens, except for the occasional victim of the coyotes, eventually ended up in the stewpot or the oven, depending on their age and toughness. She made exceptions for the beef critters, however.

And always when it came time to kill and dress them, although she would participate in the grim but vital task, she would become unusually quiet for a day or two following.

It had always been her way, and Jed had followed suit. Never was there chiding or ridicule.

"We are taking their most valued thing and that deserves some quiet and honor, don't you think?" she had told Jed a long time ago, when he had helped her dispatch chickens.

It was taken to heart by the youth and held there, coming back to him in the war, with much force. It did not prevent him from doing the job he had to do, but it did prevent him from acting as so many of his fellow soldiers did, with disregard for the very lives of the men they laid low.

They sickened him then, and had, in memory, since. The same with the various gun-happy fools he had come across in the intervening years, men infatuated with a gadget that maimed and killed. It was a tool, in his regard, no less and no more. Treat is as you might a hammer or a knife. It was built for a specific task, and the wielder should use it as such and nothing else.

All these thoughts and hundreds more whisked in and out of Jed's smoke-filled, addled mind as the hours passed.

He jousted and parried with the flames, all his efforts fruitless, but he could not comprehend the notion of stopping, of not trying to save whatever it might be he was hauling water for.

He emptied the troughs, he hauled double-buckets of water from the outflow holding pond his grandfather had dug down below the barn. And he was considering how best to get quantities of water up to the site when he was halted, struck dumb by the stupidity of his own lack of solid thought.

The water in the pond was the outflow, yes, but from the thing that fed what had always been his primary concern in life. The whiskey still.

He was a whiskey maker, and the one vital ingredient for his whiskey was water. And the source of their fine water—unparalleled anywhere in the region, so far as he knew—was the Stark's clear-flowing spring. It urged itself up to the surface, through earth and rock, to the small but deep pool that Jed's grandfather had found, then broadened and widened and deepened.

Until his time, it had been used by the various local tribes of native people, as well as by the multitudes of wild beasts whose existence, as much as any human's, depended on slaking its thirst with pure water.

The river was not far, and so the spring had not seen as much as a similar flow might in a more arid region. And thus, it was not sullied or exploited. Not until Hawcliffe Stark staked his bloody claim there and settled the land.

His wonder at his discovery of the spring had prompted him to relocate his whiskey making and home base from lower on the property. He moved from closer to the river to higher up, in the pretty glade.

The spring water was tasty, and it was the sole ingredient, the Starks all knew, that provided their whiskey with its finest quality. It was the magical portion of the recipe Jed knew as its flavor, although it didn't matter to him, folks could call it what they liked. To the Starks, it was a gift from above, and they maintained the spring and protected it accordingly.

It had been piped to the whiskey shed with care in double-layers, with overlapping joinery, gum-tight and sealed on the outside with pitchy resin. But on the inside, that layer of log piping was all oak, cut, hauled, bored, and joined over many months. And it flowed all that time into the whiskey shed. Copious amounts of sweet water.

And it had flowed, without fail, in fact, all those years, with few exceptions, save for the droughtiest of years, and even then, only for short spells. Fine, that is, until the night of the fire.

Jed realized that the flow had ceased.

He knew where the pipe lay, for he had had occasion at various times in his life to repair it, then rebury it with care in the earth-and-stone lined trench so painstakingly built so long ago by Grandfather Stark.

So why had it stopped? Jed soaked rags and draped one over his head, then wrapped another sopping, steaming rag about his face. With only his eyes visible, and with the help of a mostly unburned rail from the ruined corral, he was able to shove and pry flaming, smoldering hunks of his whiskey shed back away from where he knew the wooden pipe to be. He knew it emerged from the earth within the whiskey shed. But it was not there and the earth around where it should be was not, to his eye, wet. But of course, the heat of the fire would have seen to that.

Why was it not flowing? He would have to go to the spring and make certain the pipe inlet was not plugged. Perhaps it had burned the wooden pipe back a ways, somehow altering the course of the flow in the interim.

There had to be a seep somewhere higher up the slope, underground, along the line. He knew that once the pipe was damaged, the water, as it always did, would take the path of least resistance and travel instead in a new direction.

Jed stood, his eyes trying in vain to search the surrounding earth, beneath charred timbers and smoking, bent, twisted things that he used to take for granted and use each day—steel tools and buckets and barrels, any of their wooden parts now gone, gnawed away by flame.

Finally, he looked up, his chest heaving, his skin feeling as though it was bubbling and crackling, and coughs rose and burst from his mouth unbidden. He saw, downslope but moving his way, a shape. He squinted and tried to clear his eyes with a grimy hand. It didn't do a thing but muddy his vision.

In the glow from the fire and the slight purpling of the sky beyond, Jed made out the shape as a person, trudging and swaying. It moved stiff legged but stalwart under the load of two buckets laden with water, swaying from the shoulder yoke he himself had been using not long before. He'd left it where it was always kept, dangling from a pole down by the outflow pond.

"Mama, no!" he shouted. But even as he said it, he knew it was not possible, in her addled condition, for the woman to haul buckets.

So who was it?

The figure drew closer, closer. It was wider, stouter than his mother would ever be.

"Jed!" shouted the figure.

The whiskey man stumbled over to the person. "Loud?"

"About time you poked your head up!"

"But—what are you doing here?"

"Couldn't sleep . . ." The man lowered the two buckets and bent out from beneath the yoke.

For what felt an eternity to them both, they worked in near silence, side by side, hauling water. Each man knew the fruitlessness of the task, but went on with it anyway, each for similar and separate reasons—hope, fortitude, a bulwark against hopelessness, friendship, and many more.

Jed said, "Mama, I have to check on her."

"She was fine, resting beneath that tree"—Loudon nodded toward the big tree across the wide dooryard—"when I came down. I've been keeping an eye. She told me it was about time I showed up!" Loudon cackled, a dry, rasping sound that ended in a cough.

"Let's take a rest," said Jed. "Go see Mama."

"Oh, hey!" said Loudon. "Look what I found!" He bent over, and from beneath the charred, steaming wood behind him he tugged free a stoneware jug, intact, and stoppered.

"No idea if there's anything left, but . . ." He handed it to Jed.

The tall man took it and held it beside his head and shook it. Then he smiled, his teeth white in his sooty, blackened face. "I hear something in there. Let's go find out."

They trudged across the yard to find Lilly tending to a fidgeting, clucking Minnie.

"Now settle down, Mother Stark. I need to clean that wound or you will be in a world of hurt. I've seen such wounds before—on the railroad—my papa. Let me help you."

The solemnity in the younger woman's voice quieted Minnie.

"Lil, how . . . ?" Jed stood staring down at the two women.

Lilly looked up at him and smiled. "Jed! Are you—are you hurt?"

Her hands were busy tending the injured older woman, but her voice quavered as she looked up at the big soot-covered man.

"I'm all right, Lil." Jed stared at her a moment longer, then dropped down to his knees and hugged her in an awkward embrace from her right side. "Thank you for coming. But—"

She looked over Jed's shoulder. "Blame Loudon, there."

"It's true, odd as it might seem, I was out late, couldn't sleep. I often take walks, or if I go farther, sometimes I ride Alice. Sometimes I walk beside her. She's someone to talk with, you know?"

"But that doesn't explain—"

"It was Alice, you see. I was out this way, up on the road. We were almost to the top of your lane when I smelled smoke. Not a good smoke smell, like a campfire or a woodstove on a cold night. It was . . . this." He waved a grimy hand at the diminishing fiery mess below and before them.

"I looked to my left and saw the glow low on the sky, an orange, pulsing up into yellow, but low on the skyline. I knew what it was right away. I lived through a great fire some years ago that razed part of Providence, Rhode Island. I knew what it was I was seeing."

His small audience said nothing but waited for him to continue. "I spent two seconds trying to decide the best thing to do. That was one second too long. I slid from atop Alice and ripped out a page from my notebook. I always have it with me, you never know when a good story will come up . . ."

Once again, he saw the eyes on him. Even Minnie was staring up at him, squinty and looking to him as if she might cut loose with a burst of impatience any moment.

"Anyway, I sent her back to town, with a note on the saddle."

"And she went? Like a dog?" said Minnie.

"Sure," said Loudon. "I often do that. I don't think it's fair to ride the poor girl all the time. Sometimes I don't ride her, but walk on out, you know, as I said, to have someone to talk with."

"Then how did she reach Lil?" said Jed.

"Well, I told her to go there. She knows the way. And Lilly got my note, telling what I suspected and that if I was wrong, I was sorry. But I knew I wasn't wrong. This was a fire, all right."

"I'll say," said Jed, hoisting the jug and knocking back a mind-clearing swig, or three.

He lowered it and offered it to Lilly, who took it and wiped the rim with her sleeve, then sipped. She was set to hand it to Loudon, but Minnie piped up, "Give it here. I reckon I can use a dose of Stark's Cure-All!"

"And I reckon you've earned it, Mama. How you feeling?"

Minnie held up a finger. "Never interrupt a woman while she's sampling from the jug."

Jed said. "Now hold on a minute, Loud. You mean to say that Alice went to the café? And waited for Lilly to come down?"

Loudon nodded.

"Remind me to thank your mule," said Jed, shaking his head.

"Well, it's Polly's day off," said Lilly. "And I had to get the biscuits going. I never sleep well when I have lots to do the next morning." Lilly shrugged. "The way it is. I take a nap later, after the dinner crowd is over."

"Sensible woman," said Minnie in a raspy voice. "I always take myself a rest in the afternoons. Never fails to perk me up. And I do believe Jed does, too, out in the whiskey shed."

The quick laugh died a quicker death as they realized that there was no longer a whiskey shed. They looked across the yard and saw the smoking wreckage of what had once been a fine homestead. Here and there coals glowed and pulsed with a subdued vigor, as if waiting to be renewed. Flames licked up sporadically, but the damage had been done.

"Morning's on its way," said Loudon, dragging a hand down his face.

"Yes," said Jed, nodding. "The light's not from the fire now, not as much as it was, anyway. It's from the dawn."

"You can always count on that, anyway," said Lilly, watching the purpling sky with tired eyes.

From up the lane came the sound of a wagon rolling their way, and the steady drumming of a brace of horses.

Soon, they heard shouts, also from the wagon, and then the big thing was there, pulling up beside them. Jed walked over to the lane to greet them. He grabbed hold of the harness and calmed the big beast.

From out of the wagon, three men jumped down and two women, with another man and woman remaining on the seat.

"Jed Stark!" said the man. "It's Rupe Brown. Lilly let us know. We passed the word and roused who we might. We got here as quick as we could. I'm sorry, I guess we spent too much time fetching tools."

"And I grabbed what food I could," said a woman next to him.

Jed recognized the voice as Hazel, Rupert's wife.

The other women helped her down, and they all ferried what looked to Jed to be baskets laden with food over to his mother and Lilly.

Jed caught a glimpse of his mother's face, smiling up at the women, all of whom she knew—one she had midwifed into the world—and he felt a wash of humility and gratefulness for his friends.

Mama looked, for the moment at least, as happy as she might possibly look in the situation.

"I—I see we're too late," said one of the men who'd hopped down.

It was young Harley Thompson, Chiswick's deputy. Where the Marshal was a bought-and-paid-for Sheldrake man, Thompson was, for a young fellow, surprisingly very much his own man. And as everyone knew, he was also an admirer of Jed Stark.

"I'm so sorry about this, Mr. Stark," said the young deputy.

Jed offered him a hand. "It's Jed, son, and I appreciate you all coming out. We appreciate it mighty. And don't you be sorry about it. I'm sure it was my fault."

From behind him, in the cluster of women doting on her crowed Mother Stark. "What? What's that, Jedediah Stark?"

Mama's voice cut through the low din, quelling any of the others who might have been speaking. "You know and I know this was no fault of yours! You're a Stark, and you use fire most every day making Stark Whiskey! No sir, it's one man and one man only responsible for this, and I know that everyone knows who I mean, so I won't utter that filthy beast's name tonight!"

The finality with which she said this left everyone speechless. Except Jed. He cleared his throat. "I'm not convinced of that, but—"

She began to sputter and cut him off, and Jed spoke louder, with force, something he rarely did and almost never to his mother. "We'll let that go for now, Mama."

The folks who'd gathered there were all their good friends and knew them well. And they knew that in the infrequent event he was riled, Jed Stark was not to be taken lightly. Even Mama shut her mouth.

"I might ask the men to lend me a hand for a few minutes in shoveling more dirt on some of the trouble spots. Then maybe we could all have a bite. I'm smelling something mighty tasty."

"Bread and cheese. And pie!"

"Oh boy," said Loudon, smiling. "Save some for me, would you?"

"Oh, Mr. Paley," said Mrs. Brown. "I expect we could never bake enough pie to satisfy you!"

The group chuckled at this as the men, armed with a fresh round of tools—shovels and picks—walked back to the burning remains of the barn and whiskey shed.

"How did the fire get from here over to the house?" said Harley Thompson.

"Or vice versa," said Loudon.

Jed sighed. "Embers, maybe, carried on a breeze, I expect."

The men offered grunts, but nobody said a thing. Because they all knew that there had been no breeze in the night. The air was dead, and the likelihood of what Jed had said was slim. Not impossible, but slim.

And they all knew that Mother Stark was probably correct. Because they all knew the unceasing torment Merlin Sheldrake had been inflicting on the Stark family of late. None of the folks in the small group who'd come out were supportive of Sheldrake in any way. They were all friends of the Starks.

The women tried to coerce Mother Stark into coming home with them for a few days, to convalesce. She knew they meant well and she tried, really tried, not to say the things she wanted to say.

After several seconds of quelling the urge to round on them with her sharp words, she caught a glimpse of Lilly's face, which looked to be forming a wince, as if she knew the old woman long and well enough to know what was coming. That slight look was enough to convince Minnie to swallow back the words.

"Now look, I know you mean well," said Mother Stark, struggling to her feet and shooing off the hands that tried to assist her. "But I'm all right here. In fact, I'm not leaving the Stark place for any longer than it takes to get to town, buy what I need, and get on back home again. I like it here fine."

"But where will you stay?" said Hazel.

"Stay? Why the Starks have always stayed right here, at Whiskey Woods. Why would I want to be anywhere else?"

"But—but where will you sleep?"

Jed walked back up and said, "Oh, ladies, don't you worry none. We'll have Mama all set up as if she was on a jungle expedition. She'll be fine."

Lilly nodded. "I'll bring what she might require from town later today. Isn't that right, Mother Stark?"

The old woman looked narrow-eyed at his son's sweetheart, then grinned. "I reckon that'll suit me fine, yep."

"Thanks, ladies," said Jed. "Me and the other fellows will be done soon with what we can do down there. Now, if only we could find fire"—he glanced around grinning—"could we convince you all to rustle up some eats?"

That set the women bustling and setting up a makeshift campfire kitchen.

"Lil, can I talk with you a moment?" Jed led her away, out of earshot of the others. "I thank you for playing along. Mama would prefer to keep Stark doings close to the vest, if you know what I mean."

"About the camp," she said.

"Yep, you bet. It looks as if Mama can hold out for a while yet. But maybe after the others leave you could bring Mama on down there? She was fixing to go there for a few days anyway. You know she likes to spend a goodly amount of time there."

'I don't blame her," said Lilly. "It's the nicest camp I've ever seen."

"Then you'll help her?"

"Of course, Jed. I'd planned on it anyway. The ladies won't be here but for another hour or two, I imagine."

"Thanks, I appreciate it. She might be ornery with you—a warning."

Lilly grinned. "I've gotten used to Minnie's ways, never mind about that. Will you be all right there, down at the camp, I mean?" said Lilly.

"Oh yeah, but I won't be staying at the camp. That's Mama's when she's in residence. Like an English royal, she is. I'll stay at the whiskey shed. You remember, down past the camp."

"Of course," said Lilly.

Jed leaned down and lowered his voice. "Maybe you'll visit

me down there, ma'am?" He glanced around them, then gave Lilly a smooch. He grinned, feeling surprisingly chipper, considering he'd lost his home, his barn, and the source of his livelihood. Sort of.

Jed knew something very few people alive knew—that there was another Stark family still, indeed an entire whiskey shed, down past the camp. With any luck, he'd be able to resume making Stark whiskey within days, a week at the most.

As Jed strode back toward the smoking ruins of the house, where the men had begun work shoveling dirt over the remaining pockets of embers and flame, he caught sight of movement to his right. He paused and looked that way. There it was again, something flipping up and down again out beyond the singed brown grasses lining the path that led to the river.

"What in the world?" he muttered as he walked toward it, already suspecting it was yet another of his animals, wounded and in need of aid or a merciful death. And as he neared it, he saw a head rise up out of the grass and a familiar face offer up a big toothy yawn.

It was Redeye, and he had obviously been snoozing, as the spot in the grass, a well-padded one, was also well worn. "Redeye!" said Jed with a smile. "What in the name of all that is odd in the world aboveground is happening over here?"

Jed dropped to his knees before the big rangy hound, checking the droopy beast all over. Redeye, for his part, appeared to be even more exhausted-looking than usual.

The dog did not rise, but thumped his tail and made a low moaning noise that sounded a bit hoarse, as if the dog had inhaled a whole lot of smoke.

Jed knelt by him. "Oh, Redeye, I am glad to see you, my old friend. You all right, son?"

The dog thumped his tail and Jed looked him over.

"I see a couple of small chicken feathers stuck in the corners of your lips, pal. You want to tell me what that's all about?"

Jed didn't think the dog had killed a bird. He was forever defending them with a thump and a growl against anything that might intrude on the coop. Maybe he'd partaken of a dead, cooked bird? At that moment, it didn't much matter to Jed. He was glad to see his chum had come through the fire and somehow hadn't been hurt or worse.

The hound's legs didn't appear broken, but he was blistered and singed here and there. Jed tenderly felt the dog all over and the pup, other than wincing when the whiskey man's fingers probed a burn, didn't mutter a sound of pain.

"You stay right here. I'll fetch you something to eat. Hang on, old friend." Jed walked back up to the gathered folks who were all settling down for a feed.

"You found him? Redeye?" said Minnie, eyeing Jed with what he was pleased to see was her hawk-sharp gaze.

"I did, Mama. He's singed up a bit, and he had chicken feathers stuck to the corners of his mouth, but he'll be all right."

One of the men chuckled. "So, he took advantage of the situation and had himself a chicken dinner, eh, Jed?"

"No sir! Not on your life!" cackled Minnie, turning on the man with a fiery look. "Last I seen of him, he was darting into the coop and carrying out those hens, one at a time in his mouth! They were too stunned to help themselves, stood there like fools."

"Really?" said Lilly. "He did that?"

"Course he did. I remember shouting to him to help me. 'Help me, Redeye!' I shouted. 'Get those chickens on out of there! Herd them up!' Well, you know he's not a herding dog, so he did the best he could, I reckon. Sensible, like any Stark will do in a moment of crisis," she said, nodding and tucking into a cheese sandwich.

Jed was grateful she didn't see the doubtful looks pass around on the faces of their guests, their friends. But as far-fetched as elements of his mother's story about Redeye was, he knew it was no lie. That dog was truer than true.

Jed loaded up a tin bowl with meat and bread and brought another, empty, with a stoppered bottle of water, back down to where Redeye lay in the grass. The dog hadn't moved, which was in keeping with his usual demeanor.

But when Jed sat down next to him with the bowl of meat and the bowl of water, that dog tucked right in, first with a bite of meat, then he drank the entire bowl of water and polished off the rest of the meat. Then he belched and looked at Jed and belched again and laid back down and closed his eyes.

Jed, meanwhile, checked him over again, his feet, everywhere. He'd need salve on a few spots, burns that had bubbled and blistered, but he seemed all right. When Jed left him and went back to join their friends, Redeye was snoring. Like always.

As he walked back up the long, slow rise, he thought that if Redeye can roll along with what happened and come out okay, he and Mama would, too.

He heard a burst of laughter from one of the men, maybe young Harley Thompson. Yes sir, thought Jed, as his eyes landed on Lilly talking with Mama. Everything was going to be all right. With a little help from friends, of course.

Chapter 9

"What do you mean?" growled Sheldrake, as he stood and slammed his gut and thighs into the edge of his voluminous desk. Papers slid, and the top of his ink well slid off, spilling black ink in its wake. He didn't seem to notice. "Speak, curse you! I said what do you mean that Stark is filling his orders?"

Rollo nodded. "It's true, boss. He's back at it. We seen him making deliveries, like always."

"Wait a minute. Now, correct me if I am wrong, and I am never wrong, but the Stark place burned, yes?"

"Yes, sir," they nodded.

"And it is all gone, correct?"

"Yes sir. House, barn, whiskey still, all of it."

"Then how can he be making whiskey? And selling it? And fulfilling his orders?"

Clem shrugged. "Maybe he's got himself a warehouse, same as you got here." He looked around as if he could see the vast building all about them.

"That's what their barn was, you dolt!" growled Sheldrake.

"Oh."

The fat man shook his head. "And next I suppose you're going to tell me that useless old shrieking crow of a woman, his sainted mama, is alive!"

"In fact," said Rollo, smiling and nodding with enthusiasm. "I heard tell she's about fine. Oh, got her a knock on the bean, but they reckon she'll recover all right."

"And this pleases you, I see," said Sheldrake, rounding the desk and stalking with measured steps toward the man, whose grin was beginning to slip the closer his fat boss drew to him.

"Well, no sir, I mean, yes sir, I mean, well, it's good she ain't dead, ain't it? I mean burning buildings down is one thing, they can be rebuilt and all. But a person dying off, why, there's no coming back from a thing like that, now is there?"

Rollo said this with drawn brows, and looked at his compadre for confirmation, which he received in the form of a nod from Clem.

"That's it! You two useless cretins are through! Through, do you hear me?"

"But Mr. Sheldrake, you said if we did what you asked, you'd give us a raise in pay!"

"Ha! An increase in your pay? You'll be lucky if you get out of this office alive, you vile beasts!"

Sheldrake stopped, let his fat hands hang by his side. He turned his big pink face toward the ceiling, but left his eyes closed, then he sighed. "Why did I not begin at the top? Why, oh why, am I forever cursed with trying to save money when I should spend it? It's a curse, I tell you, boys, to be so rich and yet be so miserly at times."

He looked at the two of them. "As much as it pains me to say it, I may have uses for you two bumblers yet. But for now, get back to work in the warehouse. There are wagons to be filled. Get to it, or I will reconsider this wave of largesse I am showing toward you two . . . oafs!" He spat the last word as if it were a hair on his tongue and turned from them.

As they left his office in the warehouse, Sheldrake muttered, "There are other ways to make inroads to the Starks. And I will find them, and use them."

Chapter 10

Lilly looked up from the stove through the wide opening separating her kitchen area from the dining area of the café. It was nibbling at midday and sounds, particularly blurts of voices bursting in through the ever opening and closing door, were no surprise to her.

But this one caused her eyes to narrow and a sneer to creep upon her otherwise demure mouth. Even before she looked up she knew whose voice it was.

"I require a private table!"

She wiped loose strands of hair from out of her eyes with the back of a hand and went back to tending the sizzling, snapping bacon in the skillet before her.

The noise was the blustering, braying voice of the one person in the town, and perhaps in the world, she wanted to knock cold with her skillet. One day, she promised herself. One day.

Instead of taking one of the remaining three empty seats in the place, Merlin Sheldrake walked to the partition and leered in at her.

Lilly barely glanced up. "Find a seat, and I'll be with you in a moment. Busy time right now."

The man stood, staring at her, wearing his hat, a black bowler, atop his fleshy head, with narrowed eyes, distended nostrils, and a pooch-lipped frown nested beneath his too-narrow mustache.

It pained her to do so, but Lilly admitted to herself—and never would she say so to anyone else—that Sheldrake was a decent dresser. That is to say the clothes he wore were of obvious quality and not something made or bought locally. But that was the extent of the praise she was willing to direct his way.

The fat man cleared his throat. "Do you know who I am?"

The rest of the chatter in the café, already subdued when he'd blustered on in, grew even quieter. They were, Lilly knew, eager for some manner of conflict. She sighed, reluctant to give it to them but unable to do otherwise.

She paused and looked up at him, then felt herself gritting her teeth and she pointed her hot, greasy steel prodding fork at him. "Much to all our eternal regret, everybody in Glen Rose knows who you are, Sheldrake. And that doesn't make you any more important than anyone else in my place. Now take a seat or leave."

Lilly resumed prodding her bacon and flipping the grilling slabs of bread, before tending to the frying potato and onion slices.

For a long moment, nobody in the dining room said a thing, and Lilly knew that all eyes were on Sheldrake's broad back. She also knew, without looking up, that his eyes were doing their level best to burn holes into her as he glared at her, his jaw no doubt set in as hard a line as his fleshy face could muster.

Lilly felt like giggling. She knew what half the townsfolks would tell her later: "Merlin Sheldrake's not the sort of man to get on the wrong side of!"

And her reply would be: "And Lilly Chu is not the sort of woman to tolerate big-mouth fools in her establishment!"

He stood and gawped at her a moment longer as she turned to dish up plates of sizzling meats and eggs and bread, potatoes and onion, biscuits and gravy. She checked the latest bubbling pot of coffee, and glanced once more toward the opening and saw something she had not expected. Something that caused her to pause in sliding eggs from a skillet onto a plate.

Merlin Sheldrake was not standing there glowering at her, and had not departed her café, much to her dismay. But he was instead making rounds in the dining room, moving from one seated patron to the next, a wad of cash money in one hand and a leather coin pouch being shaken in the other.

He was bent over and grinning a wide false smile, and speaking in low but bold tones. One by one her frightened customers looked from the man's big face, inches from theirs, to the money in his thick pink hands, then back to him, then to the money. They licked their lips, they set down forks and spoons and cups, they wiped their mouths with napkins, and they held out their hands, palms up.

Sheldrake's voice grew louder as he moved from table to table, leaving behind stunned faces and hands holding money. Several of these confused customers looked at Lilly.

One woman, whom she knew well and considered a friend, was Widow Tenney, whose husband had died the previous autumn. She shrugged and offered Lilly a slight shake of her head, as if to apologize.

Lilly was saddened by the helplessness she saw on her friend's face and redoubled her intentions to oust the fat man from her eatery. For the moment, she, too, was stunned by what was happening. "Hey, Sheldrake! What are you doing?"

He glanced her way, a leer on his face, then back to his latest visit, talking with them.

She walked over and poked him hard on his shoulder. It was the first time she had actually ever touched the fellow, and he was as puffy as he looked. "Hey, I said what are you doing? Leave my customers alone!"

Sheldrake straightened, sighing and turning his face, now a beaming thing of benevolence, on her. "My dear Madame

Chu—that is how you exotics prefer to be addressed, is it not? I assure you that I am doing nothing illegal. I am merely convincing these fine folks that I no longer wish to be in their company while I dine."

Lilly felt hot rage flush her face. She pulled herself up to her full height, which she knew was not particularly impressive. "How dare you do such a thing? Get out! Get out right now!"

She turned and glanced at the people already leaving, standing and looking with regret at their partially eaten breakfasts and at her, all the while slipping unearned money into their pockets and purses. They offered her sympathetic shrugs and donned hats and tugged on shawls as they left.

"Someone go for the marshal!" She turned back to Sheldrake. "You won't get away with this, you—you . . ."

"Yes?" he said turning and standing in front of her. He was not a particularly tall man, but a bit taller than Lilly. He grinned down at her, dropping the last of his money into an inner coat pocket.

She realized he had made the complete circuit of the small, packed room, and she watched as the last of her customers edged toward the door. "What have you done?" she cried.

"Calm yourself, my dear. I only wanted to dine alone, and I did not relish doing so in the privacy of my club today, for some reason." He shrugged. "Perhaps I wanted to be out among my people."

"The ones you paid to leave here?"

"Yes. And yes, I believe I'll sit there," he pointed toward a table in the middle of the room. "But I will require it to be cleared of the previous occupants' sloppy efforts at feeding themselves. Quickly, please. I place a high value on my time."

It was all Lilly could do to not launch herself at him and drive her thumbs into his fleshy eyes, then rake them outward, taking his eyeballs with them.

Sheldrake moved to the table he'd indicated and pulled out

a chair, then dusted it off with a handkerchief. He sat down with a squeak from the chair, then turned to her with a serious look on her face. "Madame, I wish to discuss with you terms of our arrangement." He smoothed the napkin and arranged it again before looking up at her, a smug, wide smile on his face.

"What arrangement is that?" she said.

"Why, my dear, the one we are about to come to. That is, if you ever see fit to bring me coffee and food. And it all must be hot. I will not tolerate warmed over leavings." As he said this, he held up a finger, punctuating his words with a stubby digit thrust at the ceiling.

"What's the nature of this arrangement?" she said.

"Food first, woman."

"Speak first, fat man," she said. "Or I will pour hot coffee in your lap."

He gulped. "Why yes, very well. As you wish." And he once more assumed the smug look she had come to despise, even more than anything else she despised about the man.

"I intend to buy you and your establishment," he said, looking about himself with undisguised disgust. "That is to say, I will pay you handsomely to close this place, and I will do you a once-in-a-lifetime favor. Especially so for someone the likes of yourself.

"Oh, don't be offended. I merely speak the truth. People of your . . . shall we say, persuasion—a woman and, at best, a half-white woman—from what I have heard, can really expect to do no better, am I correct?"

Before she could answer, he said, "Of course I am! Merlin Sheldrake is never wrong." He waved a hand as if to dispel the very notion of himself being incorrect about something.

"Let me get this straight, Sheldrake. You want me to close my business because I offend you. Because my noble father came here from China and died helping to lay this country's railroad?"

"Oh no, no, you mistake me, woman. You see, I wish for you to close this eatery, yes, but I will retain you in my employ!" He grinned wide, his arms thrown wide. "As my personal chef! Think of it, you will be able to travel on those same rail lines that your departed father, as a pair of unskilled, grunting hands, helped to build.

"In exchange you will cook for me and—well, perhaps there will be other bonuses to come along as well. We shall see, we shall see." He clapped his hands. "Now, chop-chop, isn't that what you might say?" He chuckled. "I require food, and, I daresay, you are not off to an auspicious start, madame!"

He looked down and resumed smoothing his napkin, a wide, smug smile displaying how pleased he was with himself.

"Right away, sir," she said, and bowed down low, then backed away from hm.

"That's more like it. Money, as has been said by lesser men, certainly has its say in the end. And always and forever."

Lilly slipped into the kitchen, retrieved something from a drawer, then scurried back out to her spot, standing in front of the fat man's table.

"What on earth are you doing?" he said, looking up. "And where is my food—"

His fat grin drooped as he looked at the stick of dynamite in her left hand, a wooden match in the other. "You"—he licked his lips and swallowed—"you wouldn't dare!" His voice was a shallow, quiet thing.

She grinned and without looking away from him raked the tip of the match with a thumbnail and set the little lucifer alight.

He gasped, his eyes widened.

"Now get up and leave," she said in a calm, measured voice.

"You're"—he tried a smile—"you—you can't be serious!"

Grinning, Lilly raised her eyebrows. "This is the only thing this sad little wretch of a woman will be serving you today,

Sheldrake." She set the match to the tip of the wick wagging upward from the stick of dynamite.

For a long second nothing happened, then the wick sizzled and hissed and, as if it were a spark leaping from a fire pit, began consuming the wick, traveling at a surprisingly quick clip along the deadly string.

Sheldrake whimpered, then screamed, and shoved backward in the groaning creaking chair. He flipped over onto his back, his hands and legs clawing at the air, reminding Lilly of a flipped-over turtle. Grunting, he rolled over onto his knees, moving quicker than she would have thought a fat man might.

He did not wait to get his feet beneath him before he moved toward the door, glancing back once, then twice up at her as she advanced toward him.

He clawed at the door, rattling the glass and wood panel in its casing and clawing and fumbling at the knob, using it to drag himself to his feet.

"Hey!" she shouted, the sputtering, hissing stick in her left hand.

He tensed and spun, the door partially open.

"My napkin!"

He glanced down with wide eyes and as if the thing were a snake encircling his neck. Fat fingers snatched at it, and he ripped it off himself and threw it to the floor. He rabbited and forced himself out the door, rattling it as he went.

Lilly did not suppress her full-throated laughter as she wetted her fingers and pinched out the sputtering, sizzling wick scarcely an inch from the dynamite stick's nub of an end. Smoke wisped and curled upward.

She looked down at something by her foot, bent to it, and returned to the door in time to see Sheldrake outside, but now in the middle of the street, shouting and pointing at the café. She whipped the thing at him and stepped out onto the boardwalk after it.

The fat man's dented bowler hat sailed right into the center of his sagging paunch and dropped to the dusty ground.

"And stay out!" shouted Lilly, then she spun, entered her café, and slammed the door behind her.

She was chuckling as she thrust the stick of dynamite back into the table drawer. Her laughs dwindled as she thought about the two people in the entire world she would want to tell about this. And she realized she could tell neither.

Her father was dead. And Jed, well, he would want to kill Sheldrake. And Jed Stark was too good a man to waste on a fool like Merlin Sheldrake.

CHAPTER 11

"Nope. It was my fault," said Jed, his soot-smeared hands resting on his hips. "Who else's fault could it be?" He said this in a mutter, not to the woman who asked it, Lilly.

"Jed," she said. "Of course it was Sheldrake. Nobody but him would do this."

Jed looked over at her as if he were half asleep. Finally, he said, "Maybe, but it makes little sense, Lil. The man wants to buy us out, not burn us out. How would he gain?"

"But—"

Jed held up a big, grimy hand. "No, Lil. I can't think that way right now. Sure, I have thought about it, of course. I'd be a fool not to. But I have too much to worry about, what with Mama and work."

"But the law, Jed—"

"The law?" He shook his head and snorted. "How far would I have to ride to find a lawman who hasn't been bought by Sheldrake? No, not me. Not now. I have customers who are expecting their whiskey, and I can't let them down. I won't let them down. Not once in all our years has a Stark missed a shipment of Whiskey Woods whiskey, Lil."

He faced her in full. Any trace of a previous cloudiness in his demeanor was gone, replaced with narrowed eyes and a hard set to his jaw.

She knew the look, and she saw that pushing the notion of blaming Sheldrake any further, at least at this time, would be unwise. She'd known Jed Stark intimately for years, and she had rarely, if ever, seen him so resolute about anything.

"Fine. I'm going to go down to visit your mother. Would you like me to bring you anything when I come back up?"

"Me?" Jed had gone back to staring at the smoldering pile of charred timber that had been not long before the Stark family whiskey still, and beyond it the barn, or what had been the barn. He pulled in a big breath, let it out. "No. No thank you, Lil." He bent back to the mighty task of retrieving and sorting out potentially useful bits, planking and such, of which there was precious little.

Another few seconds passed, then Lilly nodded once and, with her skirt bunched in her hand, and with a laden basket in the other, she strode strongly away, making for the narrow trail that ran along down to the pecan grove and the river, and the camp beyond.

She knew the way to the Stark family camp, as they called it, although it was far more a house than a camp. It had been in the family for longer than Jed had been alive and added on to over the years to suit the various family members' tastes and needs.

But it was Mother Stark, Jed's Mama, who had enjoyed it and used it most thoroughly. She'd spend many but the darkest, coldest days of the winter season there, and only then in the past few years, begrudgingly allowing as how she might get along better during those few weeks back in the larger, warmer Stark family ranch house.

But of course, that was now gone. Lilly didn't doubt that once Jed had the time to devote to it, he would build it back up. For the present, he and Mother Stark were in firm agreement that his time would best be spent resurrecting the still again and making their deliveries from their secret hoard of liquor built up over many years.

Lilly had only learned of this in the past couple of years, and given how Jed had told her, and the solemnity with which he had related it to her, she knew it was a sign of deep honor and trust in her that she was being told of its existence, and what's more, of its location.

As Lilly walked down along the pretty, winding path that led to the camp, she mused on the fact that it was a trip she had made a number of times over the years, although almost always accompanied by Jed, and once or twice by his mother.

She paused and gazed at the trees in the grove and beyond, at the Paluxy River, already low but looking inviting, especially as the day heated up. No time for pleasures, such as river bathing, right now, she told herself.

As she resumed her walk, she thought back on that Sunday, a couple of years before when Jed had led her down the by-then familiar path. But he had stopped her there to admire the view, and then he had said, "Lil."

"Yes?"

"There's something I need to tell you."

She had wondered why he was acting so odd that day. Sure, he was the same, quiet, slow-to-smile Jed, but he was quieter than usual, which, for him, meant near silence.

She had long ago told herself not to expect anything from any man in her life, not even Jed Stark, not after her long, sometimes difficult life. It had been one in which she had had to depend solely on herself and put up with all manner of cruel behavior and treatment from her fellow citizens.

Despite that, as Jed turned to her that day with the most serious look on his face, a fist-size knot of fear formed high in her belly and traveled up her throat. What was Jed so serious about and what was he about to tell her? That he had grown tired of her? Unbidden, and much to her annoyance, her mind rippled through the possibilities, none of them particularly positive.

"Lil," he'd said, "you look worried." Then he'd smiled and

hugged her. "No need for concern. I only want to share something with you. Come on."

He held her hand and led her down the path, past the camp—a neat-as-a-pin structure then as now, thought Lilly. But on that day, they hadn't stopped there but kept going. Past it a ways, although the trail had gone on, angling right and along the river course, Jed had led her left. They walked along a thin path overgrown and untraveled, then toward a low rise of what looked to be a sandstone rock face.

"What—?" she'd said, but Jed looked back at her and was smiling but not talking. They continued on and she kept her growing questions to herself.

Then they angled left, then right, deeper in, seemingly making right for the rocks, as if they were going to climb them. Is that what he had in mind? Maybe there was a nice view from up there.

But no, for he paused before the rocks, let go of her hand, and she saw now there was a narrow gap in the rocks, man-high but obscured by a jumble of logs and brambles that looked to have been there for centuries.

Jed looked over his shoulder, over her head, taking in the scene, but it seemed to her he was looking for something. Something he did not see.

He turned back to the rocky, cluttered mess, and with care, Jed moved aside the logs and brambles to reveal a gap wide enough for a man to pass through without angling too much. This he did and held out a hand, a long finger telling her to wait a moment.

She did, and presently she heard a match strike, then she saw a small flicker of flame, then a squeak as a bail was raised, and then more light glowed as an oil lantern was lit.

Jed poked his head back out the gap and his eyes looked past her, all about them quickly, then looked at her and smiled. "Come on in." He took her hand and led her in through the gap.

"I would tell you to mind your head," he said, and didn't say anything more, but she knew without seeing his face that he was smiling.

He was tall and she was not, and it had been a small, infrequent source of mirth for him, and a tiny, infrequent source of annoyance for her, although she thought it was cute of him whenever he brought it up.

"What is this place?" she said, looking around as they walked slowly forward, deeper into the low rise of hillside. Lilly felt as if she were inside some great sleeping beast.

"This?" said Jed. "What do you mean?"

She'd looked at him but he was smiling.

"This is what I wanted to show you. What nobody but Starks, and few of them at that, have ever seen. It's a cave."

"Well, I can see that, Jed." she said, looking around.

"But what you don't see and soon will is—well, follow me."

She did, and within seconds, the warm, yellow light from his lantern fell on rows upon rows of barrels, wooden barrels, all bunged and stacked and neat as a pin.

"There must be hundreds of them," she said.

He shrugged. "Never really counted, but yep. Lots of barrels.

"And—and they're all whiskey?"

"All Stark whiskey, yep."

"Wow," was all Lilly could say.

"Yep."

"I've kept up the tradition of making some for customers and some for the cave."

"But . . . why?" she said.

Jed had looked at her then with drawn brows, as if she had asked her question in a foreign tongue. Finally, he said, "Because Starks have always done it. The cave was found by ol' Grandpa Stark, back when he was scouting this land as a possible site to settle. He built his first still not far from here, back along toward the river, closer by the camp. That's the first location of the Stark family ranch. Well, the house, anyway. Never really been a ranch as such, not with hundreds of head of cattle running around, as you'd expect."

"You Starks have always been too busy making the best whiskey ever made, right?"

"Well, according to Mama."

"According to everybody! I daresay," crowed a voice from behind them in the doorway. They both turned to see Mother Stark standing there with her shotgun cradled in her arm, but a wide smile on her face.

"I tell you now and true, if the entire population of the world had a chance to sample Whiskey Woods libation, there would be no more of this 'maybe it's the best' talk any longer!"

"And I daresay," said Jed, winking at Lilly, "that the Scots might have something to say about that."

"Bah!" said Mother Stark, a scowl riding her face. "Bunch of funny talkers! What they know about whiskey ain't a pinch of what the Starks know!"

Then she looked at Lilly and grinned. "Glad to see he took my advice and shared this place with you. A man can't give himself over to a life partner if he's keeping secrets from her—ain't that right, Jed? Didn't I tell you that?"

"Mama, please."

Even in the dim light of the lantern, Lilly and Minnie saw that the big bold man was blushing and annoyed.

"I thank you for sharing this secret with me, Jed. And I promise you I won't ever betray it, come what may."

There followed an awkward few moments in which nobody spoke. Finally, Jed said, "Well, not much else to see here. It's quiet, and did you notice that the temperature is about ideal?"

She was going to ask him what he meant by that, but then she knew—there was something . . . right about the air there. And it was a dry cozy feeling but not warm.

Minnie nodded. "Grandfather Stark chose right well, he did. Lived in this cave for some time while he built up the place and made his first batches of whiskey hereabouts. It's a shame we don't have any of that left."

"Mama, you don't even drink the stuff."

"That's not the point! I have a fondness for those who came before us. And I daresay you do, too, Jed, for you keep adding to this store of whiskey, the same as all the Starks have always done."

"It's where we age it," said Jed to Lilly, explaining his mother's statement.

Then Lilly heard a familiar voice up ahead, and she smiled, breaking her reverie of that day two years before when, in her mind, she had all but been asked by Jed to be his wife.

Legacy and pride in their family's life work, the Stark whiskey, meant about everything to Jed and his mother, and sharing that place with her had meant much to them, and even more to Lilly.

She advanced on up the path, smiling now, because the voice she'd heard was coming from the bustling form she saw up on the porch of the Stark camp ahead. "Mother Stark!"

The old woman looked up from shooing a slow-walking, slinking Redeye off the porch and down the three broad steps.

The old woman squinted, visored her eyes, then smiled. "Lilly! Come on up here, girl. And I told you to call me Mama or Minnie. Mother Stark, coming from you, is far too formal. Here, you help me with these rugs, if you would. I spent the last ten minutes cajoling that useless excuse for a hound up off the big braided one there and on out the door. Honestly, he can't walk two feet without collapsing from exhaustion. I swear, never has a more useless creature on the face of the earth drawn breath and remained above the soil. Amazing."

As they worked, the women chatted. Lilly noted that Minnie took more frequent pauses, unusual for the constantly moving woman. She knew Minnie suffered from that blow to the head in the fire, but for her age, Mother Stark was more than impressive.

After a while of small talk, Lilly said, "So you think the fire was no accident, Minnie."

"Course it wasn't," said the old woman, glancing up and shaking her head, as if the question itself was the most absurd thing she had heard in ages.

"I agree with you, but Jed, he's—"

Minnie surprised her by chuckling. "Jed's a Stark man. A whole lot of good qualities, to be sure, but the men of the line also come with a pile of stupid in the head, if you know what I mean." Minnie tapped her temple, then winced slightly, confirming to Lilly that the old woman's head was indeed sore.

Lilly didn't know what to say, and Minnie chuckled again. "I surprise you?"

"A little, yes."

"Oh, I love him. He's my son. I'd do most anything for him, but he's stubborn as all get-out when he gets a notion in his head. Jed's biggest fine quality is also his biggest bad quality, if you see what I mean."

"Not really, no," said Lilly, laying out the last of the rugs and smoothing it.

"He's inclined to think the best of folks, even pigs like Sheldrake." Minnie's face darkened, and she scowled. "That's the finest of him, I am inclined to believe. But the same thing, believing in the goodness of everyone else, also makes him mule dumb at times. He won't give up on a person so easy. Even when everyone else has."

"I know he has no fondness for Merlin Sheldrake," said Lilly.

"That's true," said Minnie. "You'll stay for tea with me, won't you, Lilly?"

"I'd like that."

"Good. Now, because Jed doesn't like someone doesn't

mean he's going to stop believing in them as a person. It sounds more complicated than it is. But right now, he's ignoring the obvious truth. And ignoring me, too!"

"Oh, I can't imagine he'd ever ignore you, Minnie."

"Well, he is! I told him, later on, here at the camp, that I saw someone at the fire. I know it!"

"Could you tell who?"

"Sure, I could!" She poured water into the teapot and slammed the kettle back on the stove top. "Well, maybe I didn't see a face, but I'd swear it was one of those wormy little men who work for Sheldrake. I'd bet cash money on it."

Lilly nodded but didn't say anything.

"I know what you're thinking. You're thinking that I'm calling guilty them who I'd like to see called guilty. Well, I saw who I saw, and I know what I know."

"I don't doubt you, Minnie. But Jed blames himself. He says he didn't tend the still fire as he ought to, then he rushed on out to town." She fell silent and fiddled with the placemat at her spot at the table.

Minnie laid a hand on her arm. "Oh, child. One fool blaming himself is enough. Don't you go feeling guilty, too, because Jed went to town to see you. I encouraged him to. Practically had to shove him out the door!"

"You did?"

"Sure I did, not that he didn't want to go, but he kept putting off going to town for my sake. He thinks I'm some frail old woman who can't take care of herself! Can you imagine? Ha!"

She sputtered at the bread board and brought over a plate of cookies. "So, you see, I could as well be blaming myself for the fire. But it wasn't any of our doing. It was Sheldrake, as sure as the sun will burn bright tomorrow."

"I'm sure you're right. But Jed, he won't admit it."

"Well," said Minnie, sitting down. "Maybe that's for the

best, but don't tell him I said that. After all, what good would it do if he was convinced Sheldrake was behind it? He'd get all riled, and then where would we be? He'd likely end up in jail or worse, then we'd have a pile of burned timbers and no Jed Stark. That don't bear thinking on."

Minnie had tallied the situation in her usual succinct, forthright manner. She nodded and sipped her tea. "Whoo! Bitter like me!" She cackled and smacked the table with her hand.

Lilly could not help but smile. "Mother Stark," she said, "you are a wonder."

"Thank you, I think. And it's Minnie."

Chapter 12

From the moment he smelled smoke on that awful night barely two weeks before, Jed had, of course, suspected that Merlin Sheldrake was behind the fire. He had no proof, other than the threats the man had made, and that Mama swore she saw somebody before she was knocked cold by that burning timber.

But Jed also knew that neither of these was proof enough to brace Sheldrake. And going to the law, even if the law was honest—which, at least locally it was not—would provide no solution. That Marshal Chiswick was folded and tucked tightly in Sheldrake's watch pocket made the consideration of such help impossible.

No, he had reasoned, the only thing he could do was get on with the business of cleaning and then rebuilding. As he often did when faced with a daunting task, Jed looked no further than the end of his own nose and tried to view the dogged labor it required as tiny pieces that, when stacked up, day on day, amounted to the result he sought.

Do one thing, then do the next thing that needed doing, and then the next. Pretty soon, experience had taught him, you'd have a task well in hand.

It was the only way Jed knew to face the work. Otherwise, it would be far too easy to sigh and give up, and that would never do. Not for a Stark. Besides, not only was he born to the task of whiskey making but he loved it and could not imagine doing anything other than that. Even if he had to make money in some other way, he would make whiskey. It was his blood and bone—it was more than in him, it *was* him. So, the sooner he rebuilt the big whiskey shed the better.

Before all that, however, Jed realized his most pressing need was to make money to rebuild. It would be an expensive job, and it had to be done right. As the days passed and he divided his time between cleaning up the mess left by the fire and making whiskey down at the campsite along the river, Jed felt himself growing angrier.

He didn't like feeling building anger within himself, but he knew that it was a justifiable emotion. But he also knew it would carry a man only so far, and usually not down a good trail.

No, he didn't want to travel down the rage road, because he had seen plenty of that sort of behavior in the war, the eye-for-an-eye mentality that only ended up blinding everyone and leaving no one satisfied or well served.

Despite all that good intention, the one thing that raised Jed's ire, however, was the growing gnawing urge to arm himself with more than his usual hip knife. It was not so much for himself, but because his mother had been hurt.

The next time, if there was a next time, it would no doubt be worse. He could not give room in his mind to the notion that he had had the ability to somehow help prevent a next attack and yet had done nothing.

And so, Jed Stark, for the first time since he had been discharged from the Confederate States Army, strapped a revolver about his waist with the sole intention of using it on another human. This was not because he was hunting for meat, this was because he might need to kill a man.

It was with great reticence that he opened the old wooden

trunk in a back room of the camp, into which, fortuitously or no, he had years before and without ceremony, rolled up his revolver and gun belt, and covered them over with a couple of old blankets.

His mother said nothing when she saw him haul the gun and holster and belt out one evening and clean them. He went about it as he did everything in life—with measured deliberation. And when, several hours later, he had completed the task, the gun was an oiled thing, in full operational order, its storm-cloud metal glowing dull and smooth in the lamplight. The leather belt and holster were once more butter soft and supple.

The next morning, after breakfast, he carried them outside and strapped them on, his trembling fingers betraying his calculating, methodical thinking.

Jed felt his breath hitching, his throat tightening, and his right eye twitched. He ripped at the buckle and threw the gun to the porch floor. Then he bolted from the camp and made it a dozen yards before emptying his gut behind a cottonwood tree, retching away his breakfast.

That entire experience made him angrier than anything else, angrier than he had been when he had seen the homeplace afire. For that meant that Merlin Sheldrake had already won, for he had already altered Jedediah Stark's very self, the thing that made Jed the man he knew himself to be. Sheldrake had dragged him down to his vile, pitiful level.

It took Jed two more days before he could leave the gun on his hip for an hour. Then two hours. Then much of the day. He did not wish to become accustomed to wearing it, not for the present reasons. But his mama, and perhaps Lilly, and even Loudon, too, might well need him to be capable of anything and everything.

That his mother had taken to lugging Ol' Shredder with her everywhere, including the outhouse, did not surprise Jed. Mama always had been an aggressive, no-nonsense person, and she saw no reason, from the first whiff of threats by the rich, fat Sheldrake some time before, not to remain fully vigilant. And if that meant shooting a man to protect her kin and her goods, then so be it.

The thing Jed always counted on, that unnamable something—part mind, part gut, call it instinct; he didn't need a name for it, but it had always been something for him to count on—was there within him, functioning, and for that he was grateful. Because it was telling him, more each day, that this thing with Sheldrake was not over.

"So help me," muttered Jed to himself, sweat dripping off his nose as he tended the still, "if it's not over, then fine. For I have yet to say my piece."

Chapter 13

"He's what?" Merlin Sheldrake spat the words as if they were hot coals in his mouth.

Fendall Hawkins—or "mayor," as he preferred the citizens of Glen Rose call him—stepped backward toward the door, wishing even as he did so that he had not burst in and blurted out what he had thought would be grim but defeating words to Sheldrake.

He realized that the fat man was staring at him, eyebrows raised in question. He wanted him to repeat what Fen now realized was most unwelcome news, indeed. And *unwelcome* was a mild word for what Sheldrake was feeling, apparently.

"Well?"

The doughy little mayor swallowed, ran a pink finger between his collar and freshly shaved neck, and licked his lips. "Well, yes, it's true, it's true. I—look, Mr. Sheldrake, you know I can't afford to stop serving my customers the one whiskey they request by name. For lots of folks, it's Whiskey Woods or nothing. Course, most everyone calls it Stark Whiskey, or plain Stark's . . ."

All the while he spoke, Hawkins's voice grew quieter until, under Sheldrake's increasingly intense stare, with the rich man reddening and trembling, the mayor finally let his words crawl to a stop and die.

Fen had always had a problem with talking too much—which had actually helped him when he ran for the seat of mayor of Glen Rose—but here his blabbing had landed him in trouble once again.

"I don't," said Sheldrake, forcing the words through clenched teeth, "want to hear another word about how very popular Stark's whiskey is. I want you to repeat what you told me when you busted on in here. Repeat it, and then tell me how you found out, who you heard it from, and when. Now."

It might not have been worded like a threat, but man alive, thought the mayor, Sheldrake had a way of making a fellow's innards shrivel as if he were holding a knife tip tight under his chin.

Fendall swallowed. "Jed himself, he delivered it." Hawkins nodded as if agreeing with himself. "Got a borrowed one-horse wagon and drove it right around to the back door of my two places, same as always." Sheldrake wasn't looking at him then, and Fendall relaxed a pinch.

"A full order?"

"Yeah, you bet. Same as always. And he was loaded up with barrels. Looked to me like he was making his usual route."

Sheldrake looked at him then, eyes narrowed and his voice low, but tight, trembling. "You are not the first to tell me this, in fact," he said. "But the others, I doubted them, because they are idiots. I see now it is the truth, and Jed Stark is back in business."

"Never left it, more like!" said the mayor, relieved to hear he was ranked, at least in Sheldrake's eyes, somewhat higher than an idiot.

"And yet how is it possible? My men, ah—the Stark ranch burned! I have not seen it for myself, but I have been told multiple times. It burned to the ground! Unless I have been lied to?"

Hawkins shook his head. "No, you've been told the truth, all right. House, the barns, chicken coop, the works, all burned right down to nothing, poor folks."

"Poor folks, my foot! But the still, man! The whiskey still—that burned too, yes?"

"Oh, yeah, for sure! It was sort of built on to the barn, anyway," said the mayor. "It's as gone as gone can be." He rocked back on his heels, pleased that he could be the man to verify this obviously most important information for the richest man in these parts.

Sheldrake's thick pink fist slammed the desk top, and the inkwell rattled. Steaming coffee in a low cup puckered and splashed upward. "How? How, I ask you! How can the man continue to make deliveries? It was well known that he stored his whiskey in the barn, was it not?"

Once more, Hawkins backed with sliding steps toward the door. "Yes, yes. Sure, I guess. I mean, well, I never saw that for myself, but sure! But come to think on it, he must have had a stash of it. Had to. His stuff is the finest-going quality whiskey, aged and everything. Stands to reason he'd age it off somewhere. Only aged whiskey ever becomes quality whiskey."

He nodded at this slice of sage wisdom he'd heard many times over the years from others who knew much about such things. Then he looked at Sheldrake, and Mayor Hawkins regretted his words.

It was well known that Merlin Sheldrake was touchy about the quality of his own whiskey. Touchy, but curiously enough, he didn't want to go to the trouble to make it even a low quality, plain-tasting whiskey. Instead, he paid a handful of men to churn it out, raw and fast. They were not men from town, and they were paid well to do their jobs. Nobody knew for certain what it was they put in the whiskey to "kick it off," to make it a whiskeylike drink.

But a good many folks knew by looking at it, then sniffing it. And those with little money knew even more so that it would render a man useless for days, if not kill him outright.

Incredibly, so far, there had been no provable cases of poisoning to lay at Sheldrake's feet. Rumors, sure enough. Plenty of those. But no proven instances. Or if there had been, nobody heard about them.

Mayor Hawkins had every reason to be afraid and to back toward the door, for Sheldrake's face had puffed even more, his eyes popping and veins throbbing on his temples and his coloring had faded from pink to red to an alarming purple. The mayor noted all this in increasing detail. Finally, concern for himself moved him backward quicker.

His left hand pawed at the doorknob and landed on it with his second flailing attempt. Sheldrake advanced.

"Um, sir," said Hawkins, as he jerked hard at the door, feeling great relief as the thing opened. He stepped through. "Um sir, you—you don't look so good. No, not so good at all . . ."

He did not wait, however, to see whether the rich man was in the midst of exploding, literally, or was merely displaying yet another moment of rage.

He nearly had the door tugged closed behind him when Hawkins felt the thing wrench from his grasp and the whisper of fingertips reaching for him.

Fendall was not a slight fellow himself, but compared with Sheldrake he felt quite fit. As the lesser in size of the two men, he was able to avoid the full, grasping fingers of the rich man.

"Don't you ever let me hear you say such things in my presence again, mister!" shouted Sheldrake at Hawkins's rapidly retreating back. The mayor felt aware, moments later, that the fat man might slow his retreat. A quick glance over his shoulder verified this, as he saw Sheldrake, purple about the face, sneering and huffing, with big breaths working his chest like a bellows.

He was trying to say something more but all he could manage were growls of rage matched by his flexing fingers. "You . . . you . . . ! You will not be mayor much longer!"

And yet, thought the mayor as he bustled through the sparsely crowded bar of the Money Tree. And yet I am the mayor. At least for now.

But what was he to make of that threat? Was it a threat? Knowing Sheldrake, it surely was. Bah, thought the mayor. I'll parse it out later. Right then, he had to get on out of there and fast.

Even though they were his people, it was annoying nonetheless how those folks in the bar stared after Fendall. The red-faced man made his way toward the front of the place and the door to something more comfortable and familiar, the main street of Glen Rose.

He made it, his ears throbbing with redness, even though to his mind he had done nothing wrong. He'd merely told the truth, the bald facts, and Sheldrake was so thin-skinned that he could not bear to hear it.

And then he threatened him, and within earshot of a handful of voters, as well! Perhaps threatened was a strong word for what he'd heard. But the implication was clear enough—Sheldrake felt as though he had placed Hawkins in his office, and therefore, he had the right to peel him from office. Hawkins mulled all this over as he eventually slowed his pace, walking back toward the town's small office at the far, western end of the street.

The structure housed the mayor's office as well as all the required documents and books and such to keep the town rolling along. Never mind the fact that Hawkins had never so much as cracked the spine of any of the books, much less perused the papers.

He grew up in Glen Rose, so he figured that if there was something he didn't know about the town and the people in it, he would eventually hear about it, yes sir.

By the time Hawkins made it to the office, he was feeling all right again, so much so that he had stopped within sight of the place and had complimented a woman, Mrs. Margaret McQuinnick, and her young daughter, Millie, aged seven, on how well they looked. It was a fib, of course.

Never had so homely a woman drawn breath in Glen Rose, and her daughter looked to be carrying on that sad legacy. But they would never hear such a thing from Hawkins. He nodded and smiled and patted the child's head and thought all the while how very mayorlike he was behaving, and he kept glancing up and down the street to see if any of his other citizens saw him thus engaged.

Sadly, he mused, it was the noon hour, and folks were likely nibbling away at a bite or two of food before reapplying themselves to the thing that, as a business owner himself, he most liked to see: money being spent, especially in his town and most especially in his own establishments, the Happy House saloon, the Cactus Bar, and Hawkins's Mercantile.

By the time he made it to his office, Fendall Hawkins had quite forgotten what it was that had driven him there in the first place. But Merlin Sheldrake hadn't.

After the annoying mayor had departed from Sheldrake's club, the wealthy man had spun, returned to the back room where he conducted all his professional conversations, and had almost slammed the door, but he caught himself in time. He closed the door with quiet care and paced about for a bit.

Finally, he decided that it was time. Time to do the thing he had been deliberating about for a couple of weeks. He had put it off not only because it was worrisome and perhaps things that might result from it would end up being illegal. But also, because, frankly, the man he was about to beckon to Glen Rose, a man he had chatted with briefly some months before, many hundreds of miles from Glen Rose, was none other than Pit Pritchard, one of the vast West's most notorious men for hire.

Rumor had it that Pritchard had been a wanted man in various states and territories, but that the law in those places had, as yet, been unable to pin a thing on him. In short, Pritchard was a whole lot of things, but he was primarily cautious, and most effective for those who hired his services and his men's. And that last point interested Sheldrake the most of all. He wanted results. He needed them. But how badly? This was, after all, a rather large step to take. Even for a bold and wealthy businessman such as himself.

Sheldrake decided to take a bit more time to consider this most vexing of dilemmas, whether to employ the man or no. He was doubly annoyed because when he had awakened this morning, Pritchard's name hadn't popped up in his mind for a good many days, as he had felt most assured that his problems with Stark were over.

But now he found that what those fools, Rollo and Clem, had told him was, indeed, true—that the cursed whiskey maker, and presumably his foul little cur of a mother, too, were anything but on their way to becoming a memory. They were not only back in business making whiskey, but they were delivering their gargle as if nothing at all had happened to slow them.

They must indeed have some sort of stockpile. But where? Had the fire been that little of a vexation to them? Merely a hiccup at the dining table of life? They were certainly far more than that to him.

Rather than fading away in his memory, the attempted removal of the Starks as whiskey makers only seemed to be helping them somehow, at least as far as their reputation among the doltish locals was concerned. The path that he, Merlin Sheldrake, had been clearing for so long, making him the only whiskey maker of any size in the region, was fast becoming overgrown once more with weeds and brambles.

Sheldrake barked "Bah!" and paced the room once, twice, then sat down with a grunt at his desk. He dipped his pen in the inkwell, noting that the top was once more askew. He blamed the mayor, then chuckled because he was going to have the man fired, somehow.

Sheldrake set out a fresh sheet of paper to commence the note he had thought he would not have to write. But here it is, he thought. Forced into it. He began to write.

After a few moments, he shrugged, sighed, and perused what he had written. Then he smiled and nodded and continued to write.

It took him one more start and another fresh sheet of paper, then Sheldrake grunted in approval of what he had written. He blotted it and sealed it inside another larger folded sheet, addressed it, and then went to fetch one of the two dolts he employed, either Rollo or Clem. Preferably Rollo, as he seemed to be slightly more human than Clem. Which, mused Sheldrake with a sigh, wasn't saying much.

There were many other men in his employ, of course, but the others were busy with making whiskey. And that was a task he did not wish to slow.

Rollo, the taller of the two dolts, was possibly more intelligent and was reputed to have been some sort of scout or other. He would grease the fool with the promise of money, in order to get Rollo to the town of Grindle as quick as his horse's feeble legs could carry him. There, he would deliver the letter to the telegraph operator.

The man owed him several favors and despite this, or perhaps because of this, the man didn't seem to dislike Sheldrake, as so many others did. He would send the wire immediately, or suffer the consequences of incurring Sheldrake's wrath yet again.

"And make certain you are back here in time to work at least another hour tonight, do you hear? Do that and you will receive the ten dollars." Sheldrake said this to Rollo while holding the envelope away from the man's fingertips. He saw that his offer of cash was the perfect amount to tempt the buffoon into making the ride. Any more than that and he would be wasting cash; any less and he might not get the results he desired.

"Yes sir, boss. You bet I will." Rollo nodded with vehemence, and his friend looked from Sheldrake to Rollo and back. "Um, Boss?"

"Yes . . . you?"

"I'm Clem, sir. I . . . Might be Rollo might need someone to ride along with him, right? We work well together, don't we, Rollo?"

Rollo considered this point for a moment. From the look on the man's face, Sheldrake knew it was occurring to Rollo that an answer either way would not jeopardize his promised ten dollars.

"Well, now, that's true," said Rollo. "Yep, we done all right out to Starks, you got to admit that, sir,"

Sheldrake felt his face redden.

Rollo saw what effect his words had on the boss, and he licked his lips, not certain what to say, so he shut his mouth.

"You fool," said Sheldrake in a low growl. He glanced about them at the thankfully quiet warehouse, free of the other workers, off on their midday food break, the loafing oafs.

Sheldrake spoke in a low, grating voice: "I thought I made it plain that that little venture was to forever remain sealed away in your memories, never to be mentioned again. I paid you with that stipulation hanging in the air, and you had assured me that would be the case!"

Rollo swallowed. "Um, which time, Boss? Only we have been out there a few times on your say so, ain't we, Clem?"

"Yeah, for certain. I recall each time, sure." Clem nodded in solemnity, as if what he was saying was being taken down verbatim by a clerk in a courtroom.

Sheldrake closed his eyes and sighed. "Rollo, do you want this money or no?"

"Yes, boss."

"Good. Then you will do as I say and ride this note to Grindle as fast as your horse's legs can carry you. Once there you will give it to the man in the telegraph office. His name is Alfred Jones. He is tall, like yourself, but he has a vocabulary exceeding that which you possess. He will be wearing a bow tie, arm garters, spectacles, and a black cap that covers a scar he received in the war. That last is of little consequence to your mission. Give the note to no one else, do you understand? Tell him it is from me, even though he will know it by looking at my writing. Do not wait for a response.

"Then get back on your horse and return to Glen Rose. Do not dawdle in that town. Do this, and you will earn your ten dollars. You, Clem," said Sheldrake, turning to the second man.

Clem, brows drawn, looked at Sheldrake with hope gleaming in his eyes. "Yes, boss?"

"You will remain here, and will double your efforts at work this afternoon in order to take up the slack in labor caused by Rollo's absence. Do this and you will earn yourself an additional five dollars. Am I understood?"

"Yes, boss!" said the now smiling man.

"Good." Sheldrake smiled feebly with a feeling of benevolence and handed over the letter. "One last thing: If either of you ever mention the name Stark in my presence again, I will have you publicly flogged."

"Yes, boss," said both men, looking confused but convinced that this would not be a pleasant thing to experience.

CHAPTER 14

Mr. Sheldrake:

I recall our brief conversation of several months back, and of your interest in my services. This letter will follow a wire I sent, verifying receipt and agreement to the terms you mentioned.

As it happens, me and the boys are in northern New Mexico, up Clayton way. Lucky for you I gave notice to the wire man in our stomping town of Ogallala, Nebraska, where we'd be. I expect to be finishing things for this client within a few days.

I owe the boys a day or two to lean back and blow the foam off, if you know what I mean. I recall Glen Rose as a decent little town. We will hold off on doing so here—for obvious reasons—and we will kick back for a bit once we get to your town. Then we can begin our work for you.

Mr. Sheldrake, me and the boys hope you all have a decent hotel, a decent bath house, decent whiskey, and indecent women. And we are not kidding.

Signed,

P. Pritchard

Ollie Hagar read through the letter and then paused, thinking. Finally, he began again at the top, his lips moving with the words. Pit didn't mind. He was proud of Ollie.

He had, after all, taught the kid how to read, his first success in that way, and he took much pride in seeing the younger man engaged in such a task. Of course, it would not do when they were in a rush to have the kid stumble his way through every letter and note Pritchard sent.

Pit was a businessman, after all, and had found much use for the fact that not only could he read, but he could string decent words together enough to form acceptable sentences and then put them down on paper. He had been able to get a whole lot of work for himself and his men because of that fact.

As for Ollie Hagar, Pit had found him wandering six years before, alone and without a mount. The kid was poorly clothed, thin as a four-day corpse, and footsore as all get out.

As he watched the kid work on his second pass of reading the letter, Pit let his mind tick back to that day.

He'd been riding through Jervais, Oklahoma Territory, hoping to make it across a vast stretch of flat land that offered his eyes little to give it definition. All he wanted was to keep his heart beating and his horse walking beyond the flat piece, then make it into those foothills in the far distance.

He had a new customer to please, a wealthy rancher who had been having troubles with sheep herders up in the hills beyond his spread. Pit had promised to make it to the man's ranch by nightfall of the following day, and with any luck he could commence to dealing with the sheepers and collect his fee. It was to be a good paying job and likely a quick one. And that suited him right down to the ground.

But finding a lone kid, looked like a boy from behind, limping and hatless under this sun, and with no obvious canteen or waterskin, well, Pit knew the ghost of somebody's sainted mother would never understand if he rode on past the trudging fool kid. So he stopped.

"Hey, kid," said Pit, leaning back in his saddle, resting his hands on the pommel and considering if he should hop down and water his horse.

Pit saw now that the youth was indeed not a girl but had the dirty sproutings of light fuzz on his face, wide shoulders, and no backside.

The kid didn't look terribly tall, at least not yet anyway, which was another thing Pit would come to appreciate about him. But for now, Pit was concerned with the fact that he was now likely responsible for the cursed youth.

Pit sighed, and said louder, "Kid! Hey! I'm talking to you, and from the looks of things, if you're hearing voices other than mine, it's because you're funny in the head! Sun'll do that to a fellow's egg—cook it quick, especially without a hat on it."

As if he'd been prodded on the shoulder, the bedraggled youth slowly turned a wobbly head to his right, and opened puffed, crusted eyes enough to see Pit's big black horse, Night. His gaze began to inch upward, but apparently it was all too much for him, because the boy's legs gave way at the knees and his eyes rolled back, and he toppled to the baked earth.

"Oh, no!" barked Pit, and he slid from his saddle. It wasn't yet noon, an hour or more away, and the horse threw scant but vital shadow on a patch of earth to its right side. Pit dragged the kid over there, astounded by how light the youth was.

The small cloth satchel the kid had been carrying was now dragging, too, beside his bumping body. Pit laid the kid out, then stood, fumbling for the canteen. He had been warned that it was a fair piece between water holes, so he had filled himself before mounting up early that day back in that last little settlement eastward. He'd let the horse drink its fill, then he filled his canteen and two canvas waterskins.

Since then, he'd been rationing the precious liquid, uncertain how long the trek would take and not willing to risk ending up—well, like this fool, he thought, as he wetted the kid's bubbled, cracked lips.

He forced the kid's mouth open and then gently eased in a

few drops of water, then a few more. It took some time, but the kid, or at least his nearly dead body, got the hint, and began swallowing.

"A little more, but not too much at once, lest you puke and waste it."

It took Pit a quarter of an hour of doing this, drop by precious drop, before the kid began to rouse and make sounds on his own.

Pit looked up, saw the sun and saw no clouds. Nothing but a burning light in a too-bright blue sky.

"This will never do, kid," said Pit. "I have places to go, a commitment to meet, and money to make. And your lazing about in the sun is jeopardizing the whole works."

The kid's swollen eyelids fluttered, and he licked at his lips with a thick, puffed tongue. He managed to wheeze out a word that sounded like, "Sorry."

Pit didn't know what to say for a moment, then said, "Don't . . . don't worry about it. You have a name, kid?" He was thinking that the kid was bad off enough he might not make it. Might be a way to at least bury him with a name and tell somebody in a town ahead.

"Yeah," said the kid.

Pit waited, but the kid didn't say more. He looked all done in. "Well, don't you worry about it. Pit's here, and I won't leave you to the vultures."

He'd meant it as a joke, but the kid's eyelids fluttered again, and this time they opened wide. "No, no, not that . . ."

"Don't worry. I promise. Now you have to drink more water, but not fast. That'd be a waste of good water, because you'd puke it up. So go slow—slow, I say. Now, that's too fast, kid! Slow . . . good, that's good."

"Pit?"

The voice was Ollie's. Pritchard looked up from his seat on

the nail keg on which he'd sat while working out the letter on a makeshift plank table top laid over two other kegs before him.

"Yeah, Ollie. What do you think of the letter?" He waited to hear the young man's opinion. In fact, he had grown to appreciate it and then to depend on it in the past few years. Hagar had proven to be a solid fellow, mentally and physically, and had grown in most measurable ways since that odd day when Pit found him on the trail, near death and alone.

He had become, in Pit's mind, and in Ollie's as well, a son to Pit, who had no offspring of his own—of that he was certain—and no wife. He also had no living relatives of which he was aware.

Ollie, it turned out, was in much the same situation, familywise. At least with what he could recall. It seemed that as time wore on and the kid had gained strength, he had not gained back much in the way of memories.

Or if he had and had decided not to share them with Pit, then that was the kid's choice. But they'd ridden together since, for six years, and Pit saw no reason that should change. The kid was good with a gun, better with a horse, and quick with his wits. He made decisions that Pit approved of, and the other men, four in total, all came to accept the fact that the younger man was Pit's second in charge.

It was natural for Pit to assume Ollie would one day take on the role of leader of what he had built up in the past eight years—two of working alone, then six with the kid in tow, and four or so with the other four men who rode along with them on jobs more often than not.

None of them save for Ollie was someone Pit would risk his neck for. And he knew the kid felt the same toward him.

"Pit, I think it's a good letter." He set it back on the makeshift table. "But is this Mr. Sheldrake the man we met who got all lathered because I didn't like his whiskey?"

Pit smiled and leaned back against the stable wall, cushioned by a wad of burlap sacking cut up for wiping down horses and hanging from a wooden hook above his head. He looked up at the tall, blond young man, folded his arms, and smiled.

"Yeah." He chuckled at the memory. "Man alive, didn't he go all red in the face? In his defense, you're not much of a whiskey drinker, anyway, which probably isn't a bad thing. But I thought he was going to throw down on you right there and then!"

"Well, if he did," said Ollie in his usual measured, squint-eyed way, looking toward the back wall at the sun lining in through gappy boards, "I'd say we wouldn't be going to work for him next, eh?"

"Nope," said Pit, sitting up. "Can't work for a dead man. At least not easily." He held up a hand and the kid jerked him to his feet.

"Maybe we'll find out," said Ollie, hitching up his gun belt and walking from the stable. "Okay then, I have more steers to rebrand for Whateley."

"Then they'll be Whateley's," said Pit, folding the letter. "I'll do that. Give me a chance to check on the boys' progress. You take this letter down into town and send it off, all right?"

"Sure, Pit." Ollie took the letter, then lowered his voice. "You concerned about Whateley?"

"Yeah, I am, son. But that's between you and me. I don't want the others to get wind of anything that might give them an excuse to loaf. Pit Pritchard and his men didn't get a reputation for doing a job faster than anyone else, and with all expected results fully delivered, to risk on lazy hires."

Ollie nodded. "Or a surly old tight-fisted rancher like Whateley."

"You said it." Pit walked on toward the corrals. Over his

shoulder, he said, "See you when you get back. And no dawdling with those saloon doves, you hear?" He smiled and kept walking, knowing the kid was turning red at that very moment.

Soon, Pit reached the corral where the men were working. Or were supposed to be working. Sure, the running brands were heating up in the fire to a rage-filled glow, but that was all that was happening. The rest of the cattle had yet to be wrangled, drawn closer to the corral from their waiting pen, and his men were seated on two old knobby logs upwind of the fire.

He saw a small bottle with about an inch of honey-colored liquid slopping around in the bottom. His most recent hire, a year and more back, Stubbs, received it in hand from the man to his left, Koski. Stubbs transferred a small cork from betwixt two fingers of the same hand and punked it back into place with the heel of his other hand.

They were all talking and laughing and didn't see Pit walking toward them until he was about twenty feet away. Then they did. All four jerked to their feet, reddening more than the whiskey had done to them.

"Oh, hey, boss. Thought you was off writin'."

Pit stopped, adopting his usual look of little to no expression and stared at the speaker, Stubbs, a plug of a man with bristly hair and beard and tiny round spectacles that made his eyes look piggy.

As usual, even when caught in a position none of them wished to be caught in, the man could not help himself in chiding Pit's penchant for writing and at night reading. Stubbs was illiterate and thought that such pursuits were the mark of a man with "womanish ways," and had hinted at such several times in their year-plus acquaintance.

Pit enjoyed both pursuits, and felt confident they had helped him immeasurably in securing more and better-paying jobs with clients who were discreet and wealthy. That Stubbs scoffed at him also did not matter to him. But Stubbs was poisonous in other ways, too. He had a thread of malice in him that discolored the other men at times. This had only come to Pit's attention recently, because Ollie had asked him about it one day.

The young man had, of course, been correct. He'd proven a solid judge of men's characters. And his assessment of Stubbs was interesting. Or more to the point, his assessment was correct: Stubbs's subtle, snide digs and wisecracks were affecting the other three men, and the man's poisoned attitude herded them at times like a sheep dog will a flock, away from Pit and Ollie.

Pit had had enough of him, and although he was a man who rarely hesitated once he'd made up his mind on a thing, he found himself doing so as he stared Stubbs down over the low branding fire.

It took him longer than usual to arrive at what he needed to do. This, he knew, was because he had been in a fine little mood and had been reluctant to leave it behind. But he was Pit Pritchard, a man hired for fixing problems, large or small, for others. If he couldn't do that for himself, of what use could he be to others?

"Cheever, Koski, Dooley, get those cattle branded." The men nodded, mumbled, "Okay, boss," and turned from the fire.

"And Stubbs?"

"Yeah?"

"I'll have that bottle."

The man sighed, and Pit knew that Stubbs was thinking that he'd paid cash money for that whiskey.

But Pit had also said several times over the years, and each of his men knew this, that in no situation was it acceptable for them to drink alcohol while on a job. Before and after, okay. But during, no.

He expected his men to do his bidding while they were

working. As far as Pit was concerned, they were a tight reflection of him, and he wanted each client to see him and his men as dedicated and hard at work.

Sitting down at a task when it wasn't the noon hour and sipping whiskey when they had several days to go was unacceptable. Especially not for the wages he paid, which were double what they might make anywhere else, doing anything else.

That his line of work took part largely on the dark side of a shadowy line legally and ethically played into it, too. But on that point, he was always honest with them. He was also upfront about what would happen if he ever heard that they let slip anything about him or his jobs or his clients, even long after leaving his employment.

Stubbs began to move away with the other three men.

"Stubbs, stay. I will have a word with you."

The chunky man sighed as if he were in a stage play. "Okay, boss. Whatever you say."

"We've almost had hard talks a few times. You know it, and I know it. Don't forget that you came to me looking for work. And when I hired you on, I told you how it was going to be working for me. Hard work, no lip, and no booze while we're on a job. And you agreed to it all. Right?"

"Yeah, that's about it, yep."

"But you seem to be complaining more and more. Some of the others have started that foolishness, too. And now I come upon you all drinking and sitting on your backsides. And by my watch"—Pit looked skyward toward the sun, then back to Stubbs—"it isn't midday yet. Let alone the end of the job."

"We been at this job longer than you said we would! Got a right to be a man now and again!" Stubbs was working himself into a quick lather, his nose and mouth rising in a sneer and his color darkening along with his voice.

"Yep, on both counts," said Pit. "But not if you work for

me. Tell me this, Stubbs: Where else are you going to make as much money as you do working for Pit Pritchard?"

"Shoot, boss, I done all right before I worked for you. I reckon I'll eat again after."

Pit narrowed his eyes. "Does that mean you're leaving my employ?"

"If that means am I sick of you and your riding me like a tick?—then you bet!" The man had taken a step backward and had begun to flare his elbows away from his barrel chest.

A sizable part of the reason Pit had hired him was that Stubbs had carved himself a reputation as a quick clean gunman, leaving no doubt about his abilities or his guilt, at least according to the law.

Pit hadn't liked the man all that much at the time, but he'd been hard against it on a job for a freighting company and had needed at least six men, himself included. So he'd hired Stubbs and, to his surprise, the man had seemed to fit in well. At least at first.

But time, as it always did, nibbled its way onward, and Stubbs's true nature began to show. Now he was a chafing, angry fellow.

Pit, rarely concerned for his own safety, felt the unfamiliar tickle of a seed of fear in his gut, down deep, as the plug of a gunman looked to be squaring off before him.

"What is it you think is going to happen here, Stubbs?"

"I tell you—I tell you, boss man, what is going to happen here! You are going to pay me my full wage for the job and then I am going to ride on out of here. You hear me, boss man?"

Pit pulled in a deep breath and let it blow out his nose. "Stubbs, you know as well as I do that when you signed on to my outfit, you agreed to a whole host of terms, some of which you have already violated. And when it comes to cash payments, you agreed that if you left before a job was seen through and agreed it was completed, by me, then you forfeit your money."

While he spoke, Pit didn't move a muscle, save for his eyelids, which narrowed as he focused on Stubbs's face. Any move a man makes shows on his face first. An old-timer had once told him that, and Pit had always found it to be true. It was one of those things in life he kept in what he liked to call his tool chest, a useful thing he dragged out now and again as needed, as he did now.

"I ain't leaving the job! You're firing me! There's a big difference there, boss man! You cheat me out of my money, man, and you won't live long enough to regret it. And then I will ride far and wide, and let everybody know what it is you do—or did, Pritchard! That's a fact."

Several items passed through Pit's mind at that moment, the first being that he was glad that the client, Whateley, and Whateley's own small crew were many miles and hours from the ranch. They were to make certain they were seen elsewhere by others when the rebranding took place, as Pit had instructed.

The second item in Pit's mind was that if he was shot, and if it was a fatal strike, he felt certain Ollie would be well set up.

The third and last item in his mind was that Stubbs was a fool, and that Pit Pritchard had never knowingly been bested by a fool, and he was confident it was not going to happen this day, either.

"That's the way you want it?" said Pit, keeping his gaze hard on Stubbs's face.

"It's the way it'll be. Unless you pay me and we call it quits right now."

"You know I can't do that, Stubbs. A man's word should not be taken lightly. We both agreed—" Pit wasn't through talking, but he saw the slightest whisper of a twitch on Stubbs's face, high up on his left cheek, and that was it.

Stubbs drew on him, but Pit was quicker. And since he knew that Stubbs was a right-handed gunner, as Pit slicked out his own six-gun, he stepped to his own right and angled his body to the side, providing a slimmer target.

Stubbs did not.

Pit had no time to aim for something less than vital, so his bullet did the job for which it was made—it killed. But first it plowed hard and fast, a lead fist, high in the man's breadbasket. It pummeled through cloth, into skin, fat, muscle, tendon, blood, and bone, and lodged in the burly man's spine.

It took seconds for the other three men to return to the fire, but Pit knew they had seen and heard most if not all of what had transpired between himself and Stubbs. They knew he would not wish for them to interfere, and so they had not.

And he knew them all better than he had Stubbs. He felt certain they understood why he had done what he did.

"Boss?"

It was Cheever.

"Yes, Cheever?" Pit came fully back to himself then, and slid his revolver into its holster. Another tool for which he had done another job.

"You—you all right?"

Pit looked at himself and sensed that other than his heartbeat thumping a bit faster than usual, he had not been harmed. He had not had to kill many men in his life, but it was not something he dwelt on. At least not with intention.

But in the small hours, the deaths of men, of beasts he had had to lay low, either through making meat or, due to an accident, in order to end suffering, came to him. It was always the ones whose eyes he had seen, locked on to in that last moment of life. It was those eyes that came to him in the deep dark, those quiet hours of high morning before the sun was a consideration.

At those times, Pit Pritchard was at his most vulnerable and pathetic, mewling inside like a starved alley kitten. The same as he had begun his life, a starveling in the filth of city squalor. It was what had made him and what had continued to drive him. But it was not pleasant. But he could not seem to gain distance between himself and his past. Why was that? It seemed to be a question without answer.

"Yeah, Cheever. I'm all right. Thanks."

CHAPTER 15

"I see five men before me." Merlin Sheldrake paced back and forth behind the bulwark of his desk, puffing on a nearly black cigar that emitted thick clouds of smoke.

It looked to the men before him as if he were a train struggling up a steep grade.

"Not the six I had expected. Not the six I agreed to hire."

The man who stood ahead of the other four suppressed the smile he wished to show on his face. How many such men had Pit Pritchard dealt with in these years of work as a hired problem solver? They were all, to a man, puffed with money, which always seemed to fat rich men to mean the same thing as power.

And because they invariably wielded their perceived power in cruel ways, and invariably to make more money (such men never had enough of either, money or power), they soon grew accustomed to having the world revolve about them. They behaved as if they were the sole life-giving sun and, thus, deserving of everything they demanded, no matter how outlandish or unreasonable those demands.

"I said, as of the writing of my reply to you, that I had six men currently in my crew. That was more than a week ago. One of my men met with an unfortunate situation."

Indeed, one of his men standing behind him offered up a snort soon masked with a cough. He thought it might be Cheever—he'd have to talk with him later.

"Mr. Pritchard," said Sheldrake, pausing in his slow pacing and squaring off before the standing men in his office. "It might be that you are used to blathering out all manner of excuses to previous employers, but that won't work with me, mister."

A pin-drop silence filled the room. Pit knew what his men, Ollie included, were thinking. They were thinking that nobody ever spoke to their boss that way and got away with it. And Pit agreed. He tried to be a fair man in life's dealings. Fair but honest. Well, honest to a point where the established law of white settlement was concerned.

After all, laws were mere fabrications anyway, were they not? No better, and frequently, from what he had experienced in life, they were often a whole lot worse than what a man could do on his own, guiding himself along his life's treacherous, narrow pathways.

At finger-snap speed, Pritchard went from a rising feeling of resigned mirth at this barrel of a wealthy fat man to feeling his jaw muscles bunch and jounce. He told himself to remain calm. After all, it had taken him long enough in his own life to get here. "Here" being a place in his so-called business that he didn't need to rely on any one client if he felt they were unsavory for any reason at all. And Sheldrake was proving to be a most unsavory fellow, indeed.

"Mr. Sheldrake. May I remind you that you contacted me. I did not solicit your business. If you have no need of my services, then that is fine. You will, or course, pay the agreed-upon nonnegotiable hire fee, which will account for our expenses in traveling from New Mexico to Glen Rose. Once that has been taken care of, we will be on our way, and we'll leave you in peace."

"What?" Sheldrake, behind his desk, slammed his pink fists on the blotter and glared over at Pit. "I agreed to nothing of the sort. And I never would!"

"You did when you agreed to hire me and my men, and you know it. You were told. And if you wish to make an issue of it . . ." Pritchard slicked out his revolver and leveled it on the hard-to-miss mass of the body of Merlin Sheldrake.

The effect was as Pit knew it would be—the fat man's cigar dropped from his pooched wet lips, and his fat, raging hands flew up by his shoulders and trembled, palms outward, like odd little hairless creatures.

"No, no, Mr. Pritchard! What I meant to say was of course I don't need to pay that fee, not yet anyways. because I would very much like to engage your services! Yes, yes"—the fat man nodded in agreement with himself—"that's all I meant."

"I see," said Pritchard. "Well now, that's good, Mr. Sheldrake. That's good to hear. I do believe we have the right number of men to do whatever it is you wish us to do. Which is what I would like to discuss with you in more detail right now."

Sheldrake nodded and saw his cigar slowly smoldering a hole into his leather desk blotter. Instinct drove him to begin reaching down for it, but then he recalled the situation he was in and jerked the hand back up on high, wide eyes looking at Pritchard, who he was certain was intent of driving bullets into him like a carpenter hammers nails into wood.

Pit kept his revolver aimed and cocked, but spoke over his shoulder. "Okay, men, why don't you find a good stable, then find the best hotel in town and take rooms. I will meet up with you all later."

"Right, boss," said Pit's men, almost in unison, and all doing their best to hide smirks.

The boss had done it again, they were thinking. He quietly and calmly set this rich idiot on his ear, all the while keeping the job. And on top of it, they all knew of Glen Rose's reputation as a whiskey-making town. And they had a couple of free days before they had to get back to it. It was a good deal all around.

"Mr. Pritchard, um, would you mind . . . That is to say—the gun, um . . ."

"Oh, yes, Mr. Sheldrake. Of course, how silly of me," said Pit. He eased off the hammer and slid the gun into its holster. "I'll sit here, how's that?"

"Fine, fine." Sheldrake slowly lowered his arms and swallowed.

"Mr. Sheldrake?"

"Yes?" The fat man's eyes widened again as he was groping for his chair to seat himself.

"You might want to deal with that cigar."

Both men looked at the item, which had burned most of the way through the blotter and would soon begin on the wood beneath.

Sheldrake emitted a yelp and snatched it up. With a shaking hand he set the thing in an ash tray and settled himself. He closed his eyes and let out a long breath. "This life I am leading will be the death of me."

This struck Pritchard as humorous, and he chuckled. "That is an interesting thing to say."

"What I mean is that I—people keep holding guns on me, unbidden! I—I don't know how much more of that sort of thing I can be expected to take."

Pritchard crossed his legs, his black trousers fairly clean after the last stretch of their dusty ride south. "You'll pardon me for saying so, Mr. Sheldrake, but perhaps it isn't so unbidden as you think."

"What?" said Sheldrake, his eyebrows drawn tight.

"You act as though I did something wrong, but you were all set to back out of a deal you knew we'd made. In my not inconsiderable experience, that is an unacceptable business practice."

Sheldrake opened his mouth to protest, but Pritchard held up a halting hand and kept speaking. "But as we have come to an amicable agreement, I see no reason to tread that path again. Now, something tells me that whoever else has recently pulled a gun on you might well be part of the reason me and my men are here."

Sheldrake let the words settle and then nodded. "That is exactly correct, yes!" He smacked a hand on the desktop, but as quickly winced and looked at Pritchard, as if to apologize. And to see if the man had drawn down on him again. He hadn't.

"Maybe you should tell me about it, then."

Sheldrake nodded. "Yes, yes. Where to begin? Ah, well, it's the Starks, you see."

"The Starks."

"Yes, a nest of foul creatures who are dead set on ruining my burgeoning empire."

"How so?"

"They find it acceptable to flout honest, fair offers to them on my part to purchase their ranch and their whiskey-making facility."

"Is their work all that good?"

"What do you mean? Of course it's good, why on earth would I offer to buy it if it was swill?" Then Sheldrake shut his mouth, and in a lowered tone, he said, "It is possible that some people prefer its flavor to that which I manufacture. You'll recall it, from when we met some months ago? Sheldrake's Finest."

Pritchard frowned "Hmm, no, it's not coming to me. What's the name of this Stark scoundrel's whiskey?"

Sheldrake waved a hand in the air and looked away. "Oh, they named it after their ranch. Or perhaps it is the other way around. I don't know, and I don't care."

"And the name of the ranch?"

Sheldrake sighed. "Whiskey Woods."

Pritchard's response was immediate. His eyebrows rose, and he nodded slowly. "Sure, yes, indeed. That is prime whiskey. I've had the pleasure of meeting up with it twice. And it's local, you say?"

"Yes, yes, for heaven's sake. But the Stark family, such as it is, a mother and her son, all that are left of that pathetic little brood, are anything but impressive. They are killers and thieves, and I need to have them stopped and removed, once and for all."

Pritchard did not speak for a long moment. He stared at the fat man, assessing him. At least that is what Sheldrake felt. Finally, the famed hired gunhand said, "What has been done so far?"

"What makes you think I have done anything yet?"

"Because people never call me in first. They try to take care of their troubles themselves." Pritchard shrugged. "Can't say as I blame them. Save themselves a bit of money. But I can tell you that if folks would hire me from the start, they would save money, time, headaches, you name it."

"Ah yes, well, as it happens, I did employ the services of two men who came to me with acceptable credentials in your, shall we say, line of work. That is to say they were able to make some inroads, but . . ."

"But?" Pritchard's gaze stayed on Sheldrake's face, even when the fat man squirmed and looked away, feigning deep interest in his recently singed blotter.

"They were less than successful—let's put it that way. For various reasons, none of which, I can assure you, would interest you. Now, as to what I need: I require either the recipe for the Stark whiskey or its total elimination. I am not alone in this, however! I am acting, shall we say, on behalf of a . . . a consortium of whiskey makers and sellers, all the major names in the country. Despite numerous and frankly ridiculously inflated offers, Stark refuses to entertain the idea of selling."

"What did these two professionals do so far?"

"Firstly, it is important, as I said, that you know I made frequent and repeated offers—more than generous, mind you—to purchase the recipe from them. I also offered to purchase what they laughingly refer to as the Stark family ranch. It is little more than a clot of ill-conceived structures, pathetic, starving animals, and poor land. Or it was."

He snorted and shook his head, then continued. "At any rate, it is no place for an old woman and her son to spend their lives. Truly, it isn't. But they refused me, over and over again, outright refused to even consider the, frankly, exorbitant amounts of cash money offered to them to procure their recipe."

Again, Pritchard held his tongue and regarded Sheldrake through snakelike, slitted eyes. Finally, he said, "You said, 'was,' in reference to their ranch."

"Did I?" said Sheldrake, once more not meeting Pritchard's frightening gaze.

"Yes, you did, Mr. Sheldrake." He let out a quick, full sigh. "Mr. Sheldrake, I am here at your request to undertake a job that you have failed to do yourself. If I am to be successful, which I assume you wish me to be, then I must be told all the information pertaining to the situation. Yes?"

The fat man shifted in his seat. "I see your point."

"Well, that's good. That's a good start, Mr. Sheldrake. Now, what is it about the Starks you are not telling me?"

Sheldrake looked everywhere but at Pritchard.

"I will ask around town then, shall I?"

Finally, Sheldrake sighed. "It seems not long ago that the Stark ranch burned."

"I see."

"To the ground."

"Mm-hmm. And presumably, their recipe also burned."

"You would think."

"Except," said the gunman, "that theirs is an old family

recipe, and the whiskey-making process, as far as I am aware, is fairly straightforward. The differences come in the quality of the ingredients, and perhaps the most important part—I'm only guessing here, mind you—might well come in the nuances of the process. How somebody does a certain thing a certain way, for instance. Otherwise, as I said, whiskey making is a straightforward process. More of a *way* of doing things than a *what*, if you take my meaning."

"Oh, balderdash, Mr. Pritchard." Sheldrake shook his head as if he were speaking to a simpleminded fellow.

The gunman once more had to suppress a smile. Here we go again, he thought. And sure enough, he was not surprised to see that Sheldrake had sensed a moment in the conversation in which to wedge a fat foot and bluster and blather all over again.

"It's obvious to me, Mr. Pritchard, that you do not know the first thing about whiskey making. You see, I am one of the largest manufacturers of whiskey in the country. My booze is a superior product. Some might disagree, but it has to be said that nobody knows more than I do about this art. And I know it requires all manner of ingredients. It is far from straightforward."

"I have had Stark whiskey, Mr. Sheldrake, and I will admit it was one of the finer whiskeys I have tasted in some time. Perhaps ever."

"Well, well, we'll have to get you a bottle of my own brew. Then you can compare for yourself."

"I look forward to that, Mr. Sheldrake. But getting back to the fire at the Stark ranch. Does anyone know how it started?" Pritchard watched the fat man closely and learned much of what he needed to know from the rapid reddening of the man's face.

"There was a whole lot of speculation," said Sheldrake, looking down at his blotter once more. "But I suspect it was that drunkard, Jed Stark, who was remiss about taking all the precautions a fellow in his line of work needs to take! Why, a man who is working with fire and liquids that will explode? There is no doubt the man uses the vilest of ingredients at times—gunpowder and other vile concoctions that outright kill folks. No, I am afraid Stark caused his own problems there."

Sheldrake leaned back and tried to put his hands behind his head, but his arms were too fleshy and his suit too tight. He let them slowly drift back as if he were in the act of flicking ash and lint from his lapels.

"Then at this point, Mr. Sheldrake, I must ask you what it is you have engaged my services for?"

"Oh, yes, well, the amazing thing is, after the fire, why, that cursed Stark has continued to fill his orders! And if that wasn't enough, I have it on good word that he has also continued to make whiskey. Make whiskey! Can you imagine?"

"In fact, I can, Mr. Sheldrake. Making a still isn't necessarily the most difficult thing a man will do in his life. It can be an onerous task, I imagine, and must be fairly precise in all the right places, but for a fellow who is handy and who has as much experience in the trade as does Mr. Jed Stark, obviously, I'd say it's quite possible."

"Yes, well, that's all well and good for him! But Jed Stark being back in business has put the pinch on me and my profits once again! And I won't have it, I tell you. I won't have it!" He smacked a fist on the desk top, and this time he did not shift his eyes from Pritchard's.

"Ah, that is finally the heart of the matter, then. The reason that you hired me and my men."

"You bet it is! I want that man Stark good and gone! I don't have time for this, and I certainly don't have any intention of letting that backwoods fool steal from me!"

"Or your friendly competitors."

"Huh?" said Sheldrake.

"The others you mentioned earlier. Your consortium."

"Right, well," said Sheldrake, looking at his hands. "I'll deal with them on my own. Your job"—he looked again at Pritchard—"is to deal with the Starks. I think we understand each other."

"Perhaps, Mr. Sheldrake. Now we must discuss money. And that, Mr. Sheldrake, is not something I will leave unspoken."

CHAPTER 16

"Now Mama, I don't want to sound like, well . . ."

"Like an old woman—go ahead, and say it." Mother Stark grinned. "I understand. The last thing I want to be known as is an old woman. They're annoying."

"Okay, Mama," said Jed, tamping down a smile. "But promise me you won't go looking for headaches. I have enough of them right now to last a long ol' while."

"Tell me, son, what sort of trouble you think I might get up to hereabouts?"

Jed sighed. "Mama, I only meant that I do agree with you and with Lilly and with Loudon."

"About what?"

"That it was likely Sheldrake who did all this, the fire and such. Of course I know it, and you know it, and everybody knows it. But if I went around growling and grousing to myself about it every day, I'd never get this place back in working order, would I? Once that's done, I will see to it that things are dealt with."

"I hope that doesn't mean going to the law. Least not in Glen Rose," she said.

"I'm not that much of a fool, Mama. Chiswick is Sheldrake's man. But Deputy Thompson isn't."

"Bah, Harley's a wet-nosed boy! What can he do?"

Again, Jed sighed and paused, after snugging the last buckle on the harness. Mags, his sweet brown mare, stepped in place and snorted. Jed passed a hand down her shoulder.

"Deputy Thompson has already told me that he is sent over to Grindle and beyond on a regular basis, on various law-related errands for Chiswick. And while he's there he's going to talk with whoever he knows might be out of Sheldrake's reach. As of right now, anyway. And Lilly and Loudon have offered to write letters to men who hold political office, the governor and such—"

"Bah!" she snarled again. "Politicians? A more useless, self-serving lot you'd be hard-pressed to find!"

"I can't disagree, but trying can't hurt. Loud's also sending inquiries to folks he knows back East. Newspaper types, and also more politicians, and a couple of big business owners, too." He shrugged once more. "As I say, it can't hurt, Mama. Beats complaining and doing nothing else about it."

He knew that would sting, but that was too bad. Sure, Mama knew how he felt, and she knew how she seemed to him, grousing and bitter. But he wanted her to know it was getting tiring hearing it day after day without doing a thing about it.

She stood up from where she sat on the top step of the camp's long shade porch and slowly made her way down the steps. She gripped the plank siding of the work wagon and rattled it. "This wagon Rupert Brown loaned you, it's not too bad. Mind you, it isn't a patch on ours that burned, but it's not bad. Good of him to do that."

Jed nodded. "Yeah, he's a good man. I reckon most of the town are that way. Even the ones who got their heads turned by money. It won't last, never does. They'll go back to being friendly enough."

She snorted, but he could see she was fighting the urge to light into whoever she considered a traitor. It would wind up with her howling mad yet again about Sheldrake. He moved to climb up into the wagon, then paused. "I'm all loaded up, I have to go."

He'd already wheeled three kegs in a barrow out of the cave and along the hidden winding path up to the horse and wagon. He brought Mags down from the long low shed and paddock he'd built to give shelter and protection to their critters after the fire. It served them all pretty well, save for Mama's chickens, which she set loose about the camp yard during the day. She caged them at night in a small coop he'd built for them.

"I have your list for the shops. Anything else?"

"This," she said, handing him a bulging cloth sack.

"What is it?"

"Food, of course!" She looked at Jed as if he'd asked her if he had a nose or not.

"My word, Mama, we ate a good breakfast."

She snatched his forearm and squeezed. "You're all skin and bone! You've been putting in long hours, too long for one man."

"So have you, Mama. And you won't do what I say, and Lilly says, and rest until your head is healed. And thank you for the food."

"You're welcome. And my head's fine. And since when do you and Lilly tell me what to do?"

"Hasn't happened yet, Mama," he said, bending down and kissing her forehead. "Maybe one of these days." He turned and climbed up into the wagon, smiling as she sputtered.

"You best pack a lunch of your own fixing before that, mister! I might be older and smaller than you, but I am a tough bird, and don't you forget it!" She grinned up at him.

"There's no danger of that, Mama. Now look, I don't like leaving you, given what's happened. But promise me you won't leave the camp, all right? No need to poke around back at the ranch. Nothing to see there, anyway. And nothing to do until I get back, okay?"

She narrowed her eyes and pointed a finger at him. "Get going, mister. I have work aplenty to do here. And tell Lilly I said howdy. She's welcome to visit any time. I enjoy her company."

"You didn't answer me, Mama."

She turned and made for the steps and lifted her shotgun once more. "Lilly will do more than work, grunt, and worry about me—she actually holds a conversation with me! Imagine that!"

"Bye, Mama." Jed was smiling and shaking his head as Maggie rolled them on out of the camp yard and up the long winding lane that led to the burned remnants of the ranch.

He mused on Mama, knowing she was going to do whatever she wanted to. Always had in this life and always would, he reckoned. That was her way. Like it was always going to be his way to worry about her. But she was right—they couldn't stay holed up at the camp forever.

That's why he knew she would be up at the burn, dragging whatever charred bits he had not gotten to yet. Despite his comments, she had been helping him pile the chimney stones off to the side for use again when the time came.

And she'd been saving bent and ravaged nails and other steel odds and ends, even though he had told her that many of them would be useless, having lost their strength if they had been in a hot enough spot in the fire.

He knew all this about her, as he knew and she knew that they would rebuild. And she would help every step of the way. So that was that.

Jed had accepted the fact she was not ever going to be content with bustling at the camp. And so shortly after the fire, he had been running quick trips to Glen Rose, to fetch supplies and to make scant deliveries. And today was no different. But that didn't mean he wasn't uneasy about leaving her, tough old bird or no.

* * *

Jed urged the horse forward, doing his best to keep from looking to his right at the three strangers loafing on the boardwalk. It's not that Glen Rose didn't get its share of newcomers drifting in and out of town, but there was something about these fellows that didn't sit right with him.

It was that gut feeling again, and as he had many times in life, he knew to at least listen to his gut's suspicions. Didn't mean he had to act on them. Not yet, anyway.

It also didn't help that since he'd rolled on into the eastern end of Main Street, he'd been getting at best a quick nod and then a hasty look away from folks he had known much of his life. Emmet Dalston and his wife, Ruby, and their sprout of a boy, Em Junior, were the latest of the many he'd seen in town already.

To Jed's knowledge he'd not offended Emmet any time in their lives, nor his wife, and certainly not the boy, who had to his credit, smiled and waved and shouted, "Hi, Mr. Stark!"

But that was as much as he was allowed to say because the tot's mother gave him a cross look and pulled the kid's arm down by his side.

"But, Mama—"

"Don't you say another word, now, Junior."

As for Emmet Senior, Jed looked at him with drawn brows, but his old friend gave him the merest nod of greeting, turned red, and looked at his boots as the little family hustled along past those three loafing newcomers.

Jed received much the same response to his several offered greetings, nods, and smiles. Nobody of the folks he knew acknowledged him with more than a nod, a weak smile, and then a look away. This was far more than odd.

To his mind, the only thing of note that he had done in the past few weeks was to lose his home and barn and whiskey shed to a fire. Certainly not anything he deserved a shunning over.

Jed mulled this as he guided Mags around the near edge of Hawkins's Mercantile and down the wide lane. It led to the back side of two of the three establishments he had to visit today in Glen Rose.

"Jed!" a voice shouted from behind him. He glanced over his left shoulder and saw a familiar shape, his slightly pudgy, forever wrinkled and rumpled chum, Loudon Paley, waving to him and bustling down the mouth of the lane toward him. He was not wearing his usual wide smile, but neither was he looking somber, like the other folks in town Jed had seen.

"Whoa, whoa, girl!" said Jed, tugging on the lines and easing Mags to a halt.

The horse did not mind, despite the fact that it was not a particularly brutal load that day, seeing as how it was the bare minimum of whiskey Jed needed to bring to town to fulfill his orders. But it had been a rough couple of weeks for her, hauling logs and lumber and nails and such. With any luck he'd be up to full production capabilities soon, then she'd have even more reason to relish any spare moment of downtime. He'd spell her now and again with the gelding, Stormy.

Once he was back into full-time whiskey making, Jed would feel better about taking whiskey out of storage in the cave because he'd be putting new whiskey into the cave. It was simply so that it would age and one day be worth drinking.

But he wasn't quite there yet, and it was not in Jed's nature to think too far ahead at anything in life. The present was more than enough to work on, so why trouble his mind with things that hadn't happened yet?

"Jed, good to see you!"

"Hello, Loud. What brings you hurrying on down the lane? You don't seem to share the same malady everybody else in Glen Rose is suffering from today."

"Huh?" said the newsman.

Jed smiled. "Saw Emmet and Ruby and little Junior. The

boy was the only person who's dared to say a thing to me since I got here. Except you, of course."

"Well, that is me, childlike to the end."

"End? That sounds ominous, Loud. What's happening hereabouts, anyway?"

The newsman leaned against the wagon wheel and looked up and down the street. "I don't know exactly, not yet anyway. But—and this won't surprise you one bit—I'm pretty certain it has to do with Sheldrake."

Jed rolled his eyes. "Let me guess. It also has something to do with those strangers, no?"

"Now there you have me. I saw them, of course, and there's another two of them, at least. One of them must be the leader."

"Leader? What are they, a church group on an outing?" Jed smiled, but Loudon didn't.

"You wouldn't think it was so funny if you suspected what I do, Jed." Loudon looked up and down the lane again and lowered his voice. "One of them, a fellow in black—"

"Aren't they all," said Jed, rolling his eyes.

Loudon ignored him and continued: "He looked somehow familiar to me, as if I'd seen him somewhere. Then it came to me that maybe I'd seen him at the law dog's office."

"Law dog, Loudon?"

This time the newsman blushed and shrugged. "I've been reading Beadle's again."

"What'd I tell you about all that wild west foofaraw? It'll spoil your brain." Jed tapped his temple with a long finger. "Now what's all this about the marshal's office?"

"Right, well, I thought perhaps it was at the marshal's office that I'd seen the other newcomer. The one who's not on the street right now. I thought maybe I'd seen his face in the pile of Wanted dodgers."

"And did you?"

Again, Jed's pal shrugged. "No way of knowing. Chiswick

wouldn't let me look through them. Now I don't have to tell you that that's illegal. I have every right as a tax-paying citizen of this town to look through those papers."

"I know, I know, Loud. So, the point you're trying to come to is the other stranger who I don't think I saw yet may or may not be a criminal. If he is, and if his face is on a dodger, we won't know it because Marshal Chiswick is in a pocket on that great big backside of Merlin Sheldrake."

Loudon nodded. "And we might not know of it in Glen Rose, anyway."

"What's that mean?"

"It means I am going to make a trip to Grindle this afternoon."

"Let me guess—you're going to look through the law dog's papers there instead?"

"It's the only way. The truth must be unearthed, Jed."

"Well, good luck. And be careful."

"I will."

"But none of that really explains why nobody in town except for one little boy would barely look at me, let alone talk to me."

"That is another thing I have to figure out. But I can tell you that not long after those men came to Glen Rose, the entire mood in town began to change. I can't describe it any better than that, Jed. But something's off in the air in Glen Rose. There's a raw new stink about the place that was never here before."

"Yes," said Jed. "And I can guess whose backside it's coming from."

Loudon chuckled. "Okay, then, Jed. I have told you as much as I know, which sadly is not an impressive amount."

"It adds up to more than the nothing I have to offer," said Jed. "Oh, hey, Loud, before you go—have you seen Lilly today?"

"Have I seen her? Only at breakfast time. And I was thinking a slice of whatever pie she made for today might do well in keeping me whistling on my way to Grindle."

"She's good, then?"

"Yeah, of course. She said she was out visiting you and Mother Stark the other day."

"She was, sure, but I got the impression she isn't too happy with me."

"That's because you aren't as riled up about Sheldrake as she thinks you ought to be."

Jed sighed. "Man alive, I get it from all sides. I suppose you feel the same way?"

"No, we've already talked about that. I know you want lawful justice, and so does Lilly. That's why we're writing letters and such." He glanced about them once more, then leaned forward and, in a lowered voice, said, "We certainly won't find justice in this town."

"All right, then," said Jed, nodding agreement. "I need to deliver this whiskey, visit with Lilly, buy a few things at the mercantile here, and then get back home before Mama decides to build the barn and house herself."

"If anybody can, it's Mother Stark!" Loudon headed back up the lane toward its mouth on the main street. He walked a dozen feet, then said, "If you can't find a home for those barrels, I'm happy to take them off your hands, Jed."

"Ha!" said the whiskey man, nudging Maggie forward once more. "Best of luck with that wish, mister!"

As they rolled to a stop behind the first saloon, Fen Hawkins's Happy House, Jed set the brake, wondering why Loudon would say that. It's not as if anybody had ever turned away Stark whiskey, be it in kegs or bottles. He hopped down and, resisting the urge to whistle, took the back steps to the saloon two at a time.

He was beginning to feel in a better mood, at least better than he'd been before talking with Loud. Strangers or no, cold shoulders or no, it was a fine day, and he was going to visit Lil very shortly.

Two drop-offs and then there she'd be, red in her face, hair hanging from beneath her kerchief, and eyes smiling over at him, no matter what tricky chore she was doing.

But first, he had to head on in, through the back door of the Happy House, talk with Chris, and get paid for his last shipment and today's.

Jed entered as he always did, passing through a storage room filled with bottles and crates and other stockpiled items that looked as if they had not been shifted in years. At the far end of the narrow room, he nudged open a door that stood ajar and walked on in to the barroom proper.

A quick look about the room told him there were no other customers, and Jed would not expect there to be at this early hour.

"Hello there, Chris, your boss about the place?"

Instead of the usual "Howdy, Jed!" and bear paw of a wave the big barkeep always gave him, the big bald fellow glanced at Jed and then looked away, toward the front door.

"I said hello," said Jed, making his way to the bar, but not taking his eyes from the man. "All right, what's happening here, Chris?"

The big bartender put effort into avoiding Jed's stare, and busied himself with racking glasses and drying others.

Sudden heat rose up Jed's throat into his face, forcing his teeth to grind together hard, his jaw muscles flexing. A tightness in his vision threatened to grow worse lest he do something, anything to diffuse it.

But seeing yet another Glen Rose resident who he'd known since he was a child now snubbing him as if he'd broken all the town's bylaws really made him good and angry. It was an anger that was worse, perhaps, than what he'd shown the night of the fire. Truth be told, he had wanted to ride on into Glen Rose that night and drag Sheldrake out of his comfortable bed and thrash him six ways from the Sabbath.

But today, right then, Jed realized he'd had enough.

He strode down the length of the bar until he stood directly in front of the burly barman. "Chris!" He growled, smacking his hands on the bar top. "What is going on in town? Why are you afraid to talk with me? Huh?"

The big man looked at him, head back as if he'd been struck, eyes wide. He opened his mouth, but clapped his lips together again, like a banked fish. Before he looked back down his eyes glanced over Jed's left shoulder.

Later, Jed thought back on that slight momentary motion, and he knew it should have meant something to him. It was an instance where had he trusted his gut, it would have meant something. He would have turned.

But he didn't. Instead, he was too filled with instant anger, too filled with all the rage he'd let pile up these past few awful weeks. From before the fire until now. And he half launched himself over the bar.

It was not a move Chris expected, and the barkeep didn't back away in time. The only thing he had time for was to drop the glass he had been repeatedly buffing with his half-grimed apron.

Jed's big hands landed on Chris's chest and snatched hard, balling up the fabric of the barkeep's shirts. He jerked the big man toward him, and in a low voice said, "Talk, Chris! We've known each other a long time!"

And the big man did speak, but his voice came out as a whisper. "Been told not to!"

"By who?"

Instead of speaking, the frightened barkeep's eyes communicated for him. They looked again over Jed's right shoulder, and stayed there, unblinking and wide.

As Jed turned his head, a man's voice, unfamiliar to him,

from back behind him in the far reaches of the darkened room, said, "I would let off tormenting the poor fellow, Mr. Stark."

As soon as he said this, Jed's eyes found the man in the back of the dim room. He was seated at a table well in the shadows.

"It is Jed Stark, is it not?"

Jed let go of Chris's shirtfront and spun, easing along the bar so that the barkeep would be to his right, behind the bar, but within side sight, and the stranger visible to his left. "I know you?" As Jed looked, he noted that unbidden, his left hand had already grabbed down by his side at his holstered revolver.

"No, nor I you. But that is not important. What is important is that you came in here unannounced, through the back door, not a public way, and attacked this man." The speaker moved his head slightly and said, "Isn't that right, bartender?"

Chris said nothing, but continued to look down at whatever it was he was shuffling atop a shelf behind the counter.

"I said, isn't that right, bartender?" The stranger's voice rose a pinch in volume.

Chris looked up and said, "I—uh . . ." He glanced quickly to Jed, as if to say, *Help me*, then as quickly, he looked away again.

"What's the matter, bartender? Have you been mauled by a lion?" The man's laughter filled the room, but it was hollow and brittle, and not kind in the least.

Jed regained himself and strode forward toward the seated man. A quick, steely clicking sounded.

Jed halted because he saw a revolver appear, as if conjured, atop the man's table. The rest of the fellow hadn't moved save for that hand that held the gun.

"Now then, friend, what's the purpose behind all this aggression?"

Jed halted. "I might say the very same to you."

"Then do so."

Suddenly Jed was tired, tired of this fellow who he bet good cash money belonged with those other strangers he'd seen loafing outside on the street. In fact, he was likely the fellow Loud spoke of.

"You're quick to draw a gun on a man. Why?"

"Why? Because I am protecting my person. You have shown yourself to be the contentious, warring sort, accosting as you did my fine friend behind the bar here. Then you turn on me and make your approach, your hand down by your gun. Tell me, what would you think in that situation?"

"Where's Fendall?"

"Who might that be?" said the man, sitting at his table, his pose casual save for the revolver held resting on its butt atop the table, the snout of the barrel glaring at Jed as if it were staring him down.

"Fendall Hawkins, the man who owns this establishment."

"Hmm, Hawkins, Hawkins . . . Nope, does not call to mind anybody I know. Then again, I am a stranger hereabouts. But given the welcome I have thus far received, at least by you, I am inclined to think that Glen Rose is perhaps less than welcoming to strangers. What are your thoughts on the matter, Mr. Stark?"

Jed sighed. "Stop muddying the water." Without taking his eyes off the seated man and his vile gun, Jed said, "Chris, where's Fen?"

The barkeep did not answer.

"Why don't you answer the man, Chris?" said the seated man.

For the first time since Jed arrived, his old friend, Chris, spoke in louder than a whisper. His voice nonetheless wavered in fear as he said, "I—I think he's away. On mayor business."

"There, you hear that, Mr. Stark? The man you seek is away. On official mayoral business. And I suspect you knew that. I suspect that is why you strode on in here so boldly and proceeded to—"

"Chris," said Jed in a bold tone, interrupting the man.

"Where should I put the order?" Jed noticed, even in shadow, that the fellow's face flinched.

Here was a man who did not like being interrupted. He was the windy sort who liked to flower the air with words. But, thought Jed, he might also be the sort to pollute the air with bullets.

Chris did not speak, and Jed did not expect him to. But the stranger did, and his tone matched his new look, one that was harder, colder.

"Neither Chris nor Mr. Hawkins want your whiskey this week, Mr. Stark. This week or any other week from here on out."

Jed tamped down the urge to reply in haste. He realized now that what he had suspected, back out on the main street, might be happening was indeed happening.

Of course, the strangers were here in Glen Rose working in some way for Sheldrake. He had chosen to hope otherwise, and as usual his hopes amounted to little more than a handful of mud.

And since Fendall Hawkins owned this bar and another, the Cactus, here in town, and since he was the mayor of Glen Rose—a mayor tucked neatly in Sheldrake's deep pocket, like Marshal Chiswick—he was conveniently and uncharacteristically absent from the bar this morning.

Jed didn't bother asking poor Chris if this was true. Jed might already have gotten him into some sort of trouble. He hoped not. Instead, Jed slowly raised his hands so they hovered chest height, palms out, and with a last glance at the hard, smug face of the stranger, he turned and looked at the big barman.

"I'm sorry about that, Chris."

The man behind the bar hadn't smoothed his bunched up shirts front. He looked at Jed with fear and apology on his own face, but did not dare speak. He looked back to his task.

Jed walked toward the back door.

Halfway there the stranger said, “That’s not the way out, Mr. Stark. Not for the public.”

Jed barely broke stride. He kept walking, half expecting a bullet in his left side, then his back, at any moment. It did not happen. He walked through the door, through the storeroom, and out the back door. There, waiting for him, stood Mags in the traces of the work wagon. His barrels were there as well, all as he’d left it.

Jed climbed aboard, released the brake, and proceeded down the back lane toward the east-end outlet. It would take him once more onto Main Street. His plan, as was his custom, had been to round onto Main Street, cross behind the south side of businesses, make his second delivery at the Cactus Bar, then roll further down the street and stop in to see Lilly.

He proceeded on his route, and slowed before his next stop. He was about to halt alongside the wide back porch of the Cactus Bar when he saw, emerging from the bar’s back door, another stranger. This one was a large blond-headed fellow, lean but big-boned.

He wore a double-gun rig, and as he stepped out onto the porch and let the door close behind him, he nudged his fawn hat’s brim back, exposing his full face, wide and Nordic, with a trim, wispy ginger beard.

He stared straight at Jed, no expression discernible on his big face, although he slowly rotated a sliver of wood, a match or toothpick, perhaps, and leaned back against the puckered vertical planking of the building’s backside. He folded his arms over his chest and continued his stare.

Jed halted the wagon. Once more, Jed’s urge was to hop down and walk straight in through that same back door, as he always did on delivery day. But as he did not long before, he measured that urge and found it weak. It was built on anger and the deep-down annoyance of strangers, of anyone, telling him what to do, of forcing his intentions in a direction other than what he wanted.

And if he followed through with it, he would surely be brought back home to Whiskey Woods dead, in the back of the wagon, for his Mama to see and to bury. Where would that leave her? And Lilly?

Jed decided he would ride on. But not before he continued to return the big blond fellow's stare, adding a slow, disapproving shaking of his head as he did so.

Of course, it did not fluster the overgunned man one bit, but it was the least little shred of something Jed could allow himself to do. He clucked his tongue and lightly shook the lines atop Maggie's back, and they proceeded on down the back lane.

As he approached Lilly's place, a hard knot of a thought came to him. What if one of these menacing strangers was at Lilly's? What if they had already done something to her? Even if it was intimidation—which would take a whole lot before it bothered his Lilly—it would be far more than Jed could tolerate, especially given everything else that had happened since he'd arrived in town.

The thought of it forced his jaw muscles to tighten, and he clacked the lines on the horse's back, aware he was traveling faster than he needed to along the usually quiet back lane. He guided the horse off to the side when they drew up near the rear of the café. He set the brake and hopped down, making directly for the kitchen door.

She would be busy in there, no doubt, cooking up as storm, and Polly, hopefully, would be ferrying food to the usual crowd of hungry morning customers.

Jed was almost to the kitchen door when she saw him through the screen. She pushed open the door and gave him a smile, but it was a smile of little more than relief.

She looked very tired, but there was something else there, too. In all the years he had known her, Lilly had only wept once.

That had been when she talked deeply of her father, a man she had loved beyond measure. There were, Jed realized, tears welling in her tired red eyes.

He met her in a stride, and the door closed behind her as she leaned against him and hugged him hard. He did not speak, but hugged her tight in return. They stayed standing there for some minutes like that, as he waited for her to come around, as she would.

And as he waited, holding her close, he realized several things at once—there were no toothsome kitchen smells wafting out the door to tickle his nose. There was no clacking and clunking and banging of plates and cups and pots and pans.

And more telling, he heard no sounds of people talking in the dining room, each speaking louder and louder, trying to make him- or herself heard above the voices of their fellow eaters.

Lilly did come around, stepping back from him and pulling a hanky from her sleeve—something his mother also did. Jed had wondered if that was a skill taught only to girls while they were being trained in the kitchen by their mamas and grandmas.

She wiped her eyes, her nose, and the back of her wrist over her eyes. Then she looked up at him. "Hello, stranger."

"Hello," he said.

She let out a deep breath. "I guess you noticed I don't have any customers today."

He looked past her, as if he could see through the door clear into the dining area beyond the kitchen. "Let me guess—a passel of strangers rode into town and threatened you."

"Threatened my customers, you mean."

"Hmm. But you were open earlier because I saw Loud and—"

"Oh yes, I was open, Polly was here, it was the breakfast crowd as usual. Loudon and the other early birds came and went, but we were full. Then they came in."

"They?"

She nodded. "Three cowboy-looking types, but not really. You can tell, you know? A little too much mean about them, too much swagger and not enough grime under their nails or calluses on their hands. Their clothes were too nice, and they all wore shiny guns."

Jed tensed and looked up the lane, but of the big blond man, the man in the shadows, or the other three, he saw no sign.

"What happened?"

She shrugged. "They came in, the three of them, strutting and looking as if they were the owners of all they surveyed."

"And?"

"They began going around to the tables and telling folks to leave."

"And people did? They left? Like that?" said Jed.

"It helps when somebody's wagging a revolver in their faces."

Jed felt his face go cold and his guts do the same. There were far too many strangers with guns in Glen Rose today. "Then what did they do?" he said.

Lilly sighed. "They said I'd better close up and stay closed if I knew what was good for me."

"They said what to you?" Jed clenched his teeth and looked up and down the dusty back street, as if he might spy one of the strangers lurking nearby.

She squeezed his arm to get his attention.

He looked at her, and she said, "It also might have something to do with the lit dynamite I ran Sheldrake out of here with not long ago."

"What?" said Jed, jerking back from her as if she had slapped his face.

She grinned. "It was great. Remind me to tell you about it some time."

"How about now, Lilly?"

She shook her head. "No time. I need to get this place cleaned up and sorted. And then I have to find Polly and convince her to show up for tomorrow morning's trade."

"You think that's wise?" said Jed.

"Polly's flighty, sure, but she's a solid help, and I'm not in a position to lose her. Or any help, for that matter."

"No," said Jed, "I mean opening up tomorrow. Lil, look what's going on in Glen Rose. I have to figure out how to get some proper law into this town, or there's going to be bloodshed. It feels as if we're right on the edge of something, and it isn't a good something."

"Where are you going to get the law from, Jed? Our letters are barely making their way to the folks we sent them to. From what Loudon has said, it's more than likely that Sheldrake has bought and paid for every marshal, sheriff, and deputy within a hundred miles of Glen Rose. He wants to drive you out of business, and any of the other distilleries in the region, too. But mostly you. And once he does, then he and the drummers for those big outfits can control the whiskey trade. It's that simple."

"That isn't the point, Lil. If you open up again, after you've been threatened with guns, I can't promise I'll be here to protect you. I need to make sure they don't threaten anyone else in town. And then there's Mama. This has to stop. It has to end. And I guess I'm the only one who can do it. It's all my fault, anyway, that it's come to this."

He rested a big hand atop the pistol hanging at his side. Then he looked down at his hand there, almost as if he were seeing it for the first time.

It's that easy, he thought. All the people who matter most to me are close by, and if I risk one of them getting hurt because I'm too late . . . Or I can take things into my own hands before that and save them. Or try to.

"Jed, look at you. You're thinking things that you shouldn't.

I know you well. You are not a gunman. You are better than that. Better than them. Listen to yourself," she said, shaking her head and opening the kitchen door to head back in. "You can't save the whole town. And as for me, I don't need protecting, thank you very much."

"But if you open up, they'll be back, Lil. I can't allow—we can't allow that to happen."

"I heard that slip, Jed. And I will be ready." She held open the door for him. "Well, me and my handy-dandy friends." She tugged open the drawer to her left and pulled out two sticks of dynamite."

"And what if they call your bluff?" said Jed, leaning in the doorframe.

She shrugged. "Then I guess I'm going to go out with a bang. A big, big bang."

"That's not even funny, Lil."

"Jed, I wasn't trying to be funny. Okay, maybe I was, a little. But I won't be bullied. I have spent my whole life being treated as if I'm a barnyard animal by a whole lot of people, because I don't look like them. If I show weakness, I'm through."

Jed closed his eyes and rested his head against the doorframe. He sighed and rubbed his face with both hands. "All this because one man has a craving, a greedy craving. I—I can't understand it. A desire to do a fine job with your head and with your hands, a taste for whiskey, for good food?" he looked at her. "For the love of a good woman? Now these are things I understand. But money? What a waste of time."

"Not money, Jed," she said. "At least, not for Sheldrake. I think for him it's what all that money can buy—and I don't mean things. I mean power. He wants it. All of it."

"Well, so far," said Jed, "it seems he's gotten it all. At least here in Glen Rose."

"And in Grindle, east of us, and in Finchley, to the west. Tularetta to the south, and on and on."

"So where does that leave us?" he said.

She stood a good yard from him, leaning against her worktable, and folded her arms. She looked at his gun, his hand resting atop the butt. Then she looked at his face. "As I said, Jed Stark. I know you, I bet, as well as anyone, except your mother and maybe yourself. Maybe. But I know enough to know what you are thinking of doing right now. And you can't become a one-man crusade to rid this town of these newcomers. So far, all they have done is threaten people."

"You really think it'll stop with that, Lil? These people are driven by money, and that's a big motivation. Both their employer, Sheldrake, and these men he hired. And for that matter, so is Chiswick and Fen Hawkins and a half dozen others in Glen Rose alone. No, this has to end or it will never end."

"Fine," she said, turning from him and slamming a pot on the stove top. "You go ahead and do what you think you need to do. And your mother and I will mourn you, and soon enough Whiskey Woods will no longer be the home of the best whiskey ever made, or any whiskey. And Jed Stark will soon enough not be remembered for anything more than taking a foolhardy stand to fight tyranny."

She fumed and slammed pots and pans and filled a wash tub and clattered plates and platters and cups and utensils.

Finally, Jed crossed the room and grabbed her by the shoulders and spun her so she faced him. He looked hard at her. "If I promise not to do that, not to ride in alone and shoot up the place, will you promise me one thing?"

She looked up at him, her eyes wide but beginning to narrow again. "What?" she said, scrunched but not struggling in his firm grasp.

"Don't open tomorrow. Give me a day to figure out a solution that might, might avoid killing."

"It means that much to you?"

He nodded. "It does, Lil. It really does."

After a few moments of looking deep into his eyes, she, too, nodded. “Okay, it’s a deal.”

A short time later, Jed took his leave of her, but not before making certain she had her gun close at hand. She was a solid hand at wielding the thing. She also had a rifle that he made her fetch down from upstairs.

“I hope you won’t need them. But . . . I’ll be back as soon as I’m able.”

Chapter 17

Jed swung the door open hard and heard it clunk and rattle back against the edge of the deputy's small desk beneath the street front window. Let it fall off its hinges for all he cared. He was there for one reason, and that was to see the man standing before him with a mouthful of buttered bread.

"Chiswick? There you are."

The lawman was pouring himself a cup of coffee from the pot on the small stove to the rear of the office.

He set down the coffeepot and the cup atop the stove. As he saw who was bursting in on him, he chewed the food in his mouth with haste, letting his hands rest atop the butts of his twin guns. "What is all this, Stark?"

"You know exactly why I am here, Chiswick. What's happening to Glen Rose?"

The marshal's eyes narrowed, and he frowned. "I have no idea what you mean, Stark."

"Liar." Jed watched the man bristle and square off anew, his hands no longer resting on his guns but flexing like the legs of a spider, ready to snatch and draw the gun. Itching for the final nudge of an excuse.

"That's a big word, man."

"Yep. And intended. Because you know and I know that you are allowing hired gunmen to run rampant in Glen Rose!"

"Why, what on earth are you on about, Stark?" The marshal's words sounded innocent and confused, but his smirking face wore a smugness that belied the words.

"Ah, I see," said Jed. "You're afraid to do anything to them, because they are your fellow employees."

"What's that? What?" Yet he offered Jed the smug smirk.

"And all because you are in the pocket of Merlin Sheldrake—"

"You dare say that!" Chiswick strode forward, covering the span between them in a stride and a half. They were nearly equally matched in height, with Jed rising an inch or so taller and wider at the shoulder.

But he'd known Larry Chiswick his entire life, and he knew the man was a tough devil, opportunistic and filled with self-motivation and greed, and hard-headed. Chiswick was muscled up enough that he was never interested in losing a fight. And he rarely did.

Then again, Jed and everyone knew that the two of them had rarely done more than trade a few punches as kids. But *we're no longer kids*, thought Jed. Jed didn't move.

Both men stood face to face, fists balled. Chiswick's nostrils flared, showing him as the bullheaded man he was. Jed remained his usual calm self, at least outwardly.

Inside he was a knot of building rage, and that was a feeling he did not care for one bit. And he blamed it on this fool before him. But despite all this manly bluster and bravado, Jed knew he could not, would not mention what happened at Lilly's, not her name or anything else about her.

Chiswick was exactly the sort of man who would use that as a reason to visit her under the guise of looking into a complaint. But what would he really do? Jed knew it would only make her life more difficult.

No, Jed must keep his claims general. It was enough to let

the foul man know that he was riled and would not tolerate more of this foolishness.

"Chiswick, I don't care if you admit it or not, everybody knows it, and there isn't much we can do about it, because you are the big lawman in these parts. But"—Jed leaned closer until their faces were inches apart—"it won't always be that way. And one of these days, you'll be caught with your trousers down and no guns or law badge to hide behind."

"That a threat, Stark?" Chiswick's voice was low, clean, and cold, like a knife blade in winter. "Why don't we pretend that someday is today, then, Stark? Come on. Right now."

"Nope," said Jed. "But if you and Sheldrake know what's best for your coin purses, you will run those newcomers on out of town."

"Newcomers? Oh, I guess I do know who you are talking about. And as far as I know they are but a handful of investors Mr. Sheldrake invited here. The only thing those men want from Glen Rose is to make money here. All legal, and a good bit of it will benefit the fine people of my town."

"*Your* town, huh?" said Jed, turning away from the man. "You're beginning to sound like your fellow Sheldrake employee, that spineless mayor of ours."

Chiswick walked behind him, keeping pace all the way to the door.

There was more than a trace of growling anger in the lawman's voice. "You come in here and insult me? Last time that happens, Stark!" The marshal's shouting boomed in the room and on out into the nearly empty street.

Jed caught a quick glimpse of a woman across the street turning to see what the ruckus might be, her eyes widening and her mouth beginning to open into an O.

He knew that last comment would rile Chiswick for the final time, and even as he turned, he knew he should have left without saying it. He'd already accomplished what he wished to—to let the man know more lawless behavior of Sheldrake's so-called "investors" was not going to occur without notice, or consequence.

What that might be, Jed had no idea yet. But this was the beginning of his plans, vague as they may yet be, for the day. A day that was aging. He had to get to Grindle.

But even as all this flashed through his mind, he felt the lawman's big hands slam him hard in the upper back, a shove to provoke him. He was already turning, and now it was Jed's turn to square off, right there in the doorway.

Long years ago, back when he was a thin small schoolboy, in the spring of the year before the Stark height and broadness of chest and shoulder caught up with him, he had been picked upon by a thick, meat-faced boy.

Ruddy Bollard had been twice his age and twice the height and weight of all his play yard victims.

He had, in the end, turned out amiable enough, and much later, Jed had heard with sadness that Ruddy had been killed long ago in the war and buried back East. Virginia, thought Jed.

But Ruddy had been, for a couple of years when Jed was a youth, a scourge at school to one and all, boys and girls alike, and Jed went home weeping more often than not, his lip split or an ear puffed and reddened.

His Mama had told him she would not help him fight the boy, but that if he was really a Stark, which she knew Jed was fiercely proud of, even as a wee lad, then he would have to adopt the Stark way of dealing with things. And sometimes, that meant fighting.

"But how can I fight Ruddy Bollard?" he had asked her between his stifling efforts to not sob before his equally fierce Mama.

He recalled that although she was always a tough rooster of

a woman, she had always said not to fight. He'd been confused, but she continued to explain as she danced about him, a wry smile on her face.

And so, she had given him a lesson in fisticuffs. Right there in the kitchen. And that began with the very core notion that a Stark never started a fight. But if somebody did pick a fight with a Stark, by golly, a Stark never backed down. They stood their ground, and they never lost.

She'd shoved the table to one side and told him to square off. Then she'd hiked her apron and calico skirts up, tucked them in the tops of her red wool socks, and proceeded to dance around him with her thick, work-hardened hands balled into fists, jabbing soft punches at him in the air, a foot from his face, as she circled.

At first, he flinched, but she explained what it was she wanted him to do. Then she stopped and held his hands from behind and guided them. Then she raised her knee, showing him how to strike, and it all began to make sense. It all began to seem possible that a thin little fellow such as himself might actually be able to beat Ruddy Bollard.

"I might land a lick on him!" Jed had said in his excitement.

That's when Mama had stopped, stood up, rested her hands on her hips, and frowned at him. "Landing a lick on a fool like Ruddy Bollard is easy. Any ninny can do that, Jed. What I am showing you is how to draw blood and make him cry. And when that happens, you make certain as many of the other kids are around to see it, as many as possible."

"To help me?"

"Bah! No, not that. A Stark doesn't need help in life. No, what I mean is, so Ruddy gets good and embarrassed. Then he won't bother anybody anymore, and you'll be their hero."

"Me?" Jed had said, eyes wide.

"Yep."

And that's about what had happened all those years back on the schoolyard. He'd ended up bloodying Ruddy's great nose, and the big boy had wept like a baby. No more troubles. In fact, they had then become somewhat chummy.

That nugget of memory came back to Jed as Chiswick's hands shoved him. Like Ruddy Bollard had done all those years before. And another thing that Mama had told him popped to mind: Only cowards struck from behind.

The funny thing was, thought Jed as he spun, fists balled hard and tight, and already bending low, ducking his head, Lawrence Chiswick had been one of the kids that day who had cheered as Jed had triumphed.

Apparently, the lawman had a poor memory.

Jed let Mother Stark's lesson get to work as he drove that big right fist of his hard and square into the unprepared and unexpecting face of the adult Lawrence Chiswick. Right on the nose, to be specific. Because, as Mama had said, that was the spot on a man's body that will bleed first, fast, and freely. And so it had been with Ruddy, and so it was with Chiswick.

It was painful, that much was obvious, for Jed's knuckles slammed hard like a stone being thrown from close up, and with great force. The lawman's long nose crunched and smeared and bled, right about in that order.

The marshal screamed and did the very thing Mama had said folks always do under that attack. He brought both of his hands up to cradle his freshly spurting, throbbing face.

Then he did the second thing she said folks in that situation do: Chiswick bent over double.

Jed aimed to follow through with the entire Mama Stark lesson, and with a hand atop the bent man's shoulder, he drove his left knee square into the man's gut.

Then he smacked both of his own big ham hands together to form one big fist and hammered them down in a final blow, hard, into the middle of the marshal's back.

The lawman, already making retching, gargling, screaming sounds from his blood-clogged nose and mouth, let out a quick gasp and collapsed facedown across the threshold of his own office. Jed yanked the man's double guns out of their holsters and threw them across the room. They clunked hard into the closed wooden door at the rear of the room. It led to two cells.

Then he walked up and over the flat, moaning form of Chiswick, who was trying to shove himself up with one arm, moaning and holding his face with the other hand.

Out on the shaded boardwalk, Jed paused before the nearest of a number of wide-eyed onlookers, none of whom looked more shocked than a young man. It was Deputy Thompson.

"Your boss is going to need some help, deputy." Jed nodded at the young man, who looked with wide eyes from the marshal to Jed and back again. He swallowed. "Yes, sir, Mr. Stark."

Jed strode into the street, angling to his right, toward the east end of town. He'd left the wagon there, tucked in the shade alongside the end building, Flo's Millinery. While he walked, he did his level best to not look at any of the few folks in town eyeing him, for he wanted to shout that they, too, should get angry enough to stand up for themselves and fight back.

But as quickly, it came to him that he, too, had been anything but active in reacting to the steady, relentless digging away at what had made Glen Rose a pleasant, quiet place to live. All before Sheldrake's arrival, of course.

As he walked, he looked hard at the boardwalks to his left, half-hoping to catch sight of those lurking newcomers. Now that he knew those three he'd seen loafing earlier were obviously the men who threatened Lilly's patrons and forced her to shut down, he wanted nothing more than to do to them what he'd done to the marshal. But he knew that was a quick way to get shot.

Not that what he'd done to Chiswick wasn't. And as if that

thought conjured what he heard, from one hundred feet back he heard the fast click-click of a shotgun ratcheting back as if jerked in haste. And as quickly the lawman's forced, clotted voice bellowed, "Stark! Hold, I say! Move again, I shoot!"

Jed slowed, but did not turn. He hadn't stopped, and although he gave thought to it, he decided not to. He doubted very much that Chiswick would shoot him in the back, especially in front of the onlooking townsfolk.

From behind, Jed heard uneven, scuffing bootsteps, as if someone were struggling to keep pace. That would be the lawman, coming after him. And since he was walking faster than Jed, the man, even with his recent throbbed-up head and back and gut, would overtake him in moments.

Now you're in a fix, he told himself. But he had to keep on walking. Then, to his right, he saw Lilly emerging from the café's front door, drying her hands on her apron. The sun was in her eyes, and she brought her hand up to visor them, uncertain, for the briefest of moments, of what she was seeing.

And then he saw as he strode past, in the middle of the street, that she recognized him. And then her head turned left and she saw the marshal, and then it all came to her and she shouted, "Jed! Look out!"

Oh, he thought, as he slowed and half turned toward her, this has become far more complicated than he thought it might be. You go into something with no clear idea of what you want and how to go about it, and you end up with a handful of wet river mud, Jed, you fool.

As he turned, he offered her a smile that he hoped would go some little—albeit very little—way in reassuring her all would be well. Although at this point, he did not see how it might end up that way.

He turned to see the lawman, and behind Chiswick, the deputy, closing in on his boss.

"Marshal," said Deputy Thompson, reaching for Chiswick's left shoulder. The marshal growled and with adder speed, halting and pivoting all at once, swung the shotgun up to his left hard and slammed it into the younger man's chest.

It wasn't blow enough to drop the deputy, but it staggered him and doubled him over. Chiswick ignored the gasps and shouts from the growing crowd of gawkers, and continued his churning, determined stride toward Jed, eyes hooded, face a bloodied, dripping smear, red-rimmed teeth bared and glinting wet and wide in his open mouth.

"Stark!"

Here it is, thought Jed. My end. Right in the street of my hometown, right in front of my sweetheart and all these people I know, and who know me.

As he faced the rampaging lawman he thought, too, of his Mama and of the fact that the Stark line would end with him, right there and then. It was not a new thought, but it stung, and he vowed, as he raised his hands wide and high in a sign of acquiescence, that if he made it through the next minute or two alive, he would marry Lilly.

It had to be. It made good sense. It was the only thing in his world at that precise moment that made any sense at all.

Chiswick kept that cocked barrel of the single-shot gut shredder aimed at Jed's chest as he closed in on the last eight feet separating them. And he didn't stop.

And Jed didn't budge, didn't move a thing save for his eyes which he kept fixed on Chiswick's own narrowed, intent eyes.

Jed braced for whatever it was the marshal had in mind. The man was seething, his chest working like a smithy's bellows. Without breaking stride, it seemed as if he intended to walk through Jed. As he closed in on him, he jerked the gun stock up, intending to swing it into Jed's face.

It was a fast move, but Jed was ready and he was not as riled and addled as was Chiswick. With his right hand Jed snatched the barrel of the shotgun, shoving it away and to his right, but not letting go of it, for the thing was cocked, and one light tug on that trigger would ruin his day.

He held on tight to the barrel with that right hand and stepped forward with his left boot, planting it right between Chiswick's own halted boots. Jed jerked the thing, also pulling the rampaging man toward him.

In more of the same fluid motion, with his big left hand, Jed whistled an uppercutting blow fast and solid into the underside of Chiswick's outthrust bottom jaw.

Once more the man sputtered out a strangled, yipping growl.

Jed felt the spatter of renewed blood as it sprayed from the marshal's gore-sloppy face, upward and all about the pair of men engaged in this crude, vicious dance.

The lawman clung on to his wakefulness, but his eyelids fluttered, and Jed wasted no time. Grasping the shotgun's barrel, he whipped his left arm back once more and slammed a mammoth fist with pummeling force into Chiswick's right temple.

A thin, squealing wheeze pinched off as the man's eyes jerked open wide, white and red-veined, then rolled backward in their sockets. His knees gave way and he began to pitch backward. Jed helped him with a shove to the shoulder but held tight to the shotgun's barrel.

Chiswick dropped hard to the street, his head smacking and his right leg folded beneath him.

Jed stepped backward, aimed the barrel skyward and eased the hammer off cock; then as the deputy walked up, holding his chest with one hand, Jed handed him the shotgun. Then he bent and unfastened Chiswick's gun belt and jerked it off him, the immobile man's solid frame jostling with the effort.

"Keep guns away from him, will you?" He handed them to

the younger lawman, then turned and resumed walking toward his wagon. "And lock him up until he gets his right mind back!" This he growled, not looking back.

To his right, he saw Lilly keeping pace with him some yards away. Within moments, one, two, then a few more folks offered him feeble handclaps. He ignored them, and they soon dwindled.

Lilly caught up with him at the wagon. "What was that, Jed?"

"Something a long time coming. Something between me and Chiswick. Something I wish hadn't happened."

"But you made me a promise, Jed!"

"And I am keeping it. I didn't start it, but . . . Bah, maybe I did! Look, it's complicated. But I'm headed to Grindle to make things right. Give me the time, please? I promise I'll be back."

He was ready to climb into the wagon. He held there, one hand on the wrought seat support, one holding the boot well's boards, and looked at her. "Marry me, Lil."

She took him in with a stern gaze, her jaw set tight; he saw she was nearly shaking with anger. Yet in that moment he saw a flurry of thoughts pass within her eyes. The slightest relaxation of anger and confusion, and so much more. Then it was gone, and she was stern once more.

She turned from him without a head shake or a nod, nothing to let him know that at least she understood him, and walked away, back toward the café. But she had heard him—he knew she had.

His was a long, quick, silent ride eastward. He decided not to take the Stark Spur as it was locally called, the lane that cut southeastward off this main roadway, that led to Whiskey Woods. Instead, he felt a gnawing compulsion to get to Grindle.

He felt sure that in the bigger law office there, he might find another man who wasn't yet bought and paid for by Sheldrake.

Marshal Tibbs, in Grindle, would be possibly helpful. And then there was Sheriff Crilly, also based in Grindle, but this region was all his jurisdiction. He was a sharp, straight, and true fellow. Or at least he always had been.

He had also never been a man to save money, and consequently might be tempted by someone like Sheldrake. That might not work in Jed's favor. But he'd try to find out once he got to Grindle.

CHAPTER 18

"Whoa, whoa now," said Loudon, reining up on Alice, his mule. She was shy of working up a lather, and Jed could see his newsman friend was red in the face and breathing hard, too, as if he'd been leading the mule.

"Out of my way, Loud," said Jed, looking to either side of his friend, who was jigging the fidgety mule in the middle of the roadway, blocking Jed's passage.

"What are you all worked up about, Jed? This isn't like you—Lilly and your mother okay?"

Jed nodded, jerking the lines to edge the wagon by his friend's left side, but Loudon danced the mule that way as well.

"Get out of my way, Loudon!"

"Not until you tell me what's wrong, Jed."

Jed made a growling sound in his throat, then let out a blast of breath. "I'm headed to Grindle."

"Why? It's there, same as always. Oh, deliveries?" He looked past Jed to the barrels in the wagon.

"No," said Jed. Then he remembered why Loudon went there. "What did you find out at the marshal's office?"

"That's what I was making for your place to tell you. I can't be fully positive, but my newsman instincts tell me that the fellow I thought I recognized—"

Jed interrupted. "Let me guess—he wears dark clothes, quick with a gun, trim build, lightish hair, and clean shaven?"

"Something like that, yeah. Why?"

"You tell me, first. He's who?"

"As I was saying," said Loudon, relaxing a little his grip on the reins. "I can't be sure, but I'd bet good money he's one Pit Pritchard."

A moment's silence passed between them. "Am I supposed to know that name?"

"Well, most people would," said Loudon, clearly disappointed that his friend was less than impressed with this discovery due to his diligent research work.

"I'm not most people," said Jed, looking left and right again for an opening to drive his wagon on through.

"He's a notorious man, Jed!" Loudon was sitting up straight in his saddle, a rosy hue on his face, and eyes bright.

"Seems you are some impressed with this Pritchard fellow, Loud," said Jed. He could not suppress a slight grin, despite the raw mood he was in.

"I am, I am, man! He's what they call a fixer. Mm-hmm"—he nodded—"that's what they call him. Always manages to get out of trouble before he gets nabbed. But more important, he could be the very story I have been looking for!"

"How's that?"

Loudon looked to both sides and lowered his voice. "He's a genuine outlaw character, Jed! Like in the dime novels!"

"Great," said Jed, shaking his head. "Look, Loud, I have to go!"

The reporter nodded his head. "All right, but you remember the date of this conversation, because I intend to one day make it—and me—famous."

"Okay, Loud," said Jed, looking beyond him, toward Grindle. "That sounds good. Good for you, at any rate."

"Hey, what happened to you?" said Loudon, looking at Stark's bleeding knuckles and the spray of blood droplets on his shirt and face.

"Never mind," growled Jed. "You called him a fixer, this Pritchard. What does that mean?"

"Well," said Loudon, squinting and staring at Jed. "It means he's a hired gun, essentially. Somebody, usually a rich rancher type, calls him in when they aren't getting the results they feel they deserve. Even if what they feel they deserve isn't fair."

"And," continued Jed, nodding, "even if it means breaking the law to get what they want. Sounds a lot like how Merlin Sheldrake operates."

"It sure does."

"This Pritchard, does he travel with other people? Hard men?"

"Yep," said Loud. "They're his men, his gang. They go along with him and do his bidding."

"Fixing things. Like threatening Lilly's customers with guns and making sure Fen Hawkins isn't around to buy my whiskey, and burning ranches in the night."

"Now that last one, we can't be sure it was Pritchard and his men. I don't think they were around these parts then. But then again, it does sound like something he might do, given what I've read about him in other newspapers."

"Well, they're in these parts now, all right. All over Glen Rose. The town's tighter than a drum."

"I know, I was there this morning, remember?"

"Yeah, but not long after you left, things seemed to happen fast. Maybe because I was in town. I don't know."

"From the look of those knuckles and the blood spatters on your face and shirt, I'd say more than a few things happened, Jed. You going to tell me what I'm riding into?"

Jed let out a sigh. "Let's say that Chiswick and I had it out, and he might be angrier than he's ever been in his life."

"Oh."

"Yeah. I didn't intend for it all to happen as it did, but it did, and there's no changing it. But he isn't doing his job! He's supposed to be working for the townsfolk, not Sheldrake!"

"I know, I know," said Loudon, nodding in commiseration, uncertain what to say because it was rare to see Jed Stark riled about much of anything.

"Look in on Lilly, would you? Those three loafing newcomer gunmen closed her down this morning, after you were there."

"What?"

"Yep," Jed nodded. "She's not happy, but I made her promise me she'd keep the place closed the rest of today and tomorrow. I need the time, Loud. We have to make things right, but not with guns. It can't be that way. Guns never solve anything. Violence only drags things out, makes folks angrier and breeds revenge. No, it has to be through legal ways."

The newsman looked at his friend a long moment. "All right." He nodded. "All right, Jed. I'll do what I can. Should I stop at the ranch?"

Jed shrugged. "Mama's tough. And I won't be all day. I should be back by nightfall." He shrugged again and smacked the lines hard on Mags's back. "Do what you need to, Loud, and I'll do the same. Now get along, will you? I have got to go!"

Jed jerked the lines and guided the horse hard and fast by the sidestepping mule. Loudon Paley watched his whiskey-making friend disappear eastward toward Grindle in a boil of road dust. Even as it billowed over and past him, he sat the mule and squinted, looking, hoping to see Jed Stark pause and turn the wagon in the long lane.

He was going to try to make his deliveries in Grindle, too, that much was obvious, or he would have just ridden a horse there. It was a matter of pride and principle to Jed, Loudon knew.

He guided the mule gently around and urged her into a steady, slower pace than before. "It might well be a matter of pride to Jed," he said to the mule. "But I don't see how it's going to prevent him from taking a mighty fall first."

CHAPTER 19

Loudon Paley sighed as he swung down from Alice's back and led her to the watering trough outside the Happy House saloon. He had intended to lead the tuckered mule down the street to the small news office he had set up not long after his arrival in Glen Rose four years before.

If he was going to get this week's edition out on time, two days hence, he needed to get busy and not chase phantoms and silly ideas, even if they were on behalf of friends in need, namely Jed Stark.

No, he was a reporter, a newsman, and he had work to do. Even if his efforts went largely ignored and largely unneeded. He attributed much of that to the fact that he was late of "way back East," as far too many of the local folks said of him, making him feel as if he would always be an outsider anywhere he went in the great, vast West.

He sighed again, thinking again of the most onerous and most time-consuming part of his job, which was spending time on his backside, writing and editing and then setting type.

The *Glen Rose Gazette* was at present only a weekly one-sheet—too frequent for a demure place such as Glen Rose—and much of its content merely snooze-inducing bits of gossip and advertisements. But that didn't mean that it wasn't going to one day be a mighty force in Texas letters, and perhaps in the wider world. But first he had to get there. And that meant wading through the dull drudge work.

Loudon tugged out his kerchief and mopped his brow, then looked across the street to Lilly's café. It was indeed closed, as Jed had said it would be. A renewed sense of indignation washed over him, tired as he was, and Loudon wanted nothing more at that moment than to confront this Pritchard, famous somewhat-outlaw or no, and tell him to back off, back down, and leave town! Messing about with a man's friends and their livelihoods was one liberty too many.

He turned around and saw that Alice the mule was asleep on her feet beside the trough. Poor thing, he thought. He really had worked her far too hard today. Come to think of it, he was feeling tired and rather dry in the throat himself.

He was not able to partake in his usual round of sustaining midday foodstuffs at the café, thanks to Pritchard and his oafs, and even beyond them, to Sheldrake, the piggish brute. He shifted his gaze from the mule to the structure before him.

Perhaps a cooling glass of beer would help to address his weakened state after such journeying to Grindle and back.

Loudon glanced up the steps toward the inviting doors and the cool interior of the Happy House. He licked his lips. "One glass. One glass of beer, Loudon Paley," he muttered to himself, "and then it's to work with you!"

He draped the reins over the hitch rail and ascended the steps, muttering, "Happy House, indeed."

As he ordered his beer, Loudon leaned an elbow on the bar top and looked about the darkened room. He did not expect there to be too many folks in there at that time of day, but neither did he expect to be the only patron. It made him feel a bit odd, as if he should instead be working like a prairie dog back at the office.

His vision had nearly acclimated to the darkened interior of the place, and he finished the slow casual glance about the room, darker at the back where daytime shadows grew and lingered. Then he locked in place and his eyelids rose.

It couldn't be . . . him.

Well, actually, yes it could be, Loudon, he told himself as he slowly turned his head back to the dim shape at the table in the shadows. He stared. The dim shape was a man, and that man was watching him as well. He nodded.

Loudon swallowed and returned the nod. Then he remembered he was first and foremost a newsman. Even if it wasn't who he thought it was, he was a newsman.

But he was also a newsman with a burning desire to write dime novels. He hefted the glass of freshly poured beer and walked toward the seated man. "Begging your pardon, are you Mr. Pritchard?"

The man, who had watched him advance, no emotion on his face, now said, "Yes?" He appraised Loudon. "I don't know you."

"No. No, sir, but I—I know you. Or rather I know *of* you."

"Oh? What is it you think you know, Mr., ah . . ."

"Oh, I am Paley. Loudon Paley, newspaper man, proprietor of the *Glen Rose Gazette*."

"I see. I wasn't aware that Glen Rose had risen to such lofty heights as to require a newspaper."

Loudon beamed, despite knowing he looked like a schoolboy having his feathers stroked.

"Won't you sit down then, Mr. Newsman Paley?"

"Why, thank you, Mr. Pritchard. Thank you kindly."

As soon as he was seated, Pritchard, who had not taken his eyes from Loudon, said, "So, how is it you know of me, Mr. Paley?"

"I, ah—"

Pritchard cut him off with a raised hand and a smile. "Say no more, Mr. Paley. I'd forgotten that as a reporter, such things are your business to know. No matter what it is you feel you have learned. I caution you, however, that whatever it is you may have heard, it is untrue, at least to some degree."

"Untrue?" said Loudon. "How so?"

"If something is said about someone, and it has not been said by the person himself, then by nature, it cannot be true. Don't you agree?"

Loudon sipped his beer. "Perhaps, but what if the person himself was lying?" As soon as he said it, Loudon winced as he realized it sounded as if he had all but accused Pit Pritchard of being a liar.

Pritchard shook his head. "Not me, not about me and the facts of my life. No sir, I do not lie."

"Yes," nodded Loudon. "I didn't mean to imply that you were lying, only that—"

"Calm down, newsman. I know what you meant. No harm done. But now, see here. What is it that you really want with me? Hmm?"

Loudon thought two things at once: This man was quite perceptive, and he was also the one man Loudon knew of who might be able to readily provide him with the means to write a dime novel. Perhaps the very best one ever set to page.

He regarded Pritchard with what he hoped was his very best bold, confident gaze, then he held up a hand and caught the attention of the large barkeep. "Chris? Another of the same for both, please. Thank you."

"Very kind, Mr. Paley," said Pritchard with a demure nod.

"I am not only a newspaper man, Mr. Pritchard."

"No?"

"No, you see, sir, I am also a . . . a novelist."

"A novelist? You don't say."

"Yes," nodded Loudon. "And as such, I am always on the scout, as it were, for fresh topics."

"What sort of novels do you write, Mr. Paley?"

Loudon felt stunned but a moment, then ran a finger slowly up and down the side of his beer glass and cleared his throat. "The slimmer, more active type."

"Oh, you mean dime novels."

Loudon looked at Pritchard to see if the man was mocking him. But it appeared he was not. "Yes, why, do you know them?"

"I know of them, sure. Who doesn't?"

"Well, good, because it will take far less explaining, then."

"Let me save you the trouble. You want to tell the world, or at least the folks in it who read dime novels, who I am and what I have done, what I do, and such and so forth."

"Why, yes, I guess I do. Yes."

Pritchard regarded him a moment. "And I assume you want the truth, at least as much as I do, anyway."

"Well, yes," said Paley, thinking that most dime novels, as far as he could tell, while they were exciting reads were likely as far from the truth as a dog is from being a cat.

Pritchard sipped his beer and appeared to study a spot in the air halfway between them and the bar. Finally, he said, "I happen to know that there is the distinct possibility that if you write up my story well enough, you will likely sell it to one of the many large back East publishers of such tripe known as dime novels. Am I right?"

"Well, yes," Loudon nodded, confused as to the man's rank assessment of his beloved dime novels as "tripe," whereas mere moments before he had seemed to praise them. But then again, who was he, Loudon Paley, to argue? Especially not with the likes of one Pit Pritchard, Hired Gun of the Savage Frontier!

"Mr. Paley? Oh, Mr. Paley."

Loudon was pulled out of his reverie by the loud snapping of fingers in front of his face. "Yes. Yes, sir. I'm listening."

"Good, because when it comes to money, particularly money

that should rightfully be mine, I pay my full attention to the matter, and I expect it to be the same of the people with whom I may work."

"Oh, oh, yes, of course. That goes without saying, sir."

"In my experience," said Pritchard. "A business deal that goes without saying is even more useless than one reliant on a handshake agreement."

"Well, um, perhaps if you tell me your story, then I'll be able to judge whether it is worthy, that is to say, that it would be the right sort of story to turn into a novel."

Pritchard lapsed into that unnerving stare of his. Finally, he nodded.

"Does that mean you'll consider working with me? Or rather you'll tell me your story?"

Pritchard leaned forward and in a low tone, and with his eyes locked on Loudon's, he said, "I will, in this one instance, break my personal rule. If the story is acceptable to you—and I guarantee it will be—then we shall sign a contract specifying our financial arrangement."

Loudon nodded, not quite certain what it was he was agreeing to.

Pritchard leaned forward. "If, on the other hand, you decide it is not suitable for your use, the deal, of course, is off. And if I find out someday that my story, disguised somehow, has been used, and without remuneration made to me for said use, then—well . . ." He leaned back and almost smiled.

"No, no of course not, Mr. Pritchard. That would not happen. I can assure you I am as straight an arrow as they come. An honest, ethical newsman. And novelist!"

"Then you're the first." Pritchard folded his hands on the baize surface before him. "Okay then, not only will I tell you a story, Mr. Paley, I will do you one better and tell you how I came to be the very man you see before you. The man who is now known, among many other names, and I assure you I have heard them all, as a 'fixer'—a silly word, but there it is. Are you game to hear it?"

"I—I am, yes. Would you care to walk back to my office with me so I can take it all down properly?"

"No, I would not like to do that. This is a onetime opportunity for you, Mr. Paley. You have to ask yourself if you are ready, willing, and able right here and now to take this story in."

"Yes, yes," said Paley, patting himself down. He had a fresh reporter's tablet and several pages of his older one unmarked. If he wrote small, it might work.

He would take only the larger bits and fill in the gaps and details, the flavor and the smells, the sounds and the feelings, later. Later—in the wee hours—when he could work up the story into a masterpiece. The first of many. Many!

"Mr. Paley, you're doing it again."

Loudon snapped to and opened his notebook to a clean page and worked up a fresh point on his pencil with his pocket knife. No sooner had he done so than Pit Pritchard, notorious figure of the savage West, began to speak.

"This is the story of how I came to be the man you see before you today. The man the world has come to know as a 'fixer,' a useful if mistaken label, but not wholly incorrect.

"It happened many years ago, when I was, shall we say, much younger, and perhaps dumber. Definitely greener in most ways. I was, to put it bluntly, on the run from the law. Yes, yes, it's true. I was a wanted man. I know what you're thinking, Mr. Paley. That little has changed in the ensuing years. But I assure you a whole lot has changed. Such as the fact that back then I had been accused of something I had actually done.

"Oh, it was not, as you might guess, my fault. No, no, but it was for something that did not deserve vilification. That is to say—well, there is no easy way to say it, so I'll go ahead and say it. I killed a man. I shot him, in fact."

Loudon did not respond. He continued to write with dedication, keeping his words small and tightly spaced because he had no idea how much or how long Pritchard might go on for, and he certainly wanted to capture each and every word.

But to hear the man admit to killing a man, well, that finally came to him some seconds after Pritchard said it and then paused.

"You—you killed him?"

The gunman nodded with a wise, if weary look on his face. It was the first time since they had been talking that the man looked, to Loudon, as if he were older than he had initially appeared. And even at that, the man did not appear to be all that old. Early thirties, Loudon guessed, but if he had done all the things attributed to him in life then he should be well and truly tuckered.

"I did indeed, and it was, as all men with a functioning mind would say, done in self-defense. But I am not lying. I do not lie. Unless money is involved, and then I might well be convinced to stretch things a bit."

"Well, that's good. About the lying, I mean," said Loudon hurriedly. "Not about the killing, of course. That, that must be a difficult thing to live with."

"How so?" said Pritchard.

"Oh, the idea of killing someone."

Pritchard shrugged. "No, not really. It happened, and I did it or I would have been killed myself. And that is that." He leaned forward over his folded hands. "Consider this, Mr. Newsman: Folks kill all the time. You swat a fly, it's dead, right?"

"Sure, yes," said Loudon, smiling. "But, well, that's a fly."

Pritchard held up a finger. "Ah, but to a fly, it's a living thing, no different than you or me. I'll wager, although there's no way to prove this, at least none that I know of, that a fly values its life the same as you or I do ours. Stands to reason, yes?"

It was Loudon's turn to shrug. "As you say, there's no way to prove it."

"And no way to disprove it. And how about all those beasts

that as humans, we kill in the name of food. You don't think there's terror and sadness when a duck or a chicken or a cow or a pig or a deer or rabbit feels a bullet or an arrow? Or a blade to the throat?"

Loudon nodded. "Yes, yes, I see your point all right." What he really wanted was to get back to the story. He told himself to keep his mouth shut instead of offering opinions and questions that wouldn't result in the man staying on track and finishing his story. "Now," he said. "About this fellow you killed. In self-defense, of course."

Pritchard leaned back. "No, that's not the story I want to tell you about now. The one I'm going to tell you takes place after that. Not long after that, but after it. As a result of it, you might say. But I had to tell you that in order to tell you this."

'Oh? Oh, do go on, Mr. Pritchard."

"All right, I will." The man in black slumped a little in his chair, laced his fingers behind his head, and gazed at the darkened pressed tin ceiling above. "It takes place, oh, let's see . . . six months, or so, I believe, after that initial killing. I was out—well, north of here, as a matter of fact—up Kansas or Colorado way, as I recall.

"I'd been riding my old beat horse along a desertlike river basin, making westward, and not making the way all that quickly, if I must be honest. I was tired, and the horse was far more than tired. She was drifting forward on the memory of how to walk, I do believe."

"That's good, that's very good."

"Good?" said Pritchard. "That's a hard thing to say about an old worn-out horse, Mr. Newsman."

"Oh no, no, Mr. Pritchard! I merely meant that your choice of words, your phrasing, it was good. Very scholarly."

"Oh, really? Scholarly, huh?" The man puffed visibly.

Loudon took note of that, realizing that the famed gunman liked to have his fur stroked a bit. Not unlike most folks.

"Yes, yes, indeed. Now, please continue," said Loudon with a nod.

"There I was, roving the wastes somewhere north of us, a man with men after him. Bounty men, men bent on making money off the misfortune of another. I don't fault them for this, as I have spent my life since doing much the same in a manner of speaking. But neither do I laud them for it. After all, as I said, I was the hunted man. And knowing this did not help to improve my grim outlook.

"I suspected I had little to no future. All the vague notions I had had of finding a pretty and kind and smart woman one day with whom I might marry and settle and raise children, of owning my own little place up high in the mountains somewhere, away from the filth of humanity, all these possibilities now seemed gone from my future.

"And indeed, my very future seemed a short, stunted thing that might end at any moment out there on the trail, stalked as I was. And all because I committed a crime that wasn't really a crime. At least as far as I was concerned. If defending oneself is a crime, then I'm a guilty fellow, all right. Here's what happened . . ."

CHAPTER 20

"You hear what's happening in Glen Rose?"

The speaker, Porter Sneed, licked his wet lips and leaned forward over the baize-topped table toward his two companions, who also were leaning in.

All eyes were on Sneed, and he took his time in drawing out the story, arranging his half-empty glass of beer and smoothing the flat table top before him.

"Well? Out with it, man!" Whistler Denny prompted Sneed with a nod.

"Yeah," said the third of them, fellow whiskey peddler, T. M. McCloud. "You know as well as we do that me and Whistler were together along the Altima, drumming up business for all three of us! So that means you were the only one who went through Glen Rose lately!"

Sneed kept his smug smile but closed his eyes and shook his head. "Nope, no sir, I did no such thing. Wouldn't touch that town alone, and barely with the two of you along. No offense. Not these days, anyhow. But, well, you know Sheldrake as well as I do. No, and thank you."

"Yah," said Whistler. "Wish we weren't tied up with him, but we ain't the bosses."

"Workers. And anyway, what's the big news?"

"Well," said Sneed, settling into his role as gossip once more. "I heard it from a good source—"

"Who?" said Whistler.

"Will you shut it?" said McCloud. "Keep interrupting him and we'll never find out what's going on in Glen Rose!"

"Doesn't matter who told me," said Sneed. "But I'll tell you. It was that Rollo character, who does, shall we say various tasks for Sheldrake. You know, he's the skinny one, the smarter of the two."

"That's not saying much," said McCloud.

The others smiled.

"Well, he was in his cups. His pal was off trying to buck the tiger at the faro table. He lost his pay, by the way. Dumber men you'll have to work hard to find. Anyway, for the price of a beer, this Rollo character told me that he and Clem—that's the dumber one—they were none too happy with Sheldrake.

" 'Why's that?' I said.

" 'Because the boss'—which is what they call Sheldrake—'he hired a professional outfit.'

" 'What for?' I said.

"He shrugged and said, 'Said he wasn't happy with what we done for him. Said he wanted better "results," whatever that really means.'

" 'Well, maybe I can help you,' I said to him, buying him a whiskey.' "

Sneed winked at his two chums. "Don't cost us nothing, being peddlers of the stuff and all, but it sure can be a useful lubricant at times. Anyway, he gets to really blathering on after that. I had to make sure I spaced out the drinks, because he's a thirsty fellow, let me tell you. Didn't want him to doze off or take a swing at somebody—you never can tell what whiskey will compel a fellow to do—before I heard what I wanted to."

"And what was that, Sneed? Honestly," said Whistler Denny. "A slower talker I've not met! Get to the point!"

Sneed scowled at him, then decided he wanted to share the news more than he wanted to sit there and pretend he'd been offended. "Well, Rollo, he says, 'We done some stuff for that fat man, I tell you!'

" 'Oh?' I says, then pretended I wasn't that impressed, you know, to draw him out. And it worked. He must have liked me, 'cause he leaned over and, quietlike, he said, 'We set fire to Stark's spread for the fat man.' Then he nodded."

Sneed leaned back, nodding and sipping his beer.

The other two whiskey drummers sat there with mouths open. Then McCloud said, "Well, that confirms what we all knew, anyway, which is that Merlin Sheldrake was behind all that, for sure. But you are right, Sneed. That is pretty good news."

"That ain't all of it," said Porter, looking over the rim of his nearly empty glass at his companions. "Oh, but this is thirsty work, I tell you."

McCloud sighed. "You were any more obvious, Porter, you'd be a rock. Whistler, order this man another beer, will you? And while you're at it, I could take one, too."

Whistler stood, then said, "Hey, who's paying, anyway?"

McCloud shrugged. "Same as always. The man who orders. Why change now?" He winked at Sneed as a grumbling Whistler got up and walked to the bar.

"Now, Porter. What's the other so-called professional outfit that man mentioned to you?"

"Nope," said Sneed. "Going to wait for Whistler."

And they did, although McCloud did as much grumbling about it as Whistler had about fetching beer for them all. Once they were seated and had quaffed their fresh, albeit warm, beers, Sneed said, "Well now, let's see . . ."

"The professional outfit, man! What of it?"

"Keep your hat on, McCloud. Yes, so this Rollo, he said it

was none other than"—here Sneed leaned even farther in over the table—"Pit Pritchard and his crew!" He arched his eyebrows and nodded.

"So?" said Whistler. "Sheldrake has lots of folks working for him, in his warehouses, the railroads, the distillery—not that one of them knows how to make whiskey there, mind you."

"Whistler," said McCloud, now glancing around and speaking in a low tone himself, "Pit Pritchard and his men, they're gunmen! Little more than hired killers!"

Whistler Denny's own eyebrows rose then. He whistled low. "That's something else, that is."

"Yep," said Sneed. "Sure is. A man who hires such fellows wants but one thing."

McCloud nodded. "Pritchard calls himself a problem solver or some such, but everybody knows what that really means."

"Yeah," said Sneed. "Him and his men are killers, and nothing but."

The three men were silent for a spell, then McCloud cleared his throat. "Question is, what are we going to do with this information, men?" Nobody spoke, so he continued. "I say we use it to our advantage."

"What's that, then?" said Whistler.

"Not sure yet. But it's there. A solution is there. We have to find it."

"One thing I know for sure," said Sneed. "I don't want to be accused of having nothing to do with fires or—or worse!"

"Killings!" said Whistler, far too loud, for the others shushed him.

Again, the trio fell silent. As McCloud's gaze fell on the doorway to the back of the barroom, drawn there by the entry of a new patron to the bar, he lowered his head and voice. "I think our solution has walked in, gentlemen."

All three drummers looked toward the back door. Barely skylined in the dimly lit open portal stood a large man, wide of shoulder and slender about the waist. At that distance, the fellow could well have been any of a dozen other men.

But all three men knew who he was, and they knew that other than Merlin Sheldrake, it was the one man they all disliked and were afraid of—Jedediah Stark, the very man they had been speaking of, the very man that had cost them all a lot of money over the years because of his cursed tasty whiskey. The very man Sheldrake had hired men to try to kill.

They watched Jed Stark step in slowly and look about the half-filled barroom; then he walked to the bar and set his hat there, crown down, and ran a hand through his thick topknot.

The bartender of the White Mare walked over and, although he and Jed were old nodding acquaintances, he didn't let on. "I help you?"

"Hey there," said Jed. "I'm here to deliver my whiskey."

"Huh." The barkeep looked at the shelves behind him that contained a number of bottles, many of them whiskey. "Nope, we're full up, thanks." The man resumed wiping the bar.

Jed stood silent a moment and watched him, then snatched the man's wrist and held it pinned to the counter. Nobody in the room had noticed the snakelike move, and even if they had, Jed Stark was far beyond caring.

He was bigger than the barman, and as he leaned over the bar top he spoke in a low, even tone. "You know me, and I know you well enough, I reckon, to not play these games. Who told you to reject my longstanding order for whiskey?"

The man looked at him a moment with a hard stare, then he softened and looked at the bar top. "Mister, I know who you are all right. But it ain't worth my job to tell you anything." He looked up at Jed. "Sorry."

Jed let out a quick breath through his nose but did not let go of the man's wrist. "Forget the names, I need to know if there's anybody in this town I can trust. Crilly the sheriff in town?"

"He's gone."

"Gone? You mean out tending to other places in his jurisdiction."

"Nope, I mean gone. Got himself fired, he did. Not but a few hours since. Talk of the town."

"Huh," said Jed, letting go of the man's wrist.

The fellow grasped it to his chest and rubbed it with the other hand as if he were cradling a kitten. "You ain't going to get any better from any other bar in town. You've been banned, is what I heard."

Jed considered this not unexpected information. It would likely be the same in Chisley Flats, a small settlement to the northeast of Glen Rose. It was the other town within a day's ride and back from home that he made deliveries to, although on a less frequent basis.

He nodded, plunked his hat atop his head, and turned toward the back door once more. Then his eye caught sight of three men at a poker table in the shadows to his left. They were all watching him, but when he looked their way, they glanced back to their drinks.

They were familiar to him. He regarded them, then remembered. The whiskey drummers. They worked for three different liquor outfits and spent their days roving that vast part of Texas, and he thought they operated into Oklahoma and Louisiana, too. They supplied booze to the many saloons and trading posts and mercantiles in the region. Theirs was a lucrative occupation.

But most important of all, they were in with Merlin Sheldrake. He'd seen them in Glen Rose several times over the last few years, chumming with him, braying at his pathetic jokes and nodding in agreement with his blather and boasting. Jed walked to their table.

"Gents," he said, looking down at them.

Two of them, the two fatter ones, didn't look up, but mumbled into their chests. But the third, the thinner, and apparently the boldest of the three, looked up at him. Then he stood, keeping himself well behind his thin wedge of the games table.

"Outside, mister," said the man. He tried on a growl and frown, and his voice shook, but he nodded at Jed.

Jed regarded the bold drummer, thinking that a frowning rabbit is a rabbit. If he wasn't in such a dire situation, he might well find this little play amusing. Maybe one day he could look back on all this with some sort of forgiving memory. But it was not today.

"Fine," he said. "After you. All of you."

"Why us?" said one of the fat ones in a low voice, nearly a whisper. His eyes were wide.

"Because that's what I want," said Jed. "Now."

That did it. All three of the drummers paddled on out the door before him.

As soon as they were out the door, Jed stomped down the steps tight behind and crowded them tight to the side of his wagon. It was apparent he wasn't going to make any deliveries in Grindle today, which he had suspected. But he might find out something of use from these three fools.

They all stared around themselves.

"Well?" said Jed. "You called me out here, remember? What do you want?"

The one who had tried to muster bravado inside looked up at him. "I'm . . . I'm McCloud. T. M. McCloud."

"All right, Mr. T. M. McCloud, I'm Jed Stark. But I guess you know that already."

The man swallowed. "Yeah, yep. These here are my associates. This one is Porter Sneed, and he's Whistler Denny. We all work for different outfits, selling liquor and such. We cover a pretty vast region, if I do say so. And it was all working out fine, as we agreed to not stomp all over each other's toes. We did pretty well at it for a long ol' time, if I do say so myself."

Jed nodded. "I know who you all are, and I know what you do."

"You do?" said Sneed.

"Yep. And I know that you and the outfits you sell for have all tried for years to get me to make whiskey exclusively for you. When it finally occurred to you and your bosses that I wasn't interested, you tried to buy me out. When that didn't work, it seemed, for a while, anyway, you'd all leave me alone and there'd be enough slop in the trough for all the little piggies come feeding time."

He eyed the three men, especially the two fat ones. "And it well might have done the trick. Only now we're on to running me out of business."

"Oh, now . . ." McCloud waggled his hands and turned bright red. The other two looked at their shoes and left and right, trying to figure out if they might be able to outrun the big man. It didn't look likely. "That's not—uh . . ."

"Calm down," said Jed. "I wasn't birthed under a cabbage plant. I understand that business is business and money is money."

Then the big man leaned close, and his seemingly jovial attitude slipped away, and his voice took on a low, cold tone. "But what I don't like, and what I cannot and will not abide, is when you and your chums try to get me and mine killed."

"But—but . . ." said McCloud. "That's when Merlin Sheldrake came to town! Or to all of our towns! We didn't want anything to do with him, you have to believe that! That was all his idea, all of it! You got to believe me!"

"I find that pretty difficult to buy, Mr. McCloud. I've seen all three of you chumming with Sheldrake plenty of times. What makes you think I'd believe you? And anyway, why should I care? I have bigger problems right now."

McCloud began nodding. "That's right, that's right. That's why we called you out here, ain't it, boys?"

The other two looked at McCloud, then to Jed and nodded with vigor, too. "That's right, that's right!"

"Well get to it, then." Jed crossed his arms and eyed them. "I'm busy."

"Now, here's the situation," said McCloud, looking everywhere but at Jed.

This one likes to think he's in charge, thought Jed. Fine with me.

"We have information that you will find of great interest. Great interest."

"That's true, that's true," said the one they called Whistler.

"And it is?"

"First off, we'll need assurance, a promise from you that you won't come after us. See, when I say we had nothing to do with this, why, that's because it's true, believe us or not. But this whole business of burning down your place and—"

"So, it was for certain Sheldrake was behind the fire," said Jed. As he said it, he looked right into McCloud's eyes.

The man surprised him by giving him a man's stare right back. Then the drummer nodded. "Yes, yes, that's right. It was Sheldrake behind it. Had two men who did the deed."

"How do you know this?"

"One of them told us, told Sneed here, not but a few days ago." McCloud nodded at one of his chubby pals.

"They'd be the two men he brought to town some time ago?" said Jed. "The same ones who loaf a lot and aren't too quick in the head?"

McCloud smiled. "You've met them, then."

"More than once," said Jed, not inclined in the least to crack any semblance of a smile. "What do you know of these newcomers to Glen Rose? They're working for Sheldrake, too, I assume."

Sneed nodded. "That's why we called you out here," he said.

"We?" said McCloud, rolling his eyes. Then to Jed, he said, "Those men, I don't know how many there are, but"—McCloud lowered his voice to a whisper and leaned forward—"the boss of the outfit is a man named Pit Pritchard."

"I know."

"You know?"

"Someone already told me that. But what are they planning on doing in Glen Rose? What have you heard from your boss?"

"Our boss?" said Whistler.

"Yep, Merlin Sheldrake."

"Oh, he's not our boss."

Jed said nothing.

"Okay, I get you. You've had your say," said McCloud. "Look, I don't know why they're in town. And I don't know how much your friend told you, but that Pritchard, he's a bad seed, a hired gun is what I've heard. Rich folks bring him in to fix problems for them."

"And I'm that much of a problem for Sheldrake?"

McCloud shrugged. "You were, or are." He nodded toward the wagon behind them and its demure freight of whiskey. "But then again with Sheldrake, I never quite know about him," he shook his head. "He's crazy."

"Yeah, he is!" said Porter Sneed. "He keeps trying to get us to go along with notions that are plain loco. Well, I, for one, don't hold with crimes. Not of that sort, anyway."

"Same with all of us. It's true," said McCloud. "But the thing is, Sheldrake pretty much controls our lives, or at least our jobs and our pay. Without him and his growing whiskey empire, we would be out of work."

"Heck," said Whistler Denny, "by now he might own the outfits we work for, anyway." His hangdog look almost made Jed smirk. Almost.

"So, you are telling me all this not because you are charitable fellows, but because you think I won't hold you responsible for the fire?"

None of them said a thing for a moment, and Jed continued. "Seems like a dangerous position you're putting yourselves in with Sheldrake."

"How do you mean?" said Sneed, eyes wide.

Jed tilted his head to the side and looked skyward, as if considering a tricky thought. "Well, if I was Sheldrake—a foul thought in itself—I might well wonder sooner than later who is loyal to me and who has been playing me false. That's all."

"You—you wouldn't tell him we talked with you, would you?"

Jed let out a sigh. "No, you're safe. Besides, you really haven't told me anything I didn't already know."

McCloud's face changed from worry to disappointment. The other two men looked much the same.

"But for what it's worth, I appreciate it."

McCloud nodded, and the others followed suit, solemn looks all around.

"All right, then. I came to Grindle to find a lawman I know, but apparently, he's been run out of his job, if not out of town. If I can't find him, I'm headed back home. Something tells me I have a lot to prepare for. And I have no idea what it will be, or when."

CHAPTER 21

Jed left the three foolish drummers—more pathetic and easily led than foolish, perhaps—standing in the lane behind the saloon as he once more threaded his wagon up onto the main street of town, this time in Grindle.

He had to find someone who might know more about what had happened to Sheriff Crilly. Jed really didn't know the town marshal, Tibbs. And even if he did, if Crilly was gone, there seemed little help locally for lawful assistance in the Sheldrake mess, as he had come to think of their current predicament.

He guided the horse up along the right side of main street and, at a wide patch, angled it alongside another wagon. He wouldn't be here long, for he had a feeling any more time spent in Grindle was a fool's errand. And he'd played the fool long enough. He promised Lilly that he'd try to find a lawful, peaceful resolution to all of this, and he had to give it a good go. But so far, the world wasn't playing along.

Jed set the brake and hopped down. Cutting across the dusty street, he stepped up onto the boardwalk right before the lawman's office. He didn't know Marshal Tibbs well, but he knew and liked well enough Sheriff Crilly.

He was an all right man who was perhaps a little too tough on lawbreakers. He was also an abrasive fellow at the best of times, but was, at least as Loudon had told Jed, not impressed with Sheldrake or his money.

But he was not in town. And if what the barman had said was true, he wasn't likely to be in Grindle again for some time, if ever.

The marshal's office was buttoned up—the door was shut and the curtains drawn. Despite the CLOSED sign in the window—which seemed silly for a lawman to put up; it wasn't as if he was selling hammers or haircuts—Jed rapped hard several times with his knuckles, then tried the door handle. Yep, it was locked.

He used his height to eye in through the glass over the tops of the door's curtains. The room, what he could see of it, was indeed dark and vacant. He was about to give it up when he looked to his right and saw a familiar fellow ambling along toward him mired, it seemed, in thought.

He could not help the wry grim grin that worked itself onto his face. "Well, Mayor Fendall Hawkins, as I live and breathe."

The man looked up, and as he recognized the big man addressing him, his eyes popped wide and he jerked to a stop. If Jed had tossed a pail of icy water on the little chubby fellow, the man could not have been more surprised.

"Oh—oh, Jed Stark!"

Jed nodded, offering what he felt was a warm smile. "What brings you to Grindle today, Fen?"

"Uh . . ." The mayor of Glen Rose looked about himself, as if he might at any moment rabbit on out of there.

"It's interesting to me because I was in Glen Rose earlier—you remember Glen Rose? The town you're the mayor of? Yes, that one. Well, as I say, I was there earlier today, and I was told that you were not in town, but off somewhere else, on official business or something of the sort."

"Oh, well, yes, that's right, that's right. Yes." Hawkins nodded, tugging down his vest and holding his lapels, as he was wont to do when addressing one of his citizenry. Except that Jed noticed the man did not look particularly comfortable.

"What's the matter, Fen?" said Jed, stepping closer and bending down to peer at the man's face. "You feeling all right? You look . . . odd."

"Odd?" said the man, touching his cheek with gentle fingertips.

"Yeah," nodded Jed. "Sort of . . . guilty. You feeling guilty about anything, Fen?"

The chubby little man began backing up, his eyes on Jed and his fingers touching his cheek. "No, no, can't say I am, no . . ."

Jed turned around, folding his arms over his chest and without touching him, backed the mayor against the wall of a shop.

"Jed . . ." The mayor looked left, then right. "Folks will see you! Folks will hear!"

"I couldn't care less, Fen," said Stark, peering hard at the mayor. "We've known each other for years, yes?"

"All our lives, Jed, sure, yep!"

"You could say we're old family friends, no?"

"Sure, sure we are!" Hawkins swallowed, forcing a smile and nodding.

"Then explain something to me, Fen."

"Sure, sure thing, Jed. If I can, you know I will. Anything for a citizen of Glen Rose. Anything for an old friend!"

"Good, good. What I want to know is would a friend intentionally delay a friend when he knew something bad was happening to that friend's, oh, say, to his home? Hmm, let's say, for the sake of chatter, that one fellow's home and barn and business, his very livelihood, was at that very moment being set afire by men hired by a bad fat man. A very bad fat man. And this fellow's friend, he knew it was happening, see, but instead of telling the fellow it was happening, well, he did the opposite, didn't he? He delayed the man with idle chatter. And prevented him from getting home in time to stop the men setting that fire. The men who worked for the big, bad man."

"Now, Jed, I—I don't know what you're thinking but I didn't have—"

Jed held up a long pointing digit straight up in the air between their close faces to silence the man. "Hang on now, Fen, I'm not through. See, now I'm curious . . . Is that how a friend would act? And by the way, those men who set the fire, the ones who worked for that real bad fat man? Well, I don't think they were the only ones working for the bad fat man."

"No?" said Fen, who looked to Jed as if he were melting.

"No," said Jed, shaking his head. "What's going on in Glen Rose, Fen?" said Jed in that low growl he'd come to use far too much that day. "What do those newcomers want with Glen Rose? What do they want with me, Fen? And why are you doing Sheldrake's bidding, Fen?"

That's when the man began to slide down the wall, as if his knees had jellied and he was collapsing.

"Oh no you don't, mayor!" Jed snatched the slumping man by his well-thumbed lapels and held him up, then kept lifting until Hawkins's feet no longer touched the pine puncheons.

"Help?" whimpered the little man, his voice little more than a whisper.

"No," said Jed. "The time for help has long since gone, Fen."

"It has?"

"Yep. Now, what are Sheldrake's plans for those men, hmm? He's already burned us out."

"He—he . . . oh, don't make me say it, Jed."

"I will make you say it, if I have to squeeze your head like the pustule it is! Now what are his plans?"

"He's—he told me he's going to kill me if I tell you anything, I swear it!"

"Sure, he probably will, Fen. And I don't care. Now answer my question."

The mayor swallowed again, his face now a glistening thing, streaked with sweat and tears. His voice came out in a stutter. "Sheldrake, he's angry that you're making whiskey. I thought the fire would be the end of it with him. But you're at it, making Stark whiskey. And that made Sheldrake even crazier. He hates it—hates you—wants you gone . . ."

"And those men are here to do the job, eh?"

The mayor nodded. "I guess so, yeah." He squeaked, a sound more animal-like than a word. With a last bitten-off growl, Jed let go of the whimpering man and walked off, back toward his waiting horse and wagon.

What other folks out on the street had thought of the odd assault, he didn't care, nor did he even really see them. He climbed up into the seat, uncoiled the lines, released the brake, and laid a light leathery smack on Mags's back.

Money. He thought in disgust as he rolled out of Grindle. That's all this is about—money. He realized he was not paying attention and was pushing Mags far too hard, and taking far too much of the lane way out of town. He slowed their progress with a tug on the lines.

"Sorry, girl. But I have less time now to find a lawful solution to all this, and I'm no further ahead than I was when I started the day. In fact, now I'm probably going to be arrested for attacking Chiswick and the mayor."

Try as he might, mile after mile, Jed found himself unable to quell his mounting anger. He was angry with himself and his slow response to what now seemed obvious affronts to him, to Whiskey Woods, and most of all to Mama. What he had always considered to be a fine attribute, his calm way of dealing with hardships in life, had instead made him feel like a simpering victim.

Jed gritted his teeth, his lips wide in a sneer of disgust with himself, with the entire mess. All for money. All of it. What were they all so desperate for, anyway? Didn't the world provide enough? Weren't we all waking each morning on this beautiful earth, with birds singing and the sun shining?

He was, anyway, and it was a good feeling. Good enough, at any rate. Throw in the love of a good woman, a mother who was devoted and kind—in her own way, that is—add a few friends. And a sip of tasty whiskey now and again didn't hurt, either.

He and Mama never had much in the way of worldly goods, and less so since the fire. But they'd been blessedly lucky in owning decent land. He knew that a lot of folks weren't so fortunate, sure enough, but what about Merlin Sheldrake?

If money was the man's sole big goal, and he apparently had so much that he could purchase any worldly good he desired, then what was the fat man's driving desire? It obviously wasn't money. No. Lil was right, as always. It was power. Same thing as always, same solution Jed always came back to when considering the fat, evil man.

He resented the fat man for being that way, and he resented allowing himself to bend to the fat man's will, allowing himself to get riled enough to accost folks. Sure, Chiswick deserved a good thrashing now and again, but Chris and the other bartender? Doing their work. Frightened rabbits looking to escape from the corner the slavering fox had them pinned in.

This line of thought carried Jed a good bit of the way from Grindle back along the roadway toward home, and beyond, toward Glen Rose.

Chapter 22

"By rejecting me and my story, you are judging me, Mr. Newsman."

Loudon had listened for two hours, and at his instigation, to notorious gunman Pit Pritchard telling him a story that left Loudon feeling disgusted, with himself as much as with the famed killer. And a shouting voice inside him told him, louder and louder and over and over, that he must let it go. This was a man he should not be mixed up with.

As Pritchard spoke, Loudon heard, for the first time, the clipped, snide edge to the famed gunman's voice. He cursed himself for pursuing the man and his story, for climbing into the sugary trap the man's lulling ways had laid before him.

No, that was too harsh. Loudon cursed himself for being greedy, for wanting something at all costs and ignoring goodness and rightness instead.

And it came to him in a sizzling flash that this was how Merlin Sheldrake conducted himself in life. And he, Loudon Paley, had been acting the same way, slavering for a juicy story to make his name. Like Sheldrake slavers to possess things, especially those that annoy him. Or his wallet.

But Loudon felt a flicker of hope, too, because he had stepped back from the edge of the drop in time. Or was it too late?

Pritchard was standing at the table now. Loudon saw the man's clean, trim hands, unsullied and unblemished by hard work, and the sight of them called Jed Stark squarely to Loudon's clearing mind. Jed was his best friend, and he wondered if Jed Stark considered him in the same light.

Nonetheless, Loudon had a great admiration for the quiet, kind whiskey maker, a man he knew now was ten, twenty times the fellow Pit Pritchard was or ever could be. Simply because Jed was true. He was steadfast and honest, and Loudon now saw that these traits were all that a person could and should aspire to. Not this murderous aberration before him. Never a Pit Pritchard.

"No, Mr. Pritchard," repeated Loudon Paley, standing himself. "I am not judging you, necessarily. Rather I am judging myself. And I find myself to be wanting. And so, this newsman will not, after all, be writing your story. No doubt it will entertain and make money, but it won't be written by me, nor will it make money for me. Good day to you, sir."

With that Loudon Paley slid his notebook into his coat's breast pocket, lifted his hat from the table top, and turned, making for the door.

From behind him he heard Pritchard's voice, a lower raspier version of it than he had heard minutes before. "You milk my story from me and then you dare to turn me down and walk away? From me, Pit Pritchard?"

As the man spoke, his voice trembled and increased in volume. Again, Loudon thought of his friend, Jed Stark, who had tried, and tried again and again, to take the good path, to believe in the goodness of people, even of Sheldrake, the very man who had been trying to drive Stark out of business, then out of his home, then . . . to death.

Even today, he was in Grindle, trying to do more of the same, to seek a lawful interruption to the maddening spiral of events that had somehow draped down over them all, had somehow, without them noticing, corrupted the once gentle town of Glen Rose.

"Don't you walk from me, mister!" Pritchard's voice was the only sound in the place, save for Loudon's brogans stepping firmly on the smooth, mopped planks of the barroom floor.

The newsman expected, any split of a second now, he would hear the clicking of a gun hammer, then the battering crash of a fired bullet. Already it would be in him, driving through his back and coring his heart.

But he also knew that if he did not do this, if he did not walk away when he had realized his foolishness at being hoodwinked by greed, fame, money, ambition—call it what he will—if he did not heed that last bold call from his gut, his very conscience, he would never be able to stand himself. And perhaps worse, he would never be able to look Jed Stark, or any other honest man, in the eye, ever again.

Before Loudon Paley reached the door, he glanced at Chris, the big bartender to his left, whose eyes met his. For the briefest flicker of a moment, the reporter thought he saw approval, perhaps admiration in that man's sad, quiet eyes.

It was enough, it would have to be.

Loudon caught sight of the shadow of himself in the frosted glass of the door. There he was, close up and fully there. And upright, praise be.

He twisted the polished brass door handle and walked outside, blinking once more at the brightness of the late afternoon. It was the first day of what remained of his life. Loudon Paley decided he had better make it a good one.

CHAPTER 23

A third of the way home, Jed shook his head and growled. "Knock it off, Stark!"

He glanced about and ran a hand down his face, letting go of a big breath. The day was aging fast. He reckoned it would be close to dark by the time he got back home.

The horse flicked an ear, and he said, "Yes, girl, we should get going. We've both been lagging a bit. Long day with little to show for it."

If they kept up a steady pace, he might have enough daylight to get through his evening chores without a lantern. Mama will already have tended to the chickens, and if he didn't show up soon, she would take it on herself to feed the horses, beeves, and other critters, too.

It wasn't a big spread, as ranches went. But then again, despite the fact that they referred to their place as a ranch, the Starks had never been what anyone in those parts might consider ranchers. They had always been too busy making whiskey. And it had suited them.

He came out of his reverie to see they had slowed considerably, and he saw why. Mags was limping on her front left hoof. With a groan, Jed eased the horse to a halt. She stood, her sides working a bit harder than they should for such an easy pace as they had been keeping.

He set the brake, draped the lines, and stepped down. "Whoa now, girl, whoa now. What's the trouble here?" She greeted him with a snort and a bobbing head, as if she might want to take a chunk out of his arm. "Easy, I know, I know. I haven't been paying attention. It's been a long one for me and even worse for you. I'm sorry."

He ran a big hand down her leg and leaned his shoulder into her chest. He lifted the foreleg and inspected the bottom of her hoof. Even in the day's waning light he saw or thought he spied the reason she limped.

A sharp, edged stone had driven into the softer meat of the foot, off center, and although it was gone, no doubt having fallen out again, it had driven in deep enough initially to cause the poor horse pain. It would heal, and was not a terrible wound as such things went. But it was a poor time for this to happen.

He eased the foot back down, and she whickered softly.

As he ran a hand gently along her shoulder, Jed eyed the terrain. He knew the road quite well, and reckoned even at a walk they were a couple of miles from home. Dark was coming on quick, and his horse was lame.

"Perfect," he said, sighing. "Okay, girl." he released the brake, rigged the lines so they wouldn't slither to the ground and foul the rig in the process, and grasped her bridle and tugged her back into a slow limping walk. "Let's make for home. At your pace. Nothing we can do now but get there when we get there."

It took the better part of a half hour to cover the remaining distance. By the time they reached the junction he'd been looking for, the cut-off to home, he was squinting, as if that might help to see in the coming darkness.

They angled left, along the gently sloping run of lane that marked the edge of Whiskey Woods. The homeplace, he thought, feeling slight relief at the thought that soon, once he had doctored Mags properly, he would enjoy a hot meal, perhaps a big bowl of stew topped with dumplings . . .

Jed rolled on up to the wreckage of the fire, and saw in the dusky light that it was all as he had left it, tidy stacks of old charred timbers. After a little work with the draw knife to shave off the singed, charred skin, they should be usable once more. And there were the stacks of fresh lumber and logs.

He led Mags on through this and down the lane toward the camp. That's where he'd find Mama, agitated that he had taken so long at what should have been an ordinary delivery trip to Glen Rose.

Jed noticed that Redeye had not yet made himself known. Even though he was without doubt the laziest hound in Texas, the dog always made the effort to wander on up the lane and greet Jed when he returned, no matter the time of day.

"Redeye!" he called, low but loud enough for the dog to hear. "Redeye? Where you at, boy?"

Nothing. They walked on.

"Mags, I do believe that hound has finally drifted into such a deep slumber he has plumb forgotten to greet us."

Down the last stretch of lane, he paused. From there he should be able to see the warm glow of lamps shining through the camp windows. And Mama always hung a lantern, wick turned down low, from the long iron hook at the top of the porch's broad steps.

"Hmm," he said, feeling his guts tighten once more. That feeling of dread that had become far too familiar these days was beginning to gnaw away at him, mind and body.

He almost shouted, "Mama? You around?" but caught himself. How stupid can you be, Jed Stark? he thought. Given everything that had happened to them these past weeks and months, the odds of there being something amiss were great. And he should keep his mouth shut.

He let go of the mare's halter and flexed his fingers. Thinking he might possibly be skylined against the lighter color of the slope behind them, he slipped to his left, toward the taller scrub and straggly trees and craggy rocks lining the lane way.

His hand slipped down and untied the keeper thong holding his revolver in the holster. When it was freed, he lifted it and eased it back to half cock.

What did all this mean? And why was it so blamed quiet? He wasn't yet hearing all the usual night noises—whippoorwills and crickets, cicadas, and a breeze soughing through the cottonwoods. Nothing.

And no dog. No dog and no lights. Not good, Jed, he told himself as he eased down the slope, sticking to the side and trying to pay attention to every direction at once. There was no wind, not even a light breeze. That made detecting scents a good thing, easier than otherwise.

He battled within himself, tamping down his urge to bolt forward to make certain Mama was all right versus sticking to the more prudent plan of advancing in as much silence and secrecy as he could muster, in hopes of coming upon whoever might be lurking in wait for him to return.

If that was even the case. Maybe there was an innocent and logical explanation for the fact that Mama had not yet lit a lantern. Possible, but not likely.

All the while Jed thought this he edged forward, down the slight slope toward the wider yard before the camp. As he moved forward, making his way in a roundabout fashion toward the house, he heard more of the usual chicken squawks and fluster of the hens.

That was a sign that Mama had not yet fed the critters. Then he saw, off to the right side, a dim, small shape dart by, but not terribly fast. It was a chicken; he knew it as soon as his mind had taken in the fluffed, humped hat-size thing. Then it cackled when Jed moved forward. A rooster.

As if cued by the flock, a horse whickered back in the darkness behind a lean-to he had built off to the left. That was another horse accounted for. That left all manner of other critters to go. But he was not much concerned about them. Where was Mama?

He kept on advancing, aware that it was so dark so soon down here in the trees and bottom lands by the river.

He felt that prickling, tightening sensation in his gut and along his shoulders and neck. Hope all you want, Jed, he told himself. But it's a fool's errand. Something is amiss. Something mighty.

And that's when his right boot toe snubbed short against something, something that jostled. Something on the ground, something soft and yielding, but not moving of its own accord.

Desperate, worried thoughts, even as he dropped down and began patting with his palm at whatever it was, tried to convince him it was Mama, shot and bleeding. Or already dead.

No, no, he told himself, his mind's logic warring with those dour thoughts. She is not dead, he told himself. Can't be. And then his palm felt a softness. Yes, it was flesh, a creature, but it was covered with sleekness, hair, that's what it was. Short, fine hair. Redeye.

"Redeye?" whispered Jed. "That you, boy?"

No thumping of that infernal tail, no light moan of annoyance at having had his rest disturbed. No. And yet he knew it was Redeye. Jed would know the dog's head, his ears and muzzle.

As Jed's hand trailed along the unmoving dog's body, it stopped at the shoulder, for there it felt a sticky wetness. Jed knew what it was before he probed it further. It was a wound, and judging from the size of the thing, it had been dealt by a rifle or revolver at close range.

"No, no, no . . ." he whispered, still probing the injury with gentle fingertips. It was a trough, a sizable furrow that cut into the dog's shoulder meat, but it didn't feel as if it drove deeper into the dog—deep enough, surely, but Jed's fingers felt no spot where the bullet had entered and lodged in the dog's body.

He lifted the dog's limp head once more, giving it a waggle. "Redeye," he said in a breaking voice, the hushed tones and cracking barely allowing him to utter the hound's name.

Ah, but it was no use, and Jed knew it. The dog was . . .

Then his hand felt movement, faint to be sure, but it was there. A heartbeat, breathing, something. Had to be, thought Jed. I need it to be, I will it to be!

"Redeye?" he whispered low and close, his nose and mouth buried in wrinkles of the dog's sleek hair. "Hang on, my friend. Hang on, we'll get you to safety, all right. But you have to hang on, pal!"

Harming Redeye was never something Mama would do. Sure, she groused about the dog, but she was as fond of the lazy old hound as Jed was, perhaps more so. He'd caught her a number of times slipping the dog meaty bits and talking with the half-snoozing critter as if he were a long-lost relation who'd dropped in for tea and cake.

All right then, so Redeye had been shot, hopefully only wounded and in some sort of collapsed, unconscious state. But what did that mean for Mama?

Jed tamped down the urge to bolt for the house, knowing that whoever would shoot a dog would have no worries about drilling buckshot or bullets into him. It was dark, sure, but not dark enough yet for him to rely solely on the cover of night to dash about the place.

Besides, he couldn't leave Redeye where he was, could he? What if he injured him more by lifting him? No, no, thought Jed. I have to get him to the house, have to.

He bent lower, stuffed the revolver in the holster, knowing that might well be a mistake, but also knowing this was Redeye, and he had no choice. No way was he going to abandon his dog in this moment of dire need.

Jed wormed his hands beneath the limp form of the hound

and, before he lifted him, he bent his head low and listened. Was he hearing his own thudding heartbeat? No, no there was something more, something definite beneath his ear and cheek.

And then he heard a slight wheezing sound and felt something touch his face, the same cheek that he had partially pressed to Redeye's neck and chest. Jed looked up to see Redeye's dry nose beside him, the dog's slitted eyes regarding him.

Jed shifted his left hand slightly to provide more support beneath the dog's neck and head. "Hey, boy, hey there. You're going to be all right, my friend!"

In response, Redeye closed his eyes and offered Jed's cheek a feeble lick, then laid his head down once more and groaned. But at least he's alive, thought Jed. This is a sign of good things to come. Has to be.

He lifted the stalwart beast as gently as he was able to and grunted to his feet, keeping bent and moving forward.

Jed kept on, biting back a knot of grief and rage welling and filling his throat. He had to make it to the house with Redeye, but not by the front door. All this felt as if it were taking far too long, but he knew he had to keep his attention focused and measured, or he might well end up gnawing on lead.

He cut to his left, threading his way between the chicken coop and the side yard fence, holding in part a low caged affair his mother had insisted on him building as a way to keep her chickens safe when the coyotes were about. Which to Jed's mind was nearly all the time, anyway.

The route took him longer than he liked, but he had to get Redeye to a safe place, maybe bathe his wound. He wasn't certain what he was going to do with the dog, but he thought they'd both feel better if he could get the old lazy hound into the house.

Jed was a big man, and pretty well muscled, given his work, but the sagged weight of Redeye in his arms was beginning to wear him down. Still, Jed struggled on, holding the large dog's unmoving body close to his chest.

He worked his way around to the back of the camp while doing his best to keep unseen impediments to a minimum. The darkness reminded him again that particularly down low where the camp was sited, and close by trees, it was always darker than it would be up above. In this instance, that suited him.

Jed made it to the near corner of the camp and knew that there were three windows between him and the back door. He did not want to risk the door yet, a likely spot an intruder would cover.

Since the structure was built up on four-foot posts, he figured he'd make his way under and see if he might hear somebody up there, awaiting him above.

It took him a few moments more to get situated beneath the kitchen, where he knew there was a trap door, heavy enough that it didn't need latching to keep closed from above. But it was under the kitchen table. He laid Redeye down as gently as he was able and eased his arms out from beneath the dog.

He rested his knuckles on the earth and once again leaned down close over the dog. He didn't dare speak the dog's name, but he laid his face close to the beast's wound, but higher up and along the chest, and held still.

Sure enough, he detected a movement and perhaps a sound—faint, but it was there. Whether it was the soft sound of a heartbeat or something he felt, he knew not. Nor did he care. It was enough to embolden him.

Jed laid his hand gently atop the dog's face and with his own face still close, he said, in the quietest whisper he could muster. "Good boy. Stay here and I'll be back."

He was rewarded with another slight movement, the soft touch of the dog's dry tongue against the side of his hand. He smiled in the dark and stroked with the gentlest of touches the hound's head.

Given the dog's brutal condition, Jed knew how silly it was to bother saying to Redeye that he should stay put. But he felt compelled to tell him something, anything that might lend some encouragement.

As he turned away, he once more pulled his revolver and wondered if he'd said what he'd just said to Redeye as much or more for himself than the dog. What did it matter? The fact that the dog had been heavily grazed and was still with Jed meant somehow to the big man that Mama was all right, too. Somewhere, somehow. He had to believe that.

Still under the cabin, he paused every few feet to listen, his revolver held upright, at the ready to fire should a stranger with a footfall heavier than Mama's sound above.

But he never heard such sounds, no sound at all other than those from the annoyed livestock out in the yard beyond the cabin. Their random grumblings and clanking and snorts and bellows and cackles were all he heard. Nothing out of the ordinary, otherwise.

As he crept about the place, he tried to ignore the fact that someone had tried to kill his pal, Redeye, and instead keep his mind on the fact that his mother was—well, he didn't know what she was, where she was, or if she was alive or dead. Or perhaps she was so frazzled she was tracking him at that very moment.

No, he knew better than that. If she was about the place, and able to make any sort of commotion at all, she would have. And if she knew Jed was lurking nearby, she would most definitely howl a blue streak, if only in an effort to tip him off.

He spun, disgusted with himself for wasting time in being far too cautious, and smacked his right knee against a crossmember. The sudden throb of heat and pain, as if he had been whacked there with a steel hammer, brought a groan up and out of his mouth.

He stood unmoving, a big hand clamped over his mouth, his eyes wide. If there had been anyone up there, surely that would have tipped them off as to his location, or at least set them to scouting for him in earnest.

"This is ridiculous," he growled, albeit in a low whisper. No humans were moving anywhere that he could hear. He angled his way out from beneath the house and gained the top of the back steps. He stood to one side of the door and tried the handle. Unlocked, as was Mama's habit, so he thumbed the latch fully, depressing it, and shoved the door inward.

Again, he stood to one side, but he peered in. Despite the darkness, he thought that nothing in the room appeared to be out of order. The morning's dishes had been cleared away and the room looked tidy enough. He heard and saw nothing in there that might indicate foulness had happened.

After satisfying himself that there was no one in the house, Mama or otherwise, Jed considered lighting a lantern to help him, but then reconsidered this, at least for now. It would help him, sure, but it would also help anyone who might be lurking without.

No, no lantern. Not yet, he thought, as he kept his mounting anger tamped down and retraced his steps to where he'd laid down Redeye beneath the cabin.

He carried the dog up the back steps, still easing along with as much caution as he could. He was feeling as if his chances of finding Mama well and alive were disappearing.

He snatched a quilt from the nearest bedroom, Mama's, just off the kitchen, and laid it flat on the floor of the kitchen, close by a wall and away from where anyone might stumble over the wounded beast. He hoped it was well out of harm's way, should any further trouble visit the place that night.

Jed knew that was a possibility, in this night filled with such dreaded possibilities. He did not dwell any more on this as he arranged Redeye, with as much ease as he could, on the fluffed quilt. He fetched a low-sided bowl and ladled it full with water, then wetted the dog's mouth.

At first, the hound did not respond, and Jed felt immediate fear. Surely, this was not the dog's end . . . As he scooped more water onto Redeye's nose and mouth, he felt a slight tickle as the dog's topmost whiskers and his lip twitched.

Jed kept this up and the dog's tongue touched his fingers, seeking water. He gave him all he had in the bowl, then got up and fetched more. He did this one more time, leaving the filled bowl by the tired dog's head, but not so close that should he thrash, he might tip it.

The big whiskey man had no idea how the night was going to play out, or who would next walk back into this little home. He was guided only by the moment. He considered washing the dog's wound, but decided against it.

He had to get riding. From what he felt, it was a nasty wound, to be sure, but it didn't feel as though it was something he could do anything about at the moment, save for draping one of Mama's clean hand towels gently over it.

He eased the flopped extra length of quilt over the dog, knowing from seeing all manner of bullet wounds on battlefields that some sort of shock might occur, and shivering always seemed to be a result.

Once again, Jed bent low and whispered in Redeye's ear, "Okay, my friend. Stay here and stay well. We will be back to help you. But just now I have something I need to do."

He kissed the dog's ear gently and as he pushed to rise from his knees, close by his right hand he felt movement. It was the big lazy dog's tail moving beneath the quilt. A parting thump of the tail. A sign of goodness to come, thought Jed. I'll take it.

He grabbed a lantern from atop the side cupboard and snatched up matches. Still uncertain if he was going to light the thing, he departed the cabin. Once outside and out back, he let his mounting rage guide him and paused past the chicken coop to light the lantern.

He had no idea how many minutes had elapsed since he had returned home with the horse and wagon, but a sense of panic, far beyond urgency, bloomed hot and fast within him.

"Mama! Mother Stark!" he shouted, tentatively at first, and then with more vigor, holding the revolver out and ready with one hand and the lantern in the other. He peered everywhere he was able, taking scant moments to do so.

He pulled in a deep breath and let it out slowly. "All right, Jed Stark, think, man. Think!" He looked about him, the lantern light casting its honey glow low on the ground alongside him as it hung from his lowered hand.

At the edge of the light, ahead of him, he saw a bit of a dent in the earth, nothing extraordinary about it, but it made him look closer groundward. He needed to find clues as to what had happened, who had shot Redeye, and where his mother might be.

Jed roved forward, bent low, gun held ready to fire in his left hand, lantern in the right. It took moments before he spied the beginnings of what turned out to be a clutter of horse tracks, too many to have been made by his beasts.

Amid them, he saw boot prints, here hard and deep as if someone had jumped down from horseback, then lighter, close together, then further apart as the one who made them walked, then maybe ran? Maybe. But it was enough to confirm for Jed that at least two strangers had been there.

He walked farther up the lane, passing his own hastily parked horse and wagon. The lame beast turned her head slightly toward him as he walked abreast of her, standing with her sore foot canted. He didn't speak to her but ran the knuckles of his gun hand lightly along her side to let her know all would be well. He hoped.

The horse was a good one, kind and never demanding, and he could not recall a time when she'd tried to swing on him and offer him a bite. He'd had other horses who had done that, nipping and jerking away when they were perturbed by something. Or perhaps out of spite.

He couldn't blame them for acting up. The life of a horse, or any beast of burden, was not one he himself would want.

Jed had seen plenty of mistreatment of horses, mules, donkeys, cattle, sheep, you name it, in the war. Men, often, when treated poorly by other men in charge of them in life would turn right around and do the same to whoever was in their charge, be it another person or a beast.

And men in war, as he had found, were particularly nerved up to begin with. Top that notion with the thought that they might die any moment. Yet at the same time, they were told by their commanders that not only was it allowable for them to kill another man, something that was as wrong as wrong could be in their regular lives, but that they were encouraged to do so.

That was all that many men, it had seemed to him, needed to hear to turn from otherwise decent fellows into murderous, rampaging, raping, thieving brutes. He often wondered if, when they had survived, as some always did, would the memories of their depredations bother them once they were back home with their families? Were they able to forget about those moral crimes?

Because he was not. But then again, he was good and worked up on this night, and he knew he was ready to cause grievous harm to anybody he found who had tried to kill his dog and harm his Mama.

That's when Jed saw something, up along the slope that led to the camp home, to the other side of the lane he'd rambled on with the wagon. It was a dark shape humped along the side of the lane. If he had hugged that right side when first approaching the house, he would have found this.

And it turned out to be the very thing he feared most, a human body, hunched and slumped and unmoving. He legged it the last ten feet and, holding the lantern before him, he dropped to his knees beside it.

He knelt and leaned right over it, after setting the revolver down none too easily in the dirt. Grasping the figure, the back of which faced him, he saw that it wasn't the one person he feared most it might be—his mother.

Instead, it was a man. And as he jerked the man toward him, Jed clenched and jerked back, instinct forcing him to claw for the discarded revolver.

For what he saw was the mangled mess of a man who had been blasted at close range with a shotgun. The wound was along the right side of the man's chest below the shoulder but taking part of the man's upper arm meat with it.

It was a mortal wound, that was plain to see, and Jed let the man flop onto his back. He saw that the fellow was no threat, but looked to be quite dead.

And then another shock that day visited Jed Stark, for as he pulled back to rise to his feet, the man's eyelids fluttered and his mouth worked slowly to open and close.

The man's wound looked somewhat fresh, as the blood looked shiny and not yet congealed. It pumped weakly from a couple of spots once Jed had moved the fellow from his side slump. Jed checked the man's hands, making certain the man held no weapons.

He didn't, and Jed leaned close. "Who are you?" he growled. "Where is Mama, where is Minnie Stark? The old woman!"

The man's eyes continued to flutter, not quite opening. His tongue touched his lips weakly. "Water . . ."

"I'll get you a drink when you answer my question!"

"She . . . shot me. Oh . . . water, drink of water!"

"Who are you? Where is she? What have you done with her?"

The man's eyes slowed their fluttering.

Jed bent closer and shouted into the man's face. "Answer me, curse you!"

"Sheldrake . . . Me and my pard wanted to beat Pritchard's men to it . . ."

For a moment Jed was confused, then he grasped what the fool was saying. "You wanted to impress Sheldrake? Beat Pritchard's men to—to what?"

"Kidnapping . . . old woman . . . Water, oh, a drink of water . . ."

"Where are they?" growled Jed, tossing the gun to the earth once more. He snatched up the man's coat and lifted him slightly off the ground. "Where are they? What have you done with her?"

The man's eyes ceased fluttering and his mouth leaked air, pulled in a breath, and kept on breathing slow.

Jed saw now that this was one of the two men he and Mama had driven off weeks before. With a growl, he stomped to the porch, a dozen feet away, and yanked down the water bucket.

He bent low over the man once more and saw no movement in the man's eyes, mouth, or chest. He jerked the man hard once more by the coat, but the fellow's head flopped to his side.

With another gnarling sound, Jed dumped half the bucket of water on the man. "Drink up," he growled. Then he grabbed his gun and slammed his way into the house, heedless now of any danger that might be lurking there.

He knew what had happened, or he could make a decent guess—the other of the two men got the better of Mama and had dragged her to Sheldrake as a prize offering. It was a way to show the fat rich pig that they were capable of doing his dirty work, that he needn't have called in Pit Pritchard and his gang.

Jed slammed furniture out of his way, found his rifle and another box of shells, and bolted for the stable.

With great haste he saddled Stormy, a big gray gelding, and swung up onto his back. As he tore up the lane he passed Mags, standing there, her lame foot held canted.

"Sorry, girl. No time now—pray I get back to you and Red-eye soon!"

And then he jammed his heels, shouting hard, urging growls to the horse that he intended to ride straight, hard, and fast into the very heart of Glen Rose in pursuit of one man. That one man—one filthy, greedy fat man—would, if Jed Stark had any say in the matter, not live to see the morning light.

Chapter 24

Stormy, Jed's gray gelding, hammered up the lane from the camp, then on through the site where the barn, whiskey shed, and house used to be, now replaced with stacked charred timbers, fresh logs for beams, and new lumber covered with canvas tarpaulins. Jed urged the big beast on, and cursed himself over and over again with each breath drawn for leaving his mother, for leaving Lilly in Glen Rose, for everything.

Always trying to get through hard times without a fight, without making ripples, but what had he really done all day? He'd whomped on folks, from Chiswick to barkeeps to the mayor, and it hadn't done one bit of good.

And the worst of all was that he had known Glen Rose was in the clutches of this Pit Pritchard fool and his band of gunmen, but he had gone off and tried to find a peaceful route through this mess. Even after everything Sheldrake had done to him. To everyone.

Who was the fool? Jed didn't even have the strength of will to offer the night a grim smile. It was not going to happen then or for some time to come, especially not if Sheldrake's killers continued their vicious ways.

It was bad enough that they had savaged his stalwart and true pal, Redeye, a creature who only ever gave chase to coyotes who strayed too close to the farmyard, or to chickens to herd them back in toward the same barnyard, if they strayed too far.

Other than that, the hound was a harmless soul willing to show fang and work up a menacing growl when it was required to help drive off men with ill intent in mind. For all that, his bluff hadn't been enough to repel a bullet, even if it hadn't been a mortal wound—although time would tell. The thought of his dog laying in the dirt, bleeding and in terrible pain and not understanding the why behind it was a raw, grim one.

Jed bit back hot tears of pure rage and his bootheels drummed harder into the horse's already lunging, heaving barrel. He knew he had fifteen minutes of hard riding to go to get to Glen Rose, but man alive, he wished the horse would move faster.

Over and over his mind clicked and stumbled, pawed and ripped away at memories of things he'd done that day, of the punches and kicks and hard words, of what those whiskey drummers had told him, of the disappointment on Lilly's face as she walked away from him, of the snide, sneering Pit Pritchard's threats, and his glaring men, all of them and all of it.

As the first dim little pricks of lamp and lantern light glowed before him in the distance telling him he was closing in on Glen Rose, Jed knew that one way or another, all of this, and he meant all of it, every last speck of this moneygrubbing whiskey war, would be over and done with this night.

And right there in Glen Rose. Where it all began, four years before, when Merlin Sheldrake, a fat, sweaty, red-faced man nursing a cigar as thick around as a summer sausage, had heaved himself down out of a fancy barouche.

That had happened to be a day when Jed was in town later than usual, lingering over coffee and a second helping of Lilly's tasty pie, some sort of berry as he recalled. He had, by design, been the last one to leave the café, save for Loud, who was slow to take the hint from Jed. Jed had been helping Lil clear the tables, then wipe them down, when he had paused, seeing through the window the fancy buggy pull up.

Strangers showing up in Glen Rose was not a daily happening, but one that showed up in a gleaming rig, shiny wine-red paint despite the film of dirt road dust on it, was cause enough for anyone to peer out their windows and doorways.

"Hey," Lilly had said from the open kitchen behind him. "Am I paying you to gawk out the windows, mister?"

He'd smiled at that, then had said, "No, ma'am, but look at what pulled into town. Even you might interrupt your work, even for a moment, to inspect this."

Lilly had joined him then and, in true Lilly fashion, had flung open the front door wide to get a better look. "That's some fancy buggy," she said, as much for herself as for Jed, who'd followed her out onto the porch.

And that's when the fat man had descended. He'd made a show of smacking invisible dust from what had appeared to be a spotless and well-made gray suit with dark lines up and down it. His cravat was that, a cravat in a town where most men wore work shirts and leather braces topped with a time-worn vest.

About the only time Glen Rose saw more than a few men in string ties and such with buttoned collars was on a Sunday morning. They were hustled and hounded down the street toward the steps of the little white church at the far western end by their wives who were clucking at them and the children, appalled to yet again be the one farm family late for services.

Then another family would show up. It always seemed to happen.

But this man, aside from being noticeably well dressed, was also noticeably fat. There were a few chubby fellows and women in town, but none were what you could genuinely call fat. Not only was this fellow fat, he was red-faced, and huffing on a cigar.

"Who in the world is that?" said Lilly, visoring her eyes with a hand.

Jed squinted out the doorway at the man. "No idea," said Jed, wondering what the fellow was up to. He began to get a feeling not unlike that prickling on a fellow's neck when he saw something spooky.

The fat man turned slowly, taking in all of Glen Rose that his central location in the midst of the street offered to him. Then he stopped his slow gawking turn, and faced Lilly and Jed. He plucked the cigar from out of his mouth. "See here!" he said. "You two!"

Lilly held a smile on her face, but from the side of her mouth, she said to Jed, "Maybe he's English."

Jed, too, held his own look, passive and scrutinizing. He spoke low to her. "That can't explain why he's so . . . large."

Lilly began giggling.

"Oh boy," said Jed, for he knew that whenever Lilly laughed, it was going to be difficult for her to stop.

The fat man walked toward them. From behind him, the driver of the fancy conveyance, said, "I will water the team, sir."

Without turning but while continuing to walk toward Jed and Lilly: "You will do nothing of the sort. You are paid to drive, not to think. I will tell you when it will be convenient for you to step from the buggy."

The man's tone was loud, level, and no doubt the threatening edge to it was fully intended, given the words and tone.

"Yes sir."

"You two there, in the doorway of the—does that say cafe? Excellent. I am feeling rather peckish. Yes"—he waddled closer—"I could eat a little something."

"Looks like he already has," said Jed, in a low tone to Lilly, who was struggling to suppress and desist from giggling.

But Jed knew that when she closed down for a few hours to clean up after the morning breakfast rush, and then to rest and get ready for the supper trade, that she was well and truly closed and would open the shop to cook for no one, not even him. Although she had willingly and without prompting from him fed him behind closed doors. Usually pie.

She stepped down out of the doorway, and with her hands on her lovely hips, had said, in a kind but firm voice. "I am sorry to disappoint you, sir, but the café is closed until five o'clock, when I open again for the supper crowd."

The man, much to their surprise, kept walking. "Nonsense," he said, "that's abject foolishness. I wish to eat, and I will pay you more than the going rate for your"—the fat fellow had drawn to within six feet of them in the street and stopped; he looked the café's front over, from side to side and up and down, then at Jed; he sniffed and let his gaze drift back to Lilly—"for your no-doubt delectable treats."

Jed was tempted to step down closer to the man and stop this fool right then and there, but he restrained himself, opting instead to stand back and see how long it took for this bombastic fellow to crawl for good on Lilly's bad side. She had a short fuse for fools, and this one had already lit it.

It had been a good thing, as he recalled while thundering back to town, that he'd left Lilly alone to bedevil the newcomer. Neither of them knew at that point, as indeed had no one in town, what a nightmare that fat man was to become for many of them.

For a good many others, however, in the coming few years following his first arrival in Glen Rose, Merlin Sheldrake's appearance in their midst was not a nightmare but rather a dream.

For he made a good many people a good bit of money. None of it was of much consequence, even collectively, to Sheldrake, however. He was far wealthier than any of them could ever imagine.

Shortly after he'd ensconced himself in Glen Rose, for at least part of his time, it had been rumored, in hushed tones, that Merlin Sheldrake had been left a fortune by a wealthy uncle.

Or that he had made his fortune on his own, all by himself. Or that he stole the money somehow and was in their midst in Glen Rose using a false name and desperately seeking to spend the money he stole before he was caught with it.

Nobody knew for certain what the truth might be, but the few times these thoughts had been mentioned to Jed, in whispered tones and with the tellers' eyes darting this and that way, he had tried not to laugh in their faces, because although they gossiped, he knew the folks of Glen Rose were good people.

All this and more flashed through Jed's mind as, atop Stormy, he hammered toward Glen Rose in the near dark. The sliver of moon was insufficient to see the roadway ahead, and drifting low cloud cover hindered him to an even greater extent. Jed cursed the horse and drummed his bootheels cruelly into the beast's great heaving rib barrel.

He glanced at the passing earth now and again hoping against hope and all logic that he might be able to pick out some fleeting hint, a clue showing him that a cruel man, with his mother in tow, bound but kicking and thrashing and cursing and howling, might some time before have passed through that way.

It was all for naught, as he knew it would be, but he seethed and raged inside and, betraying that inner turmoil as they thundered down the lane, he let loose a deep-throated curse, boiling up, then spitting out words he knew well enough but rarely if ever used himself.

Now, on this night of anguish, there was ample enough reason to bring them up, then spit them out into the dark night.

He did not give thought to the notion that there might be others, humans along the way, who might hear him cursing and howling in the dark. As it turned out, he passed no other humans.

There were, however, other creatures, beasts of the night, coyotes and snakes and one lion, and many smaller creatures, too, mice and rats, who heard the pounding approach and snarls and barks of rage. They soon came to recognize the sounds as those of a man. These beasts retreated, bolting back into the hills and gullies and clots of dried swale and brush, anywhere they might avoid coming close to their most feared and reviled enemy.

In this manner, Jedediah Stark made his way to Glen Rose in what for him was a record-setting brief amount of time. To him it felt as if a year and a day had passed before he saw the first of what he had longed on that ride to see—the lights of the first homes of Glen Rose proper.

As the town grew in seemingly all directions, small cottages and shacks and shanties of all shapes had begun to be built by the poorer folks who did not work their own land further out. These were people who chose to be town dwellers, a decision Jed had never understood and doubted he would ever understand.

To choose to embrace the idea of living within sight of one's neighbor, and in many cases, right on top of others—why? All so they might work in a business owned by others, for a wage that barely kept them and theirs in food and in a tiny hovel with a roof that leaked. Bah.

"To each his own," he had muttered plenty of times, passing through these modest outlying homes.

Now, however, on this night, he praised them quickly and quietly for their guiding lights, as he approached and then passed through their environs, whipping in the darkness between their scant lantern flickers on his way to town.

All the while he continued to look in vain for a sign of his mother, and yet, if he did, he knew it might be a most unwelcome sight. A scrap of clothing or a churned spot in the roadway would give him hope. But the dark, humped shape of a body strangled and shoved from atop a running horse as the thief and killer rode hard back to town—that did not bear thinking about.

Despite this, questions lingered and flickered and grew, looming large in his mind. Had the man who had shot Redeye and kidnapped his mother even ridden this way?

Even though he was obviously the other of the two oafs Sheldrake had employed, perhaps he had decided en route that he could make more money if he blackmailed Sheldrake, for the fat man obviously wanted Mother Stark to use as a bargaining chip.

Or maybe the kidnapper wished to blackmail Jed? What if the man had instead killed Mama? What then?

No, growled Jed. She was far too valuable to Sheldrake, and far too boisterous to kill. No, somehow Jed knew, he felt it in his marrow, that Mama, Minnie Stark, was very much alive. And as anyone who had ever met her could guess, she would also be very far from impressed with the treatment she had so far received that night.

Chapter 25

Hours had passed since Jed had gone to town. If Minnie knew him, he would have stopped at Lilly's for a bit of time with the girl. All well and good, she thought. But this trait, notably among Stark men, or maybe men in particular, of taking one's time, moving at a measured, steady pace, which admittedly worked well in making fine whiskey, was not the best trait when it came to wooing a woman.

It was quite late in the afternoon when Minnie stomped across the dusty side yard of the camp, making for the coop. Time to round up the hens for the night. If she waited too long, they'd take to the trees, to the roof, most anywhere they had a mind to.

And not one place they chose would offer much in the way of protection from the various night critters who'd like nothing better than a toothsome treat of chicken. Cluckers were pleasant enough, in fact she liked them a whole lot, but they were not impressive in their brains.

"Here now! Here now, where you at, birds?" She rattled a bucket with food scraps in it as she roved.

At that point, Jed had been gone most of the day. She hoped that meant that Jed had taken time to calm himself a bit and enjoy his life, particularly with Lilly, or even that pesky newsman. Oh, he was a decent enough fellow, but he was always lingering about the place—"like a bad smell" was how she put it when the chubby reporter was within earshot of her.

She always chased the comment with a quick grin, to let him know it was her way and not to be too hurt by her comments. No idea how he took it, though.

Maybe she meant it a little. He was, after all, always about the place. Or at least he had been before the fire. Cursed fire, and cursed Fat Man Sheldrake. Thinking of the rich fool put Minnie Stark's teeth together tight. If she wasn't careful, she'd damage her gnashers wasting good thinking time on that sack of grease.

No, it would be good if Jed calmed himself a bit and forgot, even for a spell with Lilly, the work that awaited him here at Whiskey Woods. Minnie had warned him he would fizzle out if he kept on, day after day, clearing the burned mess, tending small scrap fires to take care of the unusable bits.

And if he wasn't doing that, he was busy gathering materials for a new barn, whiskey shed, and, eventually, a house. That last point, reasoned Minnie, might not be too bad. After all, if Jed ever got off his backside and asked Lilly to marry him, they would need a proper house to raise the next generation of Starks.

And he had better get at it, for as much as Minnie liked Lilly, and she liked her a whole lot, half-Chinese or no—that sort of thing didn't matter a whit to Minnie, never had; person's a person, her old papa used to say, and she always thought that was about right (except for Sheldrake, that sack of wet mush)—but that dear Lilly, now, she wasn't growing younger. Nobody was, by gum, but Minnie felt it especially at times.

It was possible that she was aging. It was not something Minnie cared to admit, but there it was, every time she saw herself reflected in a bucket of water from the well, she was startled by the little apple-faced, white-haired woman with the hard look to her eyes and mouth.

Is that really me? thought Minnie more and more of late.

Yep, she'd say. And high time you were a granny, too. Do something to earn all those white hairs and wrinkles.

So, as Minnie clanked and thumped the feed bucket, calling her girls to her, back to the coop for the night, she chuckled. "Might be this is the day that that slow-moving son of mine makes a proposal of marriage to his sweetheart."

A couple of hens clucked and the old rooster strutted past her, keeping his cold, assessing, snaky eye on everything about him.

That the old cockerel wasn't in much of a rush to go on in the coop told Minnie without having to look about her that Redeye was not where she expected him to be—moseying behind her a good few yards, yawning and running his tongue around his jaws and keeping his attention half on the birds, half on a resumption of his nap.

The hound had always helped her, or so she thought of it, when she put the birds in at night, and again in the morning, when she let them loose to peck and forage about the place. She reckoned it was Redeye's way of showing the birds, especially the roosters over the years, who really was in charge of the yard.

Other than that, the dog was close to useless. But somehow the hound's lackadaisical approach to life suited them fine. At times, it was downright amusing.

But Minnie counted on the dog to be there at night. And so, on that night, she finally glanced over her left shoulder to make certain he was there, casting a cold, if somewhat sleepy eye, on the rooster. And Mother Stark received her largest surprise of the day—the lazy hound was not behind her, trailing along as usual.

In fact, as she looked about the yard while she scooted the last of the poultry into the coop for the night, Redeye was nowhere in sight. "Redeye! Where you at, boy?"

Nothing. Minnie finished latching the coop door and then roved the dooryard. The hound was nowhere she expected him to be—atop the porch steps, tucked well back in the shade, or in one of his favored dusty wallows that he'd pawed out for himself beneath the porch. It was dark under there but light enough outside that she could have spied him there, snoring away the day.

Maybe he was down toward the river. He'd seemed to have healed up well after the fire, with a little help from her greasy tinctures. She had to admit the dog had done well that night, not harming a beast but helping them, nipping at their heels and worrying them out and away from the blaze. He'd been a singed mess when Jed had found him, but that hound was made of tough stuff.

Minnie left off shouting to him and was about to go back in the house when she heard something low and even, almost as if she were hearing the deep steady drone of a hive of bees. But no, this was a more familiar sound, and lower, and closer, too.

"Redeye?" she said, setting the empty scraps pail on the steps. "Where you at, boy?"

Minnie walked away from the camp, across the leveled yard, toward the narrow lane where it angled up and curved at the same spot. That's when she got a glimpse of the dog's hindquarters, facing uphill and away from her, standing with his rigid bony tail poking straight out like a stick.

One step more and she was able to see all the way around the cornice of shadow and brush, and there was Redeye again, in full. He was all raged up, as Jed would put it, with his hound ears laid back along the sides of his head. He stood on guard, seized in place, eyeing what Minnie saw now was a man a dozen feet uphill from Redeye.

And the man carried a rifle, cocked and aimed right at her pup! The dog was having none of these shenanigans and kept up his low, slow, lip curling growl.

The man flicked his gaze from the menacing-sounding hound to the old woman.

"Hey!" she shouted. "What are you doing, mister?"

Even as she said it, Mother Stark was moving back to the steps of the house, cursing herself for not toting her shotgun with her. Blamed thing was heavy, and she only intended to shut up the chickens for the night, anyway. It really hadn't seemed necessary to lug Ol' Shredder with her everywhere. Now she knew that had been a mistake.

The man glanced back to the dog and said, "Hold it right there, old woman! And call off this here dog!"

"I will do neither of those things, thank you very much! You—hey, I know you! You're one of those idiots I peppered in the backside some weeks ago!"

She moved another step higher. Oh, but her shotgun was not far, just inside the house, leaned against the doorframe. She felt sure she could make it . . .

"I said don't move, woman! Or I'll shoot this mutt!"

"You will not!" she growled.

He glanced at her again, licking his lips. She saw that his face was sheened with sweat.

That was all Redeye needed, for once his perceived prey diverted its attention from him, he charged, covering half of the dozen feet between himself and the man before leaping.

The man's trigger finger was quicker, and he tugged it backward, more out of reflex, it seemed, for the blast of his rifle startled him and he tripped and landed on his backside.

Redeye yowled and dropped, twitching for a moment, and then lay still.

"You shot my dog!" howled Minnie Stark from the bottom step, one hand on the railing, one raised grasping at the air between her and the dropped and unmoving body of Redeye some thirty feet away.

She didn't know if the poor pup was dead, for he hadn't much quivered. Had that rifle shot driven like a deadly fist right into the dog's heart? Close range like that, had to have. There was no helping him now. Oh, but this was a raw turn.

Minnie moved fast to her right, one, two steps gained toward the top of the porch, when a man's voice shouted.

"Don't be foolish, old woman!" growled the voice, a new one, this time from behind her, off towards the trees on the river side of the yard. She glanced toward it and made out his shape, tucked into the sparse tree cover.

Minnie knew then that they were the same two brutes who had visited several times, Sheldrake's hired fools. But she hadn't thought they were bold enough to come in and kill. It sure looked as if the man was shocked to have dropped the dog.

Minnie's mind rattled fast through the possibilities before her. Why were they there? After the recipe? Or maybe they had come to kidnap her and drag her back to Sheldrake for more of his style of negotiating. Well, that would never do him any good. She'd spit in his eye and nothing more. Especially now that he had burned them out and shot their dog.

Mother Stark risked the rest of her dash up the steps, keeping low and holding her breath. She didn't think they would shoot her, but then again you never knew what their orders from Sheldrake were. Could well be he'd grown sick of it all and wanted to kill her and Jed, too.

Jed! Had they already done for him? He was in the lion's den, after all. Rode right into it this morning. Fear for her son grew fast, to match the raw rage she felt at this latest, absolute worst affront.

"I said don't move, old woman!"

She heard the man's voice, and it sounded as if he'd moved closer to the house, ready to either drop her with a steady shot or bound up the steps and nab her.

Either way, she thought, she was about to make him mighty disappointed.

Minnie yanked the screen door open wide and dove on in, keeping low and wincing as she tumbled into the coolness of the kitchen. She had overdone it and needed to get back to the gun. She spun and saw it leaning there inside the door.

From without, she heard fast boots on the big wide steps. That meant she had but a couple of seconds before the man was on her.

But Minnie was adept at wielding the brutal single-barrel popper, and she didn't bother snugging it back to her shoulder and cheek but mashed the hammer right back with her left thumb as she raised the gun. The man reached the door and must have sensed or seen her inside for he jerked fast to the left side of the door.

"Come on out of there, you old witch! You makin' this hard on yourself!"

"Fine with me, you useless idiot!"

That touched a nerve, for he heard him growl, then say, "All right, you hag! I'm coming in!"

"You do, and I'll make you into more of a gut pile than you are!"

The man wasted no time in acting on his promise, whipping the door wide and then squaring off in the open doorway.

And Mother Stark wasted no time in fulfilling her end of the deal, either. She held the shotgun at belly height and jerked the trigger back. The gun barked quick and hard, spitting a massive wallop at the fool.

The shot drove right into his torso, ripping him hard and up high on the right side of his chest. It spun his body and staggered him backward. The scream that boiled up and out of him seized in silence, as if he was gripped by the neck.

As Minnie watched, the man somehow stayed on his feet, but barely. He danced down the broad steps as if he were quite drunk, then kept pedaling backward. His own gun, a revolver, he held in a firm grip in his left hand, as if he could not bear to let it go.

He whimpered and gagged and made all manner of sounds that were drowned out by the shouts from his partner. By then the man had recovered from shooting Redeye and had begun his own advance on the house.

Minnie was bewildered that she had inflicted more than a peppering to a man's backside, to date the only thing she had done with the shotgun to a person. She stood dazed and watched the odd, gyrating, frantic mewling and high-stepping of the shot man as he walked sideways and backward a ways up the southerly side of the drive.

He made it some distance from the house before collapsing in a writhing heap, his gun gripped in his hand.

At the same time, the spell seemed to have been broken, and Minnie remembered that her gun was a single-barrel. She rummaged in her apron for another shell, which she had of late taken to keeping in one of the two voluminous pockets there, along with her handkerchief and other odds and ends she used in her days about the place.

The spare shells were no longer there. She growled and patted, and then cast her eyes about the room in the dimming light. Where could they have gone?

Yes, she thought, when I dove through the doorway, I must have lost them.

And then she caught sight of one, but as she scrambled on her knees to snatch up the closest, a boot shoved through the half-closed door and stepped on her outstretched fingers. She screeched, "Aah! Get off my hand, you pig!"

She swung the shotgun, gripped in her other hand, around like a cudgel, and slammed it into the man's foremost leg. That forced him to lift his boot from her hand. It also forced him to growl like a seething beast, and he drove his thick right hand down hard in a pummeling back swing.

His knuckles smacked hard into the right side of Minnie's face, high up between the cheekbone and the temple, and she lost her balance, releasing the grip on her beloved shotgun, and falling sideways into the edge of the side of the hutch her great-grandfather had built.

The dishes atop it rattled and one teacup danced along the

edge of the shelf and dropped, unbroken, landing on the next shelf down in a basket of dried flowers.

She grunted and fell silent, a rare thing for Mother Stark.

The man who had hit her, Clem, dithered in the doorway, looking at her, then taking a step to the right, where his own right boot stayed outside the doorframe, on the worn wood of the covered porch.

"Rollo? Rollo, you all right?"

His query was greeted with a groan and a cough. He could barely see his friend, but he knew that if this little old witch had shot him with that cursed shotgun of hers, it wasn't good.

"Rollo, I'm—I'm going to get you some help!"

Then he saw the old woman lying there dazed but breathing. She was the very reason they had come here in the first place. They knew Jed Stark, the witch's whiskey-making son, was away from the ranch that day, since they had been watching the Whiskey Woods lane all day in order to make their play.

"What do I do, Rollo? I got the old bird right here! She's—she's addled, but breathing all right!"

Clem's shot friend responded with a sound that Clem imagined only some sort of animal being crushed by a big ol' log might make as the thing rolled over it.

"Okay, Rollo, you wait. I'm—I know what I'll do!" Clem even smiled, because it was rare he ever came up with a notion that Rollo would approve of, let alone that Mr. Merlin Sheldrake would agree to. But this one would make them both proud, for sure.

"I'll truss her up, ride to town, fetch a doctor, and get on back here! You wait and see. Won't take me no time at all!"

It took Clem a good few minutes to do that, tying the old woman's hands in front of her. Then he realized that if she came around, which with her was a likely thing, that might give her more power and ability to kick up a fuss. And he didn't need that, no sir.

His backside wasn't right since that witch had dosed them some weeks back. He wasn't taking any chances with her. He tied her hands behind her. She was dazed, thankfully, so he hoisted her high over his shoulder and lugged her down the steps and to the horses.

For as much of a pain as she had been, she sure was a little thing. All anger and spit, as his gran would have said.

"Gonna have to take your horse, Rollo, 'cause it's fast. But don't you worry. I'll be back with a doctor! Then we'll drag you on back to town, get you all fixed up, you wait and see!"

Clem shouted this as he lashed the unconscious old bird facedown across the saddle. Then he got another good idea.

On account of how mouthy this old bird was, he whipped out his kerchief and wrapped it tight in and around her mouth. "Cackle now, you old hen!"

Clem climbed up into his own saddle and, with the reins of Rollo's horse in his right hand, they trotted on up the drive. He heard Rollo moaning a good twenty or more feet behind him in the fast-approaching dark.

"Don't you worry!" shouted Clem. "I'll be back, pard! You bet!"

Chapter 26

Stormy's hooves had not stopped raking the earth, pawing and prancing as Jed leapt from atop the lathered beast. He had, a half mile before, freed his boots from the stirrups, urging the horse to greater effort with drumming heels and low, snarled oaths.

He knew, somewhere in the cold night air behind him, that those sounds he flung out, that anger he exuded but could not rid himself of, drifted as his wake. It all represented some new version of himself, a man he had not been before, perhaps not even in the war, the only other time when he was consumed by the madness of a situation so out of control that he felt himself lost within it, unable to recognize himself.

He was not on this night the man he had assumed he was. He was now a man forced into a deadly situation. And he vowed, as he bolted up the steps of Sheldrake's so-called club, that while tonight may well end up being a deadly situation for himself, he would not enter into that final moment alone.

Jed jerked the door inward and it smacked hard back, to the right, against a jut of partition, spasming on its hinges. The frosted glass webbed and shattered, dropping free and clattering and collapsing.

The place was busy, as it often was of an evening, no different than the other bars in Glen Rose. But the Money Tree, owned as it was by the fat rich man, was enough of a curiosity among the townsfolk and even folks from small outlying towns, that it saw its share of patrons at times. Not lots, but enough. This night appeared to be a busy one.

And as busy and as rumbling as was the place with the spirited and spirit-driven chatter and hubbub of the customers, when Jed slammed in and stood briefly framed in the doorway, every head in the place and every eye in those heads popped wide. They grew wider when they saw who it was.

The majority of those people knew Jed Stark, many rather well, as he had grown up among them. Indeed, the Starks were the founders of the place, and on their infrequent visits to town, they always were accorded an unwanted although somewhat appreciated deference and kindness from their fellows.

Of late, however, Minnie and Jed had noticed that this had abated, and what friendliness remained was mostly a wary nod and a smile far from heartfelt. Oh, they had their stalwart friends, to be sure, namely, the few who had shown up to help at and after the fire.

But of the rest, their shifting attitude was Sheldrake's doing, because Jed had been resistant to the fat man's demands. And that meant he was unhappy, and when he was unhappy, others tended to lose money.

There were far too many stories as to why this had been fomented, often in bars, and often after too many drinks. And a brittle shell of animosity formed in town that the more bitter among them wore like frail armor.

It bothered them even more that Jed Stark in particular did not seem to care how they felt toward him. He was the same quiet man they had always known, slow to smile but always nodding and saying hello. It was humbling to them, but also annoying.

And yet here he was, that same quiet man, no longer quiet-looking. He seethed, rage emanating from him in waves, his eyes wild, his hat missing, his hair as wild as his eyes, his teeth gritted, his jaw muscles bunching and pulsing.

He glared at them from the doorway, the shattered glass door hanging askew to his right. And, most surprising of all—Jed Stark was wearing a gun.

"Where is he?" His voice was quick, deep, rasping, and loud. Half the patrons winced as if he'd smacked them. "Where is Sheldrake?"

One of the two barkeeps, having already heard of Jed Stark's wrath in town at the early part of the day, said, "He ain't here, Jed."

Stark turned on him, strode the three paces to him before the bar, the men there parting like sod under a cutting plow. "Not here? Are you lying, Jasper?"

The man shook his head fast. "No, no, Jed! I swear it."

Jed growled and shoved his way along a line of silent men at the bar, stomped down the long line of them, and to the left, barely into the dark at the back, a wide wooden door stood closed.

Jed did not slow his pace but squared off before it, his hand atop his holstered but unthonged revolver. He backed up a pace, then drove forward, his left boot raised higher than the knob and kicked the door inward.

One blow was all it took, and the door swung wide into a dark room. He barged in. "Sheldrake! Sheldrake!"

From without, the patrons began whispering, but none dared walk down near that open door, the door they knew that led to Merlin Sheldrake's private office chamber at the back of his exclusive club, a club they were currently enjoying, even if it didn't serve Stark whiskey.

But they kept their murmurings low, because they heard crashing and slamming and bellowing from within the darkened office.

Mere seconds had passed when a voice from the front doorway shouted, "What in the name of all that is lawful is going on in here?"

It was Marshal Chiswick.

Three, four, five, then six men rushed to him and began blathering about how Jed Stark had gone mad, like a rampaging bull, and was in there right now busting up Sheldrake's office!

"Oh, he is, is he?" Chiswick's words were bold, but his bandaged face, his purpled eyes, and his slowness in making for the room in which Stark raged was not unnoticed by the citizenry of Glen Rose.

They all knew, of course, that Jed had gone rogue that very morning and had beaten on Chiswick, unprovoked, so they had heard, or wished to have heard. But wasn't he hired to deal with folks who were breaking the law?

Jed hadn't been in Sheldrake's office but ten, fifteen seconds when he dashed back out and looked all over the room, bolting behind the bar, searching anywhere he thought Sheldrake might have stuffed his fat, quivering self.

Finally, he saw Chiswick, who hadn't drawn his gun. "Marshal!" snapped Jed, "redeem yourself and help me find your boss!"

That was a hard poke at a sore man, and the marshal sneered at him. "Why, whoever do you mean, Stark?"

Jed strode up to him and snatched the lapels of the lawman's vest. "Where is he? They shot my dog and kidnapped my mother! Tell me now!"

Gasps and loud murmurs rippled through the room.

Chiswick began laughing even as Jed tightened his grip, balling the shirt and vest harder beneath his fists. "Tell me now!"

"I have no idea where anybody is, Stark. And if you mean Sheldrake, I have even less of an idea. I am not his keeper!"

"No, but he's yours."

If Chiswick was offended, he did not show it, but he did smile. "That crazy old woman probably wandered off! But only after she shot that fool dog of yours!" He brayed and jerked away, stepping back from Jed. "Now keep your hands off me, Stark. Or I will arrest you, right here and right now! You caught me unawares this morning, but never again!"

Chiswick looked around the room at the wide-eyed faces staring with expectation and not a little eagerness at the two men in their midst. He offered a slight nodding of the head and a grim sneer to the crowd. "I won't tolerate dirty fighters, Stark. Nor men with ill intent." He looked back to Jed. "And you are both!"

Jed glared at the man a moment longer, then shoved him backward away from him. The marshal staggered and would have fallen but his deputy appeared in the doorway and steadied him.

"Get your hands off me!" snarled Chiswick, rounding on his employee. He had to recover quickly because Stark was nearly on him again advancing with the deadliness of a stalking tiger.

"Where is she? Where did Sheldrake take my mother!" Stark's big hands rose up and, before he snatched the lawman's collars again, a move that was already being matched with the drawing of a gun by Chiswick, Deputy Thompson dove in between the two men.

A young man slightly taller than his boss, Thompson was nonetheless on the thin side, not yet filled out to the promise of his frame.

But it looked to be that if he survived the rigors of the job, this moment included, he would grow to maturity as an impressive man, measured and kind in manner, not unlike Jed Stark, one of the few men he regarded as a role model, a consideration not accorded to his boss.

But at that moment, Thompson found himself doing the one

thing, at least not until this day had dawned, he never thought he would have to do, never thought he would need to do—protect his boss, Marshal Chiswick, a man he did not much respect, from one of the men he respected a great deal, Jed Stark.

The situation bewildered the young deputy, but he held fast as he pulled himself up to full height and looked Jed Stark right in his justifiably crazed eyes.

"This is not the way, Jed!" This was a first for the young man, unbidden and unurged, calling Stark by his given name. Yes, he needed to show friendships, but also firmness and familiarity, too, at this point.

Stark shoved hard against Thompson, swung his hands around him in an effort to get at Chiswick. "Where is Sheldrake? You're sworn to uphold the law in Glen Rose, not break it! Crimes have been committed, but you haven't even once shown up at my place, Chiswick!" Jed looked around the room at the mooning faces staring at them. "Why is that?"

"Jed," said the deputy, struggling to hold the big whiskey maker back. "Jed, this isn't the way, you'll only get yourself or someone else killed!"

"Ah, go ahead, Stark!" barked Chiswick from behind his deputy. "Get yourself killed. One less headache for me. And for the rest of us!" He brayed, and a few in the room laughed with him, although they looked uneasy about it.

"Killed by who?" said Stark. "You?"

The marshal laughed again. "You'll see, Stark! You'll see!"

Somehow, Deputy Thompson managed to hold his back to his boss and to usher Jed Stark out the door and down the three wide front steps until they were standing in the street out front.

"Mr. Stark, look, you can't keep acting this way!"

"What?" said Jed, now paying attention to the young man. He looked hard at him and shook his head as if to dispel an irksome bee. "Harley, look, son, I appreciate what you are trying to do, but I have to find Sheldrake! His men, they kidnapped Mama and shot my dog! I—I don't even know where Mama is or if Redeye will live! Don't you understand?"

The deputy nodded. "I understand, I really do. Now I don't know if you know it or not, but Sheldrake has hired some men, from the looks of them, they are hard men, fellows with guns and—"

The deputy left off, because Jed was nodding and looking past him, up and down the road, even though it was dark enough that were it not for the scanty glow of five or six lanterns hanging spaced along the street, he would not have seen far.

As it was, he saw nothing save a few lone souls rushing to get away from something. Then the street was empty once more.

"I know, I know. Pritchard somebody. But I don't think it was him or his men who kidnapped her! Now get out of my way, Harley!"

"But Mr. Stark," said the deputy. "They're everywhere!"

"Who?"

"Sheldrake's men."

"How many are there?"

"I don't know. I think five or six, counting him. Then I heard somebody else say there were a dozen. I'd wager it's a rumor, you know how these things grow in the telling."

"Yeah, especially when folks are drunk. What do these strangers want?"

The young man shrugged. "I don't know, but they're scaring everyone." He nodded toward a single soul down the street, a man hustling from a nearby shop to a waiting buckboard.

As soon as he departed the shop, Dillard's Hardware, the lone lantern in the place went out and they heard the distant clanking of keys and sliding of bolts as the door was locked from the inside.

"What's going on in this town?" said Jed, tossing out the comment as he jerked away from the young lawman's light grasp, which was holding one of Stark's sleeves.

"If I had to guess, I'd say they're after you!" The deputy's voice was low.

"Me, huh?"

The deputy nodded. "Well, anybody who knows you. Anyone who's your friend. They're gunmen, Jed. Professionals. I've seen their likes before. Look," he moved close to Jed, looking up and down the street as if they were being watched, "they'll gun you down, you won't get a hundred feet. They're patrolling the town right now. I've been told by people too scared to say any more that folks all over were threatened and abused by them. They're after anyone who they think might be a friend of yours!"

"Me? Good, let them come find me." But then Jed's face slipped quickly from a frenzied mask of anger to one of alarm. "Lilly!"

He bolted from the man, but the quick young deputy snatched his arm once more. "Don't go busting in over there! That's what they want. She's smart, and tough. I saw her not long ago, and she was fine. Lilly will look after herself. In fact, I'll make sure she's all right. Go after Mother Stark!"

Jed's wide eyes skittered as he looked for answers as if they were written on the ground at their feet. "Where?" he said, wondering at the same time if he was somehow wrong. If, somehow, he had overlooked something at the ranch. Had she been there all that time? Wounded, waiting for him to return? Hoping for his help?

Jed groaned in frustration. He didn't know where Mama was, but he knew where to find Lilly.

Jed shucked his revolver and slicked the hammer back to full cock.

"Mr. Stark, wait, didn't you hear me? They're out there waiting for you!" His voice was a rushed whisper.

"Deputy Thompson, I appreciate it. But I have spent far too long avoiding fools and killers and men of evil intent." He said this last as a grim echo of the young man's boss's own words.

"Do your best tonight, but don't do anything foolish. Glen Rose can't afford to lose any good men. And deputy?"

"Yes sir?"

"It's Jed, not Mr. Stark. Jed."

"Yes sir."

"Good. And thanks."

Jed strode the three paces to his horse, keeping his head low. He walked the big beast, keeping it between himself and the street. There were no more lit lanterns from where he was to where he was headed—the east end of the street.

Then he'd cross and make for Lilly's back door. Keeping in the shadows was the only concession he was about to make to young Deputy Thompson's warnings. But no more than that.

CHAPTER 27

A couple of hours earlier, Minnie Stark had come around, lashed, belly down, atop a horse, dazed but not a little riled. She had felt pain before in her life, but this was new, this was . . . odd. She'd been clubbed on the bean, that much she suspected, and this was verified as memories trickled back to her, of the waning day, the evening, the stranger at the camp—no! There were two of them. Two strangers!

Soon, everything that had happened at the ranch drizzled then flooded back to her in a rush. She recalled then some of what had happened at the ranch. Well, at least Jed hadn't been there. Might've been killed, who knows? Hope he's all right, wherever he is . . .

But there was something else . . . Think, Minnie, you old fool! She chided herself even as the beast she was lashed to trotted hard and fast, jouncing her up and down and racking her poor bones. They felt as if they might fly apart any moment. Think, think!

And then it came to her—Redeye. They'd shot her dog! Jed claimed Redeye was his dog, but as always with Jed, such comments were followed with a quiet, slow smile. They both knew he was her dog. Ol' Redeye, never far from her, he was. Even if he was fast asleep, that dog somehow knew when she wanted him or needed him. Oh, but this was a sore spot.

She liked that dog pretty near as much as—no, admit it, girl, you like him better than any dog they'd ever had about the place! And that had been a long lifetime with plenty of dogs, because Starks always had dogs about the place.

The place, the homeplace, the old homestead was gone, burned to a cinder pile. But they had the camp, thankfully, older than all of the rest of the place, and added on to all these years. Oh, and the secret cave of stashed whiskey!

But of the homeplace itself, the entire thing, Whiskey Woods—would she ever again lay eyes on it after this night? And what was all this for? On that count, Minnie began to remember that it all had to do with one pig of a man.

That Merlin Sheldrake! He wanted their whiskey dead and gone, since he couldn't have the recipe. But what for? As such things went, she well knew that Stark whiskey was good stuff, and could hold its own by a long chalk most anywhere in the world—she didn't doubt that. But Sheldrake, he had more money than Croesus! So why? Why did he feel the need to have everything else in the world? And if he couldn't have it, why kill it?

That man never read his Holy Book, she thought, to live and let live or some such. Oh, her head. All this was a raw thing. And Jed, he'd be taking this hard, mighty hard . . .

Oh, it was all too much, and now she was finding it tricky to keep awake. Each thud of the horse's hooves slammed her more and more, and her mouth was filled with something, too, a rag of some sort, yes, that fool had gagged her or some such. Face was numb—oh, but this was a hard night for the Starks.

And here I am, she thought, withering away on a horse. I can't seem to keep from fading off. Fading—is this it? she wondered. Am I finally headed to meet up again with Mama and Papa? And what of poor Jed?

Minnie's last thought before losing touch with wakefulness and consciousness and, seemingly, life was that Jed had better do the thing a man ought to do, even an old cranky Stark bachelor like him, and marry his girl. She was a fine one, was Lilly. She'd be a goodly mother to a brood of young Starks . . .

"You lashed that old woman to a horse? And gagged her? I can't stand the old witch, and even I wouldn't do that to her! Better to have shot her and be done with it, you idiot!"

Sheldrake waved his fat hands and raked his fingers through his thin hair and moaned. "And speaking of idiots, where is your so called 'pard'? He's the brighter of the two of you, but something tells me you are too thick up here," Sheldrake drummed a fat finger against his own temple, the red, paunchy face beneath it quivering with rage. "To come up with this—this—this pinnacle of stupidity all by yourself!"

He left off and stared at the stocky fool in the grimy clothes standing before him, wringing the life out of his ragged felt hat, and doing his best to not look Sheldrake in the eye.

"Well? I'm waiting! And you should know by now that Merlin Sheldrake does not like to be kept waiting, you dolt!"

"Boss, I—we thought we could surprise you, sort of show up and—"

"Surprise me?" The fat man waved his arms high. "Is it my birthday? Does it look like my birthday to you?"

Clem drew his brows tight together. He did not know how to answer that one. Lucky for him the old woman moaned and made a gagging, rasping sound. They both looked over to where she sat lashed in a chair. She moved her head slowly side to side as if she were shaking it underwater.

"Where . . . what happened?" She twitched and felt the rawness of being tied tight to a wooden chair, her arms behind her and lashed together, then to the chair back. Ropes had been passed over her aproned dress, pinning her thin thighs to the seat, then continued down and wrapped around her lower legs, securing her calves and ankles to the chair's front legs.

Sheldrake uttered a low growling sound and regarded her, his teeth grinding hard together. Then his hooded, dark scowl slowly lifted, and a thin, grim smile spread over his face.

"Mother Stark," he said, his voice a clipped, smooth thing. He moved over to stand before her as her eyelids flickered. "Welcome, welcome to my sanctum, as it were, the heart of the Sheldrake empire. At least in these vile parts."

She popped open her eyes and sniffed, her eyelids fluttering, working to stay open. "That you, Fat Boy? Thought I smelled gristle . . ." She tried to laugh, but it tailed off in a wheeze.

"Clem, hand me that bottle."

Clem nodded to a nearly full corked bottle on the corner of a desk to his right. "That one, boss?"

"Do you see another?"

"Well, boss, the warehouse is full of such bottles."

"In here, you abject moron! In here! Bah, never mind, back up and shut up. No, over there, by that wall, you annoying insect of a man."

"Talking to yourself in the mirror again, Sheldrake?"

The rich man's red jowls glowed with sweat and shook with suppressed anger as he snatched up the bottle and uncorked it. He took a pull, gagged, and, with obvious effort, forced it down. Then he stuffed the open top into Minnie's red, raw mouth and held her jaw so that, try as she might, she could not jerk her face away.

With a sneer of delight, he bent before her and managed to nearly pinch her nostrils closed so that she was forced to swallow. It appeared she had, and he backed away. But Mother Stark forced her eyes wide and spat a full mouthful of the amber liquid back at him.

Some of it caught Sheldrake in the face. She kept right on spitting, and swearing blue words that made both men stand back. Never had they heard a woman speak in such a way.

"More where that came from, you vile pig! I won't even call

you a pig of a man. In fact, pig's too good for you, for pigs are clever creatures and you are . . . wrongheaded!"

Sheldrake dragged a chubby hand across his face, wiping away the spittle droplets. "Keep it up, you witch! You're only prolonging the inevitable!"

"You call that whiskey? No wonder you want ours! You can't make a drop of the stuff to save your mangy hide! Granted, it's a big ol' hide to try to save!"

She chuckled at her joke and in that moment of looking askance, she did not have time, even though she was lashed down tight, to move her head to the side in an effort to deflect what was coming next.

Merlin Sheldrake had had enough. Moving with the ease and quickness of any incensed person, fat or no, he covered the stride between them in a finger snap of time. He had scarcely set down his front foot when his right hand lashed out and smacked the right side of Mother Stark's face, whipping it fast and hard to her left.

She shrieked in her welter of pain and surprise, moving her already throbbing, wobbling head in a daze. A dribble of bloody spittle leaked from the right side of her mouth.

It had happened so quickly that Clem, who had been leaning against the back wall, right where his boss had told him to stand, was taken by surprise.

He nonetheless dashed forward and grabbed at Sheldrake's arm, pulling him away from her. "You don't hit a woman, Mr. Sheldrake! Especially not an old woman! I mean, I did, but it ain't right!"

Those words did more than a thrown bucket of water could have to bring Minnie to her senses. "Old woman! Old woman!" She howled and raged at the insult, struggling anew at her ever-tight bonds, shrieking revenge the entire time.

In response to his hired man's declaration and arm grab, Merlin Sheldrake surprised Clem by turning to half face him.

He nodded in agreement, sighing. "You're right, of course, Clem. Only too right. Go on over to the desk and pour us each a whiskey, will you. I need to settle my head."

"Oh," said Clem, nodding, "okay, boss." He turned toward the desk.

As if conjured, a small, two-shot pistol appeared as a small, toylike thing, nested as it was in Sheldrake's fat hand. With no hesitation, he pinched back on the trigger and a bullet traveled the six feet between from the rich man to drive on into the middle of Clem's back.

The foolish hireling groaned and stiffened, and his arms crabbed up at the elbow as if he were squeezing his shoulders together to force the offending missile away from him. A second bullet joined it, and Clem jerked even taller.

With his back to Sheldrake and his arms held high, Clem trembled. His head jerked back, his greasy hair hanging like wet yarn on his shoulders. A gagging sound eased off in a whistle, and he pitched forward, falling prone across the desk before sliding backward and slopping, faceup, on the floor.

For a long moment neither Minnie Stark nor Merlin Sheldrake made a sound. Then he turned and smiled at her as he popped open the little pearl-handled silver hideout gun and picked out the two tiny casings. He let them drop and they clunked quietly on the wooden floor.

He tweezered his fat fingers in a vest pocket and pulled out one, two fresh bullets and thumbed them into the little gun, then closed it and waved it slowly, menacing the old woman's face from a few inches away.

She watched it, then seemed to come back to herself. That look of disgust returned to her face, but this time her voice was low, cold, rattled. "Why is it, really, that you want Stark whiskey so bad, Sheldrake?"

He leaned close, spraddle-legged before her, his meaty red face mere inches from hers. The loaded gun he held close by her left temple. "Lest you spit on me." He smiled.

"Now, as to your question—a logical one, I will grant you that. Yes, it's true I want Stark whiskey . . . I want it *gone*!"

This last he shouted into her face, giving the old woman a clear view of the gaping maw that was his mouth. She recoiled, grimacing once again at the repugnancy that was Merlin Sheldrake.

But confusion quickly replaced this look of disgust on her old, lined face.

Sheldrake pulled back and stood before her, seeing this and laughing. "You don't know why yet, do you? You honestly don't know?" He howled and howled, tears popping out of his eye corners. He shook his head.

"Priceless, I tell you. Priceless." His laughter eased and he said, "And for me to say that really means something!" This set him off again. "Oh, okay, okay," he settled once more, then regarded her.

"I'll tell you, then. Because with you and your vile son and your admittedly excellent whiskey all gone, I will control the market here, the entire booze market, mind you, not that I'm not close now to doing so, for I am! Oh, I am! But with your cursed Stark whiskey gone, I will control the market here, and then, eventually, I'll make it the entire country! Then think of the money, the fame, the power.

"Now that, you see, is the very thing that makes all this"—he waved his gun at her, then at the dead man on the floor to his right—"so very worthwhile." He pulled in a deep breath through his flared, sweaty nostrils. "Never let it be said that Merlin Sheldrake was afraid of hard work!"

It was Minnie's turn to laugh, and she offered him a grim cackle. "Not with your whiskey, you won't, Sheldrake!" She snorted and shook her head.

"What, exactly, do you mean?"

"What I said, you idiot! That vile rotgut—no, wait, that's an insult to rotgut whiskey everywhere . . . That mule pee you pass off as whiskey and all but force folks to buy, it's trash, and more dangerous than poison would be!"

He said nothing but stared at her with a fading smile and narrowed eyes. She plowed onward. "For all your talk and all your money and all your precious power, Mr. Sheldrake, there's one thing you don't know, don't have a splinter of a notion about."

"And that is?" He smiled, his eyebrows raised in curiosity.

"That you can't buy everything in life, man!"

"Ha! That's all? After your brilliant little setup, that's all the wisdom you have to offer me? You silly old hag of a hick! I have yet to find a single thing in life that isn't for sale! Everything, you sad little thing, can be bought."

"Ha to you, then," she said, wearying. "You already found the one thing that can't be bought. And it burns you up inside, doesn't it? To not own it. And so, your solution, if you can't own a thing, even if it is a very good thing, indeed, is to kill it."

"What are you talking about?"

"Oh, come on, you greasy mess! You aren't that stupid."

"Humor me."

Minnie gave a cluck of annoyance. "What do you think we've been talking about, man? My family's whiskey, that's what, you fool! What do you think?"

Once more he bent close to her, his big face an inch from hers. Subdued rage was writ large on his puffed, sweating features. When he spoke, his voice was low and raspy. "Look here, you stupid old woman. You are correct. My whiskey is liquid crap—less than, sure. I'll give you that. And because you are correct, and in exchange for your life, I want that recipe. You tell me where you have it stashed away and once I lay my hands on it, why, I'll come back here and free you, you have my word." He stood upright and looked down at her. "The word of Merlin Sheldrake is not given lightly."

For a long moment she was silent, her head bent forward,

and she looked down at her lap. Then her shoulders began to work up and down and small sounds came from her.

Sheldrake leaned his head to one side and stuck out his bottom lip. When he spoke, there was a forced softness there. "I know it must be difficult for you, but trust me, it's the only way to save your life and that of your son. It's for the best . . . Mother Stark."

She looked up at him, and he saw that she had not been weeping but laughing. Now it came out in a peal. "You idiot!" she howled. "You already possess it!"

"What?" he growled, looking around himself. "Where?"

She nodded. "It's right here, in this room! Right now!"

He looked with a sneer of disgust at her soiled and sullied dress and apron with its big pockets. "On your person, then?"

"Nope!" she shouted. "In my person!"

"Huh?"

"In my head, you big lunk!"

His drawn brow slowly relaxed, and he nodded. "Yes, fine, then. I want it written down! You will do this, and right now, or I will kill you. Wait now, surely your son possesses it, too?"

To his surprise, Minnie Stark nodded. "Yep, he does. But it ain't a thing that a Stark has ever committed to paper. Never will be, neither! It's all in our heads." She nodded. "No less than two, no more than two Starks have ever known it in full at once, from Tennessee to Texas. And nobody else, ever. Stark family rule, you see. And that's a fact." She nodded at this slice of sage thinking.

"Well, then," said Sheldrake with a grin. "If I kill you off, that leaves that buffoon of a boy of yours, one Jed Stark, eh?"

She said nothing.

"Maybe I'll kill off Jed, and you'll be the lone one to know it. Hmm."

"Won't do you no good!" she said.

"Why is that, my good lady?"

"Because I'll do my own self in, and that will be that!"

Sheldrake canted his head as if he heard something he did not comprehend. "You would do that instead of giving me the recipe?"

"Sure thing. As I been telling you, some things in life ain't for sale, you big loaf of fat!"

Sheldrake walked to his desk, stepping over Clem and sneering at the dead man, and poured himself a short glass of his whiskey. He sipped and grimaced, then rounded on her once more, smiling. "Fine."

This was not what Mother Stark had expected to hear. Her face whitened.

"I'll revert to my original plan. I'll kill you and be done with it. Then I will find Jed Stark and do the same."

"But—but you said you want, you need, a quality product to sell." Her voice wavered as she realized she had made a grave error.

"Yes, it's all coming to you now, isn't it, hag? I know what I said, but really, I don't need you alive at all. I have reconsidered my stance on the matter. I don't much care anymore. I have more money and power than most anybody I am ever likely to meet in my life. Although it must be said that I will try to beat the recipe out of that pathetic mewling whelp of a man you call a son. That is, once the small, trained army of hired killers have found him tonight and brought him to me. If that fails and he dies in a gunfight, the secret locked in his waste of a brain," Sheldrake shrugged and sipped and winced once more. "Then I will buy good whiskey elsewhere."

He set down the glass on his desk. "This game has gone on for far too long."

Any pretense of a smile was gone from his face as he advanced on her, the hideout gun once more in his hand, and once more aimed at Minnie Stark's head.

Chapter 28

Jed walked Stormy up the back alleyway behind the line of buildings that fronted the south side of Glen Rose's main street. As he had along the front street, he kept the horse between himself and the structures, which irked him because by doing so it showed he had fear, bore fear of the pathetic fools who were in the employ of Sheldrake.

And yet he was not fool enough himself to risk doing otherwise. For to tempt unnecessary risk now, perhaps of death at the hands of one of those brutes, when he was so close to finding Lilly and Mama, that would be stupid indeed.

He used the building ire he felt to help fuel his mind for the confrontation with the men, whenever it came. He had little doubt that it would come.

There were no lanterns, no lamps glowing though rear windows, nothing to illumine his path back there. Of moonglow there was little, but he knew the way well enough to find his way with little interruption. Halfway along, it came to him that there was a widening of the alleyway, right about where he was passing.

As quick as that, he decided to leave the horse there, the darkness emboldening him such that he felt secure enough in it to venture the rest of the way to Lilly's without the big horse shielding him.

Jed slid the rifle from the scabbard on the saddle, and crouching low, he cut in as straight a line as he could the rest of the way toward Lilly's back door.

Adjacent to it, he paused, half behind a gappy plank fence that was used by a number of locals as a temporary corral. Ahead, past her narrow building, a lean-to stable housed her own horse, a sweet-tempered mare named Poppy. Jed beelined for the stable, intending to pause there and eye the back door of the café kitchen.

He ran closer, aware more than ever of the grinding, scuffing sound of his boot soles on the lane. He drew up, wincing as the sounds of his boots seemed to echo in the dark. If ever a man drew attention to himself, surely, it's me tonight.

Stopping before the planked wall of the stable, he held there, then leaned closer to it. It was possible he had heard a slight scuffing sound from within. Likely a horse, but what if it was one of the men? He set his teeth hard together and tried not to feel what he was feeling—the urge to pummel one of them—no, all of them.

Not many minutes had passed since he had left the bar, for he had been moving at a determined pace through town and along the alleyway. He did not want to slow up, for Lilly might at that moment be in danger, his mother as well.

He didn't want to think of what had happened to her. She was tough, but she was an old woman. No way of knowing how she would fare as a prisoner. Her fierce temperament might well be her undoing.

In that brief pause, he heard the sound again, slight and soft, but something told him it was not, did not seem to be, any sound made by a horse in a stall.

He slid to his left along the sun-puckered planks, his cheek nearly touching the weathered wood, smelling of hot days and a sweet dryness. He had made little or no sound as he did this and reached the end of the wall.

To his right, on the other side, where the horses were kept, something—he didn't think it was a horse—was moving, too. Jed raised his rifle, his left hand gripping it low, at the throat below the hammer. It would be too close to use as a gun, but as a cudgel, it might prove effective.

With slowness, he raised it higher, pulled it back, ready to swing it at whoever was set to exit the open doorway to his right. He held, locked in that position, set to strike, and he was rewarded for his patience with the dimmest of outlines of a short man peeking, poking his head forward as if looking to see if the way was clear for him to emerge.

At the last moment, Jed decided to snatch at the man's throat and drag him out, fast, and slam him to the earth and subdue him. Speed would be all important so that the man wouldn't have time to use his own gun, which Jed did not doubt the man held at the ready.

But he needed the man awake and responsive if he was going to find out anything about Lilly or his mother, or even where the rest of the vipers were holed up, waiting him out.

He bent low and laid his rifle down as he drove forward, his right, then his left hand grabbing for the man.

Almost at once, as his steel-like fingers closed on the fellow's clothes, Jed sensed something was wrong. This man was small, yes, and while he fought back with surprising speed, Jed felt the fellow was soft, too, somehow.

The man gasped and shouted, "No!" in a quick growling bark. And it was not the voice of a man.

But Jed did not let up. He held the person down, fighting flailing arms, knees, legs, kicking, grabbing, punching all at once. Then the brute bit his hand!

Jed bent low and forced his weight down atop the person, hoping to subdue the fight somehow. And he smelled something unnamable but familiar about this formidable foe.

"Lil?" he whispered, low and close to the breathing face of this person.

His opponent held in place. "Jed?"

He bent low and eased his grasp of her, pulling her close instead. "It's me, Lil. You're okay?"

"I was until you attacked me, you oaf!" The whispered words were harsh, but she wriggled her arms free of his loosening grasp and hugged him tight about the neck.

"I'm so sorry, Lil! I—I didn't know it was you!"

"I was so worried about you all day. I didn't know what had happened to you, where you went."

"I told you I was going to Grindle—oh, it doesn't matter. Did any more of those men come around?"

"Sheldrake's hired guns? No, not much, but they tried, I think. Someone was banging on the door, then around back. They stopped short of breaking in, but when I was sure they'd left, I came down here. I was going to ride to the ranch to warn you and stay with your mother."

"You can't." He pulled back from her and made to rise to his feet.

She held him. "Jed, what's wrong? What happened?"

"Lil, Sheldrake's men," he whispered, "those first two—I'm not sure if Pritchard and his men were in on it—but they kidnapped Mama and shot Redeye. I have to go find her."

"What? But—not Minnie. Oh, and your dog!"

"Yep," he said, rising and helping her up. "I don't know if he's dead. Grazed him, but it's deep, deep enough. Look, Lil, you need to go back inside and hole up. I'm serious, never been more so! It's not safe out here. I don't know where all these men are, but Harley said they're everywhere, threatening folks all over town, anyone who knows me. I'm surprised you haven't been tracked down, taken—oh, I don't want to think of it."

"I'm going with you, Jed. No way am I staying here."

"No, Lil!" He said it louder than he meant to. Then he held her by her arms and gave her a shake.

She pulled away. "I'm not a child, Jed!"

"I have to go, Lil. Where I'm going, I can't risk having you with me, don't you see? Don't give me more reason to worry than I already have. I can't—I can't lose you, too."

"You haven't lost me, and you haven't lost Minnie yet, either. Right?"

He nodded. "Right. But I don't know where to look. I already tore about his lousy club."

"What about his distillery and warehouse?"

"Sheldrake's?"

"Who else has a distillery and warehouse in these parts, Jed? Other than you."

"Of course," he said. "I'm not thinking right. I started with his bar. But he stays at the hotel when he's in town. So, I thought in town . . ."

"Right, but I think he does most of his business deals out of the warehouse. Loudon said he had an office there or some such. According to Loudon, Sheldrake practically lives there when he's in Glen Rose. Loudon should know, he's in the business to know things, as he says."

"Right," said Jed, barely listening. "It's the mill, right? By the rail yard. Or where they were planning on building it."

"Well, it's where Sheldrake claims the rail yard's going to be."

Jed barely heard her as he bent to retrieve his rifle from the ground out on the other side of the stable wall. He pulled her close, fast and hard, and whispered in her ear. "Go back inside, Lil. I beg you. I can't worry about you, too."

She said nothing, but they kissed and he was gone, running down the alley. Within moments she heard saddle leather creaking and then horse hooves thumping faster and faster, receding away toward the far end of the lane.

Then the sound shifted as he turned toward Main Street and rounded the end of the lane. Then he was gone from her hearing. And straight into more danger than he could handle alone, that much she knew.

"Sure, I'll stay put, Jed, for as long as it takes to finish saddling Poppy." Lilly Chu was not waiting around for anyone. She slipped back inside the stable and finished rigging up the gentle mare.

"I can't worry about you, either, Jed Stark. That's why I'm going with you. At a distance."

Chapter 29

Behind him, back toward town, Jed heard random gunshots bristling in the night. He was close enough to hear the shouts, equally random, of men. Not shouts of fear or surprise, but barks of anger, of one growling dominance over another.

What that meant, Jed could only guess. Likely, given how passive the citizenry had seemed lately, particularly where Sheldrake and his foul ilk were concerned, it would not surprise him to learn the folks of Glen Rose were being ground further into the dirt.

It was not a charitable thought, but at that moment, Jed Stark had little charity left to offer anyone.

His only real concern back in town was for Lilly. He hoped she did as he had bade her and stayed put. Found a hidden corner and shot anybody who came at her. She was good with guns and was plenty gutsy, but he wasn't certain she knew the value of holing up and waiting this thing out. The more he thought about it the more convinced he became that she was not going to do that, but would somehow sneak out of town and try to help him. He moaned at the thought, but kept riding.

He could do nothing more than that. All this thinking and the sounds of random gunfire from town carried him but a minute's worth of riding the big gray hard in the direction of

Sheldrake's distillery and warehouse. Or where he recalled it might be.

He had not been out this way in what he guessed was years, although he remembered hearing that Sheldrake had bought the property for a pittance, speculating that it would be an ideal spot for a rail line to run through, and getting lots of folks in Glen Rose excited over the prospect of being a railroad town.

Others had said no, that it was too far from town, but then Loudon had told Jed that since Sheldrake owned controlling shares in a railroad, the man could likely move the entire town to suit him and his grubbing needs, if he so chose.

Jed hadn't made it far before he met up with what he suspected was going to be trouble. A man on horseback had apparently seen him coming and had pulled up and was doing a rather poor, hasty job of concealing himself in the inky shadows of the dark roadside.

Jed, too, slowed up and, as his revolver was already drawn, he peeled back the hammer. The distinctive sound would be unmistakable to the man in shadow. He could come up with no way to skirt this character and presumed the man was a sentry of some sort, lying in wait for him.

And then he heard the man mumble something, then speak louder. It was a deep, gruff voice and sounded odd to Jed, forced somehow.

"Who goes there?" said the voice.

It sounded almost theatrical to Jed. Who did he know who would talk like that? Then it came to him. "Loud? That you?"

There followed a long pause, long enough that Jed figured he had guessed incorrectly. Then a voice said, "Jed? That you?"

"Loud—you alone?" Jed urged his horse forward a step, then two.

The man in shadows did the same. "Yeah, I think."

They each rode forward at a cautious walk. Jed was not

quite convinced that it was Loudon Paley and that he was alone and not being prodded by a gunman.

"Oh, am I relieved to see you!" said the newsman, riding up on his trusty Alice.

"Why are you out here?" said Jed, not slowing. If Loud wanted to talk, he was going to have to keep up with him.

The newsman handed Jed his flask. "That's Stark whiskey, so you know."

"Well," said Jed, taking a quick sip. "Stark whiskey or no, go easy on it, pal. That's a one-way lane, if you know what I mean."

His newsman friend nodded and tapped Alice in her ribs to catch up with Jed, who was already moving on into the dark. "You should know, Jed, that before full dark I trailed one of Sheldrake's men out here. Not one of Pritchard's, mind you, but one of the others, those two that you laid out in the café a while back."

"Yeah," said Jed. "One of them's dead, shotgun blast, close range. The other took Mama."

"What?"

"Got to the ranch too late to stop it, but Lilly reckons Sheldrake might have her here."

Loudon nodded. "That makes sense. It's the place I'd come."

"Well, if you followed the man here, then—"

"Yes!" interrupted Loudon. "That's right, he was leading another horse! It was too dark for me to see, but I remember thinking that it looked like—"

Jed stopped his horse, and said, "Looked like what? Like what, Loudon?"

"That it looked like it could have been a body draped over the second horse."

Jed growled and smacked Stormy on the rump. "No time to waste! Heaven help them if they've killed my Mama . . ."

Loudon kept up, and said, "Jed, you don't want to ride in the front way. Might be some of those men there. It's the back you want. From there, I can get you into Sheldrake's office."

"How do you know? How do I get there?"

"I've been there. Interviewed Sheldrake when he began production there. But I won't tell you, I'll show you!"

"You're not coming with me, Loud."

"You bet your bonnet I am, whiskey man!"

"Go back to town and help Lil, curse you!"

"Nope. She can take care of herself."

Jed sighed and said nothing, but dug his heels harder into the horse's belly. What clouds there had been were parting, allowing the sliver of a moon to glow a helpful light down on them. Not much, but enough to make out the wagon lane, affording them more speed.

In less than a minute, they saw the bulk of the big building rise out of the darkness to their right. The facade was fronted by a massive loading dock. Despite what Loudon said, Jed rode straight for it.

"Not there, man!" growled the reporter. "Follow me!" He slowed his pace and cut to their right, along the far end of the building.

This was not what Jed had in mind. He was out of patience—hadn't had much since the morning. Any traces of it were long gone. But Loudon had been here and Jed hadn't, so he followed, clipping along beside the man, wishing they could move faster.

The lane was wagon-wide and looked to be well used, not that Jed cared much. It could have been a sheer face of rock and he would have found a way up it. Then Loudon leaned over and, in a whisper, said, "I think we're being followed."

They slowed their pace, and Jed half glanced over his shoulder. He saw nothing and had heard nothing.

"I don't care. We have to get there. Besides, it was probably our horses' steps echoing off the side of the building."

Loudon nodded. Made sense, he thought. The structure was tall, all of two, perhaps three stories, and close to their left.

"There's a smaller entrance back here. Leads to a passage that will get us to Sheldrake's office. I don't think anybody would expect us to come in that way."

"Don't care as long as it gets me in there fast!"

Loudon nodded, and whispered, "That's the plan, my friend." He pulled up short and slid down. Jed did the same with his horse and laid a hand on his friend's shoulder, steering him hard. "That the door?"

"Yep," said the reporter. "If it's locked, we'll have to find some other way in."

"Nope," said Jed, "I'll break it down."

"That will tip them off that somebody's here."

"Good. No more time for more games, Loud. Now you stay here. I'm going in there."

In response, Loudon pulled two shiny revolvers from a double-gun rig about his waist. He held them up. "And a hideout gun in my coat."

"Doesn't mean you know how to use them, Loud," said Jed, angling closer to the door.

"You don't know everything about me, Jed. I never mentioned my guns or my practice with them because you never want to talk about guns."

"For good reason," said Jed, shaking his head and moving toward the door. "Guns are a stupid, brutish way of solving a problem. But sometimes a man is forced to be a stupid brute. Now stay behind me. I don't want to have to worry about you, too."

"Okay, but I'm going in with you. This is the very reason I came west, for such a moment as this!"

"You're hopeless, Loud."

They drew to the door and found it was not only unlocked, it was not fully closed.

Jed stood to the right, Loudon to the left, and both men

held a drawn revolver. Jed nudged open the door with a boot toe, then waited a moment. He peered in.

The dimmest of lamp glow brightened the dark. He was in no temper to dither—every second might be a second closer to death for Mama, if she hadn't already been killed by the brutes.

With no more hesitation, he bent low and walked in. Loudon followed, glancing behind and seeing nothing. He eased the door almost closed, but not latched, as they had found it. The low light was scant but offered enough glow to show it came from behind a door about twenty feet ahead.

That was where he had interviewed Sheldrake. It had been a few years before, and as Loudon recalled, it was an office with fairly plain furnishings. It told him much about Sheldrake—he was all business.

There had been a desk piled with papers, and a chair behind it and one before it. Two oil lamps and a hook on the wall for Sheldrake's coat and hat.

"Don't you have a secretary or an assistant of some sort?" he had asked the fat, wealthy man.

"No" Sheldrake had barked. "Pay someone to do things I can do and can do better and cheaper? Bah! Besides, I don't trust anyone else, especially not with my money. No faster way to go penniless than to trust others."

As they advanced toward the door, Loudon recalled other details about the office. There had been two doors in and out of the office, the one they used and another that Sheldrake had taken him through that led to the warehouse and distillery.

He had also learned that this was but a small office for when he was in Glen Rose.

"On business?" the reporter had asked him.

"Of course. I am always on business," Sheldrake had said. "What an odd question!"

Loudon shook his head once fast, realizing he was musing on the past when he should be paying attention to the present.

They had nearly reached the office door when Loudon, turning to his left to get a look past Jed, who walked ahead of him, knocked against the passage wall with the butt of his holstered left-side revolver.

He winced, gritting his teeth, and in the dim light saw Jed not quite eye him over his left shoulder. Loudon didn't think that look meant the big whiskey man was pleased.

The first thing Jed saw when he shoved open the door, his cocked revolver leading the way, was the body of a man, somewhat familiar, and faceup before a massive desk piled with papers. Then, ahead, he saw Mama, lashed to a chair, but open-eyed and looking right at him.

"Mama! You all right?"

"Jed, thank the Lord you're alive! Yes, yes, I'm fine. Go! But watch him, he's got a two-shot pistol, son! Now go, get that fat sack of pond scum!"

Jed kept his eyes on her, the glimmer of a smile wanting to appear on his mouth. "That's my Mama."

He snatched Loudon by the shoulder and dragged him close. "Untie her, Loudon. Take care of Mama! Get her out of here and back to the ranch! Take my horse and cut wide around town, get her away from town! Do it, man! Do it now! Now! Now! And don't argue this time!"

With that, and a last look at his battered but nodding and smiling Mama, Jed followed Sheldrake out the door the man had taken moments before, cursing Loudon for making that noise in the passage.

Jed held in place in the dark. He smelled wood and smoke, all manner of other familiar smells, although they were draped over with a chemical pungency that he knew at once as the stink of poor whiskey.

Sheldrake made a massive amount of short-aged whiskey, something folks had been doing as long as they had been making booze, he reckoned, but it was vile stuff, doctored with poisons, dead snakes, acids, animal parts, anything the maker thought might speed along the fermentation and aging process. None of it worked. All of it was evil and wrong, plain wrong.

That was why cheap whiskeys tended at best to make people ill, and often killed them. Many men, looking for the sweet, subtle relief of a glass of whiskey at the end of a day's hard labors felt that if they drank the cheap stuff, they could buy more of it. And more was better, right?

Never had been in Jed's experience. Give him quality over quantity anytime in life, and he'd be happier and better off for it.

All these thoughts and more raced through his mind as he followed along the short, twelve-foot passage. Then the close-in sounds opened up a bit and he sensed the passage was now formed mostly by stacked crates and barrels.

Jed held a moment longer, listening. Nothing. He slow-stepped forward, aware now that there was light—low and dim, to be sure—but enough to make out general shapes and pick out the near edges of barrels. As he passed them, he could make out, too, lettering painted on the butt ends: SHELDRAKE'S FINEST WHISKEY, they read.

He wanted to snort, to say, "Bah!" but he'd save that scoffing for another day. If there was one after this night. He held in place once more, aware that the room before him was opening up, seeming vaster and darker, taller. He was obviously well into the warehouse itself. He was also aware that he'd been traveling roughly toward the front of the building. That meant the big doors and loading docks he'd seen earlier with Loudon must be to his left.

Ahead, to his right, there was a soft, sliding sound, as of cloth against a hard surface. A fat man squeezing past crates and barrels? He hoped so. He also remembered Mama had said Sheldrake had a pistol, a two-shot. Small but deadly.

A low-lit lantern hung from a hook on a beam, its honey-glow light wavering and low. The wick needed raising, but it cast plenty enough light for Jed to see the blob of a man working to reach it, trying to force himself between stacked crates, his right arm up, the pudgy fingers grasping. He almost had it, no doubt to snuff it out. Almost.

Jed stepped out in full into an open space, his big revolver on full cock and aimed square on the bulk of Merlin Sheldrake. "Hold right there, Sheldrake."

A thin squeak rose up from the fat man, but he did as he was told. His left hand, that closest to Jed, a dozen feet away, looked bunched, as if it held something, likely a hideout gun.

"Keep both hands right where they are, up high, that left hand, bend it back, up and back, and then open it up. That's it . . . No, no, you don't try to surprise me, Sheldrake. This gun is bigger than yours. Now, let that little silly gun drop."

The fat rich man made another slight sound, as if he were about to speak.

"Do it now, or I will pull this trigger, and I will not ever be bothered in my mind about doing it."

Sheldrake finally let go of the derringer. It clunked on the wood, then clattered, lost somewhere behind stacked barrels.

Sheldrake turned his face fully toward Jed for the first time, and looked right at him. The guttering, flickering flame of the low lamp danced odd shadows on the rich man's greasy, glistening face.

He licked his lips, looking to Jed like nothing more than what he was, a fat, wet bullfrog.

"This—this needn't be difficult, Mr. Stark. Jed, can I call you Jed? Look, I have more money than you can ever possibly imagine, friend. I—I will do as you ask. Anything you ask. I—oh, hey now, I will leave town! Yes, that's right, I will leave Glen Rose! For good, you have my word, my word of honor! I will leave tonight!"

Jed said nothing for long moments, feeling sickened but somehow, too, enjoying this freakish groveling. Finally, he said, "Oh, you'll leave Glen Rose tonight . . . Merlin. In fact, tonight you'll be leaving the entire land of the living. You hear that?"

Jed wasn't certain if he was going to shoot the man, club him and leave him to the rats—he didn't know. And at that moment, he didn't much care.

Mama was safe, he hoped Lilly was safe, and Loud was alive. So far things were working out. Long way to go, but the night was young, as somebody somewhere once said.

"You . . . you cretin—Jed Stark! Bah!" Sheldrake spat the words as if they were rancid hunks of meat. "How dare you threaten me! Do you have any idea who I am? I am Merlin Sheldrake!"

Even in the low light Jed saw the man's face purpling and shaking. This was amusing. "Do go on," he said.

"I can buy and sell anyone in this country, in the world! And you, you . . . peasant! You dare threaten me?"

"Yep. Now drag your beefy self on out of there—or are you wedged in too tight?"

The man didn't move.

Jed stepped one stride closer and kept the long steel barrel of the revolver aimed straight and true at the man's face. "Do it. Now."

Sheldrake complied, shoving himself back out of the tight spot he had jammed himself in. The crates, tightly stacked, barely moved as he side-stepped back toward the open space before Jed. As soon as he did, he turned to face the big whiskey man.

"Keep the hands up, Merlin!"

Sheldrake whimpered and began to make odd gagging, sobbing sounds. Jed wanted to laugh, and then he did. "My word, Merlin, it looks to me as if you have wet yourself."

"Ahh, please . . . please Mr. Stark, please don't kill me! I—oh, please!" Sheldrake, not an overly tall man to begin with, began wavering and wobbling in place, and then he dropped to his knees, closing in on full-bore weeping.

Jed moved half a step backward, and kept the gun aimed at the man's head. "More games, Merlin?"

Then, from behind him and to the left, in the dark toward the front of the building, Jed heard a throaty clicking sound of a revolver hammer being thumbed back, and a low, dry chuckle.

Jed froze.

Chapter 30

Not long before, back in Sheldrake's office, Loudon Paley worked with shaking fingers to untie the last of the knotted ropes binding Mother Stark to the chair.

"Hurry up, man!" she growled. "I ain't getting younger!"

"Yes, ma'am." He fumbled and fumbled, glancing up at her. My word, he thought. She is well and truly frightening. A sputtering tough chicken of a woman, and he didn't mind admitting she frightened him.

"Finish it off, boy. Untie me, I won't bite!" Then she chuckled.

"Yes, yes, ma'am."

Finally, the last of the ropes slid away. Minnie sat in the chair, her arms hanging by her sides. She worked her fingers slowly. "I—I need help, boy. Stiff, I reckon. I can't seem to muster the strength yet. Help me get on my feet. I'll be all right."

"Yes, ma'am, okay, then." He ran his tongue over his dry lips and then helped her to her feet, her weight fully against him as her weakened legs gave out. "Whoa, there," he said, catching her and holding her up.

"Okay, help me get to the door."

Loudon walked backward, helping her, and his boots nudged the dead man on the floor as he turned, with Mother Stark leaning on his right shoulder. He gasped.

"Oh, pay him no mind, boy! He's beyond caring!" She chuckled again. They managed to step over him, then made it out into the darkened corridor and walked as fast as he dared to usher her to the outside door at the end.

"You might want to haul out one of those fancy-man guns of yours with your free hand, boy."

"Yes, right, good thinking," he said, and tugged free his left revolver.

It took them a couple more minutes, but the odd, shuffling pair managed to make it out the door without spotting anyone else. There stood Stormy, Jed's big gray horse and Alice, Loudon's mule.

"I can't get up on Jed's beast. Too tall. Help me up on the mule. She's a good one—I've seen her when you visit. Good animals are mules."

"Yes, ma'am. I like her. She's gentle. Name's Alice."

Mother Stark grunted. "Yep, I know it. Now help me up."

Loudon did so, noting again how very slight and light she was. He grimaced as he grappled onto her, hoping he wasn't grabbing her anywhere unseemly. It must be all right, he thought, as she didn't put up a fight or shout at him, something he fully expected from her.

In short order, they were both mounted and rode out, back toward the front of the building, side by side, keeping tight to the shadows of the left hand side of the lane.

Loudon once again unholstered a revolver. "Ma'am?" he said in a near whisper. "Would you like a gun? I—I have a hide-out gun, lightweight." As soon as he said it, he realized this was the woman who could be seen about Whiskey Woods toting a heavy-as-sin single-barrel shotgun, seemingly with ease.

She chuckled. "My word, little cowboy. How many weapons you carrying tonight?" She chuckled again, then said, "No thanks. I have all I can do to stay in the saddle. Let's get on home to Stark land."

"Yes, ma'am."

In that manner, with newsman Loudon Paley riding point, holding his revolver up and at the ready, he and Mother Stark threaded their way eastward, cutting a bit wide of the usual lane out of town toward Grindle. She knew the way and so did he, so little needed to be said. The moon had decided to stay out, what sliver of moon there was, but it served to illumine the narrow roadway.

After a lull, and feeling more secure in their plight, in a low voice Loudon said, "I feel bad taking Jed's horse."

"Bah," she said. "Don't you worry about Jed. He'll find a mount. Man's resourceful. All Stark men are."

Loudon nodded. "Yes, ma'am." But he felt as he always did when speaking to Mother Stark that she was digging at him, cutting him down as a man just a little bit. He told himself to stop it, she was an old woman, proud of her son and her family. She was entitled to say what she felt.

They'd made it past Glen Rose, the lights of which shone brighter off to their right and back a ways, as if the town had awakened. The random gunfire of earlier had if anything increased in intensity and frequency, along with shouts, as if small crowds were shouting in unison.

"What do you make of that?" said Mother Stark, looking toward the flickering lights of town.

Loudon shook his head, also peering toward Glen Rose. "I don't know, but I will sure enough find out come tomorrow."

"I'm sure you will," she said.

Then they were silent once more as they rode.

A few moments later, from the dappled, moonlit darkness to their right, in a clearing off the road, a voice said, "Well now, fancy meeting you here, Mr. Newsman."

Loudon's heart seemed to turn to ice even as it scuttled up his throat. Pit Pritchard. Here. In the dark. Famed outlaw.

"Who are you?" she said to the approaching man. Then, without waiting for an answer, she turned to Loudon. "Who is this mouthy fool, boy?"

Loudon winced, his mouth all of a sudden as dry as sand. If Mother Stark had intended to keep her voice low, for only Loudon to hear, she had failed.

"He's—he's—"

"Go ahead, Mr. Newsman, tell her who I am."

Loudon spoke in little more than a whisper. "He's Pit Pritchard, ma'am."

"Huh, makes no never mind to me," she said. "He might well be the King of Siam. I don't care. I'm going home." She tried to nudge the mule forward, but the man standing in the narrow roadway stepped quick and snatched the mule's bridle with one hand. In the other he held a revolver, aimed at them.

"No, ma'am. I am no king. I'm a simple—oh, what was it you called me earlier, newsman? A heartless killer?"

"I never said that."

"No, that's true. But it was something along those lines. Now step down, the both of you! And keep your hands high!"

Loudon began to slide from the saddle but Mother Stark said, "Now see here, mister. I have been through more than enough tonight. I don't need this, too. I am going home."

"Mrs. Stark, please!" Loudon's plea was low but urgent.

"Best listen to the newsman, ma'am. Or I will kill you both and be done with it. Isn't that about what I get up to, at least according to you, newsman? Or should I call you the Rejecter. A reporter who rejects the story of the century! You know that, old woman? This fool newsman rejected me, Pit Pritchard, told me my story, offered exclusive to him, was no good!"

"I didn't say that, Mr. Pritchard. It is a compelling story, to be sure, but—"

"But?" said the gunman.

"But you didn't convince me of your innocence, sir. You revealed yourself to be what you are."

"Which is what, exactly, Mr. Newsman?"

Loudon swallowed, then in as firm a voice as he could

muster, he said, "You're a coldhearted man with no regard for life, and nothing but money in mind."

"So?" said Pritchard. "You rejected my story for that? Nobody rejects Pit Pritchard! Nobody who plans on living!"

Loudon didn't reply, but continued stepping down. He held his hands up and rounded the front of the horse. "Let her go, Mr. Pritchard. She's right, it's been a brutal day for her."

Pritchard considered this a moment. "All right, but keep those old hands high, Mrs. Stark. Don't think I didn't catch that, either, newsman. She's the old matriarch of the whiskey-making outfit me and my men were hired to deal with. Only it seems our employer has since made a botched mess of things. A shame, but it will be a big payday. I will make certain of that."

From atop the mule, Mother Stark snorted. "Don't count on it. If Merlin Sheldrake hired you, it'll be a long wait after tonight!" She giggled as if she'd taken a fit.

"Shut up, old woman!"

She kept on giggling.

He swung his gun toward her. "Shut up, I say! I will have my money!"

From beneath his thin wool coat, Loudon Paley slicked out both of his pistols, not the first time he'd worked the double-gun rig in such a manner. But it was the first time he'd drawn down on a genuine man, and not in front of his wavery mirror or a painted target.

His slight movements in the shadows, then the quick thumbing of two revolver hammers all the way back to the deadly position, returned Pritchard's attention to the newsman.

"What?" was all he managed to say. The chubby reporter's maneuvers had caught the gunman unawares. But as was his fighting custom, he angled his body sidelong to his target, dropping into a crouch at the same time. Pritchard's single gun barked flame.

Loudon Paley's two-gun assault did the same. The merest flash of fire from the deadly twin snouts came and went in eye-blink speed, and notorious gunman, the Fixer, Pit Pritchard, gasped and jerked, his arms whipping skyward as if he were at a revival, then he spun and dropped to his back.

For long moments, the only movement was the nervous jostling and chomping of the horse and the mule.

"You shot, boy?" said Mother Stark.

Loudon seemed to come back to himself then, and he pulled in a quick breath and patted himself, his guns gripped tight in his fists. "I—I don't think so."

"Good. I expect you'd know it if you was. Good shooting, boy."

"Luck, I expect," he said, his heart hammering the walls of his chest.

"No, you got the drop on him. Beat him to it, is all. You're good, and he was flustered. But no mistake, he was set to kill us."

Loudon walked over, aiming a gun at the flopped man faceup on the ground at his feet. Both of the man's hands were empty, his arms flung wide.

Loudon bent down and hesitated, then felt the man's neck. "He's dead," he said.

"Sure, he is," said Mother Stark. "You double-dosed that chatty fool."

Loudon said nothing for a long moment, then he sighed, holstered his guns, and hoisted himself back up onto Jed's big gray horse.

After a few moments of riding once more, Minnie said, "Who was that heathen, anyway, boy?"

Loudon considered this a moment. His thoughts returned to that conversation with Jed, when the big whiskey man had talked about how killing a man changes you—and not for the better, never that. Loudon understood, at last, what his friend meant. This was a hard, bitter feeling, with no glory in it.

I have met the savage, wild West, he thought, and it is not what the dime novels make it out to be. They are a fantasy, a joke. This is anything but.

Finally, he answered Mother Stark. "He—he was a bad man, ma'am. A very bad man."

With no trace of humor in her voice, Mother Stark said, "Well, where he's going, he'll be in good company. Now, take me home to Whiskey Woods, Mr. Paley. I am plum tired."

"Yes, ma'am," he said.

"And Mr. Paley?"

"Yes, ma'am?"

"Call me Minnie. All my friends call me Minnie."

"Ma'am?"

"Yes?"

"It's Loudon. Jed calls me Loud."

"He's right. Now take me home, boy." In the dark, they were both smiling.

Chapter 31

That night, the citizens of Glen Rose finally woke up. This was fueled in equal parts by a full-bore intolerance of Sheldrake's awful rotgut whiskey, by a dearth of their own, beloved hometown brew—Stark's finest—and was tipped over the edge into pure townwide rage by the braying that night of Marshal Chiswick.

His spineless defense of himself against Jed Stark only served to illuminate a growing realization of the Glen Rose folks that having their lawman deeply wedged in the pocket of Sheldrake, maker of the aforementioned swill in a bottle, was not working out to be such a good idea.

The brute-fisted treatment by the strangers in town—gunmen, it was learned—was the final straw for the townsfolk of Glen Rose. It proved to be the very thing that finally opened their eyes and smacked them about their collective faces.

It roused them from a years-long stupor fueled by a lust for money and by the promises of all manner of great and good things to come their way courtesy of Merlin Sheldrake, including prosperity for all and the prospect of becoming a railway town.

The strangers' unwarranted townwide attacks on everyone, from workingmen and women and their children to the old-timers, had popped their passivity that night like a poked blister. All day long, no one had been left unmolested by the strange gunmen who swaggered among them.

Right here, in their quiet little town of Glen Rose! And hired by Sheldrake himself to rid the town of the Starks! Think of that—and it seems they finally had. Trying to wipe out their very founding family. How on earth could that be?

Everyone in Glen Rose knew the Starks, had heard all the long tales of the family line, and even if they didn't necessarily know them as bosom friends, they nonetheless respected the fact that they were the town's founders and the makers of a fine drink.

My word, they said, anybody who makes such good whiskey should be left well enough alone! It was, after all, an undisputed fact that Glen Rose was the whiskey capital of Texas, and the Starks had about everything to do with that simple truth.

Soon enough, the citizens decided that Chiswick was no longer fit to serve them as a lawman; they surrounded the battered, purple-eyed, raging man, stripped him of his guns, and four men held him down while a howling woman in a bonnet tore from his shirt the silver star he had worn with boastful pride among them each day. Then they threw him in a cell and locked the door.

In short order, someone tracked down young Deputy Harley Thompson, making his rounds and doing his overpowered, overworked best, as he had all day long, to keep the strangers from hurting his people. They handed him the badge, held a vote right there in the street, and made him marshal.

But despite their zeal on his behalf, and despite his pleading with them to disperse and go home and cool down, there were too many Glen Rose residents out and about who were too riled up into a raging mass of citizenry. They were fresh out of tolerance for the rough-handed ways of Sheldrake's hired guns. Something had to be done, they decided. So, they did it.

The angered citizens of Glen Rose took to the streets, armed and seething, and they closed in on the first of the strangers who had been tormenting them all day.

One of the men in the crowd, a lifelong resident of the town named Cedric Dashiell, nimble of tongue and straight as an arrow, said, "There are two things a Texan will fight to the death over. One is honor!"

This drew waves of rousing cheers. And when that hubbub died down, as their captive snarled and thrashed, Dashiell said, "And the other is whiskey!"

That proclamation brought forth a louder and longer howling cheer from the crowd.

In the tumult, the cornered stranger pulled out a boot knife and lunged at the nearest Glen Rose resident. The knife-wielding stranger's effort drew little more than a scratch, and he was gunned down then and there.

Within two hours, two more of the five gunmen were dead, swinging from makeshift gibbets on Glen Rose's Main Street. Even when folks sobered up, they all agreed it had been a good job. And hang whoever might disagree.

CHAPTER 32

Lilly reined in her horse, Poppy, and held her well in shadow along the lane, a good hundred feet behind Jed and Loudon. Poppy's shoe nicked a stone, and Lilly had seen the two men pause, as if they had heard her back here.

She stroked the mare's neck, waiting for them to move on. After a few moments, they did. They cut around to the right side of Sheldrake's warehouse, making for the rear, she guessed. So, she would, too. But at a distance.

When she felt the going was clear, Lilly urged Poppy forward, and they stepped once again into the lane. They hadn't traveled twenty feet when she heard another animal's hooves close by, behind, to her left.

Lilly stayed looking forward, but reached down and unfastened the keeper thong on her pistol. Before she pulled it from the leather, the steely sound of a gun hammer clicked back once, twice. "No, no, no," said a man's voice, closer than she expected it to be. "Raise your arms, lady."

She hesitated, biting the inside of her cheek. Could she keep the gun in her hand, and turn fast?

"I don't recommend what you are thinking about, lady."

Even as the man said this, she knew it would be a fool's game, as Jed would say. Then the man rode forward. "Hands higher, that's it. Keep them up. Almost there. Now ride forward. To the front of that big building."

They reached the loading dock, and he said, "Climb onto the deck. That's right."

Lilly did as he bade her, taking her time and inching her hand to her waisted gun. But he was too quick for her and stepped close behind her. She felt his gun's barrel nudge her in the middle of the back.

"You're from the café," said the man from close behind her, reaching to her side and sliding her revolver free. He moved his face closer, until she felt his breath on her cheek. "I saw you earlier. I tried to visit you, but you didn't answer your door."

Lilly could tell the man was smiling, thinking things she did not want to know about.

"Now, my name is Ollie. Would you like to dance?"

"No," she said through tight teeth, jerking away from him. She spun and managed to see him in the scant moonlight. He was a tall young man, not as tall as Jed, but he had a square face and light hair, blond, she guessed.

She had seen him in the street earlier that day, talking and walking with the three gunmen who had rousted her customers and shut her down.

"You're one of those hired criminals," she said.

He kept his gun aimed at her, but she saw his face slip into a sneer as he grabbed her arms with his other big hand and spun her around, her back to him once more. "We'll go inside together. I have to take care of a business matter for my . . . boss, Mr. Pritchard. Maybe you heard of him? You see, somewhere in here is a man with money. A big fat man. He owes us money. I promised my boss to get it. He had something else to do."

Ollie shoved her forward and she walked toward a small door set in the wall to the right of large closed double-size warehouse doors. "In," he said.

As they stepped into the big building, Lilly felt a thin sliver of relief to see light, however slight, ahead.

"Walk," whispered Ollie behind her. "And hands up, high up."

She complied, hating that she had let this happen. Which was what Jed didn't want. Where was he? And Loudon? And Minnie?

They kept on, sometimes bumping into crates and barrels, slowly advancing toward the small dim glow of a lamp somewhere ahead in the otherwise dark warehouse. The air was heavy with the stink of odious chemicals and smoke and wood.

They shifted left and then right, and there in a cleared space to their right, backlit by a guttering lantern hanging on a hook from a beam, stood two men. One was tall and held a gun on the other, farther in, a shorter fat man. He was short because, she realized, he was on his knees, sobbing.

The big man was Jed, of course, and as quick as it took to think of it, she formed a plan. One split of a second more and she would have shouted to Jed and jerked away from this gunman, dropping low to her left, behind a cluster of crates.

But Ollie was quicker, and he clamped a big hand over her face and jerked her to him, her back held hard against his front. At the same time, he brought his gun up over her shoulder to bear on Jed.

She squealed, a muffled humphing sound behind his big clamping hand. It was enough to alert her love, but Ollie was only amused, clicking back the hammer of the pistol he had leveled at Jed.

Chapter 33

Jed looked away from Sheldrake, toward whatever it was that had caused that sound. There was someone there, toward the front of the building. The light was low, but whoever it might be was drawing closer.

He squinted in the low light at the shape, then saw it was two people, one before another. He brought the gun around to face them, glancing back once to make certain Sheldrake was on his knees. He hoped the fat man didn't have another gun hidden in his rolls somewhere.

And then the newcomers were close enough that the flickering light from the lantern lit them. Enough to see who it was.

Lilly, held from behind by that big blond brute from earlier that day, from behind the Cactus Bar. One of the gunmen. And the man had a big hand over her mouth and, with the other, held a gun to her head—her pretty head.

They had walked close enough that Jed could see not fear so much as rage in Lilly's eyes. She was a tough woman, perhaps because of all she had had to endure in her life; perhaps she was tougher than his Mama. And that was saying something.

And even in that moment, when he felt himself admiring that woman more than ever, in those pretty eyes he saw something else, that she was thinking the same thing he was: Don't stand for any of this fool's games.

At the same time, from behind him Jed heard Sheldrake laughing. Jed eased back a step and glanced toward the fat man. He had crawled back behind a wall of stacked barrels and peered out as he grunted himself to his feet.

"You there! Pit Pritchard's man!" bellowed Sheldrake. "Kill them both! Now! Do you hear me, you buffoon? I order you to do as I say! I am paying you, you oaf!"

Lilly felt Ollie tense behind her, felt it in the stiffening of his hand over her face and heard a growl of suppressed anger from his throat.

"You are not my boss!" shouted Ollie. "Mr. Pritchard is my boss, and you owe us money!"

Jed heard Sheldrake snort. But this unexpected interruption was all he needed. He and Lilly exchanged looks, he nodded slightly, and dropped low, to his right.

This caused Ollie to whip the pistol away from Lilly's head and aim it instead at the diving form of Jed.

At the same time, Lilly jerked hard, down and to her left, wrenching herself from Ollie's grasp.

Ollie sent a bullet toward the low, fleeting form of Jed.

Jed Stark did the same, driving one at Ollie. Jed's bullet found its mark in flesh and bone, yanking a shriek from the big Nordic gunman.

Ollie's bullet, however, went awry and shattered a thin wooden support arm to the right of Sheldrake.

Considering the task it had been given, that of holding back the weight of a sizable wall of filled barrels of rotgut swill, the wooden support arm really should have been made, per the head joiner's request months before, of thicker stock.

Alas, Merlin Sheldrake had told him to stop wasting money and overbuilding everything.

Ollie's bullet provided the last slim excuse the support arm needed to collapse. A loud creaking sound was followed with a series of crackings and snappings, like gunshots, and a huge wall of barrels thundered down, rolling and tumbling.

And pinning, then crushing, the shrieking rich fat man, Merlin Sheldrake, in a sea of his very own swill.

Jed wasted no time. Even as the seeming mountain of barrels toppled, he dashed forward, bent low, and met Lilly, already on her feet and making for him. She broke from his grasping hand, bent to the dead Ollie, and snatched up her revolver from where he'd tucked it in his gun belt.

Then they did not speak—did not need to—but together, Jed and Lilly bolted for the front, hearing ominous creaking and groaning sounds that seemed to rise from the belly of the vast structure itself.

She pointed to the two horses—Poppy and Ollie's mount, and Jed climbed aboard, stepping from the loading dock conveniently down into the waiting horse's saddle.

Lilly did not climb aboard Poppy but bent to her saddle bag and rummaged a quick moment.

"Lil, what are you doing?"

As if to bolster his urging, from the building more and louder sounds, the unmistakable wrenching sounds of timbers snapping and popping, rose up high and loud into the night.

She ran back to the door, thumbed alight a match, and lit a stick of dynamite.

Jed saw her pull her arm back even as she disappeared inside.

"Lilly! Now!" he bellowed. At the same moment, she reappeared, ran across the dock, leapt aboard Poppy, and shouted, "Go! Go!"

They made it far enough to only receive a pelting in the back of splinters and thumb-size debris as the big warehouse exploded, boiling up into the night in a magnificent billowing flash that lit the scene, for a long moment, as bright as a hot summer day in Texas.

"Haaaa!" shouted Lilly Chu, her fists raised in victory as they rode. She looked to her right at Jed, awe and amazement on his face.

"That's what you get when you tangle with the daughter of a Texas ranch woman and a Chinese railroad blaster!"

"I'll keep that in mind," he said, shaking his head and smiling, eyes wide.

They rode slower then, glancing back frequently to eye the exploding conflagration that was Merlin Sheldrake's warehouse and distillery of fine rotgut.

"No way one stick did all that," she said, smiling and shaking her head as she watched it.

"He probably had all manner of volatile ingredients stored in there, likely gunpowder." Jed shook his head. "Good riddance!" he shouted, riding forward. Then he held out his left hand and holding Lilly's right hand, they rode down the lane side by side.

After a bit, she said, "Hey, Jed?"

"Yeah?" he said, trying to see her beside him in the dark.

"Yes." She let go of his hand, then heeled Poppy into a hard lope, outpacing him.

"Yes?" he said, confused, then heeled his mount, trying to keep up with her as they rode back toward Glen Rose.

It took him another half mile before he understood what that meant.

He caught up with her as they passed outside of town and kept on riding. As they thundered onward toward Whiskey Woods, Jedediah Stark wore the biggest smile a whiskey man had ever shown the world.

Chapter 34

Four days later found Lilly and Minnie bustling about the camp's kitchen at Whiskey Woods, loading the dining table with steaming platters and bowls.

While they waited for Loudon, Jed poured them all a glass of whiskey. "Now this is some of the old stuff, from way back in the cave."

"To the future!" said Minnie, eyeing first Lilly and then Jed with a knowing look. They all knew what she meant.

The old woman had been clucking about grandbabies ever since she found out that the big question had finally been asked and answered, to her satisfaction.

Lilly blushed, and Jed smirked and shook his head, his ears pinking up as well.

"And to Redeye," said Jed, holding up his glass as he looked to the floor, grinning to see the limber old hound, bandaged about the shoulder but otherwise in his favorite pose—flat on his side in a near slumber.

Redeye's head was not raised, but he had worked up enough ambition to show them all one gleaming tooth. His nose flexed and twitched, taking in the heavy aromas of cooked meats, and his bony tail thumped the fresh quilts Minnie had given him that morning.

* * *

Later, after a huge meal, topped with pie and a dollop of cream, and more whiskey all around, Minnie leaned back and smacked her lips. "Well, Jed. I'm glad to see you finally recalled that lesson I gave you all them years back."

"Well, now, which lesson would that be, Mama?"

"About us not starting a fight but sure enough finishing it should someone else be fool enough to pick one with a Stark!"

"Oh," said Jed, turning away and hiding a smirk. "That one? Huh, nope, don't recall that one . . ." He winked at Lilly and Loudon.

"You don't recall?" Mama Stark was flat-out riled. She clucked back to the stove, sputtering and fuming. "Don't recall? Oh, what have I raised?"

She turned and wagged a wooden spoon at Lilly. "Good luck to you, girl! For good or ill, he's a Stark man, through and through!"

TURN THE PAGE FOR AN EXCITING PREVIEW!

JOHNSTONE COUNTRY. WHERE THE WHISKEY FLOWS LIKE WATER, AND THE WATER IS RED WITH BLOOD.

The Texas-loving, whiskey-brewing Stark family is back—in the crosshairs of an empire-building heiress with barrels of cash, buckets of bullets, and a personal army of killers. . . .

It's been a year since the infamous whiskey war ripped apart the humble, booze-making burg of Glen Rose, Texas. After the dust settled, Jed Stark rebuilt the family ranch and distillery—and now Whiskey Woods is doing better than ever, thanks to the Stark family's secret recipe. The whole community is flourishing, which, unfortunately, makes it a target for land developers—namely Mona Starret. She's the beautiful, headstrong heiress to a rail and shipping empire, and she's decided Glen Rose would be the perfect addition to her portfolio. In fact, she wants to rename it Starret City. And what Mona wants, Mona gets, come hell or high water. . . .

Or, in this case, whiskey, bullets, and blood.

Of course, Jed and his gun-toting mom Minnie have no intention of selling Whiskey Woods, not after rebuilding it from the ground up. Mona Starret would have to take the land over their dead bodies—which is exactly what Mona's willing to do. She's got her very own army of hired guns—aka "advance team"—led by a ruthless enforcer named Dalton Majors. It's not long before the two sides are trading shots, both .44 millimeter and 80 proof. Even Minnie is taking up arms with her trusty shotgun Ol' Shredder. The Starks survived the Whiskey War together. But this new war is bigger and deadlier—and it's not going to end until Mona's army is bottoms up and down the hatch.

CHAPTER 1

"Majors."

"Yes, mum."

Mona Starret sighed, shaking her head. "Why is it you people from England always insist on calling every woman you meet 'mum'? There is no way on earth or in the heavens above that I am old enough to be your mother. In fact, I think you will find I am your age or younger."

The man to whom she spoke, Dalton Majors, was her manager of operations out there in the tantalizing, promise-filled West. Despite his intention to appear to be a hard-handed, rough-and-ready character, she knew he had been born into British nobility.

It amused Mona to know that Majors's mother had been a lady or a dame or whatever they called fancy women in society over there, and his father had been a lord or a duke of some place or other.

Starret didn't really care about where or to whom a person was born, but as with all unusual facts about anyone she met, she tucked it away for further consideration and possible use. And the fact that Majors bore some shade of royal blood might well be useful to her on down the road, perhaps when she decided the time was right to broaden her business presence overseas.

Majors had told her that his family still owned the estate, but because he had been the youngest of three sons, he was obliged to leave home and explore and carve his own way in the world. It had not been particularly easy, he had told her when she hired him, but he had risen to the challenge.

Mona had rolled her eyes. "Mr. Majors, do you honestly think I would not have your background thoroughly researched? I know far more about your . . . explorations, shall we call them, than you might think. And that information shall remain where you prefer it to be—hidden. Unless there comes a time when you will have forced me to exhume it. Do I make myself clear?"

Majors nodded. He'd nod to anything she said, and if there was a directive behind it, he'd make it happen. Even though it was rare for her to pay him any form of compliment, particularly one that seemed to be offered out of kindness, Majors figured that any attention from Mona Starret was good attention.

"Mr. Majors—"

"Dalton, please," he had said, hoping to encourage her somehow into noticing that he was roughly her age and that he was a reliable, perhaps even friendly soul.

She regarded him over her spectacles, which she wore pulled down onto the end of her long, pretty nose. "Mr. Majors," she continued. "What I am paying you for is to help me secure ownership of as much of that Texas ranch land as I am able to procure. I am not paying you to be anything other than that, which certainly includes being on familiar terms with me.

"I have plenty of acquaintances, some of which I dare say I might call friends. If not, then so be it. Beyond that, at present I have no need for such familiarities and niceties in my life. I have money to take care of that. If that should change, I will certainly let you know. Am I clear enough for you on that matter?"

Dalton Majors nodded, thanking his stars that he was endowed with the capacity to absorb blunt talk in life. He had always had the ability, one of the few useful traits he inherited from his father. There was precious little else that came his way from the old duke.

You bet, thought Majors, *for a solid-paying job like this, I can put up with a whole lot of insufferable behavior.*

He had never had trouble nibbling away at brick walls that stern-seeming women built up around themselves, no matter how seemingly solid and high. That was due in part to the fact that he was English, well educated, and, judging from his considerable past successes with women, he was not a homely man to look upon.

Yes, he would wear Mona Starret down. Eventually. And he suspected that this Texas whim might well provide him with the very opportunity for that to happen.

That Mona Starret was the wealthiest person he had ever known personally and was also one of the more attractive women he had ever met, well, these twin traits certainly did not hinder his urge to keep on working for her.

Yes, sir, he would keep his mouth shut and a smile on his face, and he would endure whatever coldness and insults she might lob his way. Majors smiled and nodded, doing his best to absorb the information she was imparting. If it was important to Mona Starret, then it was important to Dalton Majors, too.

"This region of Glen Rose"—she bent once more over the topmost of a stack of maps on her massive oak desk—"looks the most promising. There is ample water and ample grazing. The river I see here, the Paluxy"—she traced it on the map with a fingertip—"looks like it might well be the solution to a lot of potential problems. What do you think, Majors?"

She looked up and caught him staring at her again. She sighed. "Look Majors, if we are going to make this new venture work, you have to pull yourself out of this infatuation you appear to have with me, understand?"

"I . . . I don't know what you're talking about, Miss Starret!" But try as he might, and despite his best intentions, Majors knew he was on the losing end of this conversation. It had been that way since he had, nearly a year before, answered her advertisement for a position for which he felt himself quite qualified.

He recalled the brief, terse wording and smiled.

Old and established firm seeks intelligent, forthright, strong person with better-than-average education to help formulate plans of expansion. Position offers long-term potential. Dolts will not be tolerated.

It was that very forthright, no-nonsense nature of the advertisement that had intrigued and amazed him and convinced him to apply for the position. That and the fact that he had recently burned the last sagging bridge of tolerance—and thus money—between himself and his stuffy English family.

Majors also bent low over the map, pushing his luck, he knew, by seeming to cozy up to her. But his defense, should he need to express it, would be that the map was only so large and they both needed to give it a thorough going over.

"According to my research into this matter, Miss Starret," said Majors, "much of the region you seek to purchase is already inhabited."

"What?" she said, looking at him with wide eyes and shock writ large on her pretty face.

It appeared as if she was truly surprised that anyone might dare settle on land that she had of late determined to be of use to her.

"Yes, ma'am. This entire riverine landscape, perhaps we can call it a valley, that stretches from here"—he tapped a long forefinger and dragged it eastward along the blue painted line of the Paluxy River—"all the way to here, and beyond, really, is most desirable land thereabouts. And as such it has attracted settlers for a good long time, well before . . ."

"Spit it out, man!" she snapped, clearly not liking what she was hearing from him.

"Well before you came along, Miss Starret."

She did not flinch, did not do much of anything save for staring at the big map and drumming a couple of her lovely fingertips on it. Finally she drew in a deep breath and said, "Mr. Majors, I want what I want and I will have it. I have my mind fixed, immovably so, on the pursuit of building the largest cattle ranch in the world. That is my intention and therefore that is what will happen. I am Mona Starret and I deem it so."

Majors held his tongue a moment then said, "I never doubted that for a single moment, ma'am, but . . ."

"But, man? *But?* But *nothing*! You, as manager of this bold new plan, will represent me there, in person. Yes, this is how we shall begin." She rubbed one hand along the other, over and over as if she were washing them.

This was a trait Majors recognized as indicative of excitement in his employer. He liked seeing this, for it meant she was about to smile. Even if that dazzling look was not directed at him, he reveled in its reflection.

"You shall travel to this Glen Rose place, and you shall interact with the local populace, such as it is, and you shall proceed to purchase as much of the land from them as you can in person, without arousing ire or suspicion. Never that. We must entrench. From there, we shall usurp. This has been my method in every business dealing I have ever had, and so it shall be with this."

"Yes, ma'am. Pardon, but what do you suggest as a course of action when a landowner will not sell up to me, er, you?"

For the second time in that conversation, Mona Starret looked at him as if he had suggested they try swimming nude together under a full moon. "Frankly, Mr. Majors, you disappoint me. What is the use of having ample amounts of money, you dolt, if you don't use it? Whatever the cost, make it happen. And do not take no for an answer. We shall return together and deal with any holdouts. For surely there will be a few fools whose greed will lull them into thinking that if they wait, they will receive more compensatory money.

"Nonetheless, promise them anything, offer them more money. Pay them as little as possible but make as many purchases while you are there as possible. Attract as little attention to yourself as possible. And for heaven's sake, do not mention my name."

"Shall I take anyone else with me?"

"Why? Is the task I've assigned you so very onerous and perplexing that you feel you might need assistance?"

"Well, no, ma'am. What I meant to say was—"

"Mr. Majors, you appear to be operating under the delusion that my plan is open for discussion. It is not. I am your employer, you are my employee. You will therefore do as I command. The initial foray will be made by you. Secure the land, Mr. Majors. At all costs. At some point, there will be no more resistance. That is the magic of money, Mr. Majors. Perhaps someday you will learn this.

"In the interim, while you are there, inquire as to the availability of workers. I have a detailed list of needs in this packet." She patted a thick sheaf of papers folded double and wrapped and bound in tooled leather.

"Very good, ma'am," said Majors as he bowed, took the bundle, and backed toward the door. As he took his leave, tucking the paperwork under one arm so that he might open the door, he heard her voice reach him from back by her desk.

He turned. "Yes, ma'am?"

"I doubt I need to remind you, Majors, and yet I shall: Failure to accomplish this task, Mr. Majors, is unacceptable. By this I mean that if you fail to do as I wish, then I will find someone who will succeed. Therefore my intentions will not fail.

Weak people fail. Prove to me you are not one of them and I see no reason why we cannot both enjoy a long and fruitful relationship. As employer and employee, that is."

"Yes, ma'am. Understood, Miss Starret."

"Good." She dragged another stack of papers before her and seated herself once more behind the massive desk. "Now, on to the ice hauling enterprise on the New England coast." She regarded him once more. "You may leave now, Mr. Majors."

"Yes, Miss Starret." He smiled and bowed slightly and closed the door behind him. Out in the hallway, he readjusted the bulky bundle and proceeded on down the long, carpeted hallway that led to the middle of the mansion. As he walked, he glanced left and right.

Yes, sir, he thought. *When I am the man of this house, then we shall see who orders who about.*

He grinned. "Just a matter of time, my good man," he whispered to himself. "You heard the woman, Majors. Do the job or else. So I shall most certainly do the job. And soon enough, all of this shall be mine for the plucking."

By the time he reached the first floor once more, Dalton Majors was whistling.